Mercenaries and auxiliaries are useless and dangerous; and if one holds his state based on these arms, he will stand neither firm nor safe
Machiavelli: *The Prince*

Table of Contents

Author's Note	7
Prologue	9
Chapter One	23
Chapter Two	30
Chapter Three	39
Chapter Four	48
Chapter Five	59
Chapter Six	68
Chapter Seven	77
Chapter Eight	87
Chapter Nine	97
Chapter Ten	108
Chapter Eleven	117
Chapter Twelve	126
Chapter Thirteen	138
Chapter Fourteen	153
Chapter Fifteen	164
Chapter Sixteen	174
Chapter Seventeen	186
Chapter Eighteen	196
Chapter Nineteen	207
Chapter Twenty	220
Chapter Twenty One	233
Chapter Twenty Two	242

Chapter Twenty Three	252
Chapter Twenty Four	264
Chapter Twenty Five	273
Chapter Twenty Six	284
Chapter Twenty Seven	295
Chapter Twenty Eight	307
Chapter Twenty Nine	316
Chapter Thirty	327
Chapter Thirty One	337
Epilogue	345

Author's Note

The troubled East African state of Zambute (pr. ZAM-BOO-TAY) is, of course, entirely fictional. If Zambute did exist, it would be at the apex of the borders between Ethiopia, Kenya and Somalia. For the purposes of our story, Zambute has annexed a disputed slice of Somalia, bisecting that country south of Kismayo, and this coastal region is where *The Devil's Work* is set.

Suffice it to say I have taken significant liberties with reality. Place-names, people, politics and geographical descriptions have been designed to be *notionally* sympathetic to the region (Zambute is a majority Christian, Swahili-speaking country with both Kenyan and Somali cultural influences). Nonetheless, any balance between geo-political accuracy and artistic license has inevitably favoured the latter.

DA
London, August 2014

PROLOGUE

Derecik, Turkish / Iraqi border

The bullet smashed into a tree, two metres to my left. I froze, belt buckle pressed into the dirt, sweat stinging my eyes. Crows swirled skywards from a knot of trees, croaking in protest. I reckoned that put the shooter just shy of three hundred metres away.

I first heard the myth as a lance-corporal in Bosnia, a lifetime ago. A Yank from an armoured recce unit told us the story over coffee and donuts, said he'd picked it up from the Intelligence guys up in Zupanja. And although it sounded like an urban legend at the time, Balkan service had a way of degrading your faith in human nature. A few years later we all deployed to hot and sandy places and I forgot all about it. Iraq confirmed my lack of faith in our species, but that's another story for another time.

Anyhow, the American was a long-service Master Sergeant called Nolan. He didn't strike me as a man given to bullshit. He spun us a dit about an outfit called *Die Jagd*: The Hunt. Wealthy Germans, big-game hunters, paid Serb criminals big bucks to take up a sniper's post. They'd snipe Bosnian Muslims as they ran back from getting food or going to prayers. For the Serb militias it was a win-win: some other fucker was paying to do their day job, and the hunters experienced the ultimate murder porn, slotting civvies through the scope of a Dragunov. It sounded too twisted to be true. But, like I said, I should've known better.

The sun was behind me and I was in good cover; long grass in dead ground, leading to a copse of gnarly blackthorn bushes. My camouflaged jumpsuit matched it well. I'd threaded yellowish grass into slits slashed in the shoulders and sleeves. I'd lost three stone for this role – head shaved and body inked with Russian prison tattoos, a wolf's head on my arm and pentagrams across my shoulders. Orthodox crosses and stars stretched across a newly-found pectoral. Oz beasted me every day for six weeks, I'd given up booze and was as fit as I'd ever been.

The operation to take down The Hunt had come through a BKA informer called Bernard Schmidt, a convicted people-trafficker. The *Bundeskriminalamt*, the German FBI, wanted nothing to do with it directly. Oh no. Maybe send them on a sensitivity awareness course, or confiscate their hunting licences. So we'd been sub-contracted to do it for them.

"They only come together in one place for a hunt," said Schmidt nervously, flanked by two stony-faced BKA handlers, "at the site where the kill takes place, so you won't get them all anyplace else. They are very careful." I'd seen Schmidt's file. He'd trafficked girls, illegal immigrants and refugees. He was a sleazy bastard, with dead eyes and bad breath. He told me he was fifty, but looked older by a century or so. He was the sort of man I was usually sent to kill, but now he was my lifeline.

"Get that?" said the BKA agent coldly. "They must all be... *managed*, simultaneously, no German government involvement."

"Then we'll 'manage' them out on a hunt," said Oz. "Won't you Cal?" Oz was my team-mate. Still recovering from a bullet wound to his arm, he was out of the active roster for another couple of months.

The Hunt had moved to eastern Turkey, where the border with Iraq is lively enough to absorb casual murder. Schmidt had been contracted to provide fresh meat, which he reported back to the BKA. The Germans even put up a reward, showing that virtue is sweeter with a briefcase of used Euros attached. Schmidt reported The Hunt had set up a new game: They would hunt a paid volunteer who won a bounty if he crossed the playing field without getting sniped. Inevitably, these volunteers were people with serious debts to criminals, or drug addicts or other losers.

It was meant to be Darwinian.

It was also an opportunity.

"They shoot up a village on day one," the people-trafficker told me during our briefing in Cologne. "That gets blamed on bandits or terrorists. The local police get paid off. Then, on day two, they hunt the professional target."

Schmidt reported The Hunt had good OPSEC, or operational security. The criminals who provided logistics and targets were compartmentalised from the guys who looked after the murder tourists. Schmidt had been tasked with providing 'The Hare,' the stupid fucker who agreed to be hunted. There were enough trafficked people desperate enough to do it.

For the next hunt, I was going to be The Hare. Yeah, that's the type of job I have. It's not like I volunteered. My legend was Mikhail Susenov, a Russian ex-squaddie and drifter with a heroin habit. I was qualified: I spoke fluent Russian. I'd worked in Siberia in energy security. And I'd be lying if I said I hadn't had my fair share of problems with recreational chemicals. I not-very-reluctantly smoked some Afghan heroin, as I knew they'd give me a blood test, and we stuck needles in my arms and feet to try and make track marks.

Bernie flew me to Turkey on a professionally forged EU passport. I even grew to tolerate him, in the way you get used to rising damp or toothache. We stayed in a flophouse hotel, on the outskirts of Istanbul, to meet The Hunt.

The organisers were German, apart from a guy from Marseilles called Henri. Henri was a rangy, skin-headed psychopath with a pock-marked face. He was suspicious of me from the start, asking detailed questions about the prisons I'd been in and pretending he could check. Bernie looked at me hopefully as we sat drinking and smoking. I told Henri I'd done a four-stretch at Lgov for assault. He nodded sagely, slinking off and making a show of getting his mobile out. His German colleagues took over the questioning, which wasn't as hard-core as I'd anticipated.

They offered me a syringe to see if I'd inject, which I did. It was so good it reminded me why I'd taken that trip to The Priory. I was offered ten thousand Euros to be the hare on the next hunt.

BANG. The second round was much closer. The shooter had seen something, but I was lying statue-still and a stiff breeze was moving the trees like leafy puppets. I looked at the map I'd recovered from the tiny plastic tube up my arse and tried to orientate it to the ground. The map, that is, not my arse. Schmidt had agreed to hide the weapon on the plot, which as far as I could work out from the map was on top of the Yew trees where the shooter was. I'd told him not to hide it anywhere a hunter might choose as a firing position. It would be an interesting de-brief.

I decided to wait a while, see if the shooter got bored. Good hunters are patient, and the playing field wasn't big. To make the game more fun for the customers, and in case I loitered in one place too long, they had beaters with dogs to flush me out if I lost my bottle. I hadn't heard them yet.

After half an hour I saw movement near the yew trees. Amongst the foliage I saw a camouflaged figure, wearing a full ghillie suit and mask, crawl to one side and out of view. I began to inch slowly towards him, at an angle in the dead ground using the thorn bushes for cover. The hide I was looking for was ten metres away from the shooter and now two hundred from me. There was barking in the distance. These weren't The Queensbury rules I'd been promised - maybe the hunter was bored and wanted his kill in time for dinner. I crawled forward, trying to make as much progress as I could without showing out. After another ten metres I found a shallow trench, possibly an old irrigation ditch, to my left. It ran towards the yew trees. Screened by long dry grass, this was the best luck I'd had all day, allowing me to crawl quicker, knees bloodied and raw. The elbows of my jump-suit were torn to shreds in the gravelly grey earth.

When we'd trained for this, Oz had taught me to stalk. An ex-SBS commando, Oz was once an instructor on the Royal Marines sniper course. "Right, Kurdistan ain't exactly Woodbury Common but we'll do our best!" he'd said, loading an air rifle to punish me with if he spotted movement. Stalking ain't rocket science but it is tough. You need to think exactly where you are going to move next, in a range of inches rather than feet, and be fit enough to haul yourself for hundreds of yards in tiny, stealthy increments. I wasn't a natural, but I'm a stubborn bastard and I threw myself into it.

"You need to move faster!" said a voice in broken Russian through a loud-hailer, "or we send dogs." It sounded far away, from the direction where I'd last seen the hunter.

I figured the hide was about fifty yards away. Standing up on the brow of a hill was one of the guys I'd seen in Istanbul, wearing a dusty camouflage jacket and scanning the field through binoculars. Slung over his shoulder was a Kalashnikov.

He couldn't see me.

The barking louder, I took my chances and loped forwards in a low run, like a lunatic doing a monkey impression. I dropped to my belly and crawled over the top of the ditch, towards the hill. The guy with the Kalashnikov was gone. If the hunter was where I thought he was, he was stalking in the wrong direction, but would still be able to bring his rifle to bear if he heard me. I painfully clawed forward, inches at a time, across rough ground and through thorns. I tried to tuck my bloodied hands into the cuffs of the jumpsuit so I'd be able to pick up my buried weapon. I finally made it to the yew trees, spotting the crushed foliage and disturbed earth where the hunter had crawled away. Spent brass from two .357 rounds lay by the base of the tree.

I looked again at the tiny map, blood from my fingers smudging the waxy paper. Schmidt said he'd buried the weapon next to a distinctive mauve and orange coloured rock, three yards from a dead yew tree. I tugged off my boot and pulled away the heel. Hidden in the sole was a thin piece of hardened plastic which I used to scrape away the earth next to the rock. I saw the edge of a black canvas bag when the voice threatened me again over the loudhailer. "Faster you fucking junkie! I swear we'll put the dogs on you."

I heaved at the edge of the canvas, the loose earth packed round it crumbling. I got both my hands underneath and tugged with all my strength, a tool bag emerging from the ground. I unzipped it and pulled out the plastic-wrapped rifle. My hands felt like I'd been rubbing them on a cheese-grater, slippery with blood and sweat.

Finally I ripped the weapon free. It was a compact Russian SVU-A sniper rifle with a bipod and PSO-1 scope. There were five thirty-round magazines in the bag, which I tucked into my pockets. In a separate bag was a canvas belt with a holstered Browning pistol. Less than three feet long, the SVU-A is easily hidden but the shorter barrel only gave me an effective range of four hundred metres. It would do. I assembled it quickly, slid a magazine into the housing behind the trigger group and made ready. I crawled on my belly into the firing position, the low branches of the yew tree providing cover. Opening the bipod I settled myself into the weapon.

The Russian PSO scope is arse-about-face, the stadia marks and chevrons the wrong way round from NATO weapons, so it took me a moment to orientate myself. I peered over the top of the scope and saw the guy with the loudhailer walking across the plot, a hundred metres away, cigarette in mouth. There was no clue as to the hunter's position. I guessed he was stalking towards my last hide.

I lined up loudhailer guy in my sights and shot him in the chest. He crumpled to the ground, but I was already panning right, looking for the first hunter. I saw movement in the long grass three hundred yards away, then a dark shape. I lined it up in the scope and fired again, my bloodied finger too fast on the trigger. Startled, the hunter broke cover, a fat guy cradling a rifle. He put his hand in the air, as if a referee was going to make this stop. I squeezed the trigger again. The hunter's head exploded like an over-ripe piece of fruit, his body flopping back into the sea of grass.

Dogs appeared, three grey-brown blurs loping through the grass. The dog-handler, wearing green fatigues, was crouching in the trees fifty metres away from where I'd shot the hunter. I fired and he tumbled backwards into the shadows. I switched my aim to the dogs, three mutts barrelling through the grass like furry sharks. I did some time, pace and distance math in my head and squeezed off another shot. It missed. The second took out one of the animals, which disappeared in a crash of blood, teeth and fur.

An incoming round hit the embankment to my front, sending up a geyser of dust and grit. A second zipped past my shoulder. The other two hunters had risen to the challenge. I heard the rattle of assault rifles as men began to riddle every possible piece of cover with lead. I began to crawl backwards, the SVU-A cradled in my arms and out of the dust. Another bullet smacked into the tree where I'd just taken cover.

Then the dogs were on me. They looked like pit-bulls crossed with crocodiles. Dead black eyes rolled backwards into sharp, angular heads as they attacked. The first hound sank it's fangs into my leg, just below the knee. The second went for my neck, fetid breath and foam-flecked teeth inches away from my face. I rolled onto my back and dropped my rifle, pulling the pistol from my belt and firing at the beast as fangs sank into my shoulder. The bullet smashed into the dog's skull, the animal scrabbling into a ball. The second was tearing my leg, crazily shaking its head from side to side.

Instinctively I kicked it with my free boot, which did nothing. Waves of pain crashed through my leg as I sat up and rammed the muzzle of the 9mm into the side of the dog's head. I pulled the trigger five or six times before the creature died.

Holstering the pistol, I staggered to my feet and picked up my rifle. I had puncture wounds in my shoulder, blood oozing slowly from the bite. My leg, from calf to knee, was bleeding freely from multiple injuries. I tore off the bottom of my jumpsuit and bound the wound as best I could. Crawling away from the yew trees, I headed back towards the irrigation trench.

The Frenchman, Henri, was creeping along the top of the trench, an AK tucked into his shoulder. I aimed and fired a hundred metre sense of direction shot. It hit him in the arm and he fell out of sight. Rolling into cover behind a pile of weed-covered rubble, I waited. He crept back the way he'd come. I whistled. Henri's face turned towards me, centred in my sights. I fired, his head evaporating into a red mist.

I scrambled on my belly towards the trench, leg burning with pain. I lay on my back, rifle cradled in my arms as I looked up. The sun burned in the midday sky and I heard movement through the grass. Rolling onto my belly I put the bipod on the lip of the trench. I could see the last two hunt organisers, but not the hunters, walking towards me with their AKs ready. I sank back into the trench, put my rifle down and slid a new magazine into my pistol.

They were less than five metres away.

I counted to three and stood up, firing the Browning and hitting the first guy in the belly. I hurled myself back down again. My target swore in German and fell sideways as I heard the crack of the first huntsman's rifle. The bullet hit the baked mud wall of the trench behind me. The other shooters were on the ball, and now knew my position. "Get in the trench or you're next!" I shouted in English. I put my hand over the top and let off three rounds with the pistol.

"OK!" gibbered a terrified voice, a man scrambling down into the trench in a cloud of dust and grit. He was in his forties, paunchy with a red baseball cap and a deep suntan. There was no sign of his AK. "What the fuck is going on?"

"Payback," I said quietly, "it's usually about payback." I aimed the pistol at him and smiled. "Now strip."

"Huh?"

"I said strip. We're swapping clothes." I unzipped my jumpsuit to the waist and tugged off my boots.

"No way," he said.

I shot him in the soft part of his left arm, just south of his elbow. He winced and fell to his knees, hand clutching at the exposed, glistening meat of the exit wound. "Strip or the next one is in your head," I said slowly.

"You're not Russian" he said, his eyes watering.

"No, Sherlock, I'm not. Give me your hat."

"Why?" he said, gazing at the blood running freely down his arm. "I don't understand."

"We're swapping places. You're going to dress as me and try to get away, like bait. Come back towards me and I'll kill you. Get spotted by your customers and they'll try to kill you. So you're better off heading in their direction. I'm a good shot and I'm closer."

"The first guy you killed was an idiot. He couldn't shoot, but the others? They're big game hunters, experts. I won't stand a chance!" If his eyes had gotten any wider they'd have fallen out of their sockets.

"You've got a better chance than the villagers you shot yesterday, or those Bosnians back in Sarajevo, right?"

"Sarajevo? That was before my time…"

"Tough shit. Get your clothes off." I pushed my pistol into his head and treated him to one of my deranged smiles. I have about fifty to choose from and they all seem to have the desired effect.

We swapped clothes. I pulled my pistol belt tight around the waist of the shorts and rolled up the bloody sleeve of the camouflage shirt. Finally, I put the red baseball cap on my head. "Off you go," I said, picking up my rifle.

The man looked down at the filthy jumpsuit he was wearing. He gripped the bullet wound in his arm and started off in a low run along the trench, then broke cover, waving his arms in the air and shouting. I peered through the scope of the SVU-A, my finger taking up the trigger pressure.

CRACK!

The faintest heat shimmer, and a wisp of smoke, rose from my adversary's rifle on a ridge some five hundred metres away. I wasn't watching the guy I'd shot in the arm, who I knew was already dead. The hunter was outside the effective range of the SVU-A but I took the shot, aiming off for windage and slightly high. I imagined where the largest part of the hunter would be, in relation to the smudge of smoke I'd seen from his rifle.

I waited. After half an hour I crept along the trench to the tree line, entering the woods where I'd started the engagement. I limped towards the hunter's position. Apart from a whistling breeze and the chirrup of crickets it was eerily quiet. The ridge ran for about ten metres at an angle to the wood, edged with dirty grey-green and yellow foliage. I flipped the fire selector on my rifle to automatic and patrolled into the copse slowly, painting arcs as I went.

The boot was brown and waxy. It was sticking out of the bushes, attached to a camouflaged leg. Groaning and swearing, I hauled the body out of cover, a big bearded man who must have weighed eighteen stone. He was wearing a ghillie suit, jungle hat and a green net over his face. My bullet had hit him in the shoulder, underneath the clavicle, and exited his body below his shoulder blade at the back. He'd bled out, trapped in his fire position by his bulk. Beneath him was a rifle, a custom '98 Mauser. "You missed the other guy," said a voice behind me.

I spun around, rifle shouldered. It was Bernie Schmidt, wearing jeans and a checked shirt. A Kalashnikov was slung over his shoulder, a cigarette smouldering in the corner of his mouth.

"Don't *ever* creep up on me," I hissed. My head was pounding from the heat and the stalking. The bleeding had stopped on my leg, a swarm of flies buzzing around the scab-encrusted wounds.

"Come on, there's a first aid kit in their truck," said Schmidt, offering me his hand.

I nodded and went with him. "Where's the other hunter?" I said.

"Also in the truck," he smiled. "I was just behind him when you shot his friend. He radioed to ask what was happening."

We walked the half mile to a rusty pickup, Bernie offering me some water and a Russian menthol cigarette, which was a worse experience than the dog bites. In the back of the wagon was a sorry-looking man, hands and ankles bound with duct-tape. "What's your name?" I said to the prisoner in English.

The hunter was in his early fifties, as lean as his dead friend was big. His grey hair was cropped close to his skull. His flinty eyes narrowed. "Martin Weiss," he said carefully.

"How much did you pay for this trip?" I said, resting my back against the truck.

"More than I anticipated, I suspect," said the German. "Is that a SVU-A?" he said, looking at my rifle.

"Yeah," I said.

"That was a good shot at five hundred metres, the one that got Wili. You shouldn't be able to do that."

I shrugged. "Wanna know how this ends?" I walked to the tailgate with his rifle, a Steyr.

"I would be lying if I said no."

I cut the hunter loose. "You get your hunt, Martin. Same rules I had. Except you get to keep your rifle. Here, have some water."

Weiss rubbed his wrists then gulped down the water. He closed his eyes for a moment, then smiled, "how unexpectedly generous. May I ask you your name?"

"Cal Winter," I said quietly, mouth dry. I passed him his rifle and told him to shift his arse. He jogged back up the hill.

"That was very noble of you," said Schmidt, shaking his head.

"Not really. I unloaded his rifle," I replied, shouldering my SVU-A. I took a bead on Weiss' back.

I'm a low-life wet-worker. I hate the life I'm in, the never-ending cycle of kill-or-be-killed. Still, I try to find some merit in my trade, and any scrap will do. This man had chosen to kill people for pleasure. Even I'd never done that.

Schmidt was laughing as I took the shot.

CHAPTER ONE

From *'The Daily Telegraph'*

Johannesburg - The Zambutan Foreign Minister, Joseph Njenga, has alleged a British Private Security Company supported an attempted coup. Lt. Col. Mel Murray, 52, was arrested last week in Marsajir, capital of Zambute. Murray, a former SAS officer, is chief executive of *Focus Projects*. The company, based in Mayfair, specialises in providing protective security services to overseas energy, construction and mining industries. Doctor Kwame Nwebe, President of the African Union, said 'despite the current conflict, UN-monitored elections in Zambute must go ahead. We urge President Aziz to honour promises made to The AU and the UN.' President Omar Aziz, a reclusive and paranoid figure, has signed controversial trade agreements with China, but the regime is threatened by nationalist rebel groups and Islamist guerrillas. Zambute's annexation of the disputed border with Somalia has intensified the conflict, displacing Al-Shabaab terrorists and their latest off-shoot, *The Shadow of Swords* militia. The crisis has also thrown the new Somali government into fresh turmoil, foreign Islamist fighters travelling from Yemen, Sudan, Pakistan and Syria to join the fighting.

The regime has been persuaded to hold UN-monitored elections, on pain of suspension of Western aid payments. Zambutan authorities have yet to release any specific allegations against Murray, who was arrested with political activists linked to Gen. Kanoro Abasi of the Free Zambutan Army (FZA). Tanya Rigby, Executive Director of Focus Projects, said 'Mel Murray was on a feasibility trip for a Russian client in Northern Kenya, conducting routine logistics and security survey. Mel was not involved in any activity detrimental to the Zambutan government and we urge the authorities to release him immediately...'

La Rovellada, Catalonia, Spain

The Firm's 'decompression facility' was a crumbling stone *Finca* overlooking the Mediterranean. An ask-no-questions local doctor visited to check my dog-bites. To begin with, they'd leaked stinking puss. Now they just leaked puss. The doctor said I'd be fully recovered in two or three weeks. Whereupon we'd just be given another shitty, high-risk job... rinse and repeat.

I mooched around, itching for a fix after the stuff I'd taken in Istanbul. Choosing the lesser of two evils is the story of my life, so I settled for cognac and tranquilizers. Sitting on a lichen-covered wall, I took another swig. I picked at scabbed-over bites, making them ooze. Everyone needs a hobby. Now and then I wondered where I could score some brown. An addict is always an addict, even when you're more or less clean.

"It would be easier to cut it off," said Oz, looking at my leg.

"I might still make striker for Crystal Palace," I replied.

Neither of us wanted to be here. The Firm blackmails us all. I'm looking at a life sentence for murder after stalking and killing my former CO. I don't regret it as much as I should, because the glory-hunting bastard deserved it. We get paid, but the money is held back until we're time-served. I had fourteen months to do. Then I'd supposedly be free with just over three million quid in my back pocket. I wanted out, the sooner the better. Most of us died on ops before we got the pay-out anyway. "Please give us somewhere warm for the next job," said Oz, basking in the afternoon heat.

"Be careful what you wish for."

"Have you spoken to Sam recently?" Sam Clarke was the nearest thing I had to family, and even she was wary of me. Oz thinks we're an item, or it's a severe case of unrequited love. The truth was Sam and her kids were my window on normality. I spent three months in a mental hospital after I was invited to leave the army, via military prison. Her visits stopped me making a noose from my bed sheets, or slashing my wrists with a piece of glass. Then she let me kip on her sofa, until I got a job.

Got back on the straight and narrow, right? What a joke. I became a security contractor, straight back to the sand-pit. Then the murder, and The Firm... Sam's late husband, Clarkie, was my platoon sergeant in Iraq. We'd done our infantry training together, before I became an officer. He died near Amara when a Yank airstrike went wrong. It wasn't the pilot's fault, it was mine - I called it in. "She thinks I'm still doing energy security work" I said uneasily, tapping the rubberized satellite phone on the balcony. "When will this bloody well ring?"

It rang. "You can't teach that," Oz grinned.

Harry's voice was scratchy over the encrypted line. "When are you two good to go?"

"According to the Doctor, I'll be match fit in a couple of weeks."

"I said when are you good to go, *not* what some local quack's diagnosis is," he snapped. Something in his voice sparked me up. He sounded in a hurry, which was unusual. "I need you in London on Thursday. I've also assigned Syndicate Three, they'll arrive after you."

I sat up in my chair, "what's the deal?"

"What if I said you're going to break into an African prison?"

"I'd put my head in my hands and cry," I replied, taking another gulp of cognac.

"Prison breaks are the most fun you can have with your clothes on," he said, lightening up a bit. "It gets even better – you've got a new handler. You'll know him as Monty. And you'll be picking up a new team member, to replace Andy."

When Andy died on Salisbury Plain, trying to disarm an IED, he saved my life. "You can't *replace* Andy," I said.

"Sure, I understand. Anyhow, the new fella is American," Harry continued. "A hard bastard, but this is only his second operation for us."

I'd never met Harry. He was a just voice on the phone, my remote control gaoler. But I still felt a sort of closeness to him, which I put down as some especially twisted type of Stockholm syndrome. "Where are you going?" I asked.

"Retirement. I'm too old for this shit."

"Is that it?"

"More or less, anyhow I hope you make it to the end of your contract."

"Why," I snorted, "do you know something I don't?"

"I know lots of things you don't. Just be careful with Monty and keep your head down. Stuff's happening on The Firm, it's going through one of its reinventions."

"What does that mean?" I said quietly. Harry had never elaborated about The Firm before.

"It means there are new butchers operating the meat-grinder, and you poor bastards are the cheap cuts. Just do your job, ask no questions and you'll be OK."

"Harry, give me a break. What's going on?"

I heard him exhale smoke, his gravelly voice lowered to a growl. "I know how you feel about The Firm. Fuck it, I used to feel the same way too. Maybe I do again. I tell you what, in London there's a tailor's shop off Old Street, run by a man called Isaac Samuels. Tell him *The Saint* sent you. He can help you…"

"What's this about, Harry? Why help me?" I tried to keep the note of pathetic gratitude out of my voice.

"Two reasons," he said. "First, once upon a time I was sat where you are, with The Firm holding a gun to my head. Second, if things ever go tits-up, I'm going to need you on my side. Are we agreed?"

"Yes," I said. "We're agreed."

"Roger that," he replied. "Good luck with Africa."

"You know if I can take The Firm down one day, I will," I promised.

"You won't be the first to say that," he sighed. "Chances are you won't be the last either." He hung up.

"What was that about?" asked Oz.

"Harry's retiring, we've got a job in Africa and we brief in London on Thursday. And we've got a new handler." I decided not to tell Oz about Harry's strange offer for now.

"Is there any good news?"

"You wanted to go somewhere hot?" Oz shot me a look as he left the room. He doesn't see The Firm as a prison sentence like I do. He must have done something beyond the pale to end up on it.

My head booze-heavy, I took a shower and went to bed. I dozed for an hour, under wrinkled, sweat-stained sheets. Sam was in my dreams, skin pale and cool as I undressed her. She straddled me, freckled breasts squashed against my face. Then the roof disappeared from her house, armed men peering in, laughing as they readied weapons. Planes circled above, dropping bombs on a desert. They dragged Sam away and attacked me, bullets tearing into my chest, freeing me from the crushing black fist of guilt…

I was woken, gasping, by the trill of my sat phone. Looking around, there was no sign of Oz. My body was slick, sheets stained with blood where my bandages had slipped.

"I'm Monty," said a man with a nasal Northern accent.

"It's Winter."

"I know. I've *heard* about you," he sniffed, like I was some sort of venereal disease doing the rounds. "You'll be met at Heathrow on Thursday by a man called Jackson. Questions?"

"None," I said, remembering Harry's warning.

"Good. We might get on at this rate." The phone clicked off.

Time spent in reconnaissance is seldom wasted, so my next call was to Marcus. He's a serving Secret Intelligence Service officer. On my last UK job, circumstance led to me doing him a big favour. Off-policy. He owes me one in return, which is the way these things are meant to work. "It's Cal, how's tricks?" I said.

"Synchronicity, Calum. I was going to call you later," he purred. "I take it you're relaxing in that Spanish bolt-hole you think we don't know about?"

"We're heading back to the UK on the hurry-up. Would that be for your lot by any chance?"

"It might be," he said carefully. "We need to meet. Toulouse, I think. Lose Mister Osborne. I'm sure you'll find an excuse." He gave me the address of a budget hotel near the airport, on the Avenue du Général de Gaulle. "Let's say ten o'clock, the day after tomorrow."

"Has this anything to do with Africa?"

"Yes, it's all about Africa," he replied. "And if you help me, you might get back from the place in one piece."

CHAPTER TWO

Toulouse was spitefully hot. At the hotel lobby I stood under the air-conditioning unit and scanned the room. Marcus had brought hired muscle, a sinewy, olive-skinned dude sitting on a sofa reading a magazine. He saw me, raised an eyebrow and tapped a message into his smartphone. My phone buzzed. The message said *Room 308*.

308 was a conference suite, decorated in grey and beige. The window looked out over the cargo terminal, UPS planes lined up like giant toys. Marcus, all twenty-odd stone of him, was buttoned into a heavy woollen suit, a stained club tie knotted around his chins. He looked at a pile of croissants like a greyhound eyeing a rabbit. "Not like you to have a bodyguard," I said.

"Times have changed," he shrugged. He shuffled over to a percolator and poured me a coffee.

I took a seat. "How can I help?"

"I need a favour," said Marcus easily, like he was asking me to lend him a tenner. His accent suddenly sounded harsher, more Scottish. He'd shifted from friendly Highland GP to Glaswegian docker.

"This relationship seems one-sided," I replied. "Once upon a time you told me to think of you like a kindly uncle."

"*Uncle* Marcus will make sure there's a quid pro quo." He smiled, returning to friendly Highland GP mode. Then he mashed a croissant into his mouth.

I raised an eyebrow, "hopefully with the emphasis on *Quid*."

"Quite," Marcus replied, dabbing at his mouth with a napkin. "The senior management at SIS trust me to carry out reviews into internal... *issues*."

Marcus was an inveterate rule-bender. I suppose poachers make the best gamekeepers.

"Generally speaking," he continued, "SIS has a remarkably honest workforce. But we occasionally pick up a bad apple. It's inevitable in our line of work. The responsibility is great but the pay is awful."

"Like Philby?"

"Ideological traitors? How *very* twentieth century. No, generally speaking our bad apples want money. Either that or they have a Damascene conversion about the ethics of our trade and squeal to *The Guardian*."

"Which one is worse?"

"The second," he shrugged. "The first type can usually be persuaded to go with a pay-off. The second are childish narcissists. They want publicity and a safe billet somewhere open and free. Like Russia."

I peeled open some marmalade and scooped it out with my finger. It tasted bitter and sweet. "How does this concern me?"

Marcus' eyes hardened. "My bad apple is involved in a delicate operation. Yes, in Africa."

"So my next job is already compromised?"

"Perhaps," he conceded. "I'd be remiss not to consider you as an asset, perhaps flush out the suspect."

"Who's your traitor? And what does it have to do with a prison break?"

Marcus fixed me with piggy little eyes, shining with cunning. "I don't know *who* the traitor is. All four suspects are in the field. I don't want to scare them off with a formal investigation, not in the middle of planning such a risk-laden operation."

"Where do I fit in?" I replied. "It's not like we ever meet spooks." It was a golden rule that we never directly interacted with intelligence agencies. That way we remained deniable and they kept their arses covered. When I'd first met Marcus, entirely unintentionally, my handlers found out and went apeshit.

"Ach, you're too sharp for me. We're deliberately exposing you to them, breaking a rule. It will make them feel more trusted and therefore more likely to make a mistake. Usher them into the inner sanctum, see what they do…"

"I'm not sure I like being bait," I said.

"You didn't seem to mind on your last job for the Germans."

"I had a rifle and a target," I shrugged. "I can handle that, but not your spy-games."

"Oh come now," he cooed. "The current DIADEM agrees. We've ensured all four suspects are DIADEM-indoctrinated."

DIADEM was the codename of the deniable MI6 officer who tasked The Firm via our handlers, an arm's-length proxy. And I only knew that because Marcus' late wife, also a career spook, had once been DIADEM. His knowledge of The Firm was one of the things I intended to prise out of him.

Marcus pushed a steel key-ring towards me. It looked like one of those novelty bottle openers you get in upmarket Christmas crackers. Mind you, I drink a lot of beer so it was less of a novelty and more of a lifestyle essential. "There's a

GCHQ-grade encrypted memory stick hidden in that. It contains profiles of the four SIS officers. Their operation was called CORACLE. You're tidying up, getting an asset out of there."

"Who thinks up operation names?" I asked. "Isn't a coracle a little round boat?"

"It is," Marcus smiled. "And this one's sprung a leak. And the leaker is, I'm convinced, siphoning intelligence to the Chinese Ministry of State Security."

I knew the Chinese were buying up Africa piece by piece. Corrupt African politicians were in the pocket of Beijing, China aggressively seeking resources to fuel its relentless economic expansion. Mind you, they weren't doing anything we hadn't pioneered a hundred years ago. "I'm being asked to play detective again?"

"Don't be modest, Cal. You're an excellent problem-solver, I like that about you."

"I don't like it," I replied. Playing spook Cluedo in some hostile East African war-zone wasn't my idea of fun. I'd rather be in a field in Kurdistan, being shot at by big-game hunters.

"I'm afraid it's Hobson's choice. The alternative is to explain to your new handler why we've had this meeting." Marcus looked sadly at his next croissant.

"True," I shrugged.

"Alternatively," Marcus continued, "go on this operation anyway and get killed because you didn't identify the treacherous bastard planning on selling you out."

"So what's in it for me?"

"This life you're in, an indentured gun? You *do* want out, don't you? Maybe knowing more about The Firm might help?"

"Sure," I said. "We both know my chances of surviving 'til the end of my contract."

"If it doesn't send you mad first, Calum. Are you still on medication?"

"Booze, mainly," I replied.

Marcus sighed. "I'm prepared to give you information. In fact, you might find a report on that memory stick, just to whet your appetite. It will automatically wipe itself after you've read it, just to be safe."

First Harry, now Marcus... It was like The Firm was a dam, holding back a dark reservoir of secrets. Was I being offered the chance to make the first crack in it? "Why are you offering me this?"

"It's in my interest," he shrugged, offering me a sticky pastry.

"What happens when I've identified the target?"

"I've yet to decide," he glowered. "I've a range of options to manage the... *traitor*." Marcus took the mobile he'd given me from the table. He replaced it with a compact satellite phone. "From now on use this."

"Okay," I replied, studying the phone. It was a good quality commercial brand, the type a security contractor would take into the field.

"It looks normal enough," said Marcus, "but it's been through the propeller-heads at GCHQ. It's as encrypted as it's going to get." He stood up, the meeting over.

"How often do you want me to call in?" I asked. I had no option but to accept. Seldom had a rat been put in such a baroque maze, and with such a compelling piece of cheese at the end.

"I'll call you," he replied. "And, for what it's worth, thanks for…"

"Please don't say *help*," I interrupted. "It suggests a level of choice."

"OK, how about *understanding?* Will that do?"

"I guess," I replied. I walked towards the door, the satellite phone clasped to my chest.

"There is light at the end of the tunnel, Cal."

I shot him a look.

"There's change in the air, Captain Winter, it's like a bad smell. Men like you and I need to seize any opportunities from it, if we're to survive. I'm going to need you."

"Everybody's talking in bloody riddles at the moment, Marcus."

"I know." The SIS man smiled and returned to his breakfast. "We'll talk after you get back from Africa." The bastard was toying with me. Along with what Harry had said, I was sure big wheels were turning.

Leaving the room, I took a taxi to an electronics store on the Rue de Toul. I bought a tablet computer and a small digital camera and returned to my hotel. It was a quiet back street place, anonymous but comfortable. Plugging in the memory stick, I brought up the files. Navigating through the device, I could see that they were copy-protected. I tried to use a screen capture tool, but the program knew what I was trying to do. A dull pinging noise warned me it wouldn't work. I suspected as much. Scanning the material, I decided it was like low-alcohol beer. It tasted like beer but lacked the bite you needed for it to *be* beer. I needed context. I photographed each page with the camera, uploading the lot to an encrypted online drop-box.

Oz was due at any moment. I hid it for later. I'd sold the trip to Toulouse as R&R while we waited to fly back to London. So when Oz turned up we hit the bar, ordered cold beers. "What have you been up to?" he said, chugging back a cold *Kronenbourg*.

"This and that," I shrugged.

Oz patted me on the back. "You look like someone pissed in your cornflakes."

"I've had enough of The Firm's bullshit."

Oz looked over my shoulder, into my room, and sipped his drink. "What are you going to do about it? All this dripping about The Firm is starting to get on my tits."

I gave Oz a look. He wasn't stupid. My plan, to screw over The Firm, on the other hand, was. "How can they stop us going public, blowing the whole thing open?"

Oz rubbed at the bags under his eyes. "For starters, you've been in the nut-house. You ain't the most credible witness. And all you've got is a phone number for a Handler you've never met."

"But... what if I recorded all my conversations with them?"

"If they thought you were playing that game you'd be dead already."

"Oz…"

"Don't you think that for every job The Firm isn't back-stopping you as a rogue head-case?"

I shook my head. "They can't watch us all the time. I wonder if they watch us at all."

"They do, but they can't watch us all the time. They check up on us now and then. I know they do. They use paranoia to keep us in line."

I had that itching feeling, like the one you get when you have a discussion about fleas. "Who are *they*?"

"You must have heard the stories," said Oz. "They've got people who used to be like us. And if we get too lively, they're the ones who make us disappear."

"How do you know all this?"

The ex-SBS man shrugged. "I see people now and then, in the crowd or in a car near my place. People who used to be in this line of work. It's not a coincidence."

I scratched at my neck, felt it redden as I swallowed my drink. "Doesn't it drive you nuts?" Something squirmed in my brain, the demons that I fought so hard to keep away. Hatred, for The Firm, for Marcus, for *everything*, buzzed in my head.

"No," Oz shrugged.

"How do you deal with it?" I said, voice cracking.

"The Firm is better than the alternative. And when you're time is up they let you go." Oz patted my shoulder, "dig in, son, that's my advice. Hack it for a bit longer then get out and enjoy your dough. It's a clean slate, right?"

"It's never a clean slate. I want The Firm gone, fucked up."

"Why? What do you get out of it? And don't say revenge."

"Revenge."

"Man the fuck up," Oz laughed, finishing his beer. "Let's watch the world go by. It might be the last opportunity we'll get for a while, if we're off to hot and sandy places."

"Sure," I half-smiled through gritted teeth. I felt the hate suddenly dissipate, like poison gas, from inside my head. "I wonder who we're rescuing in Africa?"

Oz pulled a face. "Well, whoever the poor bastard is, they must be desperate."

"Why?"

"They've hired us, haven't they?"

CHAPTER THREE

London

We were taken to a decaying office block overlooking a stretch of motorway. The room smelt of mildew, cobwebs hanging from the ceiling like little silk nooses. Briefings follow a familiar script; they wheel in bosses who won't set foot on a two-way range, but want to meet the tame killers who will. They give you a plan full of holes and expect you to make it work.

Studying my fingernails, I ignored the spook at the door. At Heathrow he'd introduced himself as Hugo Jackson. He was a mixed-race guy of Chinese heritage, all spiky black hair and hipster clothes. "Shall I get us coffee?" he smiled. His accent was cut-glass English public school.

"I thought you'd never ask," said Oz. He wore a new suit and a Royal Marines tie. He looked like he was dressed for a court appearance, or maybe a funeral.

Hugo was the first CORACLE suspect Marcus had identified. His report, anodyne and stripped to the barest details, contained nothing more than a skeleton resume for each suspect. I'd studied his file the night before. 'Hugo Jackson' was Hong Kong Chinese, with fluent Cantonese and Mandarin. English educated, he'd attended Harrow and Oxford. His British father, a bigwig at HSBC, landed him a job in cyber-security after Hugo graduated from Balliol. He was one of four officers entrusted with operation CORACLE, a cluster-fuck of epic proportions. That, and his links to China, made him a suspect.

He left the room to get coffee. Hugo struck me as a decent enough bloke: laid-back and polite. And for a posh public schoolboy, he was happy to fetch a brew. But experience taught me it meant nothing. Ten minutes later Hugo returned with a tray of chipped coffee mugs, "Princess Juliet's here," he whispered.

A smartly business-suited woman and an ex-colleague of mine strode in behind him. "I'm Juliet Easter," said the woman. She was thirtysomething, with glossy chestnut hair and a wind-burnt, freckled face. Her accent had a trace of Africa in it, her voice exuding authority. She had a prettily broken nose, just wonky enough to be cute. "But, please, call me Juliet."

Juliet Easter, CORACLE team leader, was the second suspect.

"Can we get a drink?" I said bluntly. I'd been dry for a day, and Easter's confident manner irked me already. Weren't we here to sort out her fuck-up?

"Cal… Relax," Oz whispered.

"I was warned about your legendary interpersonal skills," she replied easily, eyes locked playfully onto mine. I noticed that her fingernails were chewed. No wedding ring, either.

The guy loitering next to her was Tom Dancer. He'd been a company commander in my old battalion, half a lifetime ago. Unlike me, he'd been successful in SF selection, leaving as a Major after a tour on 22 SAS. He had a head of thick, fair hair and a broad, handsome face. He'd been a popular guy, tipped for high rank. "Cal," he said, offering his hand. "You're looking great, good to see you after all these years."

"You don't, you fat bastard," I teased.

"Too many business lunches, old boy," Dancer grinned, patting his paunch. Well over six-feet tall and barrel-chested, he wore a bold pinstripe suit and a Hermes tie. He looked like something out of a City of London investment bank.

"There's a lot to cover and not much time," said Easter. "Then, you never know, we might find you that drink. Tom, please begin. Hugo, you can go."

Hugo nodded obediently, performed a theatrical bow and sauntered out of the office. "Of course, my moon and stars!" he purred over his shoulder. So, he was a George RR Martin fan, too. I wouldn't like to be spoken to like that, and wondered if Hugo did either.

Easter rolled her eyes. "Geeks," she sighed.

"What's Hugo's speciality?" I asked.

"What, apart from being an arse? Hugo's role isn't relevant at the moment," Easter replied, firm but polite. "Tom?"

Dancer shot his cuffs. "You've heard about Mel Murray?"

"I saw the news," I said, the penny beginning to drop. "He was taken prisoner by government forces in Zambute, right?" Zambute was your standard-issue basket-case African dictatorship, forever teetering on the brink of failure. It was like North Korea with wildebeest. Oz nudged me and rolled his eyes.

"Yes," Easter added. "The CIA world fact book describes the Zambutan-Somali annexed Zone as *possibly the most dangerous place on earth.*"

"You're not selling this job to me," I said.

"I don't have to," Easter replied, eyes sparkling. I couldn't work out if Easter was agreeably jaded or simply trying to lighten the mood. She slipped off her jacket and sat down, revealing a neatly-ironed white blouse that contrasted nicely with her tan. I noticed Dancer quickly brush her leg with his hand below the table. She didn't seem to mind.

Oz sipped his coffee. "Mel Murray owns Focus Projects, right?"

A Private Security Company, Focus Projects boasted Mayfair offices and a corporate box for the rugby at Twickenham. Retired Generals queued up to beg their former juniors for a chance to sit on the board, earn a small fortune for a couple of days work a month 'consulting.'

"I'm Ops Manager for Focus Projects," said Dancer proudly. "Mel Murray isn't just my boss, he's a good friend. And his work in Zambute wasn't about energy security."

Friend? That wasn't the gossip I'd heard on the private security circuit. Apparently Murray was a bastard when he was CO of 22 SAS, fucking-up Tom Dancer's chance of promotion to half-colonel. Then again, Dancer wasn't the sort of bloke to hold a grudge, especially where a boatload of money was concerned.

"Since when does SIS care when a deniable drops in the shit?" I replied, straightening my leg. It still hurt when I flexed it.

"Murray was my responsibility," Easter replied, not taking the bait. She pulled a file from a treble-locked case. "This contains what you need to know about Operation CORACLE, which *was* our effort to covertly disrupt Chinese economic expansion in Zambute."

"CORACLE is fatally compromised," Dancer added. "We're implementing an exit strategy. Scooping Mel up is the last piece of that jigsaw."

"The Chinese?" said Oz. "Ain't we mates with them now?"

Easter shrugged. "The Treasury's *volte face* on China hasn't exactly... helped our position."

Britain, like everyone else, was selling their crown jewels to Beijing. We were like a crippled war widow, shuffling off to a pawn-broker with her husband's old medals. Meanwhile the Russians were creeping back across Eastern Europe like poison ivy while we junked our military capability. "No disrespect to Colonel Murray," I said, "but why is he so important?"

"Yeah," Oz added, "doesn't he just get a token show trial and a couple of years in prison?"

Dancer put his hand on my arm. "Mel has..."

"...royally fucked up," Easter snapped. Her steel-grey eyes flashed, a frond of glossy hair falling across her face.

I shouldn't have noticed, especially not during a mission-critical briefing, but Juliet Easter was smoking hot when angry. There was a slight flush on her face, flinty eyes almost feline when they narrowed. Her lips formed a lush pout, which made me think bad thoughts. Oz saw the look in my eye and guffawed. Like I cared - apart from booze and schadenfreude, nothing cheers me up like a beautiful woman. "Colonel Murray is a grand-standing buffoon," she scowled. "He's wrecked two years of intelligence work playing *Lawrence of Arabia*." She was even cuter when she sneered, discretely painted lips drawn back over a neat row of teeth.

Dancer sighed. "Well, I suppose Mel did step a tad outside his brief."

"*Outside his brief…?*" she snorted. "There's blatant electoral gerrymandering down to Murray, as well as weapons procurement via groups the CIA have decided are linked to terrorists. It's a diplomatic and political disaster if he cracks under torture."

"Not to mention SIS," I smiled. "And you too, right?"

"I think we can safely say I'm not the issue," Easter shrugged. "My career trajectory is now fixed firmly in the *crash and burn* position." I got the feeling she meant it. "My brief is to ensure that we get Murray back," she continued, "before he's tortured and coughs everything he knows. This is damage limitation, pure and simple."

Oz ran a hand over his perfectly smooth scalp, "anything else we need to know about this cake-and-arse party?"

Tom Dancer stood up like he was giving a Sandhurst briefing, except we were in a deserted office with sticky grey carpet and rising damp. "The plan is to extract Colonel Murray from the *K*ivuli *H*atua secure facility, inside the annexed zone. I envisage an in-and-out job." He tried to smile and lighten the mood. "After all, Seal Team Six bagged Bin Laden, didn't they?"

"Seal Team Six had twenty-three fully-equipped Tier One operators, two secret stealth choppers, satellite cover and the CIA," said Oz, "and a dog. I know, 'cos I've seen the movie. And they only had to kill their target, not an exfil."

"And one of the multi-million dollar stealth helos crashed," I added helpfully. I'd seen *Zero Dark Thirty* too.

Juliet Easter studied her fingernails. "I'll see if we can get you a dog, if that will improve morale, Mister Osborne. There's a second objective. You need to escort my team into the prison."

"This gets even better," I sighed.

"I appreciate your concern, but my team aren't helpless civilians," she replied. "Apart from our technical expert, the rest are experienced officers."

"I didn't say you were helpless."

"You didn't need to," she replied, cocking her head.

I finished my coffee and sighed. "I apologise if it came across that way. There's a lot of new information being dumped on us in a short space of time."

"Apology accepted," she replied, rewarding me with a smile. "By the way, your fee is generous by SIS standards: a hundred thousand per operator, plus expenses and a successful completion bonus of twenty-five per cent."

Dancer stroked his chin, pretending to be impressed. What a load of bollocks. It was chickenfeed compared to some of the dough I'd made for The Firm. "Wow," I sniffed. "I won't spend it all at once."

Easter caught my expression, a smile tugging at the corner of her mouth. "You should see the pittance *we* get paid. As a bonus, upon completion of the contract you'll be provided with a credible alibi for the Belov affair."

You couldn't put a price on that. It appealed to me more than money, even if I had to go to war to do it. I wasn't going to tell Easter that half of my work on that job was for SIS, my first taste of skulduggery for Marcus. "So why don't you use your own covert operators?" asked Oz, "Special Forces or a legitimate PSC?"

"This has to be *completely* deniable," said Easter. "I don't know if you've noticed, but right now we're a piss-poor little country with an army the size of a cricket team and the force projection capability of My Little Pony. Being sneaky bastards is all we've got left."

"It has to be The Firm," Dancer continued. "Nobody else has the capacity to integrate into an operation like this *and* remain genuinely deniable. Things need to look as normal as possible, until Mel's safe."

"There's another problem," said Easter. "The Zambutan elections are scheduled for early September. Whatever the result, there'll be an army marching on the capital and then we'll never extract Murray. I want him back within three weeks."

I caught a laugh in the back of my throat, "three weeks? I'll get out my pointy hat and magic wand. I'm a mercenary, not a magician."

Easter smiled. She knew we weren't in a position to turn the job down. "Abracadabra," she replied.

I picked up the thick green SIS file, covered with protective markings. "OK, let's see if you're trying to kill me or not."

"I'll get Hugo," she nodded, picking up her stuff and leaving the room. "He'll look after you for the rest of today."

Dancer caught me checking her out and smiled. "How did you get wrapped up in this?" I asked.

"Mel head-hunted me in the early days of the company. I had nothing else going on at the time."

"And what went wrong in Zambute?"

"Mel got too involved with the locals, went native," Dancer shrugged, rubbing his jowls. He looked tired now, bags forming under his eyes. "Some men buy a Ferrari when they have their mid-life crisis. Mel started a war of liberation."

"OK, and SIS going into the prison?'" said Oz. I could tell that escorting a bunch of civilians into a hostile environment concerned him. "What the fuck is that all about?"

"I'm not cleared to know," said Dancer conspiratorially. "But Juliet gave me a heads-up. The Chinese use the prison as an electronic warfare station and listening post. They've discovered the People's Liberation Army have a piece of their latest kit stashed there. It's too good an opportunity to miss – SIS wants to steal it." He went to say something else, but Easter stepped back in the room. Dancer looked like a naughty schoolboy and fiddled with his iPhone.

"Right," Easter announced, "accommodation is ready. You can begin planning there."

"You're the boss," I replied, standing up and shouldering my bag. Dancer led us out of the dingy office, towards the bare concrete stairs.

"Captain Winter?" said Easter.

"Yes, Juliet?"

She handed me a bottle of Maker's Mark in a duty-free bag.

"That's my favourite bourbon," I said.

"I know," she winked. And then she was gone.

CHAPTER FOUR

Hugo drove us to a derelict army barracks near Heathrow airport. Nestled amidst industrial estates and derelict pubs, stray carrier bags flapped like surrender flags along the wire. "Welcome to the Hounslow Hilton," Hugo chuckled.

"We're expecting a new team member," I said, cracking open the car window for some fresh air. It was time to put on my team leader's hat, pretend to be the guy in charge. My fingers gripped the duty-free bag and the bottle of bourbon inside.

"He's here already," Dancer replied. "My guys scooped him up from Heathrow."

We were ushered into the long-abandoned NAAFI, which still smelt of spilt beer, Kiwi parade gloss and pies. A pit-bull of a man was sprawled across a threadbare sofa, napping. He wore dusty Kuhl mountain pants with lots of pockets, sneakers and a faded blue muscle vest. He opened an eye, leathery face creasing into the type of smile a crocodile might give a lame antelope. "Cal?" he asked in a husky, half-strangled American accent, "Alex Bytchakov."

"Yeah, I'm Cal Winter. This is Oz," I said, jabbing a thumb in the direction of the ex-Marine.

Bytchakov was squat, no more than five-foot eight, but carved from a block of heavily-tattooed muscle. The American's face looked like someone had re-shaped it with a hammer, scars snaking across his closely-cropped scalp. His close set eyes scanned us up and down. "I guess I'm the Fuckin' New Guy," he said, offering a paw.

"It's good to meet you," I replied, shaking his hand. I noticed the scar at his throat, two star-shaped gashes inches from his jugular. It explained the voice.

He caught me looking. "That was a 5.56 round, I was lucky as hell. It hit my throat and sailed straight through my jowls. The bullet stopped in some unlucky sonofabitch's eye."

"Where was that?" I asked.

"Tajikistan," he replied. "I wouldn't recommend it for a vacation."

"What's your CV, then?" said Oz, not unpleasantly.

"You mean *resume*, right?"

"No, I mean CV," Oz dead-panned. "After all, we're not in Butt-Fuck Ohio, are we?"

Bytchakov laughed. "I served in the 82nd Airborne, 508th Parachute Infantry. After that it I graduated Ranger School and onto Delta for five years, with a tour on The Activity. I've got seven tours in total, plus some excursions to other shitholes where Uncle Sam ain't meant to be." Yank ops tours were usually twelve months – which meant Bytchakov had been fighting longer than the length of World War Two. They've also got more elite military units with dodgy names than I've had parking tickets. *The Activity* was another one of those black ops outfits, full of deniable snake-eaters and heavily-bearded killers. The kind of outfits they make video games and straight-to-cable movies about.

"MOS?" said Oz. American servicemen had a set Military Occupational Speciality, a number which denoted their trade.

"18B" he replied. "It's the only way to fly."

"That's Special Forces Weapons Sergeant?" I said. There were lots of trades in the American SF, but the 18Bs were the pointiest of the pointy-end.

"Hey have a cookie," Alex shrugged.

"And then?" I asked.

He pulled a face. "I fell out of love with the army, which I guess was mutual. I left and got a gig with Steel Patriarch. That lasted three years, but I quit after Tajikistan. Then… shit happened and I end up on this outfit. I've spent the last year working out of Trieste, learning the ropes."

Steel Patriarch was a Russian PSC. The pay wasn't great and the discipline brutal, but you were guaranteed action. I also knew that The Firm's central and Eastern European operations were run out of Trieste. "What happened?" I said. "For The Firm to get you?"

Alex sat down and lit a cigarette. "Mister, that ain't none of your business. Don't ask again."

"Fair enough," I replied in Russian.

"What did *you* do?" replied the American in the same language. His Russian was fluent.

"I killed a man."

"No shit?" he snorted in English. "Your Russian is good. Where did you learn?"

"Here and there," I replied. "I pick up languages easily."

"It's his only talent," said Oz.

Dancer reappeared. He was in shirtsleeves and tailored linen slacks, a pair of steel-rimmed glasses perched on his forehead. He looked around the gloomy NAAFI and shrugged. "Let's get on with it, shall we?"

"What's the prison like?" I said.

"It's called *Kivuli Hatua*. It was built by the Italians in the late twenties. The regime uses it for political opponents."

"Why in the south of Zambute?" asked Oz, studying the map. "That's bandit country, right?"

"It's their version of Guantanamo Bay, but without the customer service."

I picked up a sheaf of surveillance imagery. Kivuli Hatua was an angular, *Beau Geste* fort perched on top of a rounded cliff overlooking the sea. A broad, flat beach stretched further north, sweeping into a crescent as it met a lightly-wooded headland below the prison.

Oz turned his attention to the satellite pictures, sipping coffee and munching on biscuits. Crumbs dropped on the castle. "Dancer, there's an airbase three miles northwest of the prison. There's what looks like a mobile antiaircraft gun down there. What's the score?"

Dancer nodded, "oh, that's Quaani airbase. They've two ground attack jets there, and two Hind attack helos. Yes, that's an exported ZSU 23/4 with radar."

"Are you fucking kidding me?" said Oz.

"Magic Eight Ball says this is a battalion assault," Alex offered, rubbing his stubbly chin. "If we were doing this for real we'd deploy SPECOPS teams with Rangers runnin' a hard perimeter. Right now, though, I see four of us."

Dancer saw the look on our faces. "Only one of the jets is operational, they use ancient radar that occasionally works if their generators aren't broken. The helos are in good nick, there's a Russian PMC providing maintenance and pilots. However, fuel is a problem, those Hinds haven't moved for almost a fortnight."

"You need to take those helos out," said Oz, "right off the bat."

"Damn right," I said. "What air assets do we have?" I cracked open the Maker's Mark and poured a beaker-full.

"Two helis, a Super Puma and a Dornier, a bit like a Huey. The rebels can help with the air base, I've got that covered."

"And how's that covered?" I asked. "It's hardly a small detail."

Dancer shrugged, "the Zambutan Freedom Army will launch an assault on the Quaani air base at a time of our choosing."

"Why?" asked Oz.

"They love Mel," he replied. "His links to the rebels might have dropped him in the shit with MI6, but we can exploit it to our advantage." I thought about it for a moment. If the rebels attacked in strength, it might just work.

"In which case I reckon infil by sea," smiled Oz, tracing a finger across the map. I looked at his eyes, darting back and forth across the map and schematics. I knew he was getting a buzz out of the thought of doing this for real. "This looks ideal." He pointed to the comma-shaped beach north of the prison.

"If I wanted to storm fuckin' beaches," drawled Alex, "I'd have joined the marines."

"Nobody has stormed a beach since Korea," said Oz. "When I was a marine I only ever *crept* up 'em." He accepted a plastic beaker of bourbon from the American and smiled.

"Guard force?" I asked, shuffling maps and plans of the prison.

Dancer didn't need to look at his notes, "a reinforced platoon from the Presidential Commando and twenty prison staff. Sometimes the Chinese get up there to do interrogation," said Dancer.

"Chinese spooks?" I said.

"Probably," he said. "There's also a battalion of Chinese marines up in Marsajir. They're part of the international anti-piracy task force, but I doubt their Rules of Engagement extend to fighting rebels. If we go in early doors they'll be tucked up in bed anyway."

"A battalion, you say? A quick-in-and-out," laughed Oz. "What do you think, Cal?"

I thought about it for a moment and looked at the glowing tip of my cigar. It was crazy. "Fuck it," I groaned. "Who wants to live forever? Being a mercenary and not liberating a small African country? It's like being a rock star and not throwing a TV through a hotel window."

Dancer grinned. "You sound like Mel Murray, you stupid bastard!"

Alex Bytchakov shook his head for a moment. Then he laughed, which sounded like someone starting up a high pitched buzz saw. "Jesus, gimme another drink," he croaked, pointing at the Maker's Mark. I sloshed Bourbon into a beaker and pushed it towards him. "I didn't know what to expect when I got screwed into this," he said, "but it sure weren't a Kamikaze mission."

"Welcome to The Firm," said Oz. "You pick up your rising sun headband tomorrow."

Dancer produced another bottle. He opened his laptop, showing us maps and pictures of Zambute. He explained the Americans had already sanctioned drone strikes in the south, on alleged High Value Targets from the Shadow of Swords *mujahedeen*. "So if we're not only dodging the Chinese, we need to worry about Reaper drones." We watched some video he'd taken in-country. Zambute was the colour of yesterday's porridge, spindly trees littering the blighted landscape. The battle-scarred towns were made of breeze-blocks and corrugated iron. The only thing that cheered it up, like every Third World war zone I'd been to, were kids playing football.

My Firm-issued satellite phone rang. I picked it up and headed for the door. It was Monty. "Did Bytchakov get to you?" he said. "He's a useful man."

"Yeah, he's here. They've put us up in a barracks in London."

"OK," said the Handler sourly. "Don't show your faces. I'm still managing the fallout from your last operation."

"I'd prefer to talk about this Mission Impossible you've lumbered us with."

"Let's not get off… on the wrong foot," he said haughtily.

I blew cigar smoke as I gazed over the parade square. "I'll suck up as much crap as you can throw. But we need more operators."

"Syndicate Three arrives tomorrow," he replied. Monty didn't sound like a soldier, not like Harry did. "And I doubt you have any idea how much crap I can throw at you."

"We need more men," I repeated.

"Stop whining or I'll put someone else in charge," he whined. "And you'll be floating in the Thames with your bloody hands sawn off."

"Threats don't change the fact that we're under-staffed."

Monty thought about it for the moment. "I've been given authority for *Fallen Eagle* support on this operation. Does that help?"

I'd heard the term before, another of The Firm's legends.

Fallen Eagle was The Firm's codename for UES, Urgent Exfiltration Support. It wasn't offered lightly, but if a job was deemed especially politically risky, we were given 'Fallen Eagle' status. If we activated the protocol, we would be given 'Extraordinary Assistance.' It was The Firm's own arrangement, compartmentalised from whoever was sponsoring the operation.

None of us knew what the 'assistance' was. Some of us reckoned it sounded like the CIA, as the Americans used macho codenames. So, we figured, perhaps their Special Activities Division would appear, like the Seventh Cavalry with big beards and Oakley sunglasses, to magic us away. Seeing as we were British, I guessed it was more likely we'd get a mini-cab.

My view was if they could extract us that easily, they could extract Mel Murray too. Why chuck good money after bad? A more realistic outcome was assistance in lying low in-country until we could escape. Nonetheless, some of our best operators, men who should have known better, relaxed when Fallen Eagle was offered. It was a bullet-proof comfort blanket, for men sent on pointlessly risky missions like extracting Mel Murray.

Like everything else on The Firm, I knew a little, but not enough to leverage any advantage out of it. I felt like a prisoner in an old prisoner of war movie, slowly figuring out the guards' patrol pattern and the timing of floodlights… "It's better than nothing I suppose," I told Monty. "Whatever the hell it is."

"It's a precious operational resource," he snapped. "You should be grateful."

The temptation to tell Monty to fuck off bubbled at the back of my mouth, but I kept schtum. "Sure," I replied.

He rang off.

Back inside, Dancer walked over. "I'm coming too. That's one extra gun. Juliet's team will need some muscle, and I know Zambute well."

I slapped him on the back, "No offence, but you're out of shape." I liked Dancer, who'd been a formidable special operations soldier in his day. But years of working lunches and drinks parties had taken their toll.

"Bollocks," he replied easily, patting me on the back. "I know the area, I speak passable Swahili, fluent Arabic and the locals trust me."

"Tom…"

"Cal, I'm still a field guy, not a suit."

"Ok, you've two weeks to sort yourself out," I shrugged. "Get yourself down the gym. It's not like I'm going to be overwhelmed with volunteers."

Dancer and I went outside for a smoke, leaving the others chatting as they pored over the maps. We walked past the barrack blocks and stood in front of the old officer's mess. I pulled my cigar case from my pocket, "Tom, what's the score with Juliet Easter?" I remembered how he'd touched her back at the office block.

"Ah, Jools," Dancer smiled as we crossed the parade square, trailing cigar smoke. "Juliet was born in Zimbabwe, moved here as a kid. After college she joined the army, made captain in the Intelligence Corps. During the Basra fuck-up she went on secondment to SIS. They were impressed enough to offer her a permanent job."

"What's her speciality?"

"HUMINT and languages," he replied. "She's the real deal, speaks Swahili, Creole, French, Pashtun and Arabic. She even passed the army Commando course." She sounded like one of those sickeningly epic over-achievers you meet in some of the more exotic corners of MI6. It fitted in with the pen-picture I'd been given in Marcus's report.

"And she's very attractive," I shrugged, although I wasn't going to share what it said about Easter on her profile. She was a hundred grand in debt, her tiny London flat re-mortgaged to the hilt. Her younger brother suffered from cerebral palsy and needed around-the-clock care, which she was never going to afford on a spook's salary. "Sounds like you two are close…" I said.

Dancer treated me to a cat-who-got-the-cream grin. "She's only human. We've been seeing each other on and off. It's only a fling, nothing else."

"Can we trust her?"

"Fuck no," Dancer sputtered. "Cut Jools in half she'd have *Secret Intelligence Service* running through the middle like a stick of rock. We've an understanding, that's all. It gets lonely out in Northern Kenya."

I knew Dancer had been divorced twice. Some of the other officers in the battalion used to think he was a bit too flash, but I took the view they were jealous of his moneyed background. Easter didn't seem his type compared to the posh, willowy blondes that hung off his arm while he skied around Switzerland or caught some rays on the Cote d'Azur.

"CORACLE can hardly help her up the greasy pole at Vauxhall Cross, can it?" I said, fishing.

"True," Dancer shrugged. "Jools wishes she was a shooter, not an intelligence monkey. I know it when I see it, Cal. I did the same thing, gave up promotion to get posted back to The Regiment."

"I always wondered what happened to your brilliant career."

"I could've made brigadier," he sniffed. "Jools isn't realising her potential. And by the time she does, it'll be too late. If she's not careful she'll end up a bitter, childless re-tread with a hatful of war stories she's not allowed to talk about."

"You old romantic."

"The truth hurts."

Pissed off at how Dancer could be so flippant about a relationship with a woman like Easter, I changed the subject. "And you think this operation could work?"

"Yes, I think it could, but we need to be fast and aggressive. I want to get Mel out of there. He's a good man, whatever mistakes he's made."

"That sounds like the only reason to do this job in the first place," I said.

We finished our cigars and went inside, to plan our nasty little war.

CHAPTER FIVE

It was just after eight in the morning when Syndicate Three arrived. I stood on the derelict parade square as they emerged from a Range Rover with tinted windows.

First out were two lithe, good-looking guys in their mid-thirties, dressed in designer sports gear and sunglasses. Both had creamy-brown skin, high cheekbones and dark, narrow eyes. Physically, they were identical. It was the Grey Twins, Raphael and Ruben. They claimed to be Jewish-Moroccan-Turkish, by way of Romford. The scions of an East London crime family, they scarpered off to join the Royal Marines after being acquitted of murdering their father. They chose the Marines because Ruben liked the look of the Commando Dagger. Inseparable, they served together in 42 Commando and specialised as raiding craft coxswains. They earned themselves a reputation as hard men with a love of combat, either in the field, the dojo or the nightclubs of Plymouth. "Cap'n Winter," said Ruben cheerfully, throwing up a mock-salute, "still smoking those fuckin' 'orrible cigars?"

"Yes, *mon ami.*"

The twins spoke terrible 'Legion French' from their brief spell in the *Légion étrangère*. That ended with a shoot-out in Marseille that left the head of a drug syndicate dead. The boys had been running drugs out of Corsica in a military landing craft. "You speak French like a frog," Ruben replied. "I speak it like a... *warrior*." Raphael grunted his agreement. "You see?" said Ruben, "even he agrees."

Raphael Grey was famed for his lack of verbosity. Graveyard quiet, he rationed words like water in a legionnaire's canteen. If I ever turned on The Firm, these two would be a good prospect, as long as there was enough cash in my war chest.

Next up was their syndicate leader. Duncan Bannerman was a rangy, foul-mouthed Scotsman, coppery-red hair worn in dreadlocks. His face was mortuary-white, with a long nose and a grim slash of a mouth. All he needed were fangs and he'd look like a Caledonian version of Dracula. He wore baggy cargo pants and a *Motorhead* tee-shirt, a desert camouflaged Bergen on his back. Strapped to the rucksack was a hessian-wrapped object, some four feet long. "Hello wankers!" he hollered.

"What's that on the side of your Bergen, Duncan?" said Oz, shaking the Scotsman's hand.

"It's ma Claymore," he replied proudly.

"Do you mean a fucking *sword*?" said Alex Bytchakov.

"Aye," he replied, eyeing the American up and down. "Don't I know you?"

"Yeah," growled Bytchakov. "I kicked your skinny Scotch ass in Kabul."

"*Scotch* is a drink, you ignorant Yank cunt. There were six of you meatheads, if I remember correctly," said the Scotsman breezily, un-shouldering his rucksack. "You were working for that shower of wanky Russian pussies, the ones who think they're the Waffen-SS, right?" He pushed his face a few inches from the American's.

"No fighting," I grumbled.

"Another time then," Alex scowled.

The Scotsman was a good operator, but a gobshite. You could put him in a room on his own and he'd start a fight. Luckily, this job was all about starting fights. "Ah, Captain Crap-Hat, MC," Bannerman smiled, clenching my hand. "It's good to see you." *Crap-Hat* was what Paras called non-airborne soldiers who didn't wear their beloved maroon beret.

"I suppose you've led a bayonet charge?" Oz replied defensively. He'd never stuck up for me before, and I wondered if it were affection for me or a dislike of Bannerman that prompted it. In any case, everybody who knew Oz rated him and respected his opinion.

The Scotsman was referring to the Military Cross I'd won in Iraq, leading a platoon attack with bayonets fixed. I didn't deserve it. It's in my safe. One day I swear I'll put the bastard thing on eBay. "Easy, Oz," said Bannerman. "It's all banter."

Duncan Bannerman had served in 2 Para before being court martialled and discharged from the army. He'd gone on a post-Afghan wrecking spree during decompression leave in Cyprus, after a gang of drunken holidaymakers from Liverpool picked a fight. Two of them were still being fed through tubes.

"Good to see you again," I said, pointing at his dreads. "Get a fucking haircut."

"Ma locks are like Samson's; if you cut them off I lose all ma strength." He slapped the glowering Bytchakov on the shoulder.

"Leave it, Duncan," I warned, following him inside the NAAFI.

"Fucking yanks have no fucking sense of humour."

"Give the guy a break."

"Which arm?"

We settled, the men dumping bags and lighting cigarettes while Oz fixed us all a brew. Shaking my head, I explained the job, to groans and jokes about suicide missions. Then I let them loose on the maps and the CORACLE file. Finally Tom Dancer arrived, looking every inch the ex-army officer in claret jeans, suede brogues and a salmon pink shirt. I made the introductions, the table now littered with maps, photographs and notes. "We've a big shopping list," I said.

"I'll speak to my contact in Poole," Dancer replied. "You'll want a boat, too, I presume?" Poole was where the SBS were based. I presumed Dancer knew a friendly quartermaster from his Special Forces days.

Oz smiled. "Yeah, I'm thinking of a RIB, I'm sure they won't miss one."

The Grey twins nodded in unison when Oz suggested a Rigid Inflatable. Between them I knew that we'd get to the beach nearest the prison undetected. All three ex-marines were maritime operations experts and trained landing craft coxswains. "A Pacific 22 would work," said Ruben. "It's got three hundred nautical miles range and it's a piece of piss to sling under a heli. A bit noisy, but the beach looks like it's in the arse-end of nowhere. I used to run 'Luca from Tangiers to Gib in a 22."

"*Luca?*" said Dancer quizzically.

"It's rhyming slang, innit? Gianluca Vialli – *Charlie*," said Ruben, looking genuinely surprised. "As in fucking Coke, White, Colombian Marching Powder, Chisel... don't you speak English, Major?"

"I *thought* I did," Dancer replied.

"Fucking Ruperts," Ruben laughed, using the derogatory expression for posh army officers. Raphael Grey sniggered, dark eyes roaming up and down Dancer like he was figuring out where to stick a knife.

I sucked on my cigar and made notes. "What's the tide looking like?"

"No dramas," said Ruben, returning to leafing through nautical charts. He showed them to Raphael, who simply nodded. "The sea's pancake flat in East Africa this time of year. It's a smuggler's dream."

We studied the plans of the prison. We'd looked at the geography and decided against a helicopter assault dropping straight onto or near the target – the plot was covered with machinegun towers. They'd also stretched steel cabling over the exercise yard to deter helicopter rescues. The terrain directly in front of the fort was a killing zone with no obvious natural cover.

"We're gonna need antitank," said Alex, tracing a finger across the satellite imagery. "That's a BMP-2. Then we'll need wall-breaching equipment for dynamic entry."

"Agreed," I said. "I'd go for the wall nearest the cliff: it's furthest from the guard towers." We could easily tab the kilometre from the beach, using the trees for cover. I looked at the grainy satellite image of the AFV. The BMP was a small tracked vehicle, resembling a tank that had shrunk in the wash. It was Soviet-era piece of kit, equipped with a cannon and a rocket launcher.

"I reckon we should site an OP in there first, mebbe up on this hill." Alex pointed to a lonely stretch of high ground southwest of the prison.

"That only leaves five of us to assault," said Oz.

Bannerman lit a cigarette and took a deep drag, ash tumbling onto the map. "Granted, but the Yank has a point. A guy on that wee hill with a light fifty, a machinegun and a couple of rockets could cause a lot of trouble. I can take any sentries on the headland over the beach with a suppressed rifle. I'd like a VSS, if we can get one." The VSS was a near-silent 9mm Russian rifle. I'd used one before but didn't like the way the weapon was configured, thinking it back-heavy. But Bannerman was a better sniper than me, and we all chose our own tools for the job.

"Shouldn't be a problem," Dancer nodded. "I've yet to find a weapons system we can't get hold of in the region, for the right price."

"That's settled then," I nodded. "Dancer, tell us more about the plan for the airfield."

The ex-SAS officer cleared his throat. "We've got an agreement with the rebels, the FZA. When we give the signal, they'll attack the airfield in company strength, at least eighty or ninety men. Their assault will provide a distraction."

"How good are they?" asked Oz, scribbling in a notebook.

"Good enough to keep the airbase buttoned-up for a couple of hours," he replied. "When the attack starts, the guard force will seek to reinforce the airfield. That just leaves the warders."

"That could work," said Bytchakov warily, "as long as the guards take the bait."

"I can't see why they wouldn't," said Dancer. "Then we heli in the SIS team, they do their bit and we all bugger off sharpish." I had to admit that the mission was looking more feasible.

"So we get our kit?" said Oz.

"OK," said Dancer, an impatient note in his voice. "Your requests will be passed on."

"Will the kit we ask for be the kit we'll get?" I said. We'd all been on jobs where the kit promised never appeared. In my case it was called 'The British Army in Iraq.'

"Yes," said Dancer. "I'm not going to pretend that there aren't issues, but weapons and equipment isn't one of them."

"Amen," said Bannerman. "The last PSC I worked for sent us out with fucking Elastoplast and cough sweets, but saying that, I'm nae too fussy about kit. The prime components of warfare are ammo, Mars Bars and water. Anything else is for schoolgirls and Americans."

Alex raised an eyebrow. "You talk big, Bannerman. It'll be interestin' to see how you walk the walk in the field."

"Whatever," the Scotsman shrugged. "I've no need to impress you, wee man. I've got a blue Drop Zone flash that tells you everything you need to know about me."

The American's eyes narrowed. "Cal, you gonna ask this asshole to develop some manners, or am I gonna teach him?"

"Save your aggression for the mission," I snapped, "both of you."

"My money's on the Yank," Ruben Grey guffawed.

"So much for loyalty," Bannerman replied, "Cockney wanker."

Dancer's secure phone suddenly chirruped inside its ballistic case. He picked up the rubberized handset, nodding occasionally as a scratchy voice spoke to him. "OK, I'll get back to you in the hour." He slammed the receiver down.

"Anything we need to know?" I asked.

Dancer checked his Rolex. "They're moving Mel Murray next Sunday evening. He's being taken to Marsajir for a show trial, which means we'll never get him back. Fall in gents, we fly tomorrow."

I shook my head. "That gives us just over a week."

"Good," said Bannerman. "The less time we're over there the better."

"I've got stuff to do," said Dancer, striding towards the door. "I'll be in early tomorrow with an update."

I heard a car idling outside. Looking out of the window I saw him get into a Volkswagen driven by Juliet Easter. Despite myself, I felt a pang of jealousy. *Grow up, Winter.*

The six of us talked some more, kicking the plan about. Then we chalked out a plan of the prison on the parade square and spent the afternoon doing walk-throughs and actions-on. I turned in early with a brew to study the maps and diagrams of the area. Zipping myself into my doss-bag, I thought about the remaining suspects on Marcus's list, both in Africa. Having met both Hugo and Juliet, neither of them struck me as obvious wrong 'uns. I hoped the two remaining spies would seem better prospects - I'd read their files but wanted to meet them in person before drawing any conclusions.

Eventually I slept. My dream about Sam morphed into a nightmare. It gripped my heart like a claw, and I woke clammy and gasping for air. My hand fluttered to the Maker's Mark, which I gulped from the bottle. Staggering to the shower block, I stood under freezing water, teeth chattering.

I couldn't go on like this. I'd resolved to rescue Murray, but I was damned if I wasn't going to find a way to get out, screw over Monty and The Firm. The need to strike back was like any other addiction I'd suffered, all-consuming and destructive. And if that meant Operation CORACLE collapsed messily, leaving a load of spooks and politicians with egg on their faces?

I could live with that.

CHAPTER SIX

Waking early, I showered and dressed in my linen suit, artfully crumpled and very un-soldierly. Breakfast was black coffee and ibuprofen, although I'd be lying if I said I wasn't tempted to splash bourbon in my Gold Blend. I took a deep breath and chose not to, feeling an itch of despair as I left the bottle behind.

I was going to find Harry's contact in London, the tailor called Samuels. I imagined him as the guy at the end of the Yellow Brick Road, the one who knew what lurked behind the curtain. Why else would Harry send me his way? His cryptic offer was too tempting to resist. It was like heroin, booze and violence, all the things I enjoyed but shouldn't. The Firm's secrets hooked me like the cotton-wool embrace of heroin, like the first glass of my second bottle of vodka. And, if I'm honest, like the feeling I get when I pull the trigger on some bastard who deserves it.

After two London hours on trains and buses, I found myself in a shadowy street behind Moorfields Eye Hospital. The shop was a yellow-windowed relic, frozen in an eighties time-warp. It was shut by the look of it, headless mannequins modelling Biscuit-coloured suits and the sort of sweaters golfers would reject as too garish. The grubby sign over the window read ISAAC SAMUELS – MENSWEAR SPECIALIST. I rang on a buzzer. The front door swung open, security chains rattling as a battery of locks disengaged. "Can I help?" asked a reedy voice.

"The 'Saint' sent me."

An old man appeared. Beyond was a corridor with peeling wallpaper, ankle-deep in junk mail. There was a strong smell of chemicals and something that might have been paint. "I'm Isaac. Isaac Samuels." His gravelly voice was fifty-fags-a-day rough, pure East End.

I gave him the once-over. Samuels was a stooped old geezer with waxy skin and wet eyes, strands of oiled hair carefully arranged across his scalp. He wore flared slacks, grey slip-on shoes and a tangerine-coloured sweater. He should have moved the shop east, towards Hoxton, where his dress sense had probably come back into fashion.

"Hello," I said. "Can I come in?"

Samuels said nothing, offering only an obsequious smile as he ushered me along the corridor. Finally we squeezed into a tiny lift, treating me to the smell of body odour and cheap aftershave. The lift wheezed and shuddered as it climbed the building. "Here we go," he said as the doors clanked open. "Please, come in and take a pew."

The room was an airy studio, looking out over rooftops and office buildings. City noise was muted by treble-glazed security windows. Air-conditioning hummed in the background, a sports channel on the radio. "How do you know The Saint?" asked Samuels. He shuffled over to a kettle and started brewing up tea, fussing over cups and saucers with long, delicate fingers stained blue and black. "Do you take sugar?"

"No thanks. I used to work for The Saint," I replied, settling into an office chair. "He said you'd have something for me if I called."

"Yes," he smiled. "I do." He whistled merrily. "I've met men like you before, squire, if you don't mind me sayin' so. It's in the eyes: proper naughty. They never lie, do they, your eyes?"

"Maybe I should get some sunglasses."

I took in the room. Whatever he was, Samuels wasn't a tailor. The studio was equipped with a phalanx of industrial-grade laser printers, some sort of optical equipment and a row of top-end Apple Mac computers, the type I associated with graphic designers. Rows of neatly arranged lockers and drawers lined the far wall, secured with padlocks. Wall racks held bottles, tubs and phials, next to neatly arranged ranks of stationery.

Finally Samuels brought lemon tea and a plate laden with cake. He sighed contentedly as he fell into a moth-eaten armchair. "My daughter makes a lovely cake," he smiled. "Battenberg, you see? Very difficult to bake, you have to get all the pieces just so. It takes seven different processes to get the flavour and colours right. If all the elements ain't done proper, the whole thing's a disaster."

I nodded indulgently and took a slice. "That's good," I said, telling the truth for a change.

Samuels smiled, "I knew you'd like it. Where were we?"

"The Saint," I replied. The old man was clearly going to take his time. I decided there was no point rushing him. Besides, I like cake.

"Of course," the old man sighed. "He told me I'd get a visitor one day who'd mention him by his codename. He said

I should tell them my story. I don't know why, and I know better than to ask." He winked and tapped the side of his rubbery nose.

"The whole thing's a riddle to me too." I was expecting a parcel or a memory stick and a hurried *on-your-way-please*. Not cake and lemon tea.

Samuels read my face. He cut another fat slice of Battenberg and slid it on my plate. "My story concerns a man I hate with a fucking passion." I saw his tongue slide over wobbly, ivory-coloured teeth, "maybe you could cause him a few… problems."

"Perhaps," I agreed. "I'm in the problems business."

"The Saint told me that whoever came to see me wouldn't judge me, or betray my confidence," said Samuels nervously. "Am I correct?"

I laughed, brushing crumbs from my lap. "I don't like to brag, Mister Samuels, but whatever your sins, I've done worse and with a cherry on top."

"Fucking marvellous. Call me Isaac," grinned the old man.

"You can call me Adrian," I replied, using my usual legend.

Isaac gave me an *Adrian-my-arse* look. "I'm what they call nowadays a *Full Spectrum Asset Replicator*," he said proudly. He produced a pair of wire-rimmed spectacles and pushed them onto his face. "Fucking spies, they love flash names, don't they?"

"Huh?"

"I'm a scratch-man. Y'know, a forger," he laughed. "I started making dodgy MOT and insurance certificates. Then I moved on to copying anything that could be copied."

"I can see why that might interest a spook," I replied.

"I got sent down for a nine-stretch in '85. Pentonville. Ever been there? They got cockroaches the size of cats."

"I've never done porridge in a UK lock-up, unless you count military prison."

"Keep it that way, my son. Anyhow, I'd done six months when a fella called Robert came to see me, along with a couple of Special Branch men. He said he could get my sentence reduced if I helped him with a project."

This was sounding familiar. "Robert was from the intelligence service, right?"

"Yeah, MI6 I think. He wanted Russian and East German papers for people coming across the Iron Curtain. The work was easy: old communist-era documents were shit. They gave me pukka paper and inks and took me to an old warehouse out near Bath. Robert was as good as his word, if not better."

"Did you get your early release?"

"Yeah, sweet as a nut. I only did twelve months in open prison. Then they sent me to learn about different forgery techniques. I even went to America, once. I was a fast worker. "That was what I was known as, *The While You Wait* forger."

"I'm glad it worked out for you, mate," I said easily. "Except I'm guessing it didn't in the end?"

"No, it all went pear-shaped after 9/11," Isaac replied, crumbs dotting his chin. "This new bloke took over from Robert, an arrogant prick called Owen. I just got on with it, but it wasn't the same. One day, I remember it clearly 'cos I'd won an accumulator on the two-twenty at Sandown, some nag called *Likely Lad*. Anyhow, what was I saying?"

"You were talking about Owen after 9/11."

"That's right. Anyway, one day Owen told me to create a full re-settlement package: Passports, driving licences, health cards, insurance policies… the lot. It was for a bloke from Belfast, they were moving him to Croatia. For Owen, nothing was ever good enough." He went on to tell me the Irishman, a geezer called Declan Cross, disappeared in the field. Owen arrived one night with two other Irishmen. "They gave me a proper kicking," he said. He pulled up his sweater, revealing a cross-shaped scar on his chest. "They did that too, with a Stanley knife."

"Why would they do that?"

"Owen was bent, I'm telling you," Isaac spat. "I might be a criminal, but I'm not a fucking traitor. I swear Owen was making a pound note on the side from these IRA men. The Irishman got involved in a gunfight with Old Bill, in the Balkans somewhere. Well, you don't fuck about with the filth over there, do you?"

"Don't tell me," I said, shaking my head. "It went tits-up and Owen blamed you?"

"You've worked for these cunts too, ain't you?" Isaac beamed. "When they'd finished stabbing me up, Owen said the Irish wanted fifty grand to make things right. I paid up, of course. Then he disappeared and said my contract was finished. If I said anything, the Irishmen would come back and kill me and my family." His eyes burnt with hate. "Threatening my family like that. Taking a fucking liberty, they were."

"Did you ever suspect he was getting you to work off the books?" I said sympathetically.

"No," Isaac replied. "It was routine. I never asked questions and was always paid on time. Anyhow, about a year after 'Owen' left, I got a visit from a bloke calling himself *The Saint*."

I assumed this was Harry. Isaac told me The Saint offered him work, which I guessed was for The Firm. "After I knew The Saint for a while, we started to get on. Y'know, like friends," said Isaac warmly. "He paid better than the spies, too. One day he told me he knew Owen professionally. The Saint didn't like him either."

I sat forward, locking eyes with the old forger. "Go on."

Isaac smiled. "That's when he told me that one day someone like you might come. He said it was an insurance policy. You know what it's like in this game, don't you Adrian? You need something in your back pocket for a rainy day."

I nodded sagely. "Yes you do."

"He told me Owen's full name was Owen Montague. He'd been with MI5 until he was sacked for dishonesty. And the reason that Irishman died in Croatia? Owen was trying to save his skin. He'd been caught with his greasy fingers in the till, so he gave up Declan Cross as a terrorist, trying to buy guns and explosives in the Balkans. The Croatians had him bumped off, I imagine."

"I don't know what this story has to do with me, to be honest."

"The Saint told me to mention that everyone knew Owen as *Monty*." Isaac saw the flash of recognition in my eyes and smiled. "It's important, The Saint insisted."

Harry's present to me was a get out of jail free card with karma attached. It was generous, and I was pleased. "Oh yes," the forger continued, excited at my response. "He works in an office down in Kent. I've got the address and everything. There's also a safety deposit box number, for a bank in Switzerland."

"Is the bank called *Tete Noir*?" I asked. It was The Firm's main hidey-hole, a very private establishment in a Zurich backstreet.

"That's the one," he replied, pulling an old betting slip from his pocket. On it was a code written in immaculate copperplate handwriting. "There's something in there for you, don't ask me what it is."

I took it and nodded. "Thank you, Isaac."

"This is like Christmas, innit?" he grinned, reaching into a drawer and pulling out a blue cardboard folder. "Here's two copies of passports Owen had me knock-up for him. There's one Irish passport and one Canadian passport, both in the name of Owen Ross.

I smiled and drained my tea. Monty had a moon-shaped face, close set eyes and a beard, dressed in a tweed jacket and tie.

"Does that make any sense?" said Isaac, chewing his lip.

"It does mate, yes," I replied. I peeled five hundred in twenties from a roll of cash.

"Why are you giving me a monkey? There's no need for that," said the old man.

"Do me a favour," I laughed, slipping the passports in my jacket pocket. "Have a drink on me and The Saint, or put it on the two-twenty at Sandown." As a wise man once said, always make a new friend if you can... especially if he's a hyper-skilled underworld forger.

"I will son," he winked, pocketing the cash. "Will it fuck Monty up, what I've told you?"

I looked over my shoulder as I opened the door. I let him look into my eyes, the ones in which he'd seen the monster.

"Yes, Isaac, it'll fuck him up proper, and the bastards he works for."

The old man's eyes shone with tears, "I wish I could see it."

"Trust me," I replied, fists clenching in my pockets, "you don't."

CHAPTER SEVEN

On my way back I bought a padded envelope and some stamps. I posted the passports to my apartment. At the barracks I changed into jeans and a polo shirt, before crossing the weed-strangled parade square. Inside the NAAFI Hugo was cheerfully rustling up tea and bacon rolls. He told us he'd studied Classics as well as computer science. Oz explained that a bacon roll with brown sauce was a classic, and Hugo was therefore amply qualified to make breakfast. Hugo's laugh was a happy boom as he passed me a roll and a cuppa. "Thanks," I said, "must make a change from silver service at Vauxhall Cross." Dressed in skinny jeans, Converse sneakers and a vintage rock tee-shirt, he looked more like a student than a spook.

"Oh, absolutely, you're better off here when it comes to food," Hugo laughed. "Naturally, it's all cucumber sandwiches with the crusts cut off at Babylon-on-Thames. Then, after the nursery school food, they push a button and you drop in the shark tank."

"How many guys are there on your team?" I asked, casually as I could.

Hugo thought about the question for a moment. "There are two more of us winding CORACLE down in Northern Kenya." I ate my bacon roll and waited for him to fill the silence. After a second or two, he obliged. "They've stayed on to cover Mel's extraction. Meanwhile Princess Juliet and I fly out with you tonight."

"Well, you know my role," I said easily. "What's your thing?"

"Cyber-operations and technical surveillance," he shrugged, running a hand through waxed shards of spiky black hair. "It's geeky shit, very dull." He tapped his nose conspiratorially.

Good tactics, I thought – using good humour and a neutral answer to deflect further questions. "Yeah, straight over my head," I agreed. "What type of support do the rest of the team provide?" I wanted to see if there was any inconsistency between my briefing and Hugo's version.

"There's Alan, our GCHQ guru. Jesus, I thought I was an apex-geek. He's a comms genius, designed all our counter-interception measures. Meanwhile, the lovely Amelia looks after HUMINT with Juliet. Juliet and Amelia are both ex-military, our girls with guns – they cover me and Alan while we deal with the technical stuff."

This was more or less what I'd read on Marcus' background report. Except that Alan had a drink problem that made mine look trifling. Amelia on the other hand, was a model officer except for her tendency to clash with management. "Girls with guns," I laughed.

"They're both hot, too," Hugo smiled wistfully. "But sadly out of my league, you know, service hierarchy. The two of them can be competitive, alpha-female syndrome."

"Who's the Alpha in your opinion, then?" I said good-naturedly.

"I've probably said too much," he said quickly. "But Princess Juliet is the mistress of all she surveys. In any case, they get on well enough."

"OK, tell me about Mel Murray."

"Mel?" he laughed. "The crazy bastard's a one-off. He'd have been happier on the Northwest Frontier in the eighteen-hundreds. The modern world has too many rules for him."

"Juliet seems especially pissed off with him."

Hugo nodded. "Princess Juliet's a... perfectionist. She's invested a lot of effort, not to mention political capital inside the service, into CORACLE. And now it's collapsed." His tone was laconic, almost mocking.

"You don't sound troubled by it."

I thought I saw a shadow of a frown cross Hugo's face. "I'm disappointed, naturally," he replied. "I just can't see the point of moping about it - what's done is done. I just try to get on with everybody and focus on the next job."

I nodded and thanked Hugo for his time. If he was lying, he was a natural. We sat on the moth-eaten sofas and chatted until Dancer and Easter arrived. Light flooded the dingy canteen as the door opened. Easter wore a smart business suit and heels, hair tied back in a simple plait. The Grey twins grinned wolfishly when they saw the attractive SIS officer. "This is Juliet," said Dancer to the new arrivals. "She's the team leader."

"Sweet," said Ruben.

Juliet fixed him with a laser-beam stare, which shut him up. "Thanks, Tom," she said. "Colonel Murray is still in the prison facility, one hundred and twenty miles north of the Kenyan border. However, he *will* be moved next Sunday."

"Are we all up to speed on the plan?" said Dancer.

"Yes," I said. "If the distraction assault on the air base works, we can do it."

"Note Cal's use of the word *if*," Bannerman added.

Easter smiled. "I understand your concerns, but I wouldn't agree for my team to go in if I weren't satisfied."

"OK," I agreed. The SIS team were following us in to do their secret squirrel stuff in the prison, putting boots on the ground. It deserved respect. There was no shortage of keyboard heroes in the intelligence community.

"General Abasi of the FZA is a personal friend of Mel's," Easter continued. "He assures us the assault on the airfield is on."

"Kanoro Abasi?" I said. "We really have fallen in with thieves." Abasi was leader of the FZA, the Free Zambutan Army. He was meant to be as bad as Aziz.

"Abasi is the only rebel leader capable of delivering an assault of this scale," Dancer shrugged, seeing the look on my face.

"And does he realise that the wheel has come off Mel's plan to overthrow Aziz for him?" I replied. Abasi might not commit to an attack if he knew CORACLE was folding.

Easter nodded. "That's a reasonable question, Cal. Abasi isn't aware that CORACLE is dead in the water, nor will he be until Mel is out of the country."

I appreciated her candour. "Well, as long as we keep it that way," I replied.

"Any questions?" asked Easter.

"Yeah," said Oz. "Who else knows about this?"

"Just my team, Dancer and my immediate boss," she replied. "Why?"

"Loose lips sink ships."

"I agree," she nodded. "So, Mister Osborne, your team can help with operational security by handing over your telephones and internet-capable devices."

"Not yet," I said quietly. The satellite phone Marcus had given me was still at the bottom of my bag. And I didn't like the way she'd tried to turn the operational security problem around on us.

Ruben Grey shook his head, brandishing an iPhone. "Out in the field, yeah, I get it. But not here, I've still got business to worry about. We're busy people, you know." Raphael nodded. "See?" said Ruben, "Raph thinks you're taking liberties, too."

"Don't worry, boys, the book-maker's is open 'til twenty-hundred," Bannerman chuckled.

"I understand," Easter replied. "Tom, you can manage this… *issue*? I'll see you at Biggin Hill later." She turned on her heel and left. I could tell she was angry.

"Sorry about that," said Dancer sheepishly.

"She's a stuck up cow," said Ruben, "although I'd still give her one." He pronounced 'cow' the common-as-muck London-way, *cah*.

"Yeah, I detect control issues," said Alex Bytchakov. His fingers traced the outline of the scar at his throat. "Just like my third wife. Or was it number four?"

"Juliet's under a lot of pressure," Dancer replied. He bit his lip, wondering if I'd told the men he was involved with her. "I'd just ask you bear that in mind."

"Yeah," I added, "give her a break. This job's tricky enough without pissing off the customers." I stood up. "Dancer, when we fly out tonight we'll hand over our phones."

"Agreed," he said. "Transport to the airport will be here at sixteen-hundred. Please be ready."

"You heard the man," I said. "Get your shit sorted, police your personal items, email your wills to Monty and be fell-in for fifteen fifty-five." The men nodded and headed for their billets. If I'd learnt one thing as an army officer, it's not to let the guys see that you might be as shit-scared or sceptical of the mission as they were. I needed to show that now, despite the dark thoughts swirling around my head.

Outside, Easter huddled with Dancer next to her car. Hugo joined them, pulling out a mobile and making a call. Back at the white-washed billet, the men were packing. The only kit we'd take would be boots, wash kit and personal items like knives, eye protection and compasses. All identification would be left in the UK and swapped out for false papers. Combat uniforms, body armour and weapons would be picked up in-theatre.

At the bottom of my bag were my satellite phones – one for The Firm and one for Marcus. I took Marcus's out of the case and emailed him to call me in ten minutes. Pulling a cigar from my pocket, I waved it at Oz to let him know I was going for a smoke. He put his thumb up and went back to packing his faded green Bergen. The camp had a warren of crumbling prefabs, once used as classrooms. I stepped into one, brushing cobwebs from my face. The place smelt of dead mice and mould. While I waited for the phone to ring I had a drink, hands shaking on the neck of the bottle. Exactly ten minutes later it buzzed. "Are you OK?" said Marcus, "you're flying out tonight."

"Yes, I'm good. I've only met Hugo and Juliet so far," I said.

"What do you make of them?"

"Hugo's sharper than he looks. Easter's feeling the pressure, I think. But everything about her suggests she's a loyal employee."

"Those are the ones I tend to watch. Mind you, I watch the moaners and groaners too."

"She's having an affair with Tom Dancer," I said. I felt like a dirty grass saying it, but I had my men's lives to consider. And, if I were honest, I didn't think Dancer deserved her.

"Did Dancer tell you that?"

"Yes."

"He's a flash wee bastard, from what I've heard. What's your assessment?"

"I haven't seen him for years," I replied, "but he was a solid officer back then. Tom seems more interested in rescuing Mel than anything else."

"OK," Marcus replied. "You should know we've traced a message, received by a Chinese spy ship bobbing about off the Somali coast."

"Saving the best news 'til last again, Marcus?"

"Quite. The Chinese have intelligence that General Abasi is mobilizing to support an operation in the south..."

"Is that from the bad apple?" I asked, my heart sinking.

"Possibly," said Marcus, "the SIGINT is inconclusive, but it didn't come from inside Zambute."

"I feel so much better now."

"Find the bastard for me, Cal. Find them and end this."

"So you've decided?"

The old spy's voice was icy. "Yes. Let the sun bleach their bones."

"Very Old Testament," I replied, although I'd already decided the traitor, if there was one, wouldn't be leaving Zambute.

"You're a good man," he said quietly. "I knew I could rely on you."

"Wrong on the first point, possibly correct on the second," I replied, switching the phone off and taking a gulp of booze. Emptying the bottle of Maker's Mark, I licked my lips and pulled out my other phone. The second call I made was to Sam Clarke. "It's been a while," I said. "Did you get the money I forwarded?" I'd paid twenty-five grand into an offshore account I'd set up for Sam recently. The rest of the money I'd earned from taking down The Hunt was donated anonymously to a veteran's charity. It's not like I'm a saint – there's enough banked for me to afford my generosity. Sam hardly touched the money I gave her, but I felt better knowing the cash was there if she needed it.

"Yes, I got it Cal," Sam replied. "You know you don't need to."

"Yes I do," I replied.

How's your leg?" she said, changing the subject. I'd told her I'd hurt myself climbing through a broken window on a training course. "I got the postcard from Turkey."

"The leg's good, thanks."

"Where are you off to next?"

"Oh, you know, abroad. Energy security," I replied.

"Ah," said Sam, an awkward note in her voice. "*Energy security* again…" She knew I was lying, but rolled with it. These were the boundaries we'd created, the game that allowed me an occasional slice of her life. Although I was never going to live a peaceful existence, a *normal* life, I could at least step into one now and then. Sam Clarke's reality was like an exhibit in an art gallery, something I could covet but never touch.

"I want to see you," she said finally.

"Why?" I said, laughing to mask my surprise. Usually it was me who wanted to see Sam and the kids, not the other way round. I supposed I reminded her of Clarkie too much, of the army and Iraq.

"The kids keep asking when you're coming over next," she said quietly. "They want to know more about their dad, stuff he did in the army. They're getting to that age."

"I'll be back in the UK in about six weeks, early October I guess. Why don't you all come up to London? I'll put you up in the best hotel you've ever seen."

"They'd like that."

"Would *you* like that?"

"Of course," she said. I heard a trace of exasperation in her voice. "You swear all the time, you're usually pissed and I can't ask you anything about what you've been up to. When you're not drunk you're liked a coiled spring, with a shitty temper. Cal, you're not exactly the ideal date for me, or a role model for the kids."

I laughed it off. "Believe it or not, you guys keep me sane. Just put up with me for a couple of days." She'd used the word *date*. I'm pretty sure that's a boyfriend-and-girlfriend thing unless you deliberately insert the word 'platonic.' It was wrong. So why did it make me feel good? I remembered the dream I was having about Sam, about her grinding on top of me. I felt my cheeks burn.

"Sure," she said. "I've got to go now, but ring me when you get back."

"I will," I promised, and rang off. The prospect of the trip in October would keep me going. They could screw decompression facilities and debriefings and lying low. I was coming home after Zambute. I told myself I wasn't going to have another drink.

Then I did.

CHAPTER EIGHT

Kenya

The pilot of the private jet wished us *bon voyage* as we descended into Nairobi. The plane belonged to a Russian oil company, its crew untroubled at having a bunch of cutthroats like us aboard. We hurried through customs at Jomo Kenyatta. Two uniformed officials escorted us with quiet efficiency, no doubt delighted with Dancer's pre-arranged bribe. We picked up our kit and waited outside the terminal's fire exit, luggage buggies zipping past. "It's gonna rain later," Alex yawned, dressed in cargo pants and a tee-shirt. He looked up and sniffed. There wasn't a cloud in the sky, the sun scouring the tarmac like a laser.

"I thought there was a drought on," said Ruben Grey.

"Yeah, but I've been here before."

"Doing what?" Ruben asked.

"Killin' folks, mainly. It rained then, too."

Dancer led us through a maze of humid service tunnels. Eventually we emerged into a car park, where a tired-looking lorry waited. We piled in the back as it bumped off, the donut-shaped terminal disappearing in a heat haze behind us. We were driven to lonely corner of the airfield, suspension creaking and groaning beneath us. We rolled to a halt, my face already coated in a film of sandy dust. Dancer arched an eyebrow, "get in the cab chaps." He pointed at a helicopter –

a Super-Puma painted in lurid tiger-stripes. It looked like a box of Frosties with rotor-blades. The livery on the fuselage read ZAMBUTE AIR SAFARIS.

"You're taking the piss, right?" laughed Bannerman.

Alex Bytchakov put a meaty hand on the Scotsman's shoulder. "Hey, Bannerman… I make that for a Breeze-Eastern cargo winch, hydraulic external hoist and a SH20 door mount for crew-operated weapons. Forget the comedy paintjob dude, that's a properly pimped SAR combat bird."

Bannerman laughed. "Good spot. I bet you're a fucking scream down the pub, you sad fucker."

Waiting by the Super Puma was a pudgy European and a tall African, both wearing grimy flight suits. The European was in his late fifties with cropped grey hair. His face was as red as an Arsenal shirt. "Dancer, 'ello mate," he said.

"Steve, meet the team," Dancer replied. "Cal, this is Steve Bacon. He runs our helicopters, used to be an aviation tech in the REME." The Royal Electrical and Mechanical Engineers were the technicians who kept the Apaches flying and the Challengers rolling, back in the days before we sold all our tanks. Bacon had the air of a man who could strip down the Puma blindfolded. "Come on fellas, load your kit and get in the taxi," he said. "I'm loadie today. This is Idris, the pilot."

Idris was a lanky African guy wearing big 70's Ray-Bans. He looked mixed Kenyan-Somali, with high cheekbones and a hawkish nose. "*Jambo*," he said. "Welcome to Kenya."

I shook his big, dry hand and nodded. "I'm Cal, team leader." We climbed into the narrow fuselage and stowed our kit. We squeezed into the forward-facing seats and strapped ourselves in, Steve checking us and speaking into a headset. He handed out packets of squidgy yellow ear protectors, which we rolled up and plugged in. The whining of the engine drowned out all conversation. I picked up a spent 7.62 bullet casing from the deck and smiled. "Air safaris?" I shouted.

"Of a sort," Steve grinned. "Let's go."

"How far is the trip?" I hollered back, the airframe vibrating alarmingly.

"Too far," he replied, "top end of the Puma's range, but Idris flies this cab on fumes all the time." He offered me a cigarette from a pack of Camels. The Puma took off in a whirlwind of dust and grit, wheeling away from the landing strip. When we'd gained altitude and cleared the city, the heli swung northeast. Steve sat on the edge of the open door, feet hanging in space. "I love this place," he shouted into his mic, "but it's like the sea – turn your back on it for too long and it'll do for you."

We were in the air for ninety minutes. Juliet Easter sat in a huddle with Dancer and Hugo, deep in discussion. Idris treated us to some low-level flying as we approached the base, the tiger-striped heli barely fifty feet from the ground. "Can he go any lower?" I asked.

"LOWER," Steve bawled as deer scattered in panic, the heli skimming the ground. Then the Puma roared up into the sky, pushing us back in our seats before jinking left and heading to a lonely cluster of buildings below.

The heli-pad was made of segmented aluminium tracking laid over rough brown earth. As we descended we saw the other heli, a small Dornier painted sandy-yellow. Beyond was a cluster of pre-fabricated buildings. Parked nearby were a couple of trucks, a fuel tanker and a small fleet of 4x4s. One of the buildings had a satellite dish and looked newer than the others.

"Welcome to *Focus Projects*," said Dancer. "We've got a South African guard force of eight men," Dancer replied. "They've been told you're all contractors, doing something hush-hush they don't need to know about. Don't talk to them or associate with them. You'll have separate accommodation and mess areas."

"Look over to the east," crackled Idris' voice in our headphones.

I shuffled across to join Steve on the starboard side of the Puma. I saw dust trails streaming towards the camp, running parallel with the border. The terrain was predominantly flat, bush-land interrupted by shallow hills. "Are those vehicles?" I asked.

Steve peered through a pair of binoculars. "Yeah, I reckon."

Dancer unbuckled his seat and shimmied forward in the cramped aircraft. "There are only two possibilities; Kenyan army or Vultures."

Oz raised an eyebrow, "Vultures?"

"They're Xaboyo tribesmen, some linked to the *Shadow of Swords* militia," Dancer replied. "They prey on the refugee camps. Land pirates, I suppose. They've never been bold enough to attack us before."

"*Shadow of Swords* is a mujahedeen group, right?" I said.

"Maybe, but junior league wannabes by East African Muj standards," Dancer sniffed. "The CIA thinks they're the next big thing." I'd seen the refugee camps on TV, bigger than anything thrown up by the Ethiopian invasion of Somalia in 2006. There was a sprawling tent city roughly seventy miles to the east of the camp, on the disputed tri-nation border between Zambute, Somalia and Kenya. Both of the warring factions in Zambute viewed the Shadow of Swords as enemies, and since Al-Shabaab had taken a battering by US Special Operations forces, the *Shadows* were on their own. But sometimes the most dangerous animal is one that's cornered, and East Africa's Jihadists were far from de-fanged. And as usual, the filling in this grief sandwich were the local civilian population.

"I reckon we should take a look-see," said Steve.

"OK," Dancer agreed, looking at me. "I'll get on the radio to Hester. He's in charge of the guard force."

Ruben Grey's eyes flashed. "Do we get a bonus for having a tear-up on day one?" The heli groaned as it banked, surging towards the dust trails. It was a convoy of battered pick-ups, camouflaged with mud and streaks of dark paint. Each held a motley crew wearing grey hooded cloaks and mismatched uniforms. Through my binoculars I spotted Soviet-era small arms and RPGs. One of the pick-ups had a crudely-mounted Soviet heavy machinegun, a DsHK. We all called them *Dushkas*. I felt a spasm of fear. The weapon's 12.5mm round would rip through the fuselage like tissue paper.

"Yes, they are Vultures," said Idris over the intercom. "It is strange for the Xaboyo to raid this far from the camps."

"The situation across the border is boiling over," said Easter grimly. I was suddenly tossed backwards, harness cutting into my shoulders as the airframe shuddered. "Incoming," said Easter calmly. "Get on the radio now, please, Idris."

I couldn't hear anything over the sound of the helicopter engines, but saw a neat line of holes in the fuselage above Oz's head. It was small arms fire. "Steve, do we have any weapons on board?" I shouted.

The technician shook his head. "Never take tools on a run to the airport."

We gained height, trying to clear the effective range of the Dushka. With a half-decent gunner and a stable firing platform it could take down a heli at two thousand metres. Steadying myself on the bulkhead, I looked down again. I saw puffs of smoke from small arms from the moving vehicles. "I'd say thirty men," I reported.

"Hester's aware," said Idris. "I'll land on the westernmost side of the camp, next to the armoury. He's waiting for you with weapons."

Dancer strapped himself back in his seat. "Change of plan," he shouted. "We're going all-round defence. When we land, follow Mister Hester's instructions."

"Hester's a good bloke," said Steve. "He knows what he's doing." The Puma started to descend. I saw the approaching dust cloud to the east, no more than two miles away. Tiny figures scurried in the camp below us. I looked back towards my team. All of them looked untroubled by the attack, Oz counting the bullet holes stitched across the top of the fuselage. The heli landed next to a low-level concrete building with no windows. A tanned, bearded old dude wearing fatigues and a bush hat crouched outside.

"That's the armoury," said Dancer, "move!" Easter and Hugo were first out, heading towards the security guard.

"Oz, grab me a gat and get back on board," I shouted. "Duncan, take the other guys and follow Dancer." Oz nodded and leapt into the billowing cloud of orange dust thrown up by the rotor blades. The others followed him, Bytchakov slapping my back as he jumped down onto the deck. I grabbed the intercom. "Idris, have you got enough juice to fly back around and drop us behind them?"

"Yes," he replied, "but only just."

"We need to take out that Dushka," I said. "Else they'll rake the compound to pieces." My mantra is the best form of defence is attack. The Vultures would expect us to hunker down in our compound, letting them snipe away. They wouldn't expect us to take the fight to them.

Steve nodded and hopped out, "Idris give me a second," he said. I squinted out of the square Plexiglas window, streams of dust trailing across it. Beyond the armoury several armed men strode towards a boxy, sand-coloured beast of a vehicle. Next to the vehicle a striking, dark-haired woman was strapping on body-armour.

"Here you go," said Oz, passing me a well-used G3 rifle and a bandolier of magazines. I took the weapon and hauled him into the heli. He had his own G3 and a canvas bag containing a clutch of grenades.

Steve came puffing behind him, sweat making a spider's web across his dust-plastered face. He cradled a General Purpose Machine Gun in his beefy arms, belts of ammunition snaking around his neck. "Help me with this," he gasped.

Idris took off as we dragged Steve onto the deck. He scrambled to his feet, hooked a karabiner into his safety harness and attached the machinegun to the door-mount. The heli gained altitude, dropped its nose and hurtled on a parallel course to the pick-ups. The little convoy had stopped, a huddle of bandits discussing what to do next. I guessed they expected a lightly defended survey facility, not well-armed mercenaries. On the rear-most vehicle, men wrangled with the Dushka, shielded by a metal plate welded to the weapon's tripod. We were coming out of the sun, the men shielding their eyes. "You're in range, Steve," said Idris over the intercom. He used that slightly bored, cold-as-ice tone pro-pilots adopt when faced with danger.

Steve nodded his helmeted head, body shuddering from recoil as he opened fire. The mount stabilised the machinegun, allowing him to hose tracer down onto his target. Bullets raked the line of pick-ups, scattering men as they sought cover. The vehicle with the Dushka pulled forward, into cover behind a cluster of spindly black trees.

"Put us down," I shouted.

Steve nodded as he continued to fire, shouting into his intercom. Hot cartridge cases bounced off the deck, gun smoke swirling about our ankles. Idris circled the pick-ups again, this time drawing fire. I saw a puff of white smoke as the bandits opened up with their RPGs. The rockets flashed beneath us, close enough for me to see the sparkling warheads.

The Dushka gunner opened fire, their position marked by a shimmer of dust thrown up from the recoil. Beer-can sized blobs of tracer arced into the baby-blue sky. Their aim was off, but the glowing snake of tracer began to slither towards us. Idris lost height, like he was dumping the heli into the ground, before levelling no more than five metres above the desert floor. He aimed for a hillock two hundred yards from the leading vehicle. "Get ready," warned the pilot.

I snapped back the cocking lever on the G3 and shouted my acknowledgement. The Puma hovered for a moment, the undercarriage almost touching the ground. We bundled out, rolling into cover. The black shadow of the heli washed over us and was gone. More blobs of tracer zipped past us, along with the steady *chug-chug-chug* noise of the Dushka. Oz and I scrambled to the top of the high ground and fell to our bellies.

We found ourselves on a baked-mud escarpment overlooking the convoy. The rebels had parked a Dushka-equipped technical in a dried riverbed, flanked by straggly trees. The tracer from the Dushka was chasing Idris, the gunners aiming ahead of the Puma. They would hope that the heli would fly into the stream of 12.5mm shells, but Idris was better than that. Losing speed, he jinked the chopper again, hurling the Puma in a tight circle and flying away in the opposite direction.

I could see part of the armoured shield protecting the Dushka, obscured by a clot of acacia and thorn trees. The G3 fired a punchy 7.62mm round, and the weapon crew were well in range. "I can see it," Oz hissed. "Where are the other tangoes?"

I glanced left. The rest of the bandits had taken cover near their vehicles, weapons aimed skywards. Some were shouting, urging the others to head towards the camp. I lined up the top of the shield covering the Dushka in my iron sights and aimed off a fraction into the trees, where the crew should be. The G3 bit into my shoulder as I fired, Oz joining in. We fired ten shots each, peppering the area around the vehicle-mounted weapon. The Dushka stopped firing. I saw something crash into the trees, flailing and tangled in the thorns. The other bandits suddenly switched on, realising they'd been flanked. A ragged burp of machinegun fire swept the ground in front of us. We ducked as more gunfire sailed over our heads. "A tenner says there'll be an RPG in five seconds," Oz grinned.

"Not a bet I wanna take," I replied. We shimmied down the embankment on our arses as the first rocket hit the top of the hillock, earth raining down on us. The rest of the enemy were to our left, another hundred yards towards camp. "Oz, I reckon they'll try and flank us with that Dushka, once they've got their shit together."

He nodded, sliding a fresh magazine into his G3, "agreed – assault towards them with grenades, go firm and wait for the cavalry." He handed me a smoke grenade from the canvas bag slung across his shoulder. I pulled the pin and nodded. "Throw that," whispered Oz, "then cover me, I'll head for those trees." He pointed in the direction of where we'd hosed down the Dushka crew.

I scurried up the embankment, digging my feet into soft, gravelly sand. I was glad I was wearing my trusty Lowa boots. Peeping back towards the enemy, I saw gunmen rushing for their vehicles. Now we were closer I noticed black banners with white Arabic lettering fluttering from the aerials. They were lovingly made, the script surrounding a curved sword motif. They'd left a couple of guys with a light machinegun covering them, another dude scanning the sky with an RPG. I could hear, but not see, the Puma. "Go!" Oz hissed, rifle ready.

I nodded. Sweat stung my eyes as I tossed the smoke grenade as far as I could, and opened fire.

CHAPTER NINE

The grenade spat red smoke, drawing fire from the rear of the convoy. I thumb-flipped the Happy Switch on the trigger group, opening fire on automatic. The weapon spewed hot brass, my ears ringing at the metallic bark. The lack of return fire meant I was keeping their heads down, allowing Oz to move forward. The ex-SBS man darted through the smoke, across open killing ground. He rolled into cover as he neared the trees, hurled a grenade in the direction of the Dushka. I heard a dull crump, and Oz was back on his feet, weapon spitting flame as he advanced.

I slid another magazine into my G3 and emptied it in short bursts. The breeze was dragging the smoke away, back towards the camp. A skinny guy darted into the open to my left in a flanking move. I had no idea where he'd come from, but he had an RPG launcher balanced on his shoulder. Muzzle flashes from a dozen weapons sparkled, incoming fire forcing me back down the slope. I had no comms, no grenades and only three more charged magazines.

I took a deep breath, blood pounding in my skull. I heard the sound of RPG rockets fizzing, men excitedly shouting instructions. Sliding back down the slope, I scurried towards where I'd seen the RPG operator. We almost ran into each other as I broke cover. The RPG guy was a wiry Somali. He dropped the launcher, his fist scrabbling for the canvas holster strapped to his belt. My G3 was already pointed at his belly. I squeezed the trigger and a burst of 7.62 rounds tore into him, lifting him off his feet and shredding his guts in a spray of wet gristle. Bawling, he writhed on the ground. I shot him again, in the temple, and picked up his RPG. I felt bullets cracking through the air around me as I took a knee, aiming at the boxy shape of a pick-up truck through the swirling red smoke. The convoy was still in a neat row, awaiting the signal to advance. The launcher was already armed.

I fired.

The RPG grenade spun like an oversized firework as it slammed into an old Toyota. The pick-up was shrouded in fiery smoke as men tumbled from it, groaning and yelling. As they tried to scurry away they were torn to pieces by heavy machinegun fire, the heavy thud of the Dushka ringing in my ears. Through the acacia trees I saw Oz stood on the back of a bullet-riddled pick-up, huddled behind the Dushka. I dropped the RPG and sprinted towards him. The smoke was thinning now, revealing the burning Toyota and shattered corpses. I saw the remaining four pick-ups speed towards the camp. "Jesus," said Oz. "That was close." There were three bodies scattered around the blood-stained pick-up, the metal shield pock-marked with multiple bullet strikes from our G3s.

I climbed into the cab, hand searching for the ignition. The engine was dead, the hood pock-marked with our incoming fire and tyres shredded by grenade-shrapnel. "Where's the heli?"

"Fuck knows," shrugged Oz. "They might have taken some incoming. It was like bullet soup when they dropped us off."

We advanced towards the Toyota I'd brewed up with the RPG. A body draped across the bonnet wore a crude canvass bag with three RPG rockets stored in it. Tugging it from the dead man's back, I retrieved the launcher. "Let's go."

Oz nodded, helping himself to an AK and stuffing his pockets with spare magazines. We moved forward, the line of shabby buildings two hundred metres to our front. The pick-ups had formed a ragged line halfway between us and the base. Two out-buildings had been hit with RPGs, dirty black smoke roiling skywards.

"The fuckers haven't seen us," said Oz, a smile on his dirt-smeared face. The pick-up closing the distance between us at speed, I aimed the RPG at the centre of the convoy and fired. Oz joined in with his G3. My aim was low, the rocket skittering across the ground and exploding against the wheel of a truck. The explosion tossed men out of the vehicle like fiery rag-dolls.

Fire from the base intensified as an up-armoured vehicle lumbered out of the gate. It was a sludge-coloured Unimog, an ugly pig of a wagon. I saw a flash of red hair from a weapons mount atop the vehicle, Bannerman crouching behind a machinegun. The attack had been blunted. The remaining rebels began jumping back in their vehicles, gunning engines and driving crazily towards the baked-mud track. Sliding another RPG grenade into the launcher, I aimed and took out the leading vehicle in a ball of white and orange flame. Oz nodded approvingly.

Machinegun fire from Bannerman's MG raked the little convoy, another Toyota skidding off the road. The last vehicle zigzagged across the open ground, rear wheels spewing dust. I went to aim, but couldn't track the fast-moving target. "Welcome to Kenya," hollered Bannerman from the top of the Unimog. He swept his hand towards the burning pick-ups and bodies, "getting to know the locals, Cal?"

Sweat streamed down my face, my breathing raw. I tried to think of something nonchalant and witty to say. I failed.

Dancer approached, along with the older guy who'd handed us weapons earlier. Both carried tricked-out polymer AK rifles. "We need to get this cleared up," Dancer sniffed. "The last thing we need is the Kenyan authorities poking their noses around here."

"You OK?" The older man nodded at me. "I'm Willem Hester, security manager. These men are Vultures, they won't be missed." He sniffed the air, looked at the black flags fluttering in the breeze, "but the fact they're travelling over the border is bad." His accent was unmistakably Afrikaner.

"Why?" I asked, offering my hand.

He took it, giving me a knuckle-crunching squeeze. "They usually operate on Zambutan territory. The fact they've been forced into raiding over here means they're desperate or they were targeting us deliberately."

"I doubt they knew we were here," Dancer shrugged, taking a deep breath. "Willem, can you organise a work party and get rid of the bodies?"

The Afrikaner nodded. "We'll burn them west of here, out in the boondocks. Nobody will ever find them, and the jackals will eat what's left. We'll tow the vehicles with the 'mog and dump them." He pointed at the chunky Mercedes.

Bannerman jumped down from the Unimog. "There's lots of kit here," he said. "Should we strip them for ammo?"

"Trust me," Dancer replied, "we've no shortage of bullets."

Bannerman shrugged and strode over to one of the dead bandits, splayed obscenely in the baking sun. Flies were already feasting on the bloody holes punched in its torso. "They've got money on them," he said, pulling a wad of dollar bills from a bloodied ammunition pouch.

"How much is there?" I asked.

Bannerman flicked through the bills. They looked crisp and clean, "five hundred US, not too shabby for out here, I'd say."

"Yes, that's a lot of cash," said Hester, scratching his leathery forehead. "Have they all got that much?"

We were searching the corpses when Easter appeared with a tall, dark-haired woman. I recognised her from Marcus' file as Amelia Duclair, the third SIS officer and HUMINT specialist. She was sharp-featured, with full lips and large brown eyes. Dressed in jeans and desert boots, the form-fitting tee-shirt under un-zipped body armour showed off the well-honed physique of a serious gym bunny. She had an icy, harsh beauty about her. "They've got new US banknotes?" she asked.

"Yes," Dancer replied, checking another body. "This guy has two hundred dollars."

I searched another corpse. It stank of body fluids and charred meat. I found a wad of money tucked away inside a pocket. A yellowing slip of paper was stuffed in-between the banknotes. I examined it. The lettering was in Mandarin. I slipped it in my pocket. "My guy's got a hundred," I called.

"Do you think they've been hired to do this?" said Easter. She ran a hand through her hair, eyes hidden behind sunglasses. "We've never seen them this far out before."

"How?" said Duclair, "who knows we're here?"

"I don't know," Hester shrugged. "I say we put the money in the end-of-operation beer fund."

"I knew I liked him," Bannerman laughed.

"I'd better call this in," said Duclair, shaking her head. She put a hand on Easter's shoulder, "are you OK, Jools?"

"Sure, it's just another shitty day on this shitty operation," she replied glumly. "It's cursed."

Duclair shot me a look. "Are these the increments?" she asked, like we weren't there.

"Cal," I replied pointedly, offering my hand.

She looked at my paw like it might bite, decided it wouldn't and gave it a squeeze. "Cal, this is Amelia Duclair," said Easter.

"I'd better put a report together for Vauxhall," Duclair replied, surveying the carnage. She seemed more bothered about the admin than the dead. I mentally filed her under the *hard bastard* category.

The sun was half-sunk by the time we'd helped the South Africans dig a grave. We dumped the corpses in the shattered pick-ups and towed them behind the Unimog. We blew up the trucks with plastic explosives and doused the bodies in petrol. Dancer's operational security plan went to rat-shit, as the Saffas were switched-on enough to twig that we were Brit mercenaries and obviously up to no good. To their credit, they kept their mouths shut and didn't ask too many questions.

I'd done a lot of bad things on The Firm, but burning those poor bastards in the desert was memorable even by my blood-stained standards. The meaty, almost sweet smell of charred human flesh made me gag as the funeral pyre flared and crackled. One of the Saffas stopped and said a prayer. *God our Father, your power brings us to birth, your providence guides our lives, and by Your command we return to dust…*

Bannerman nodded and lowered his head respectfully, Bytchakov doing the same. The Grey twins chuckled as they counted the dollars they'd looted from the bodies. "Mate, they're Muslims, ain't they?" Ruben said to the Saffa.

"I don't know any Muslim prayers," the Saffa shrugged, "but it's all the same God."

"If you say so, geezer," the little ex-Marine shrugged, rolling his eyes. His twin nodded sagely in agreement.

Finally we returned to camp, showered the stink of the dead from our bodies and stowed our stuff. Our quarters were in a pre-fabricated hut on the far side of the complex, the men chatting among themselves and brewing-up tea. Easter finally appeared, calling me to the doorway. Dancer lurked with his satellite phone nearby. I'd seen Steve and Idris examining the Puma, which had been hit by a couple of rounds from the Dushka. Three fist-sized holes dotted the fuselage just behind the cockpit.

I wanted to tell someone about the money band I'd found, marked with Mandarin script. Given the number of Chinese in Zambute, was it normal? Had the Vultures stolen it, or been hired? I was itching to crack open my satellite phone and call Marcus, but everyone was twitchy and on high alert. The guards wore their rifles slung across their chests, even the SIS officers wearing pistols on their belts.

Easter nodded, Hugo at her shoulder as usual. "Gentlemen, if you could follow me," she said. "We've got to start work right away." We followed her towards a rusting hangar, to a corner partitioned off with chipboard sheets. A bank of chuntering air-conditioning units fed cold air inside, neatly arranged laptops sitting on a row of desks. It was a briefing area, with a large screen mounted on a steel frame.

Dancer cleared his throat. "We don't have much time, but we do have a good idea of the prison layout. These laptops are programmed with a three-dimensional map of the interior of the complex."

"What's the source for these plans?" sniffed Bannerman. Like most of us, he was instinctively suspicious of intelligence product.

Easter smiled. "Our colleagues from the Security Service found a taxi driver in South London, a refugee. He'd served an eighteen month sentence in the same prison as Mel for opposition activities. While he was there he worked as a cleaner, with access to the staff areas, offices and barracks. He was fully debriefed and the computer model put together by Hugo."

"Well," said Oz, "not only does Hugo make a mean bacon roll, he's also a computer genius."

"He speaks Mandarin too," Dancer added. "He'll be translating any intercepted Chinese product we get, fast-time."

"I also do weddings, funerals and bah-mitzvahs," Hugo grinned. "It would be false modesty for me to deny my technical genius."

Ruben Grey rubbed a hand over his cropped head and smiled. "If you're a genius, why are you earning government pay?"

"Touché, sir," Hugo replied. "Perhaps I'll go for gold in my *next* career."

"Hugo will stay here to help with any technical issues, I'll be in the comms hut if you need me," said Easter. She frowned as she left, fumbling at a pack of cigarettes.

We settled around the laptops and began exploring the prison in 3D, as if we were playing a computer game. Steve Bacon appeared with a tea urn and sandwiches. We spent a few hours familiarising ourselves with the interior of the prison and surrounding terrain. "There are missing areas on the map," I said. "Like the basement, for example."

"Yes," Hugo nodded, scratching his head. "That piece of the complex is part of our retrieval operation. Sorry about that - it's sensitive, so I've left it off your version."

The men started to groan at the need-to-know bullshit, but I quietened them down. There was no point arguing, not least because I intended to ask Marcus what the score was. I rotated the computer model of the map so we could see the main complex from the small hill. "Alex, you can cover us from your OP when we go in and come out. When we extract we can spot any movement towards the LZ."

"I got it," the American replied.

"It needs to be aggressive and it needs to be quick," said Dancer. "I want the enemy to think he's being assaulted in battalion strength, so lots of things that go bang."

"I've got that covered," Bannerman grinned. "Making stuff go bang is my speciality."

"Alex, we'll put you in at dusk tomorrow," I said.

He nodded. "Sure, ain't a problem." I asked Alex to join me over at the control room, a low-rise building with a satellite dish on the roof. A sign on the door read BASNEFT SURVEY GROUP – ENERGY IN ACTION. Inside was an office, three table fans moving milkshake-thick air about. Sat behind a desktop computer was Juliet Easter, wearing desert fatigue trousers, sandals and a loose-fitting shirt. Body armour and helmets were neatly stacked near the door, the walls covered with maps, photos and satellite imagery. She looked up and gave me a wan smile. Sat next to her was a stocky man in his forties, tinkering with a laptop. I recognised him from the file as Alan Brodie, the GCHQ technical officer. His file described him as an electronic warfare expert, specialising in encrypted networks and satellite communications. I remembered a warning note – Easter had caught him drunk on duty. There was an email in the file from Brodie to his boss at GCHQ, berating Easter's management style.

Brodie wore the global uniform of the techie: baggy cargo pants full of pockets, chunky outdoor trainers and a polo shirt. A laminated BASNEFT ID card hung from his neck on a lanyard. He looked up and nodded in acknowledgement. "Hello there, I'm Alan," he said, offering a pudgy hand. He had a soft Scottish accent and the flushed complexion of a heavy drinker. "Alan runs all of our comms," said Easter matter-of-factly. "We'll be escorting him in on the raid."

Alan's unshaven, doughy face twisted into a frown. "I'll only need about twenty minutes when we're inside. Is that OK, do you think?"

"It'll have to be. What comms have we got?" I asked.

"Satellite and personal role kit - we'll be using Yank military radios," he said, "but I've tweaked them, made them more reliable. They'll have better range, too."

Easter looked up at Alex. "Ah, Mister Bytchakov, I've read your file. Promising career until that unfortunate incident in Iraq..."

"An unfortunate incident in Iraq, lady?" he replied. "Take your pick."

"Quite. Well good to have you here," she said.

"Will we get any more intelligence on Murray?" I asked.

Easter nodded. "We'll have fresh imagery of the prison and airfield in the morning."

"Good," I said, "how are we for night-flying?"

"No problem. Idris is good, flies us in and out at any hour. We've got two South African pilots. They're both ex-military, used to night work."

"Is there anything else?" I asked, walking towards the door.

"The RIB gets flown in tomorrow," said Easter. "In the meantime, just let me know when you're ready to put your OP in. There's one other thing..."

"Yes?"

"When you put Bytchakov in, I'd like to come on the heli to take a look at the ground." She fixed me with those cool grey eyes. I think Easter half-expected me to challenge her on it.

"No dramas," I said, "it'll be a good opportunity to talk a few things through."

She raised an eyebrow. "That's good to hear, I thought you might see me as a passenger."

"It's your operation."

"We've all got our crosses to bear."

"Well, maybe together we can drag this one somewhere quiet and forget about it."

"I hope so," she said. "I better finish this report. We'll talk later."

"Sure." We strode outside. "Alex, I'll meet you back in the briefing tent." Alex headed off as I lit a cigar, a thin mist of rain enveloping the camp. Raising my face to the sky, I enjoyed the sensation of moisture on my face. Alan Brodie walked outside, nodded to me, and shuffled off towards a cabin resting on breeze blocks. It was dusk now, the sun a shimmering fireball as it sank into the horizon.

I waited until he was out of sight then followed him.

CHAPTER TEN

Alan Brodie shuffled into his cabin, reappearing a few minutes later holding a wash-bag. He'd changed into shorts, sandals and a tee-shirt, a towel around his neck. I watched him plug in some ear-buds, head nodding in time to music. He traipsed towards the shower block, a warm wind blowing dust devils around his ankles. I ducked out of sight behind the cabin. Brodie's billet was unlocked, which didn't surprise me given we were hundreds of miles from anywhere. Nudging the door open with my boot, I peered inside. The cabin looked like something by Tracey Emin. It smelt of cigarettes and old socks, clothes and empty bottles strewn over a sleeping-bag lying atop a camp bed. I noticed his poison was vodka, the odourless stealth-nectar of the veteran alcoholic.

I should know.

More empty bottles of Smirnoff were lined up on top of pallets of cola I guessed he was mixing it with. He'd taken to drinking the local stuff too, dirty yellow bottles of it jammed under the bed. I took a mouthful of vodka from a bottle under the bed and sighed happily. Glancing out of the window, I reassured myself I was alone before carrying out a quick search.

The only personal effects lay on a scuffed wooden desk: a laptop computer, magazines on computer hacking and economics, a stack of personal papers tucked into a sticky copy of *Men Only*. Analogue porn – how retro. I decided to leave the laptop alone, figuring that tampering with a GCHQ officer's computer was like trying to break into Fort Knox with a wire coat hanger. Instead I leafed through the papers in the porn mag, sandwiched between Gemma from Stoke and a reader's wife. There was some general correspondence, mainly in Brodie's cover name and relating to his 'employment' as IT specialist for BASNEFT. There was also a National Crime Agency report on money-laundering, an open-source document and not protectively marked. I also found cash in US dollars and sterling and UK lottery tickets. Carefully tucked in the slim stack of banknotes was an SD card. I examined the lottery tickets. On the back of each was part of a carefully drawn grid, the boxes labelled from one to thirty-two. Each had a short alphanumeric code neatly printed underneath in black ink. Perched on the end of the bed, I took my digital camera from my map pocket and photographed the paper several times, then replaced it.

Next was the SD card. It was a normal SanDisk 32 GB card, the sort you might put in a camera. I slid the card into mine, the device humming gently as it processed data. A series of photographs appeared. I scrolled through them. Most of them were of local wildlife and landscapes. A third of the way through, the images changed.

They were of Juliet Easter.

In all of them she was in the camp, usually on the telephone or her laptop. In one or two she was smiling, talking to Hugo. From the look of the images, I guessed Easter was unaware she was being photographed. In most of them she looked ravishing. Navigating back to the thumbnails of the snaps, I noticed there were eighty images on the card. Thirty-two of them featured Easter.

Was this linked to the GCHQ man's apparent grudge against Easter, or was he some kind of stalker? Easter was so far out of Brodie's league it was possible. Then again, the photographs appeared to align with the grids drawn on the back of the lottery tickets. If he *was* a stalker he was an unorthodox one. None of the photographs could be remotely construed as sexual – no attempts to photo her in the shower or in any state of undress, although they captured her earthy beauty, especially in black and white. To me they looked like surveillance photographs. There was nothing else of interest in the room. Copying the images from the SD card to my camera, I put everything back and stepped back outside.

"What were you doing in there?" asked Amelia Duclair sharply. Her hand rested on the grips of her pistol, worn in a drop-thigh holster. She looked like she was preparing for a tactical entry into the trailer.

"I'm looking for my accommodation."

"It's certainly not this festering pit, is it?"

"OK," I shrugged easily, "my mistake."

Duclair shot me a look and walked off. If I'd been busted, I'd stick to my story – I was looking to bag a half-decent room. Unless Brodie wanted to make a big deal of it, in which case I'd ask him why he was taking sneaky photos of his boss. I headed for the briefing tent, where Dancer was in conference with Easter. I went to join them, not least to see if Duclair was going to mention my nosing around in Brodie's room. "OK," said Dancer, sipping mineral water. "We'll sort out weapons before we crash. We zero and test fire in the morning."

"I'll leave you with your toys," said Easter. "Amelia and I have stuff to do, Vauxhall wants more updates."

"How many ways can you write *we slotted some bandits?*" I shrugged.

"You'd be surprised." Easter looked tired, dark smudges under her eyes. "The legal officers are considering the Human Rights implications of the firefight."

We all laughed.

"Come on Jools," said Dancer, "I'll walk you back."

"No, its fine," she replied. I caught her shooting him a look. "Crack on with weapons and kit, Tom."

Dancer smiled ruefully. We left the trailer and headed to the warehouse. Inside, the air was hot and stale, smelling of unwashed bodies and machinery. The men were unpacking weapons under the glare of arc lights. It was like Christmas morning for gun-nuts. "What've we got?" I asked.

"It's a Heckler Koch party pack," said Bytchakov. "I prefer Russian or American hardware, but hey."

"Yeah, why aren't we using Soviet kit?" I agreed. I'd have preferred to use the same weapons as the locals, in case we ran out of ammunition and needed to scrounge in the field.

Dancer smiled, rifling through the olive green crates. "The HKs were part of a *Bundeswehr* shipment headed for UN forces, until some friendly pirates intercepted the cargo. There's as much ammo as you can carry."

"It ain't all Kraut kit, the sniper rifles we ordered are here," said Bannerman approvingly. "I've got my VSS." He held up the suppressed Russian rifle and grinned.

Bytchakov nodded and produced a SOPMOD, a modern version of the classic M-14 battle rifle. "Sweet. They've delivered my weapon of choice."

"Over here!" shouted Ruben, crouching over some more BASNEFT crates marked DELICATE SURVEY

EQUIPMENT in Cyrillic script. "We've got a Barrett 95 in here with peripherals." The 95 was a compact .50 rifle. "Fuck me," said the ex-Marine as his twin hauled a green tube from a crate, "we've got AT-4 and Stinger too."

It was serious, war-fighting hardware. The seven of us would be as tooled-up as a rifle platoon and I could see the men were happy. Firepower builds confidence like that. I tapped Alex on the shoulder, "Alex, sort your kit and pick up a satellite radio from Alan. Then find me in the office for a briefing OK?"

"Sure," he replied, working the action on the M-14.

The men busied themselves with improvising a range. They found a stack of man-sized targets and began adjusting sights, optics and peripherals for their weapons. I walked outside and found Steve Bacon talking to the South African pilots. Both men wore shorts, flip-flops and fatigue shirts, Oakley sunglasses perched on their heads. The Dornier had been fitted with a machinegun on each door and a winch. "This is Peter and Henry," said Steve. They said their hellos in thick Afrikaans accents. Overhead, a thin slice of moon hung in the sky.

"You OK with the helis?" I said.

"Yeah, the Dornier is fine - it's even got a winch," said Steve. "You could use this for the extraction or the Puma, just this has the advantage of being smaller. Steve will patch it up, it took some bullets earlier."

"You want to go in at night?" said Peter.

"Yes," I replied, "that OK?"

"No problems, man," said Henry, who had a Robinson Crusoe beard and bad teeth, "just let me know who's choosing the LZ and I'll speak with him. The Puma would be better for hauling your boat in my opinion, man."

"The guy going in is called Alex," I said. "I'll send him over soon OK?"

"Cool," said Peter, rolling an exotic cigarette, "the Dornier is a good bird, we have no problems with her. Steve is a good mechanic."

"Hey, let's find this Alex guy," said Henry, punching Peter on the arm and belching loudly.

Peter lit the jumbo-sized reefer. He saw my expression and grinned, "I fly better when I'm relaxed."

I went back to where the men were still checking weapons. Bytchakov was sitting quietly, poring over maps. Bannerman passed me a HK G36 rifle. "Take that one Cal, its fine. I think I'll take the MG4 for extra firepower." The Scotsman picked another machinegun from its crate, "these MG4s are mega, like a Minimi but German. It's like the difference between a VW and an Audi," he grinned. Quickly stripping the weapon, he pulled some spray cans of firearms paint and masking tape from his bag. He started camouflaging the weapons in streaks of sand and grey.

At the end of the line were the Grey Twins. They were fluidly practicing weapon-switching between their G36 rifles and suppressed HKSD5 sub-machineguns. They spoke quietly among themselves, adjusting sights and tactical weapon slings. "OK fellas?" I said.

"Yeah, sorted boss," said Ruben, "more metal 'ere than there is buried in Epping Forest. All the kit is brand-new Magpul, too." They pointed to a pile of weapons peripherals and rails to customise their weapons, all made by the popular American tactical manufacturer. Another box contained gloves, knee-pads, load-carrying gear and similar kit. Raphael simply nodded, studying his weapons with dead, hooded eyes.

At the end of the line was Oz, wearing floral shorts, flip-flops and a 42 Commando tee-shirt. In front of him was a selection of Very Dangerous Stuff: plastic explosives, grenades, a brace of AT-4 antitank weapons and a Stinger antiaircraft rocket. He'd also found a General Purpose Machinegun and a M224 60mm mortar. Belts of ammo, like sharp bronze teeth, snaked across the floor. "Decisions, decisions," said Oz lightly, waving a hand at his armoury.

"It's an in-and-out, Oz, not bloody D-Day," I smiled.

"Yeah, right, I've heard that one before. I'd take it all if I could," he said. "I'm taking the '36C and two AT4s. The twins are taking the last MG4 and a Stinger. You should take the rest."

"I'm not hauling a mortar in there," I replied.

"You'll regret it."

We'd been provided with a selection of German army-surplus *flecktarn* desert camouflage fatigues, American AirFrame helmets, British Osprey body armour and load-carrying gear. None of the equipment had any insignia or identifying markings on it. The men rifled through it carefully in the dimly lit warehouse, looking for familiar kit and adjusting it to their own requirements. I found a close-fitting wicking under-armour shirt, baggy German combat smock and trousers. Easter turned up and issued vacuum-packed bundles of dollars, in case we were split up inside Zambute and had to pay bribes to get out. We each had ten thousand in twenty and fifty dollar bills.

"Shit, this is like Christmas," said Alex Bytchakov. He held up a tiny, toy-like heli he'd found in one of the crates. "This baby is a PD-100." The PD-100 was a small, palm-sized recce drone. I'd heard of them, but never used one.

"How many are there?" said Ruben eagerly.

"Three, all good to go," Alex replied. The drone looked like a mix between a helicopter and a dragonfly, small enough to fit in the palm of your hand. "It's got a thousand metre line-of-sight with a tilt and pan camera."

"OK, shall we split them up?" I asked.

"I should take two," said Alex. "The battery life is pretty short, and if one breaks I've got a spare."

"That makes sense," said Oz. "Plus, you'll have something to play with when you're bored."

I rummaged through the remaining weapons and kit, making sure I had two water bottles and a body-worn rehydration system. Along with the G36 rifle I chose a Walther P99 pistol and a thigh holster. The clothing was well-worn and comfortable. I would wear my own boots, kneepads, scarf and goggles. Scooping up all my kit, I returned to the hangar alone. I'd moved my bunk into a quiet area, screened off and positioned behind a rusting tractor. As team leader I reserved the right to privacy, not least if I had to send a message to Marcus. A cigar and a drink helped me relax while I adjusted my body armour, getting it just right. Then I stripped down to shorts and a tee shirt, ready to sleep. My bunk was comfortable enough. I lay down and blew a smoke ring, then reached for the fresh bottle in my rucksack.

Then I heard a noise, the faint creak of metal and footfall on concrete.

Rolling off the bunk, I drew the Walther from its holster and readied it, tracking movement in the tritium rear-sights. There was definitely someone in the shadows, a darkness scudding across the bare flesh of an arm. "Who is it?" I barked. "I'm armed."

"I'm sure you are, Captain Winter," said an amused female voice.

Someone stepped out of the shadows.

It was Amelia Duclair.

CHAPTER ELEVEN

"You're good at sneaking about," I said, lowering my Walther.

"You were concentrating on all those... straps and zips," she replied, nodding at my armour. Her lips were glossy in the half-light

"Quite."

"Are those Russian tattoos?" she asked, nodding at the wolf and pentagram on my bicep. "They're very... unusual."

"Yes," I replied. "Long story." I swung my legs over the side of the bed and plugged the cigar back in my mouth.

"I wasn't going to ask," Duclair smiled, pushing a bang of thick black hair behind her ear. I noticed she was wearing a wisp of makeup that had been absent earlier. I've been fooled by enough women to know when the charm's being switched on, but that didn't mean I didn't like it.

Amelia Duclair was the last of the suspects Marcus had identified. Her file was sketchy, noting only that she'd completed a short service commission in the Royal Engineers. She'd proven adept at field survey, leading to freelance work in the energy industry before joining SIS. Mentioned in dispatches in Afghanistan, she came across as a seasoned operator. I noted that her brother, a lieutenant in the artillery, had been killed in an IED attack in Helmand.

She'd been on leave during one of the compromised ops, reducing her status as a suspect. "I wanted to talk through the infil plan for my team once you've secured the perimeter," she said. I tried to establish eye contact, which she avoided. I'm sure if she put her mind to it, she'd make an excellent liar. She wanted me to *know* she was making up an excuse. "Dancer's leading on that," I replied, playing her game.

"Sure," she replied. "Dancer's a good guy."

"Dancer's all-round awesomeness isn't the reason you're here."

She smiled and sat on the bunk next to me. "Tom told me you were a sound person. He said I could trust you."

I felt her thigh touch my leg. "Did he?"

"Yes, he said that you'd been in this sort of situation before."

"I've never broken into an African prison, if that's what you mean."

"No, that's not what he meant," said Duclair, rolling her eyes. "But you're neutral. I mean, you're not linked to SIS *or* Focus Projects." There is a first time for everything. Being described as an honest broker was one of them. The intelligence officer leaned forward and glanced at the door. "Our last two operations in Zambute went badly wrong." Her voice lowered to an urgent whisper.

"What happened?" Of course, I knew already, but wanted to hear Duclair's version.

Duclair glanced at the door. "The first operation involved a meeting with one of President Aziz's ministers. He wanted to come across and give intelligence on Zambutan money-laundering and trade negotiations with the Chinese. He never made the appointment we'd set up, he'd been arrested for corruption by the secret police and hung."

"How did you know it was a compromise?"

"I didn't, until the second op. We'd managed to get a virus into a computer in the finance ministry, one Hugo had written. It was going to flag every corrupt Zambutan account in the Swiss banking system." She brushed away a flying bug and frowned.

"Don't tell me, they executed the computer for treason." I opened a bottle of Chivas Regal and produced two plastic beakers from my rucksack, "fancy a drink?"

"God, yes," she said, shaking her head at my awful gag. "Whisky seems to keep these bastard mosquitos away. No, they spared the computer. Instead, Aziz's circle transferred their loot back to Zambute three hours before we went live. It was a blatant leak. It could have come from outside the CORACLE team, but it's unlikely." She chugged down her drink and motioned for me to pour another.

I stood up and started stowing my kit. "Rooting out spies isn't my speciality. If you think you've got OPSEC problems then why are we even flying in tomorrow?"

"Balance of risk," she shrugged, sipping the whisky. "If Mel ends up in Marsajir it's nothing short of a disaster for HMG." She stood up and put her hand gently on my shoulder, "we're taking a risk if we go, but a bigger one if we don't."

"So what do you want me to do?"

"You can help me find out who leaked those details."

"How am I meant to do that? We fly in less than twenty-four hours."

Amelia reached into the pocket of her cargo pants. "Hugo ran some diagnostics on our encrypted network here. Alan manages it, but Hugo deputizes. He was able to put a covert packet-sniffer into the system."

"A packet-what?" I laughed.

"It's a program that monitors ingoing and outgoing data packets from a network. It allows us to monitor all email, satellite phone and internet traffic on every device connected to CORACLE, either going in or coming out."

"How do you know Hugo isn't the leak?"

Amelia's eyes narrowed. "Hugo hates the Chinese regime. His mother's family were persecuted for opposition activities."

"Shouldn't you be a suspect too?" I took a slug of the golden whisky, felt the burn and sighed happily. Then I took another.

"It's a fair question," she replied grudgingly, handing me a tightly folded piece of paper. "The minister who was executed was *my* agent. It took me a year to recruit him. We had a good rapport going, but I sweated fucking *blood* getting him to turn. I go on leave and when I come back he's swinging from a gibbet in Traitor's Square. The idea I'd do that is bollocks."

I raised an eyebrow. "You would say that, though, wouldn't you?"

Amelia's nostrils flared. "I wasn't here when the op was actually compromised. The details of the meeting were caveated for OPSEC reasons. It *couldn't* have been me."

"So it's either Alan or Juliet?"

"Yes, I think so," she nodded. "On that piece of paper is the CORACLE team's telecommunications data for the dates around both operations. Interestingly, they were wiped because of a 'critical systems failure' Brodie reported. Hugo scraped them back."

"And what am I meant to do with them?"

"Get them back to SIS, by any means you can. We're locked down for the exfil and Brodie has full control of all our comms. The slimy bastard probably has kit we don't know about. There's no point me pointing the finger until I have proof. I'm sure you've got independent comms."

I remembered Easter had asked for all of our phones and internet-capable devices. I'd complied with the rest of the men, but kept the satellite phone Marcus gave me. "Break a rule?" I said. "Never."

"If you say so, but that data might hold the answer," said Amelia urgently. "If it can be looked at independently, investigated, then we'll see who was talking out of school."

"If the camp is locked down comms-wise, how can I help?"

"I'm DIADEM-indoctrinated," Duclair replied. I detected a hint of pride in her voice. "I don't know much, but I do know within SIS your organisation is viewed as a bunch of wily and resourceful bastards."

"Why, thanks," I smiled. She was good at what she did — attractive, personable and an outstanding flirt. But I know when smoke's being blown up my arse.

"You're in charge, Cal. You're my best chance of getting a message out of this place before we either get killed by bandits or die in Zambute."

"So who do you think it is?" I asked.

She shrugged. "It doesn't give me any pleasure saying it, but Alan Brodie doesn't strike me as ruthless enough to crucify an agent, even for money. But Juliet's a hard bitch, and penniless. We all know it, and it's the oldest motive of all."

I didn't tell her about the list I'd found in Brodie's trailer. It looked like he shared Duclair's suspicions. "Why is Juliet broke?" I asked innocently.

"Her brother, poor bastard, has cerebral palsy. He's about to lose his place in a private care home. There are big problems with his health insurance." She shook her head sadly.

"I'll see what I could do, OK?" I took the paper from her and put it in my pocket.

"I'd appreciate it if you kept this between us," she whispered, leaning forwards. I could feel her breath, hot on my ear.

"Of course…"

She kissed me, slowly, on my unshaven cheek. I felt her tongue just shy of my ear. It's not normally a part of my body I'd describe as an erogenous zone, but Duclair managed to change my mind. She smelt of perfume and body spray, which made a change from unwashed men and weapon oil. Her teeth brushed my ear-lobe, a buzz of pleasure travelling down my spine.

"Thanks, Cal," she said. She smiled, drained her cup and left the hangar, a swing to her hips.

I looked at the slip of paper. It was a densely printed table of IP addresses and meta-data sorted by dates and times. It might as well have been written in Sanskrit for all the sense I could make of it. Booting up the satellite phone hidden in the bottom of my day-sack, I walked out to the moon-washed vehicle park. I found a battered cargo truck rusting in a corner and climbed in the back. I didn't know if this was progress or not. The truth was I liked Easter. And selling out some corrupt Zambutan government minister to earn enough to look after your critically ill brother?

I'd have done exactly the same thing.

I made the call. Marcus answered immediately. "Do you have an update?"

"We were attacked by bandits," I said.

"I know," Marcus replied. "Duclair made a report."

"There's something she doesn't know," I replied. I told Marcus about the slip of paper with Mandarin writing I'd found on the dead Vulture.

"*If* it was the Chinese, that's a massive tradecraft balls-up," said Marcus.

"There's also suspicion within the team. Duclair shares your concerns." I told Marcus about the conversation I'd had with Duclair, and the strange note I'd found in Brodie's trailer.

"So Juliet Easter's team have lost confidence in her, *and* she's having an affair with the hired help?" Marcus said gently, "what do you think?"

"Duclair's smooth, very smooth. And Easter is very capable. It could be the GCHQ guy, Brodie. I'm going to reserve judgement."

"That's very wise. Can you read out the material on Duclair's note? I'll record the conversation and transcribe it later."

"Why did she ask *me*?" I said suspiciously.

"She's not aware of my investigation, if that's what you're suggesting. Duclair is smart. If she's marooned in an area where a potential hostile has access to all comms traffic and records, it makes sense for her to approach a third party. It's what she's trained to do, take calculated risks."

"Even with someone like me?"

"It's an indicator of her desperation, Calum," the old spook replied.

I read out the data. It took almost five minutes. Marcus told me to wait for a message, and to check the phone on the hour. I grunted in acknowledgement and hung up. The monster in my brain, the crushing depression, was being held back by booze for now, but what I really wanted to do was sleep. I crossed the shadow-dappled compound and returned to the hangar.

I was pleased to see Oz talking with Alex. The Yank took a while to unwind, but seemed a decent guy. After Andy died I was worried that it would take some time for Oz to accept a new team member, but he seemed to like the croaky American. Even Bannerman seemed to warm to him when Alex showed off some moves with the Scotsman's claymore. Despite my thirst, I shared the remainder of the whiskey with the men. It was gone in twenty minutes, and Alex produced some more. After some more booze, a brew and some banter we turned in for the night.

The next day began with heavy rain, the sandy earth transformed into rich ochre mud. The men cursed as they prepped weapons in the hangar, brewing up tea and coffee. The South African pilots came and cooked porridge and scrambled some eggs, which was the first time I'd ever had a cab driver make me breakfast. After they'd eaten, Bannerman announced that he would set up a range and zero the weapons. "If it ain't raining, it ain't training," Ruben shrugged.

We all trudged outside. The rain was warm enough to shower in. All of us had ran enough ranges to take turns playing instructor and safety officer, and we sent a thousand rounds each into a series of targets. We trained, got plastered with mud and trained some more for the rest of the day. Then, after some more walk-throughs on the computers, it was dusk. Idris, the pilot, appeared in the doorway. Juliet Easter was at his side, wearing a green flight suit. "Ready when you are," she said.

"Hell, I'm ready," said Alex. He wore a ghillie suit over his fatigues, camouflaged with strips of fabric, scrim and hessian. He carried his scoped M-14, a pistol, the .50 AM rifle, a compact satellite radio and an antitank rocket. It would be difficult to be more dressed for war. "This is my disco gear, you like it?" he croaked.

I laughed and checked my G36. I would ride shotgun and cover Alex at the LZ. I followed Alex out of the hangar, towards the waiting helicopter.

Standing watching us was Alan Brodie. He waved as we passed. "Good luck!" he said cheerfully. Slightly pigeon-toed and awkward, he didn't seem a likely candidate for prime bad guy. Then again, if you've seen *The Usual Suspects*, you'll know all about Keyser Soze.

"Cheers," I said. He thought I'd turned away, but I saw his expression change when Easter walked past. His bloodshot eyes blazed angrily. The guy was unhinged. And he was in charge of our mission-critical communications. I sighed and boarded the Puma.

CHAPTER TWELVE

"We're crossing the border now," Idris reported, his sing-song voice crackling in my headphones. Easter peered into the gloom through night-vision goggles while Steve chugged coffee from a flask. He sat at the fuselage door, feet dangling over the deck. The sky looked bigger, somehow, in the inky-blue African twilight.

"You OK?" I asked Alex.

"I'm fine, boss," the American replied easily. "I'll put in a SITREP soon as I'm dug in." He gave thumbs up and plugged his headphones into an MP3 player.

We sat in silence, the throbbing engines pounding in my skull. Easter scrambled over and strapped herself into the seat behind me, "what do you think?" she said.

"The flying suit is a bit last season, but it complements those lovely grey eyes," I said, "and your hair looks better down."

"Fuck off," she laughed, "and good luck, Alex."

"The harder I work, the luckier I get," Alex drawled. "Now I'm going to listen to some music to get me in the mood."

Easter touched his shoulder, "what's on the iPod tonight, DJ Alex?"

"Mussorgsky: *a Night on Bare Mountain*."

"Cheery," I noted.

"Lovin' that Mussorgsky," said the American, plugging in his ear-buds.

Easter smiled and shook her head. I wondered if Duclair was right, if Easter really was selling out her team to the Chinese. I'd spent years surrounded by liars, mercenaries and thieves. Dammit, I was all three myself. So I liked to think I knew a wrong 'un when I met one. "Anyhow, I agree with Dancer," I said. "We need to be fast. Whatever your team are doing in there, do it quick."

"Roger that," she replied. "Alan assures me it'll be twenty minutes at most."

"Is everything else OK?" I said.

"What do you mean?"

"Maybe I'm being out of turn, but is there a bit of atmosphere in camp?"

Easter sighed. "Alan Brodie is an arsehole and a drunk. The rest of the team are just freaked out by the operation going so badly wrong."

I nodded. "I can understand that." I remembered Hugo seemed sanguine back in London and hoped she wasn't just seeing what she wanted to see.

"Thanks," she replied. "How about you - are you OK?"

I pulled a face.

"You stink of booze, you look like a tramp and I'm wondering if you're actually up for this."

I looked at the steel deck beneath my feet. "I'll be alright on the night."

"No more booze until we get back, OK?"

I shot her a look. "I didn't say that."

"Look, I don't know what it's like to be in your shoes. We know very little about The Firm."

I let my head rest on the bulkhead behind me. "Did you know we're all blackmailed? That none of us want to work for them."

"No I didn't," she replied. "I've only heard rumours."

My laugh was bitter. "Want to share?"

"I've heard eighty per cent of you die before you finish your contracts, that most of you don't have any place else to go."

"Those are facts, not rumours."

Easter touched my hand, felt the scrape of a fingernail on my skin. "No more booze, Cal, OK?"

"I'll try," I said. I couldn't meet her gaze. "It's not like I want to be like this."

"Who would?"

"I've been in this life a long time now, and I'm still alive. That'll have to do."

She nodded. "Just let me know if I can help."

I had to remind myself she was the prime suspect for treason, the person I might have to execute in twenty-four hours. It would make sense for her to make a connection with someone like me, someone vulnerable. I ground my teeth and studied my boots. We spent the rest of the flight listening to the roar of engines and watching the trackless scrubland zip by below us. My guts churned as the Puma descended sharply, hugging the coast. The bone-white sand sped by beneath us, dotted with scrubland and rocks. Alex was fast asleep, so I nudged him with my boot. "Wake up, mate," I said.

"Sure," grunted the American. He fished a sand-coloured Boonie hat from his pocket and jammed it on his head. "I was dreamin' 'bout my first wife and a vacation we had in Baja."

"Was it a good vacation?"

"No, she stabbed me with a broken Tequila bottle and had me arrested by the *Federales*."

I left it at that.

"Hey, let's do this thing," he bawled over the throb of the heli's engine, pulling on his heavy rucksack.

I nodded, adjusted the strap on my helmet and readied my G36.

Steve Bacon emptied his coffee over the side of the Puma then clambered behind his door-mounted machinegun. We banked sharply left, away from the coast. In the distance I could see the sodium glow of lights on the horizon. "That's the Quaani airbase," said Easter, business-like again. We were five miles from the prison as the heli slid through the darkness, towards the desert floor. Bytchakov reckoned he could march there in full kit and be dug in by daybreak.

Just as the Puma's wheels connected with the ground, I jumped out to cover Bytchakov. Scanning threats as I sprinted clear of the heli, the patchy scrubland looked clear through my NVGs. The American hopped down, a rifle in each hand and an AT4 rocket strapped across his giant Bergen. He looked like an armoury on legs. He scurried past me with a nod and began the long tab to the prison. When Alex was clear, I jogged back to the heli and climbed in. "Go!" I called.

The Puma's engines whined as we pulled up into the night, Idris throwing the machine through one hundred and eighty degrees. I kept my NVGs on and watched Alex turn slowly into a small glowing blob. Keying the handset on the satellite radio, I shouted over the engine noise, "Charlie Seven Oscar, this is Charlie Seven Alpha, comms check, over: Alex you getting this?"

"Hey, I guess it's too late for a career change?"

"I think so," I laughed. "Good luck mate."

"Like I said, harder I work, the luckier I get," he grunted.

"Do you think he's really as tough as the macho posturing suggests?" said Easter.

"Tougher, I reckon. How's the schedule for the rest of our kit?" I asked.

"The RIB is coming in first thing. Amelia's chasing it up."

"What's Amelia's speciality?"

"There's not much Amelia can't do," she shrugged. "She's good with agents, can blow stuff up, survey an oilfield *and* she's handy in a fight."

"Can she reverse a family-sized saloon into a tight parking space?"

"Hey sexism," she smiled, "how edgy." She looked happy that I'd cheered up, punching me playfully on the shoulder. "Look, despite it all, the team will come together when push comes to shove."

I didn't suppose she'd want to admit that her technician was a drunk and her second-in-command suspected her of espionage. "I still think you got the rough end of the stick with this operation," I said.

"Coming from a member of The Firm, I'll take that as a rare display of sympathy," she replied.

"I'm not a member of The Firm," I said, "I'm one of its prisoners."

"I understand. Look, all I want to do is get Mel and the rest of my team home and salvage something positive from this mess."

"And what's the plan after that, another overseas posting?"

"Hopefully London," she replied. "I've been abroad constantly, with the army or SIS, for almost nine years. I need a break."

We landed back at camp, the rest of the team sat on a low wall smoking and chatting in the dark. The Grey twins were working on a make-shift punch bag. "Alex is in," I said, taking off my helmet.

Easter ran a hand through her wind-tangled hair. "I'll call an intelligence briefing in the morning, as soon as I get it. OK?"

"Guys, get some zeds," I said, looking at my wristwatch, "It's late and the rest of the kit arrives in the morning. Briefing is at 08.00."

Alan Brodie wandered over. He was sipping from a mug of hot chocolate. "Captain Winter?"

"Yes, Alan?"

"There's a call for you on the secure net, from your… *management*."

"Thanks," I replied. I walked over to the HQ building, into the cramped comms room. Alan handed me a handset connected to a suitcase-size satellite radio. I waited until the GCHQ technician left the room. "Monty?"

"Yes" he replied in his nasal whine, "SITREP, please."

"We're on schedule," I replied lightly. Now I knew Monty's real name and what he looked like, I felt empowered. The forger's story about the operation in Croatia fitted everything I suspected about the creepy bastard.

"I'm not happy you're being exposed to SIS personnel," Monty sniffed, "any problems?"

"No, they're OK," I lied. "Although I agree with you, the decision surprised me too."

"Well, it was imposed on me from above," he replied carefully, not expecting me to agree. "Nobody listens. Just don't mix with the spooks too much. Watch what you say."

He'd said *no-one listens*. I'd never heard a handler criticize the hierarchy before, except for Harry's warning in back in Spain.

"The Fallen Eagle protocol is engaged," he continued. "If you can't make a voice call, send this code to the emergency number using your sat phone."

The code flashed up on the LED display on the radio, a short alphanumeric sequence. I scribbled it down in my notebook. "I've got it."

"Support will be basic," he warned. "No dramatic rescue, but we'll get assets to you in-country. Remember Winter, it's only to be used if we are *completely* compromised."

"That's good to know," I replied.

"OK," he said, relaxing. "Keep me updated."

Returning to the hangar, I showered and crashed in my bunk. Pulling my camera out of its neoprene pouch, I punched in the password and opened the pictures I'd taken of Marcus's file, the taster I'd been given as a bonus. It was an MI6 report from early 2002 about The Firm. I'd read it twice already, but kept getting drawn back to it. I had to squint to re-read it:

DIADEM URN 00/031/908 TOP SECRET UK EYES ONLY

Briefing note re. Independent Covert Asset 031-A20-5300

ICA 031-A20-5300, previously known as SAWBUCK, has adopted a new cover name, apparently derived from a colloquialism used by employees to describe the organisation. This is 'The Firm.' Previous cover names known to DIADEM include:

STREGA	(1953-1965)
GREY ORCHESTRA	(1965-1975)
THE BOATCLUB	(1975-1986)
PANTHEON	(1986-1995)
SAWBUCK	(1995-2002)
THE FIRM	(2002 - present)

Re-naming usually coincides with the appointment of a new executive committee (known as *The Evocati*, symptomatic of the sense of theatre enjoyed by founding members of the STREGA project). The Firm's projected demand tempo since the 9/11 attacks on the Twin Towers and Pentagon prompted the latest restructuring, including renaming for OPSEC reasons. DIADEM has corroborated expansion in the operative base and utilised their services on operations: ABEMARLE, BASELINE, MACHINE and NOTIONAL.

DIADEM COMMENT: The last of the original 'STREGA COMMITTEE / EVOCATI' (see URN 00/031/1999) died in 1999. The direction taken by the organisation since the Op. PANTHEON incarnation is more profit-driven but professional. The centre(s) of gravity for 031-A20-53 remains London, Washington DC and Trieste. The Firm has hitherto aligned itself with causes broadly sympathetic to HMG interests. However, since the 2003 Iraq War, the organisation has 'chased the dollar,' aligning itself with state and non-state actors of whom previous Evocati would have disapproved. At the time of reporting, this is an observation rather than a concern, but the situation will require careful monitoring. Operation BODYLINE, the exit strategy from any linkage to The Firm, is the official contingency in place should this position become untenable.

The Firm had been started in *the fifties*. I tried to guess how many poor bastards had been press-ganged into service since then. I knew that *Strega* was Italian for witch or sorceress. My mother was Italian, and the word popped up fairy tales she'd tell me. The only other Italian link was Trieste, where Bytchakov worked recently. I Googled the word *Evocati*, discovering they were Roman ex-soldiers who, having completed their service, re-enlisted voluntarily. They enjoyed favoured status as a result. Harry had been a pressed man, became a handler. Was he one of the Evocati? And once, the report suggested, The Firm had been on the side of the angels. For a second I wondered if it could be again.

I laughed.

There wasn't enough water to hose out those stables.

I punched the pillow and tried to get comfortable, but the report gnawed at my brain. The old forger, Samuels, told me that Harry's codename was The Saint, like the old TV series. I knew that Monty was a disgraced ex-MI5 officer. The more I learnt, the less I knew. The only way to find out was to get Marcus the result he wanted, get him to give up his dead wife's secrets. And to visit Zurich, prise open that safety deposit box.

I slept fitfully until my bladder woke me. Stuffing my feet into my boots I shuffled next door, creeping through the men's billet. There was the usual snoring and fug of bloke-odour, and the fresh air outside was a relief. I checked the luminous dial on my G10 watch: oh-three-hundred. I made for the wash block, seeing movement over by the trailers where the SIS team lived. I heard a noise and froze.

Duclair and Easter were standing by a trailer, deep in conversation. Duclair was smoking, the amber tip of her cigarette bobbing like a firefly. Fifty metres beyond them, near the gatehouse to the camp, I saw the silhouette of a South African guard sitting behind a sandbag emplacement, rifle pointed into the wilderness beyond. Staying in the blue-grey shadow of the hangar, I broke cover from the building line and slid behind the trailers to eavesdrop. "Are you sure?" said Easter quietly. "I know we've been over it a dozen times…"

"You've read the product, Juliet," Duclair replied huskily. "The source is reliable. If he says it's there I'm inclined to believe him, and fuck the management."

Easter sighed. "In any case, it's an opportunity we should take. Chinese EW capability gets better every month."

"I agree," said Duclair. "Returning home with the equipment shows something tangible for all this effort. I know how much graft you've put into this job."

"Thanks, Amelia. Are you sure we need to take Brodie, though? I'm sure Hugo can manage."

"Hugo could do it, I suppose," Duclair replied, "but Brodie's the expert. If anything went wrong they'd ask why he wasn't there. They'll be looking for ammo to shoot at you, why give it them?"

"Yes, they'll have me on health-and-bloody-safety," laughed Easter.

"I know you don't like Brodie, but he's good at his job."

"If I can smell a drop of booze on him, he can fuck off back to GCHQ and play with his gadgets. We're going into a hostile environment, I'm not taking baggage." Easter's voice dripped venom.

"I'll keep an eye out," Duclair replied. "And did you see Cal mallet those vultures earlier? It was murder-as-performance art."

I heard the low-pitched warble of a satellite phone. "It's Vauxhall," Easter sighed. "We'd better go back."

They walked away, which was a shame. I like it when attractive, intelligent women talk about me in favourable terms. At least I'd learnt from their conversation that Dancer's tale of Chinese electronic warfare equipment seemed accurate. I went for a piss then returned to my bunk, crashing into a deep sleep.

I was woken by the sound of a heli, the chug of heavy rotor blades rattling the hangar roof. Pulling on my fatigue trousers and a tee-shirt, I ambled outside. A colossal Mi26-T cargo heli lumbered through clouds of orange dust. It was liveried with the Red and Grey logo of BASNEFT, the Russian energy giant. Slung underneath in a cargo net, like a toy, was the 28' long rigid inflatable we'd use on the operation. Wearing goggles, the Grey twins scurried beneath the hovering giant, releasing the fastenings on the stowage net as the pilot lowered his cargo. Juliet Easter strode towards me. "They're taking food supplies to the refugee camps on the border," she shouted above the howling engine noise, "good PR for BASNEFT and better cover for moving contraband."

We approached the heli, the men ready to unload our kit. The crew, wearing orange flying suits, opened the curved rear doors. Bannerman took a list from the loadmaster. "It's in Russian!" he bawled.

I went over and read it. Everything was in order: explosives, wall-breaching kit, a battering ram, spare radios with batteries, NVGs and enough to medical kit to equip a field hospital. The loadie nodded as I gave him thumbs up, and he disappeared back up into the belly of the aircraft. They weren't hanging about, the giant turbo-shafts increasing in volume as the pilot prepared for take-off. I went to step off the ramp at the rear of airframe when the loadie waved at me to join him. "Here," said the Russian crewman. He passed me a box marked GRENADE, RGD-5 x20 in Cyrillic lettering. "This is for you."

I raised an eyebrow.

"Hey, don't look at me," smiled the loadie, "this is from a friend of yours, on the quiet. You understand?"

"No," I said. "I don't."

"The fat Scottish guy sends his regards," said the Russian.

"OK, thanks," I replied, taking the box. Whatever it was Marcus wanted me to have, I doubted it was grenades.

CHAPTER THIRTEEN

The evening air was warm, dirt-grey clouds scudding across the sky. In the shadow of the Puma, I paced around the line of armed men. I felt like a camouflaged quarterback in my body armour and Crye Precision helmet. The only insignia I wore was a Velcro blood-group patch on my armour. Luckily, I had too much to think about to be scared. As per my promise to Easter, I hadn't touched a drink. My fists were clenched, to stop them trembling. I had to survive this job. There was unfinished business to take care of.

The Dornier sat on the neighbouring landing strip. The SIS officers sat by their equipment, Easter and Duclair checking their weapons while Hugo and Brodie sat drinking coffee. All of them looked calm and relaxed, like the mission was no big deal. I wouldn't look down on spies again, at least not the people they sent into the field. It was just a shame one of them was a traitor. "OK, double-check for any operationally insecure items: no phones and no ID," I ordered.

"I'm an operationally insecure object Cal," Bannerman protested. "Ma life-story is tattooed all over ma beautiful body."

"He's a fucking criminal," Ruben grinned, jerking a thumb at Bannerman. "Nobody would be surprised to find him wrapped up in wrongness like this."

"The wee Cockney bastard's got a point," the Scotsman nodded.

In the army they'd have called Bannerman *ally*, which means looking effortlessly cool. The ex-Para wore a faded Denison parachute smock over pea-dot camouflaged fatigues and armour, fiery red dreadlocks flowing from the back of his AirFrame helmet. The MG4 was across his chest, a Claymore sheathed in a camouflaged scabbard on his back. A black fighting knife and a Walther were strapped to a drop-thigh holster. On his smock were para wings and a dark blue rectangle, the Landing Zone flash for 2 PARA. "I got those inked on my arms too," he shrugged, "plus, they're good luck."

Oz and the Grey twins double-checked their weapons and inspected each other's lightweight life vests in case we ditched at sea. The three ex-marines were small, wiry men, all wearing identical German army camouflage fatigues and chest rigs, without adornment or affectation. They'd swapped out every item they could to make room for extra water, grenades, explosives and ammunition. Steve Bacon, a cigarette smouldering at the corner of his mouth, inspected the rigging for the cargo nets. The Rigid Inflatable lay nearby like a beached dolphin. The heli now had machineguns mounted on the side doors.

"OK," I said, "mount up."

Dancer, wearing old-style British desert camouflage, held his thumb up and started stashing the AT4 antitank rockets in cargo nets inside the fuselage. His only concession to combat fashion was a silk scarf, worn to stop his body armour chafing his throat. "That's a rare blood group, Dancer," I said, pointing to the blood patch on his armour. It read AB NEG.

"That's OK, I don't intend on losing any," he replied smoothly.

Easter strode over, eyes narrowed, "Cal," she said quietly, "for Christ's sake, just in-and-out OK? I'll have Vauxhall wanting updates every ten seconds as it is."

"Agreed," I said, offering my hand.

She grabbed my arm and kissed my cheek. "Thanks for not having a drink," she whispered into my ear, "I need this. I appreciate what you're doing."

"We'll be fine," I replied. Glancing over her shoulder I saw Duclair looking straight at me, head cocked slightly. Her look said, *don't get taken in*.

Finally, we were ready. Alex Bytchakov, in his dusty OP, gave the order. "It's a go," he croaked over the satellite radio, a hundred and thirty miles away.

Idris, who'd spent hours doing pre-flight checks, like a midwife expecting quadruplets, started the engines. Engines pulsing, the tiger-striped Puma lifted into the air, the Grey twins squatting behind the door-mounted MGs. Sitting in the seat nearest the side doors, I felt the airframe tug as the heli took up the slack of the RIB slung underneath. Idris spoke into his mic, "ETA to LZ One is an hour and five minutes."

I peered over the side of the deck. Easter stood in the swirling dust, shielding her face from the stones and grit thrown up by the rotor blades. She waved at us, a grin on her sun-tanned face. Duclair, hands-on-hips, stood next to her.

"There's no shortage of fit birds in MI6, is there?" chuckled Ruben. Not even the threat of imminent death can stop British squaddies thinking about sex.

"Shame none of them go for street-urchins or Neanderthals," Dancer replied.

"You ain't an officer anymore, and I ain't a marine, Mister Dancer," Ruben grinned. "So you can fuck right off."

Dancer grinned and flipped him the bird.

The men bantered some more as we gained altitude, before settling for gazing out into the hazy blue night. I left them to their thoughts. Our route would follow the border, flying low to avoid radar, then jink north and hug the coast. Through my headphones I could hear chatter between Idris and the Saffas back at base, until they too were quiet. Next to me was the satellite radio, tuned into Bytchakov's frequency. I keyed the mic, "Charlie Seven Alpha?"

"Yup," said the American with an engaging lack of interest in correct radio procedure.

"This is Charlie Seven Oscar actual. We're an hour from Lima Zulu One, over."

"Copy that. It's quiet here," he whispered, barely audible as I squashed the receiver to my ear, "primary target is quiet - no aircraft movement from the secondary."

The heli's interior lights went out as we tracked towards the coast. The guys lit their red tactical torches to check and re-check their kit. I joined in the obsessive-compulsive routine that allayed fear. My shakes had gone, adrenaline trumping the craving for booze. First I unloaded 5.56mm rounds from the magazines of my G36 rifle and cleaned each with a cloth. I slid them back into the magazine and tapped it on my heel to settle the rounds. Then I slid it back into the weapon. I did the same with my pistol before re-checking the protective cap on my rifle optics. My fingers tapped the boot-knife. The razor-sharp blade fitted snugly into a hidden panel in the top of my Lowas, handle flush to the leather. The grenades on my body armour were all secure, spare magazines positioned in pouches angled just-so for fast re-loading. Sitting on the other side of the heli, Bannerman, Ruben and Oz were asleep, surrounded by neatly-stacked weapons and kit, including the explosive wall-breaching equipment. Raphael Grey, silent as usual, was checking his first aid bag and collection of flares, ropes, night-vision and communications kit. He looked at me approvingly as I fussed over my stuff.

Marcus' present, retrieved from the package the Russian loadmaster gave me, was tucked at the bottom of my assault pack. It was a multi-channel receiver that allowed me to secretly patch into the CORACLE team's secure comms. Although Brodie had rigged a main working channel for the operation, the SIS team were using a separate, dedicated secure net. Now I could listen in to not only their team channel, but personal radio-to-radio traffic. I checked my watch – 20:05. The rebels where scheduled to attack Quaani air base in thirty minutes. The landscape, grainy and flat through my NVGs, looked like an alien planet as the heli banked starboard and headed out to sea. Losing altitude, it felt low enough to reach out and touch the waves. "Wake up ladies," hollered Steve Bacon cheerfully. "We're at the LZ."

The Puma slowed to a hover as the Grey twins moved to the winch. Raphael hooked on with a scuffed green karabiner and stepped out of the heli, clothes squashed to his body in the rotor's down-wash. His job was to release the RIB and steady it as we fast-roped down. Ruben stood and operated the winch with Steve. The wind was light, the sea calm as Idris held the Puma steady. I dropped into the night, following Oz down into the RIB.

Raphael caught the shoulder strap of my webbing as I landed. "Over there," he grunted from behind the controls, pointing to my position at the front of the RIB. It was the most I'd heard him say since we'd arrived.

Dancer roped down last, surprisingly agile given his bulk. He settled next to me and gave a thumbs-up signal. Bannerman was to my front, stubby VSS rifle cradled in his arms, bulbous night optics mounted on top of the weapon.

Oz chopped his hand towards the mainland, the faint glow of the GPS illuminating his face. Raphael said something into his throat mic and the Puma began to turn, the harness and cargo net disappearing above us. We waited, bobbing gently in the choppy black water, for the heli to disappear. Now we were on the start line, and there was no going back. Even with noise-reduction alterations, the sound of powerful diesel engines sounded deafening in the night-time quiet. Raphael let them run before throttling down to a gentle chug. "Twenty minutes to the beach," Ruben announced.

The RIB edged forwards, the coast a dark strip ahead of us. Minutes ticked by, and I saw lights atop the vertical cliff edge marking the perimeter of the prison. From the sea, the most prominent feature was the angular block house and pale yellow walls. The beach, a thin grey crescent, lay to my right. It was less than a kilometre away now, partly screened by acacia trees. I studied my watch. The attack on Quaani was five minutes late. "What was that?" whispered Dancer. In the distance I heard a percussive pop-and-roar.

"Mortars," Bannerman replied matter-of-factly. "I hope it's friendly."

I held my breath for a moment, felt a wave of relief at the chorus of explosions and the unmistakable chug of HMG fire. A warbling siren chopped through the night-time silence like an axe. This was the part of the plan that had been laden with risk, relying on the rebels to be on time. It was looking like they'd delivered, testimony to their loyalty to Colonel Mel Murray.

"Two 'undred metres to the beach," said Raphael Grey, crouching at his pilot's position.

"See, it speaks!" said Ruben.

"Shut the fuck up, you mug. I'm working."

"I agree," I hissed, scanning the beach with my NVGs. I saw a grey-green blob in the trees. "Look left: the tree nearest rocks, possible tango."

"Seen," Bannerman replied. He cricked his neck and settled into the optics on the VSS. "It's a sentry. I think he's having a piss."

"Take him," I replied.

"Roger." Bannerman lay on side of the hull, pulling the rifle tightly into his shoulder to off-set the movement of the RIB. The suppressed VSS coughed once, a waft of cordite tickling my nose. Through my NVGs I saw the figure crumple and fall. "Targets *will* fall when hit," the Scotsman whispered.

Raphael increased the power. Within a minute the RIB nudged onto the beach. We hopped out, water lapping our knee-pads, weapons covering arcs through three-hundred and sixty degrees. Raphael set a timed charge in the RIB, set to explode in an hour. I scanned ahead of us, into the trees. The steeply-wooded slope led directly to the parking lot next to the prison. I saw nothing, but heard vehicles manoeuvring on the cliff top above. We threaded our way through the trees, Oz leading us towards the target. We passed the body of the sentry, clad in neatly-pressed fatigues. I noticed the orange-and-black flash of the Presidential Commando on his sleeve. Bannerman's bullet had hit him in the sternum, a dark patch of blood spreading across his uniform.

As we crept forward, floodlit prison walls loomed above us through the trees. Originally built by Italian fascists, Kivuli Hatua was every inch the ham-fisted thirties tribute to imagined Roman glory. Through night vision it was a grey-green monstrosity of barbed-wire draped walls and rectangular turrets, rising from a scab of rock like Mussolini's chin. "It reminds me of Govan," Bannerman whispered, "barbed wire, guns, gloom and the prospect of imminent violence... makes a man homesick."

"Nah," said Ruben Grey, "it's gotta be the flats off Ripple Road, the ones you can see from the A13..."

A solitary light burnt in the guard tower nearest us, flaring in my NVGs. Behind was open ground leading to the cliff edge. To our front a metalled road ran past the gatehouse, due north towards Quaani. Lying at the edge of the treeline, I made out the shape of an armoured vehicle, the BMP we'd seen on the satellite images. The stubby AFV made strange shadows through my NVGs. We cleared the trees at the top of the slope. I ordered the team to halt, the men dropping into all-round defence. "Alex, can you see us?" I whispered into my mic.

"Copy that," he replied. "You've got three tangoes approaching the BMP."

A trio of Zambutan soldiers morphed out of the gloom and clambered aboard the armoured vehicle. The driver tried to start the engine, which sputtered and died. The BMP was directly in front of our route to the prison wall, turret-mounted gun pointing towards Alex's position. The 30mm cannon could fire up to 800 shells a minute and had to be neutralised.

Now we were on higher ground, I saw the flash of explosions, due north of our position. Blobs of tracer rose and fell in shallow parabolas, fire-tinged balls of smoke drifting on the wind. I heard a voice in my ear. "They ain't got any idea you guys are there," Alex reported.

I tried to focus on the Alex's OP, on the hill over three hundred metres west of us. I couldn't see it. "Can you take the BMP crew?"

"Yup."

Dancer crawled forward, face streaked with camouflage paint. "Look," he whispered, the urgent chop of his hand pointing towards the prison, "the blockhouse?"

"Seen," I replied.

He shifted his hand right, my eyes following it, "top floor to the right of the blockhouse, rectangular window - that's where we reckon Mel is."

The blockhouse was a three-storey stone box, jutting bulwark-like from the prison walls. A staggered series of towers could be seen beyond. "The first MG tower is on the far side of the blockhouse," Oz reported. "It can only cause a problem if we end up inside the prison yard." The machinegun towers were set at different levels, each with its own arc of fire. It was a 1930's design flaw, the prison built before the advent of helicopters. No single tower enjoyed a three-hundred and sixty degree view.

Bannerman took my night vision binoculars and scanned the prison, "I'm going tae blow the wall next tae the blockhouse, the floor-plan shows a door in the facing wall behind there."

Dancer shifted on his belly, reaching for the binoculars. "I'm sure you've done the maths, old chap, but those walls are eight inches thick."

Bannerman pulled a circular camouflaged bag from his pack and pushed it in front of him. "Meet the *Ensign Bickford* rapid wall breaching kit, Mister Dancer. It'll blow clean through ten inches of reinforced concrete. And if it doesn't then I'll give the wall some lovin' with an AT4. My only concern is not blowing the fucking blockhouse over the cliff and intae the drink."

"Sounds good to me," Dancer smiled, "apart from the bit where we blow Mel into the sea, of course."

My radio, tucked into the top of my assault pack, bleeped. I keyed the handset. "Charlie Seven Zero?" said Juliet calmly, "we'll be on the start line in five minutes." The Dornier had landed at an LZ fifteen kilometres southwest of Bytchakov's OP.

"Roger that and good luck," I said.

"You've got movement by the gate," said Alex over our tactical net.

"Let them go, Alex," I said.

"Copy that. The gates are opening, three jeeps manoeuvring outta the gates, about six guys in each..."

We watched from the trees as the three Land Rovers roared past us. Heavily-armed Zambutan soldiers jeered at their colleagues with the stricken BMP and zoomed north. I waited until the vehicles were clear of the prison. "Alex, take out the BMP crew, then the sentry in the tower nearest the blockhouse." The only acknowledgement over the net was the crackle of static. Then muzzle flash from the .50 rifle as I heard the supersonic crack of the round breaking the sound barrier. The first crewman was torn in half by the high calibre bullet, torso thrown in one direction and legs in another. The second soldier, perched on the turret, evaporated from the shoulders up. The third Zambutan darted towards us. Bannerman's VSS coughed twice, both rounds hitting the soldier in the chest. "Go!" I barked.

We formed pre-agreed fire teams, Oz and the Grey twins sprinting for the BMP while the rest of us covered them from the trees. I heard the men's boots padding across the dusty ground and the creak of equipment as they advanced. Alex's .50 barked again. The top of the guard tower rocked, a second shot blowing the sentry out of his perch. His carcass toppled fifteen metres to the flag-stoned deck below. The aught-fifty rounds were designed for fucking up lightly-armoured vehicles. A guard tower posed few problems for its velocity and killing power. Bannerman's team went firm and it was our turn to dart forward. We fell to our bellies, weapons covering arcs. "Go," I spat into my mic.

The Scotsman nodded and scurried up to the blockhouse. I could still hear the boom of the .50 mixed with the crack of Kalashnikovs. Bannerman motioned for us to back off as he busied himself with the wall-breaching kit. I squinted through the sights of my own rifle, ready to engage anything that moved.

"Contact!" Dancer barked. He coolly fired up at the wall, like he was at a Northumbrian game shot. The ragged burp of an MG4 followed. I looked up at a shadowy shape darting along the battlements and snapped off two shots.

"GRENADE," Oz warned, stepping forward and scooping something up. He tossed it back over the wall and fell to his belly. I ducked back down as the grenade exploded. The Grey twins opened fire, dragon's breath spewing from their automatic weapons, raking the tops of walls and guard towers. The one-in-six tracer made distinctive glowing blobs, like fiery snowballs arcing into the night.

Bannerman aimed the MG4 up at the lip of the guard tower, raking its entire length. The muzzle flash lit up his face like some sort of avenging demon, a thin smile on his face. There was a groan as a dark shape fell and was caught on the dense coils of barbed wire. "Re-loading!" he called, flipping the cover of the feed tray. I nodded in acknowledgement and fired a controlled burst. The rhythmic *TAK-TAK-TAK* of aimed rifle fire filled my ears, the familiar smell of cordite and burnt weapon oil in my nose.

All the time I could hear the boom of .50 rounds as Bytchakov covered us, his high-pitched voice inside my earpiece, "you got tangos trying to get out of the towers onto the walls, keep up that coverin' fire 'cuz they're pinned down."

"Get back!" Bannerman ordered, doubling away from the explosives package.

We all sprinted towards the parked BMP when, with a thunderous roar, the block house wall evaporated. The vortex of flame, smoke and debris rocked the armoured vehicle on its axles. The wall wasn't breached as much as demolished, a ragged chasm splitting the blockhouse asunder. A steel door hung off its hinges like a coffin lid. A cloud of smoke and dust rolled towards us. "Go," I said into my PRR. Beyond lay the courtyard, swathed in smoke.

Dancer and the Grey twins were already there, weapons aimed into the courtyard. Taking cover by the rubble, Bannerman fired a long burst from the waist, tracer bouncing across parked vehicles. Oz took advantage of the covering fire to move forward, taking his turn to hose down the open yard with fire. Uniformed bodies littered the ground. The Grey boys darted across the yard, firing at anything stupid enough to move. A body flopped from a shadowy corner, hitting the floor with a wet crunch. "RPG," Bannerman hollered. He shrugged an AT4 onto his shoulder and pointed it at the furthest guard tower. Shielded by steel plates, a helmeted figure desperately tried to bring a RPG launcher to bear.

I rolled out of the way as Bannerman fired, the gout of orange-white flame from the back-blast filling the breach in the wall. The guard tower disappeared in a cloud of white fire and smoke.

"Ma fucking 'dreds!" the Scotsman hollered. The rocket's back-blast had singed his long copper dreadlocks, "bastard-fucking-piece-of-shit-Yank-fucking-rocket!" He tossed the empty rocket tube onto the ground and kicked it.

I slipped past him, to the blockhouse door. I kicked it off shattered hinges, "on me!" I bawled. I made a hand signal to Dancer: clear the room.

"GRENADE!" he acknowledged, tossing a M67 inside the doorway. A flash illuminated the night, smoke spewing from the corridor.

I emptied a magazine into the darkness, bellowed "CLEAR!" then called out my re-load. Dancer was already ahead of me, rifle pushed forward, into a dimly lit office with white-washed walls. The Surefire torch attached to his rifle lit up the corridor. Dancer's face was sweat-slicked, his breathing laboured. Nonetheless, he was keeping up.

"It's OK out here," said Oz over the PRR. "Eight dead tangos."

"Roger that: go firm on your position," I said into my mic. "Wait for us and provide cover, then meet Easter's team when I call them in."

"Roger," said the ex-SBS man. He and the Grey twins would run an outer security cordon for the extraction.

Through the corridor was an open prison wing, flanked by flights of metal stairs. "Fuck," said Dancer, "what do you want me to do with this lot?" Rushing down the steps were a dozen terrified Zambutan prison guards, hands aloft. They wore a hodgepodge of sweat-stained khaki uniforms. Most of them looked like they'd just woken up. The others smelt of sweat and cheap whisky.

"Get them to lock themselves in a cell," I grunted, pushing past them and heading up the stairs.

One of the guards gave me a look, reached for his revolver. Dancer shot him, barking orders in Swahili at the others. The guards fell to the floor, begging for mercy. The dead man collapsed at the bottom of the concrete steps, blood pumping from the fist-sized exit wound in his back. The high-velocity bullet had sailed through his trunk and hit another guard in the shoulder. "Cal, shall I do for the lot of them?" said Dancer, eyes gleaming.

I looked him up-and-down, "If you were going to do that, you wouldn't have asked my permission. Lock them up." You could tell a lot about a man in the heat of battle. With his blood up, Tom Dancer liked the taste of it. It wasn't a trait I admired.

The first floor was smaller secure wing. Four-man cells lined a dark corridor. It smelt of the familiar prison cocktail of urine, sweat and vomit. One of the guards must have understood English, volunteering a collection of steel dungeon keys that looked like they belonged to a fairy-tale giant. We made it to the top floor, up a spiral staircase. A grey-green painted steel door with a sliding wicket dominated the wall, a sign in English reading SOLITARY CONFINEMENT WING. The recessed lock had a blob of flaking orange paint above it, which matched the paint on one of the keys. Even I could work that one out. "Murray, we're friendlies!" I called as I slid the key in.

"About fucking time," came a voice from the other side of the door. I put my shoulder to the door, Dancer adding his weight. It swung open. "Come in," said Lieutenant-Colonel Mel Murray. "But I hope you realise we've got a traitor in the camp."

CHAPTER FOURTEEN

Murray looked like a leader of men, even dressed in a grimy boiler suit and sandals. He had a thicket of wavy grey hair, a hawkish nose and deep-set eyes. He slapped Dancer's shoulder. "Jesus, Tom, it's good to see you..." I looked him up and down. Murray had taken a beating, eyes swollen and hair matted with blood.

"This is Cal Winter," said Dancer. "We hired The Firm to get you out of here."

"So you're from The Firm?" Murray replied. "They do the Devil's work, so I'm told."

"If that's true, what does it make you?" I said. "Let's go."

Murray shook his head. "Hold on."

"This is Charlie Seven Zero, we've got the package. Alex, call in Easter," I said into my mic, ignoring Murray. I looked at my watch, hoping to hear rotor blades at any moment. "SITREP" I growled into my PRR.

"Easter's team ETA three minutes," said Bytchakov. "But it's lookin' sweet out here. All the action is back towards Quaani."

Oz's voice came over the net, "Charlie Seven Zero, you OK in there?"

"Roger, we've got the package," I replied. "He's in good health." *This is actually going to work…*

"Listen," Murray snapped. "When I was captured there were two MSS agents with the security police. The

Chinese…" Chinese spies? This was running too much to Marcus's script for my liking.

"Mel, there's no time," Dancer replied.

"… The Chinese knew I was going to be there, dammit. I was betrayed."

"Tell me about it in the heli," Dancer sighed, leading the way back down the stairs.

"Hold on, Tom," I said. "Colonel Murray, what did the Chinese say?"

"I said let's go," Dancer pleaded.

"No, this is important," I growled. "If we're compromised…"

"I'm glad *you* understand," said Murray. "They knew too much about CORACLE, I tell you. I know when I've been played..."

"This is Duclair," said a voice over the PRR. "We're going to be with you imminently. The rebels have sent a flash signal – they're getting counter-attacked. You need to move."

"Cal, we need to shift our arses," Dancer shouted. We navigated back through the warren of dimly lit concrete corridors, here and there an empty cell. I saw a suspended landing, cages crammed full of men wearing dirty red boiler suits and chained at the ankles.

Murray said something in Swahili and tossed the keys to one of the prisoners. The guy that caught them nodded and set about undoing the shackles, "red boiler suits are for political prisoners," he explained. "These men are from opposition parties. We should let them go, it will cause havoc."

I keyed my PRR, "All call-signs from Charlie Seven Zero, we're coming out on the opposite side of the courtyard, hold your fire. There are also prisoners in red boiler suits. They're not hostiles."

"Roger that," said Bannerman. "I can hear the heli, let's go." We exited the prison and fanned out, weapons ready.

"Sarn't Bannerman, nice to see you again," boomed Murray, spotting the Scotsman prowling across the body-strewn courtyard. The Colonel stuck his chest out, switching on the bluff bonhomie obligatory for British officers in the field. "I haven't seen you since, when? You were with the Pathfinders in Basra?"

"It was Baghdad, but hello anyway Colonel," the ex-Para replied, touching the edge of his helmet in salute, pointing towards the smouldering breach. "The helis are that way."

"What's happened to your bloody hair?" said Murray, pointing at the singed dreadlocks.

"It was the back-blast from ma AT4, bastard Yank rocket."

"That's why you're not allowed exotic hairstyles in the army."

"In case you didnae notice, Colonel, I'm nae in the fucking army," Bannerman grinned. "I'm on The Firm. Fuck off over there and we'll take you to the LZ."

Murray nodded, stooping to pick up an AK from one of the dead guards. Dancer and I strode across the courtyard behind him, the throb of helicopter engines in the distance. "What can you see, Alex?" I said into my mic.

"It's still looking OK," he reported. "But there's war brewin' back towards the airfield, I see tracer and explosions."

"Keep an eye on the main road," I said. "Engage targets moving towards us."

"Copy that, Captain," he croaked.

The dun-coloured Dornier swooped in low, thumping onto open ground west of the prison. The Puma would hang back until the first extraction was complete. "Get ready to cover Easter's team," I shouted.

Oz nodded, leading the Grey twins across the yard. My plan was to wait for the SIS team to do their thing while Oz's team covered the road leading to Quaani, supported by Alex in his miniature fire support base. The four SIS officers trooped towards us, Duclair in the lead. They stepped through the shattered wall, Hugo and Alan shouldering empty kit bags. "What an awful mess," said Hugo, tut-tutting as he surveyed the carnage. "You really are a bunch of hooligans."

"We aim to please," I replied.

"You OK, Cal?" said Easter from beneath a helmet. She wore body armour, an M4 carbine cradled in her arms.

"Yes, it's gone as well as we could have hoped."

She took in the bodies and flaming vehicles, nodding grimly. I wanted to be in a position to keep an eye on the SIS team, but the exfil came first. There was no point finding more clues if the end result was getting stranded. And if one of these agents was a traitor, why had all of them set foot in the danger zone? It didn't make sense. "You're good to go," I said to Duclair, who was looking at a schematic of the prison on a hand-held device of some sort.

"Thanks," she replied coolly. "Mel, it's good to see you."

"We need to speak," said Murray. "Juliet?"

"It's over," she replied, her face a mask. "CORACLE is terminated."

Duclair nodded at the two technical officers. Hugo and Brodie walked towards the prison, ducking into a bullet-riddled doorway. "The staircase is next to this corridor," he said to his colleague.

"OK," Brodie replied, voice shaky. He fished a rubberized torch from his belt kit.

"What are they doing here?" said Murray archly.

"We've got equipment to extract," Easter replied, looking at her watch. "We'll be twenty minutes at most." She hefted her rifle and looked towards Quaani, a smoky orange pall settling on the horizon.

"*Equipment?*" snapped Murray.

"Calm down Mel," urged Dancer. "It's an SIS matter now."

Murray stepped forward to remonstrate. "Juliet, you've got a problem. The bloody Chinese *knew* I was going to be at that meeting." His eyes bulged, hands tightening on the grips of his Kalashnikov. He looked like he was going to flip out. I had plasticuffs on my belt kit, just in case.

"*None* of your meetings were authorised, Mel," Easter snapped. "No wonder you were compromised, so spare me a lecture. You probably led the Chinese straight to us, monitoring our comms all along. We'll have a post-mortem back in the UK."

"What if Mel's right?" said Duclair. "Juliet, I think we've got an OPSEC problem too." I watched Duclair's finger slide off the trigger guard of her M4.

Bannerman looked bemused. "Ladies, if you don't mind, we're in the middle of a fucking war zone. Any chance you can have your fucking argument on the fucking heli out of here?"

"Amelia, I'm inclined to agree with Mister Bannerman," said Easter. "This needs a formal de-brief when we get back. Right now, we've an operation to finish."

Duclair went to speak, eyes flashing. "Jools…"

"Contrary to your expectations, this isn't a democracy," said Easter icily. "Please, join the others inside and get this thing finished." Duclair almost snarled with anger and headed downstairs.

"OK, are we sorted?" I said, watching Duclair disappear inside.

"Yes, Cal, we're sorted," Easter replied. "I'm sorry about that."

"We're leaving as soon as your team extracts," I replied. "Let's get on with it, shall we?"

"Come on Mel," said Easter, expression softening.

Murray stood, head lowered. Bannerman passed him his water bottle.

Murray thanked him and took a gulp, "Glenlivet?"

"Aye, Colonel. Good to see an African prison hasn't jaded your taste buds."

I passed Murray an energy bar, which he took gratefully, peeling off the foil with trembling fingers. "I'll check the perimeter," I said. Pushing past a knot of fleeing prisoners, I headed to the breached wall and jogged to the BMP, bodies scattered about it. I wanted to know what the hell was going on with the CORACLE team. From the cold glint in Amelia Duclair's baby blues, I honestly thought she'd shoot Easter.

She wasn't to know that the only person authorised to murder MI6 officers on this trip was me.

Rummaging in my assault pack I pulled out Marcus' transmitter and plugged the jack into my radio. A list of call-signs scrolled down the display, like I was searching for a Wi-Fi signal on my cell. I flipped on the SIS team's private talk-group and waited. "It's clear," said Duclair. "Get on with it, before Mel fucks this thing up."

"I heard someone upstairs," replied Alan. "Is Easter clear? I don't trust the bitch."

"It's OK, it's only Tom…"

"Jesus," said Hugo, laughing with delight. "I'm in. This is unbelievable, there's bugger all security to speak of. It's like a day one training exercise."

"What is it?" said Duclair expectantly.

"We've got the whole bloody lot" Hugo replied, "just like I predicted."

I heard something to my right, beyond the BMP and main road. It sounded like the grinding of metal on metal. I switched back to our tactical net. "Alex, talk to me – what's coming up the road?"

"I can't see," he replied. "Whatever it is, it's beyond those trees where the road dog-legs."

The noise grew louder, the deep bass roar of powerful engines and the creaking and clanking of machinery. I felt fear, the *oh-fuck* sort of fear that makes you want to empty your bowels. I knew what the noise was, wanted to believe I could be wrong.

I wasn't.

An armoured beast groaned and clanked towards me, felling trees like a demonic lawnmower with steel-shod tracks. It was a tracked ZSU anti-aircraft vehicle, oversized turret bristling with cannon. Armed men, some of them wounded, clung to the sides. The Zambutan army was retreating from Quaani airbase, back towards us.

My sleuthing would have to wait.

The ZSU was painted in a dirty grey and tan camouflage pattern, four cannons mounted in a lozenge-shaped turret. It stopped, the turret jerkily panning left and right, exhaust fumes roiling through the trees. I held my breath, praying the guns wouldn't come to rest on my position. I scanned the terrain – to my front the road snaked past the trees, where the ZSU lurked. Then there was the parking lot, where I crouched by the armoured BMP. Further back behind me were the prison and the extraction point. That made me the meat in a tank sandwich.

A screen of infantry broke the tree-line in platoon strength, fanning out in front of the ZSU. Several bullet-riddled jeeps limped along the road behind. I could still hear explosions back towards Quaani, the dull crump of mortars and the lazy *pop-pop-pop* of Dushkas. I flipped my radio back to the main channel. "Contact - we've got enemy armour and infantry to the north. I need antitank."

Alex Bytchakov's croak filled my ears, "Copy, engaging with AT4. Get your head down Cal." He made it sound as stressful as ordering a burger. A monochrome flash lit up the hill as the HEAT round, an incandescent fireball, streaked across the open ground and slammed into the ZSU. There was an explosion and a plume of smoke, infantry scattering from the blast.

Taking cover, I lined up the first of the advancing troops in my sights and opened fire. Behind me, near the shattered prison wall, Oz and the Grey twins hid in a shallow ditch. They set up one of the MG4s and began pouring fire into the trees. A return volley of gunfire splashed against the BMPs armour. The damaged ZSU's turret changed direction, quad-cannon inching towards the hill where Bytchakov was hiding.

The wave of infantry surged forward, firing wildly. Red tracer from one of our MG4's stitched across their ranks. The first wave of Zambutans faltered then broke. Bytchakov's rocket had struck the ZSU in the running gear and lower hull, flames licking around the underside of the vehicle. Aiming at the turret, I saw a head emerge. I opened fire, rounds striking the armoured steel. The head disappeared in a dark splash. The rest of the crew leapt from the vehicle and fled. "The ZSU is disabled," I said, keying my radio. "Begin exfil."

"Roger," crackled Dancer's voice in my ear. "And thank The God's of Fuck for that!" The Zambutan jeeps reversed into the trees, sweeping the road with machinegun and rifle fire as they went. An RPG streaked towards me, flashing by and striking the prison wall.

Behind me I heard rotor blades.

A Land Rover zoomed up the road, the front passenger spraying Oz's position with machinegun fire. The vehicle suddenly rocked on its axles, as if punched by a giant fist. Aught-fifty rounds from Alex's heavy rifle shredded it, the gunner leaping down from his weapon. Fire from Oz's team tore up the road, killing him instantly. More bullets raked the cab, front passengers flailing like bloody dolls. The open ground surrounding the prison now worked against the Zambutans, a killing field with no escape. "Oz, Alex and I will cover," I said into my mic. "The rest of you fall back to the heli."

"Roger that," said Dancer.

I saw the rest of my team, dark shapes moving across the desert floor, lope away towards the prison. Thumbing the fire selector on the G36 I emptied the magazine into the treeline to my front. The Zambutan assault had been half-hearted, too easily broken. I guessed they'd fallen back to re-org for a second assault.

Alex continued to fire at targets of opportunity. Now he was using his M-14, the sharp crack of 7.62 rounds echoing across the desert. So far, the decision to put him in the OP had been solid, saving our arses from a variety of threats. Scrambling to my feet, I headed back to the prison. The SIS team were formed up in a text-book stack by the wall, ready to go. Hugo and Alan both dragged bulging kit bags, secured with heavy padlocks. "We've secured the treasure from this fell citadel," grinned Hugo, in a mock-Shakespearian voice. He was as excited as fuck. I could literally smell adrenaline.

"I'm glad you're having fun," I shouted. "Juliet, you good?" Chilled sweat ran down my back, the stink of cordite and brick-dust in my nose. I tried to make out what was in the bags but the shapes were too indistinct.

"Roger that," said Amelia Duclair calmly from the front of the stack. She could have been on Salisbury Plain, not in a war zone. "We've retrieved the kit, we're good for exfil."

Easter nodded, leading Murray and the others away, Dancer following closely behind. Bannerman brought up the rear, Oz and the twins covering them. Their weapons covered every arc, their pace slow but steady to avoid stumbling on the uneven ground. I saw the dark shape of the Dornier ready for take-off, rotor blades churning up a tempest of gritty sand. The team approached the heli, pulling down goggles to cover their eyes from the swirling dust and grit. In the inky-black distance I heard the steady beat of rotor blades. "OK," I hollered, "here's the Puma." We darted forward to join the others.

The metallic cough of cannon-fire rang out over the engine noise, the flash of weapons flooding my peripheral vision with searing light. "That's nae fucking Puma," Bannerman yelled, "take cover!"

CHAPTER FIFTEEN

A volley of cannon-fire tore a strafing line through the Dornier's cockpit, chewing it up like plastic. We hit the deck as another smashed through the fuselage, smoke billowing from the airframe. The South African pilots lolled lifelessly in their seats, like crash-test dummies. The Dornier's engine exploded with a dull thump, followed by ammo from the door-guns cooking off. The SIS officers scattered, hurling themselves to the pancake-flat killing ground. Another heli flashed low overhead. From the glow of the burning Dornier I saw the glint of a sleek fuselage and weapon pods. Ice-cold sweat pooled at the small of my back.

"Get down, Raph!" howled Ruben Grey. A dark shape zoomed overhead only to be replaced by another, spraying the road with cannon-fire. Raphael Grey disappeared in a hail of steel and smoke, body twisting as if spun by a giant hand.

"Who the hell are they?" said Dancer, flat on his belly. I strained to hear him over Bannerman firing his MG4 into the sky, hot brass tumbling onto my arms and back.

"Z9's," said Oz, appearing next to me. He went through the prep drills for his Stinger shoulder-launched rocket, "looks like the Chinese navy by the markings." A third heli howled overhead, then a fourth.

"What the fuck is the Chinese navy doing here?" I shouted. The blazing helicopter lit up the open ground beyond the prison, exposing us like rabbits cowering from a circling hawk.

"Shit," said Oz, looking at the rocket tube in disgust, "it's fucked."

There were at least four helis. They circled hungrily, lining up for another strafing run. Orange and white flashes lit up the night as cannon pods fired, shells gouging jagged holes in the road. Now I knew what the Iraqi Fedayeen must have felt when we called in attack helis, like the entire sky was trying to kill you, crowded with psycho Valkyries. Murray appeared at my shoulder. "We need that ZSU," he said, pointing at the anti-aircraft vehicle. "I can operate the guns, assuming the on-board radar is still working." I guessed Murray, an SAS veteran, would have mastered any number of foreign weapon systems.

Flash bastard.

I got on the radio and ordered the SIS team to find cover. Easter's team complied immediately, dragging the bags of stolen EW kit after them. They scanned the inky night sky as they headed towards the prison. I heard helicopter engines change pitch as the Z9s began to turn for another attack run. The muzzle of Alex's .50 flashed over on the hill. A hovering Z9 lurched in the sky, began careering drunkenly. It was too dark to see where it had been hit, but it lost altitude and chuntered back towards the air base. "The Yank's a mega-fucking-shot," grunted Bannerman, reloading his MG. "I'll give him that."

I led Murray into the trees, towards the crippled ZSU. The smouldering vehicle lay abandoned next to a clutch of burning acacia. Murray dropped into the belly of the armoured beast, bellowing instructions. Oz lowered himself into the turret as the chassis jerked unhappily, power-assisted servos creaking.

I heard Ruben's voice behind me, high-pitched and desperate, "over here!" Crouching by the roadside with Bannerman, they worked on Raphael Grey. They'd dragged him from the killing ground, into a semblance of cover by some rocks. Emergency medical kit was scattered like confetti, bloody dressings and IV lines snaking across body parts. Raph was groaning, his right leg blown off above the knee by a cannon-shell. Another had hit him in the shoulder, tearing off his arm and leaving a gaping, meaty void in the side of his torso.

Bannerman had stuffed Raph's shemagh scarf into the wound to staunch the bleeding. Ruben was speaking quietly to his twin, sliding a morphine shot into his remaining arm. The ex-marine's body armour gaped open, exposing a mess of blood-soaked uniform, entrails and charred meat. "Just shoot me," groaned Raphael, face ashen and slick with sweat. His eyes rolled wildly. "Do it!"

Bannerman shook his head. Ruben looked at me grimly and nodded. "Do it, Cal. Please, mate, I can't…"

I shouldered my '36 and shot Raph in the heart, twice. "Move," I grunted. "We'll fetch him later."

Ruben followed Bannerman towards the trees, weapons painting arcs as they advanced. Taking a last look at the shattered corpse, I ran after them. On the tree line, the guns of the ZSU tracked the Chinese helis. I'd been a soldier and mercenary for over twenty years and never come under attack from aircraft: a Twenty-First century First World warrior fights with air supremacy. It was terrifying, helis disappearing and diving at will in the blackness, the rasp of weapon systems roaring fiery death far beyond reach.

The ZSU 23/4 guns, when they fired, weren't as loud as I'd expected, or maybe I was just deafened by the noise of explosions and gunfire. Gouts of white flame licked from the quad-barrels, streams of glowing tracer spitting into the sky. The high-pitched whir of mechanical components continued after the guns finished. The Chinese helis weaved and banked when they saw the AA gun open up, engines whining. "BLOCKAGE," Oz hollered from inside the ZSU.

I heard muffled cursing and swearing as Murray, huddled in the turret, struggled with the guns. For the moment the skies were clear, the Chinese Z9's spooked by the unexpected flak. The ZSU's guns roared again. There was more swearing from inside the turret as Murray tried to explain the finer points of antiaircraft gunnery to Oz.

"Cal," shouted Bannerman from behind the ZSU, "listen!" I heard the thud of rotor blades again, slower and steadier than the little Z9s. The orange and black Super-Puma sped in low from the south, skimming the tops of trees and bushes. It landed two hundred yards from our position. I could see Steve Bacon crouched in the side door, scanning the LZ with the mounted machinegun.

"They're fucking mad" said Bannerman, "the magnificent wee fuckers!"

"GO, GO, GO!" I shouted into my PRR mic.

The men nodded and began sprinting towards the Puma.

I heard arguing as Murray refused to leave the turret. "Get out, before I throw a fucking grenade in there, Colonel." I yelled. "You're the only reason we're here."

Murray grunted as the ZSU's guns swivelled jerkily, the radar dish fitted to the back of the turret sniffing out a new target. They let rip again, shell casings spewing onto the ground. I heard the sound of metal-on-metal, then a groaning crash as the cannon shells ripped through a distant target. I could see fire in the distance. "That will buy us time," said Murray, "OK, let's go."

I wasn't going anywhere without Oz. "Get to the heli. I'll be there once I've got Oz out." Murray nodded, levered himself out of the turret and disappeared into the night.

Oz watched him go. "Cal, that Puma won't cover ten miles if they know the AA gun is abandoned," he panted, wiping sweat from his forehead, "let's hold 'em off, then exfil on foot or have one of those jeeps away."

I nodded and keyed my PRR, "This is Charlie Seven Zero: All call-signs bug out. We're staying with the ZSU to cover you. We will exfil via vehicle and issue coordinates on the sat phone later. That's an order."

"Roger," Bannerman replied over the net. "We're almost at the heli now, good luck Cal..."

"Mortars," I shouted.

Bannerman and Ruben fell to the ground, a stick of bombs exploding near the roadside. I saw Murray running towards the heli, limping and holding his thigh. I flinched as the flash-and-smoke of high-explosive strikes crept towards the LZ, the plot swathed in smoke. "Go!" I heard Bannerman shout over the PRR, and then he was gone. I couldn't make out if he'd made it to the heli or not, among the flaming clouds and flickering shadows from burning wreckage. Then, engines roaring, the Puma took off, turning one hundred and eighty degrees and thundering back towards the border. Next to me, from inside the ZSU, came a pinging noise. The ageing Soviet radar had acquired a new target. The ZSU's AA guns opened up again, joining the sound of mortars and small arms.

I hopped off the open-topped turret and rolled under the tracks. "Easter," I spat into my mic, "are you getting this?"

"Roger," she replied. "We didn't pick up Bannerman or Grey. We're doing a sweep now."

"I think they've been hit," I replied. "If you've got Murray, go. We'll find them."

"Keep heading south," she said. "We'll find you." It was the sort of thing you were expected to say, like a medic reassuring a dying man he'd be OK.

Dark shadows appeared to our front, enemy infantry ghost-like through night vision. There was a crack of a sniper rifle and one of the men fell, then another from our left flank. It was Alex, still plying his trade with deadly accuracy. More mortar bombs fell like rain, a non-stop barrage of fire and steel. I hugged the earth and screamed as my eardrums threatened to pop. "Fuck this," yelled Oz. "I'm bailing out."

I tried to raise Bannerman on the radio, heard nothing but static. Engines rumbled to my right, near the tree-lined cliff edge. I glanced over and saw two armoured cars trundling towards us, stubby cannon protruding from their Dalek-like turrets. Oz flopped down next to me, "Cal, I think for us the war is over."

I looked over my shoulder. The Puma was gone. Hopefully the time we'd bought would be enough for them to make the border. I heard the drone of engines from the Z9s nearby, prayed they wouldn't catch up. "Do I call *Fallen Eagle*?" I said.

Oz scowled. "If they could realistically help us, why are we here in the first place?"

I pulled the sat phone from my assault pack. "Are we fatally compromised or not?"

The ex-SBS man looked at the approaching troops. "Not yet," he grunted. "Murray's been rescued. We haven't failed." His eyes bore into mine. "Understand? *We haven't failed.*"

"OK," I agreed. I wondered if he knew something I didn't.

Alex appeared out of the gloom, a rifle in each hand. "I'm Airborne. I'm meant to be surrounded," he puffed, sweat trickling down his face, "but there's a company of infantry out there with support weapons. Where the hell did they come from?"

"You didn't believe the intelligence reports, did you?" I said. "We're surrendering. Keep schtum as long as you can."

"Schtum?" said Bytchakov.

"Don't tell them anything," said Oz.

"We all spill our guts in the end," Alex shrugged. "Ask my second wife."

"Was that the one who stabbed you in Baha?" I said, smiling. I dropped my rifle and stood up, hands in the air. I cringed as a bullet whipped past me, a shrill voice shouting something in a language I assumed was Mandarin. Perhaps we'd be executed, cut down where we stood. It bothered me more than I thought it would. I hadn't stood over Monty, a gun pointed at his scrawny throat, watched him piss himself with fear...

The voice belonged to a Chinese PLA marine. He stalked towards me, assault rifle tipped with a bayonet. He was joined by the rest of his squad, clad in blue-grey camouflage uniforms, faces streaked black.

Their officer was a tall, arrogant-looking bastard with high cheekbones and narrow black eyes. He wore a faded fatigue cap and hooded camouflage jacket, a cigarette smouldering from the corner of his mouth. He stood just out of striking distance, rifle ready. "I am Colonel Zhang Ki. You are the British mercenaries?" He gave a thin smile, his English flawless.

"Fuck you," growled Bytchakov in Russian.

"I see," replied Zhang Ki easily, in the same language. "You've shot down one of my helicopters and killed at least seven of my men. You've entered the sovereign territory of Zambute illegally and destroyed half of their air force. You realise the sentence for mercenary activity here is death?"

"Forgive my friend," I said in Russian. "He's had a bad day."

"Trust me, it's going to get worse," said the Colonel, a smile on his thin lips. "Drop the façade. I know you are English."

"I ain't English," spat Bytchakov. He looked at Oz and me. "No offence, guys."

"None taken," I shrugged.

"No, Mister Bytchakov, you are an American are you not?" Zhang Ki's expression was almost apologetic, "and you are Mister Winter and Mister Osborne?" Duclair was right. We'd been set up. I didn't know how, and I didn't understand why the People's Liberation Army were involved. After all, the Chinese were known for their doctrine of non-military intervention. Their anti-piracy taskforce had a strict mandate, and fighting rebels wasn't part of it.

"Colonel," I asked politely, "is the People's Republic now formally fighting for President Aziz?"

"Of course not," smiled Zhang Ki, studying his cigarette. "We're simply part of the anti-piracy effort. We were moving aviation assets to Quaani, part of a routine deployment order, when we were attacked by terrorists and... *you*. My hand was forced. Our rules of engagement entitle us to defend ourselves."

"How convenient," I replied.

"Ask the families of the men I've lost before you speak of *convenience*," he spat. "There will be an investigation. *Shang Shi*! Take these men, search them and take them to the airbase!"

A wiry Chinese sergeant, uglier than sin, bound us with plastic handcuffs. We were bundled into one of the armoured cars, a Russian army-surplus BDRM-2. The drive back to the Quaani airbase took fifteen minutes at full speed, the sergeant looking daggers at me. Finally the BDRM stopped, engine chugging and wheezing like an old man. The dawn light was rose-coloured, lighting up the blackened skeletons of aircraft and charred corpses that littered the concrete apron. The buildings were pock-marked with bullet holes and damage from RPG strikes, stinking black smoke rolling out of shattered buildings.

Zhang Ki was already there, tapping a cigarette on the back of his hand. He looked at his watch and smiled, "I have a few hours to question you before the Zambutans arrive. I've just learnt that Colonel Murray is missing. It would be easier for you to be... frank."

"What do you want?" I said.

The Colonel produced a sheaf of papers in Mandarin and English. "I'd like a video confession. You can read from these statements, which outline your rogue mercenary activities for the British Secret Intelligence Service. Sign them." I had a feeling that it if I signed it, the statement would be the last thing I would ever put my name to.

"Fuck you," snarled Bytchakov.

"I have to agree," I added, as bravely as I could.

"Very well," Zhang Ki shrugged. "Let it begin."

CHAPTER SIXTEEN

The interrogation was simple but efficient. The Special Operations marines of the People's Liberation Army stripped us naked, dragged us into an aircraft hangar and kicked the shit out of us. Bytchakov responded with the most foul-mouthed rant I've ever heard in Russian, a linguistic achievement in itself. Then he bit the pig-ugly sergeant. The marines gagged him, kicked him in the balls and stubbed cigarettes out on his chest and scrotum. Bytchakov laughed and called them pussies.

They noticed my Russian prison tattoos and the leg injuries I'd picked up in Kurdistan. The Colonel apologised as he cut the suture with a knife and stamped on them, waves of sharp pain doing circuits through my lower body. "Sign your statements. I will order them to stop." I clenched my teeth, breathing bloody snot as I shook my head. "The Zambutan secret police are much worse," said Zhang Ki gently. "They have men with AIDS on hand to rape you, pump you full of killer seed. On the other hand, if you confess to me I will have you dealt with leniently."

Oz sat cross-legged, looking around for a weapon or escape route. Bytchakov was curled up in a bruise-coloured ball. During a brief hiatus from torture, the Colonel rifled through our equipment. "Enough for now," he said. "Whatever you are being paid isn't worth your fate. Confess and I will deliver you to the multi-national anti-piracy force headquarters in

Mauritius. The commander there can either render you to the People's Republic for trial or hand you to the International Criminal Court."

"Can you do that?" I said, trying to disguise my incredulity. Neither sounded appealing, but better than a cell in Marsajir's secret police HQ.

Zhang Ki shrugged, eyes shining, "who is there to stop me?"

"Let me see the statement."

"At last," said Zhang Ki, unable to disguise the relief in his voice. He pulled the papers from inside his jacket, holding out the English version out for me to examine. The statement bore a passing resemblance to the truth. It confessed that we'd been hired to rescue Murray as a pretext for stealing Chinese technical equipment by unnamed British intelligence officers. Either the Chinese knew less than they were letting on or it was a version of events tailored to suit an agenda. Nonetheless, the entire CORACLE rescue plan had been compromised.

We'd been well and truly stitched up. "I'm not signing *that*," I grunted.

Zhang Ki kicked me in the guts. "This is my only promise – you will get a slow death, but a quick ride to hell. I will be watching as the Secret Police set their worst dogs on you, watch them fuck you up the arse!"

Oz pulled a face. "He's obsessed with buggery, ain't he?"

That earned us another beating.

We were plasticuffed and left naked in the hangar as the colonel led his men away. I lay curled by a petrol drum, face resting in a pool of oily gunk. "As long as the satellite radio is switched on we can be tracked," I whispered. My comms kit was lying on top of my Bergen. The sat phone had been switched off, but not the modified US satellite radio. I lost track of time in the sweltering hangar. When I almost fell asleep a marine appeared and poured a bucket of tepid water on me, which at least allowed me to sip some fluids. Slipping in and out of consciousness, I heard the chop of rotor blades. There was soldierly hollering as two Chinese civilians swept in. One was tubby, one was skinny but they wore identical grey poly-cotton suits and black-rimmed glasses. With them was a plump Zambutan wearing a summer-weight khaki uniform, followed by two other local soldiers in camouflage fatigues and berets.

Zhang Ki arrived and spoke with the Chinese guys in suits. I watched warily, in case this meant a one-way trip to Secret Police HQ. "These men are from the... foreign service," he explained. I assumed they were Chinese spooks from the MSS, the Ministry of State Security.

"We should move them to the prison," said the Zambutan in the khaki uniform. He had a crown on his epaulettes, red tabs on his collar and a Sam Browne belt which strained against his hefty gut. A shiny, well-oiled .38 revolver sat in a holster on his waist.

"Of course," said the second Chinese suit.

Zhang Ki barked more orders. His marines bundled us back into the armoured cars and drove back to the prison. Daybreak revealed bodies strewn by the roadside, the area littered with smoking vehicles and the detritus of battle. We arrived at the slab-like fortress, walls streaked with bullet holes and pock-marked from the impact of rocket strikes. The breach we'd blown in the wall was a jagged black scar, smoke still drifting from the rubble. Alex Bytchakov grinned bloodily. "This is a professionally satisfying level of destruction," he croaked.

Kicked out of the truck, we were herded towards the gate. I studied the marines, expecting another beating or worse. They were too busy covering their noses from the stench of death. We passed a detail of Zambutans piling the bodies of prisoners by the gate. No doubt our raid had been used as an opportunity for some extra-judicial administration. Zambutan soldiers were dousing piles of bodies with petrol and burning them, the stink of charred flesh and burning hair drifting on the breeze.

We were led through the courtyard and thrown into a sweltering office in a flurry of slaps and rifle butts. The Chinese sergeant was competing with the two uniformed Zambutans for who could hit us most. Another marine arrived and dumped our stuff on the floor, presumably for further examination.

Grey suit number one, who smelt of sweat and garlic, glowered at the soldiers with a raised eyebrow before returning our fatigues and boots. "Please, gentlemen, get dressed. Major Kito, may I have a moment alone with the prisoners?" he said to the burly Zambutan. The MSS agents pulled their pistols and covered us.

"If you must," Kito sniffed. He looked around the office disapprovingly. Like everywhere else on the ground floor, it had been shot up by either us or escaping prisoners.

"Yes, I must," replied the Chinese intelligence officer icily. His English was excellent, with only a trace of Oriental inflection.

We pulled on our fatigue pants and jackets while nodding our thanks. I wanted the spooks to like us, think we were compliant and grateful. Stuffing my feet into my Lowas, I checked the concealed boot-knife. When we were dressed, the spooks re-cuffed us. Grey suit number one pulled up a chair and plucked an *Ashima* from a white-and-gold pack. His English was fluent. "The fat Zambutan major is from army intelligence. He found out about this incident first – so you are lucky. If you play the game properly we can keep you from Aziz's security police. The army hates them."

"The army hate the secret police?" I grunted. "That sounds pretty par for the course."

"Indeed, the secret police are out of control and completely incompetent. We try to avoid dealing with them when we can. The army intelligence people are slightly easier to deal with, for Africans that is."

"Yes," said Grey suit number two quietly. He had a reedy voice, acne-scars and a shaved head, "the story is simple: a group of mercenary soldiers manipulated by British intelligence rescue the spy, Murray. This is more or less the truth, no?"

"We could make it look like rebels shot down our helicopter," said Grey suit number one, a sly smile on his waxy face. "The whole incident was the result of an unfortunate mistake by trigger-happy... *bandits*."

"That would be better," agreed Grey suit number two.

"What if I sign your statement on the condition I make a couple of amendments?" I said.

"It would depend what the amendments were," said Grey suit one easily. "But we are reasonable men."

"Something that spreads responsibility more fairly," I said, injecting a note of desperation into my voice. "There's more to this affair than you know – we shouldn't take all the blame.

I could tell you about the organisation I work for, which isn't MI6…"

"As you wish," the MSS agent replied, smiling at his luck. Spooks love talkative prisoners, it makes it easier for them to write reports and impress their boss. They released my plasticuffs, Grey suit two producing a notepad from his pocket. They ushered me to a rickety desk. I took a pen in my bloodied fingers and started writing in the margins of the statement, scribbling down stuff about the CIA and other random bollocks. The Chinese read with interest over my shoulder. One of them produced a satellite phone from a chunky black briefcase and began talking excitedly in Mandarin.

I coughed and reached down, catching Oz and Bytchakov's eyes. I tapped the top of my boot-knife. They both nodded. My hand swept up. The curved blade caught the first MSS guy in the throat, just north of his Adam's apple. Dragging the blade across his neck, I slashed the brachial artery and pushed his blood-slicked carcass into the second intelligence officer…

But Oz and Bytchakov were already on him, pummelling the spook with their fists. I planted my boot in his mouth to stop him screaming. I tossed my knife to Oz who opened his neck, spraying us with a fine mist of blood. Within five seconds both men were dead. Oz cut Alex's plasticuffs and patted down the shocked-looking corpses. Each wore a small black pistol in a shoulder holster, with a spare magazine each.

I picked up the blood-stained statements and stuffed them in my pocket. "We go out of the side door, see if we can make for one of those armoured cars."

"That's not a plan, Cal, that's a suicide note," Oz hissed.

There was a knock on the door. Oz readied his pistol, tossing the second to Alex. He nodded and took cover behind a desk. I held my knife loosely by my side. The Zambutan, Major Kito, opened the door and stepped in. Oz pistol-whipped him, the butt of the handgun bouncing off the side of his skull. I stepped behind him and closed the door. "Shut up," said Oz, tucking the snout of his pistol into the Zambutan's chubby jowls.

Major Kito winced. "I cannot say I will miss those Chinese bastards," he said, rubbing his swollen temple. The MSS men were in a tangled heap of limbs, blood and bad tailoring.

"I'm not feeling the love," said Oz. "Between you and the Chinese."

"They say they are here to help us, but behave like they *own* Zambute. Just like every other bastard foreigner who comes here," he snorted. "They buy everything for a fraction of its true value."

Although I was sympathetic to his views on Third World exploitation, now wasn't the time for a chat. I pulled Kito's revolver from its holster and cut the lanyard with my knife, "How are you going to get us out of here?" I said, stuffing the .38 into the waistband of my fatigues.

"I wouldn't be surprised if that Chinese Colonel doesn't kill us all when he sees *them*," said Kito, pointing at the dead agents sprawled at his feet, "Zhang is a ruthless bastard. He spends more time with spies than he does hunting pirates."

"Start thinking," I grunted. "How did you get here?"

"In a Chinese helicopter, with those two," he replied. "We were going to take you to Marsajir for interrogation, before the secret police discovered we'd arrested foreigners."

"Well that's fascinatin', but how you gonna get us outta here?" Bytchakov growled.

"That is possible," said Kito nervously. "I will say you are under arrest and escort you to our helicopter at Quaani, if you can get out without these bodies being discovered. You will have to disarm my men, of course. I would be grateful if you let them live."

I narrowed my eyes, hefted the revolver in my hand, "what about the Chinese?"

Major Kito rolled his eyes in disdain, "those yellow bastards can go and fuck their mothers. I have to take direction from their spies... but their *navy*? Besides, there is a tunnel that leads from the governor's office to the service road. Zhang won't know about it."

"A tunnel?" said Alex.

"Yes," said Kito nervously, a bead of sweat tracking down his chubby face. "The Italians built an ammunition resupply tunnel in the thirties, when yet more bastard foreigners interfered in Zambute."

"Call your men Major," I said. "I swear you'll come to no harm."

Kito pulled a radio from his belt and ordered his men to join us. Hiding our pistols, we stood sullenly in front of him like obedient prisoners. I picked up my assault pack, our radio and satellite phone tucked safely inside. Alex and Oz checked their belt-kit and chest-rigs, clambering back into their fighting rig. Outside, in the courtyard, I could hear Chinese troops moving about.

I again considered calling in the Fallen Eagle protocol, although I wondered what The Firm could do to get us out of Zambute. The direction was clear – Fallen Eagle was only to be used when there was unambiguously no hope of mission success. As far as I knew, Murray was safe and nobody had mentioned The Firm or our status as anything other than mercenaries. I decided to hold fire. I still tapped the code into the sat phone's memory, to save time if the worst happened.

We left the office. Kito's men trudged along the corridor, rifles slung over their shoulders. One of them threw a lazy salute towards Major Kito, who returned it smartly. We drew our pistols. "Lower your weapons," said Kito to his men, hands spread in front of him. "They have given me valuable information, but want nothing to do with the Chinese. Unload your rifles."

"Are they paying us?" grunted the first Zambutan soldier in good English.

"A thousand dollars each," said Bytchakov. We still had the cash sewn into our clothing, part of our escape and evasion kit.

The soldiers lowered their weapons, lit cigarettes and chatted to each other in Swahili. They didn't seem bothered about the situation, not with a thousand dollars attached. When we demanded their AKs, they shrugged and handed them over. We made off down the corridor, led by the parade-ground smart Major Kito. We reached a bullet-riddled office. Two dead prison officers lay nearby, a neat bullet hole in their foreheads where prisoners had taken their revenge. "This is the place I remember," he said. Kito motioned for the two soldiers to move a desk, a black wooden monstrosity the size of a piano. Underneath was a panel with a flat metal ring fitted flush into it. Threaded through the ring was a piece of nylon cord. I tugged on it. The metal panel lifted with a creaking sound, revealing a hole tunnelled into the rust-red earth below.

"Lead on, Major," I said, motioning with my pistol. My mind raced... was this a trap? I looked at Oz and Bytchakov, both men looking straight back at me.

"In for a penny," said Oz, who I'm pretty sure can read my mind.

I took one of the AKs and re-loaded it, relieving the soldier of his ammo-stuffed chest rig. Bytchakov took the other. The tunnel dropped horizontally for ten feet, a rusting ladder set into the wall. I flicked a metal switch and a tear-drop bulb cast a sickly light in the darkness. There was more shouting. "Move," I barked. The Zambutans lowered themselves into the tunnel.

Oz plucked a grenade from his webbing. Looking around he found an old fruit tin on the desk, now used as a pencil holder. Emptying it, he slid the pin from the grenade and pushed it gently into the tin, so the lever was held in place by the rim. He crept towards the wooden door and placed the tin behind it. "Go!" he whispered, nudging his improvised booby-trap into position.

I dropped down behind Alex, already scurrying along the circular tunnel. The air was dank but cool, a relief from the stifling heat above. Decaying rails for ammo trolleys ran along the floor, electric lights fed by rotting cables snaking along the walls. Oz crouched behind me, rifle trained on the return path. We jogged along the tunnel, breathing hot, stale air. The grenade detonation, when it came, was a dull thump. "Run," I hissed.

"They'll search for more IEDs," sniffed Bytchakov approvingly. "It'll slow them down." The tunnel curved to our left before straightening out into the distance. The lights dimmed then went out completely. One of the Zambutan soldiers flicked on a torch and we tip-toed forward.

"Here," whispered Kito. The tunnel began to slope upwards, another metal ladder set into the wall. There was a circular opening in the ceiling. "This is the way out."

Oz pushed the Zambutans aside and told them to wait. I trained my rifle on them as he shimmied up the ladder. I climbed up next, emerging in a clearing several hundred metres from the prison, shielded by a sad clutch of outbuildings. The Zambutans emerged and we scrambled away, Alex dragging the rusty metal grille back over the exit. He wedged another grenade into a gap between the rim of the tunnel and the cover.

I realised we were parallel with the road that led from the airbase to the prison. Parked nearby were some battle-damaged soft-skin vehicles. The most serviceable was a Land Rover, scarred with bullet holes from last night's fighting. A dead soldier lay nearby, flies swarming over a gelatinous mass of entrails. "Get in," I said to Kito. "One of your men will drive."

Kito nodded and gave an order in Swahili.

"When we get to the Chinese aircraft, will it have enough fuel to get us to Kenya?" I asked.

"I'm not a pilot," said Kito cussedly, "but I expect so. It is a large helicopter."

We were pulling out onto the road when Alex's booby trap went off. The Zambutan driver hooted with laughter and gunned the engine, sirens ringing in our ears.

CHAPTER SEVENTEEN

Quaani shimmered in a distant heat-haze. Above us, impatient vultures circled. We slowed down to negotiate the chicane of wrecked vehicles littering the road, weaving in and out of debris and bodies. A pall of black smoke hung over the air base, and in the distance I spotted teams of Zambutan soldiers working on clearing the runway. "Abasi's men were repelled," said Kito haughtily. "The Chinese arrived with helicopters and the terrorists fled."

"It feels like everyone's a terrorist nowadays," I said, hunkering down in my seat.

"*You* are terrorists," he snapped. His men murmured their agreement. "Or in your world do terrorists only have brown skin?"

I suppose he had a point. "If that puts me against your President Aziz then I can live with it," I replied. And I meant it. If I was going to wade in blood again, it would be on the least-worst side. From the file I'd read, The Firm used to send bad men to do good things. I guessed that was the best I could hope for. The sentry on the gate saluted Kito and raised the barrier. I saw three Chinese Z9 helicopters parked on the apron nearby, beyond them stood rows of rusting hangars and a control tower. On the apron, two Chinese pilots examined battle damage to one of the helis. "Where's your helicopter?" I asked.

"It was on the other side of the hangars." We drove by the bullet-holed control tower, no one taking much notice of Kito's Zambutan military detail. Driving straight into the belly of the beast was audacious, bordering on crazy and I hoped it was the last thing Zhang Ki would expect. The alternative was to risk getting lost in the desert in a rickety Land Rover. We chugged past the tower and took a right, into a warren of workshops and more hangers. "There," said Kito, pointing to a bulbous grey transport helicopter. A pair of Chinese pilots wearing dark blue flight suits lounged nearby. He waved at the pilots, who nodded back. "They will want to know where the two MSS agents are," he said nervously.

"I'm sure you'll think of something," I replied, fingers curling around the grips of my AK. "Tell them the spies have discovered a new lead to investigate."

"Cal, look," said Oz.

A heavily tooled-up squad of Presidential Commandos prowled towards us, led by a stiff-backed officer wearing a beret. They wore camouflage fatigues, closely-fitted in the French style, parachute wings on their sleeves. "Major Kito," said the officer, saluting smartly. One soldier can easily tell if another's got his shit squared-away, and these blokes did. They moved with a purpose, weapons and equipment well-maintained. They looked like the sort of operators you killed before they killed you. My finger slid to the trigger of my Kalashnikov.

"Intruders!" Kito hollered, leaping from the Land Rover. Alex shot him twice with his AK before rolling deftly out of the vehicle, shooting the commando officer in the chest. Oz slid his pistol against the skull of our driver and fired once. The last of Kito's men cowered in the front. I emptied my magazine at the commandoes before kicking the driver out of his seat and clambering in. Revving the engine, I reversed into cover behind a neighbouring hangar.

Soldiers scattered, taking cover behind the grey heli, the aircrew sprinting away as well-disciplined shots rang out. Alex and Oz tossed grenades in the direction of the Zambutans. There were two explosions, shrapnel zipping off concrete and the helicopter's fuselage.

"I'm going back to the control tower," I said, hitching a grimy thumb behind me. It looked like the largest, most defensible building on the base. Which was when I realised I was going to die. There's never a good day for it, but I'd always promised myself I'd die well. Not rotting in a Third World prison cell.

I looked at Oz. He grinned back, reading my mind again.

"Well move then," said Bytchakov. The Land Rover jolted over smouldering rubble as we headed for the tower. The white-painted building was streaked with smoke and scarred with bullet holes. Every window was broken, the ground littered with spent brass and blood splashes. Airfield staff, from mechanics to men in civilian clothes, scattered as they looked for cover. They were Russian and Zambutan, the Russki contractors making straight for any unattended vehicles so they could flee the carnage.

Two soldiers crouched by the front door, looking for the source of the gunfire. Alex hosed them down with his stolen AK, men tumbling to the ground, legs flailing. I edged the Land Rover closer to the doorway, Alex and Oz scrambling into the lobby. Scooping up the dead men's weapons, I sprinted up a broad flight of concrete stairs. My lungs burnt from the exertion, my muscles aching from the beating I'd taken.

"This'll do," said Oz. The top floor of the tower offered a three-hundred and sixty degree view. The air traffic control consoles and radio equipment were pock-marked with shrapnel, the windows splintered and cracked. In an attempt to make the building defensible, a sand-bagged .50 calibre machinegun had been positioned in a loophole looking out over the gate house.

Bytchakov huddled behind the MG. Behind him were boxes of ammunition and a heap of rifles, shotguns and grenades. "Apart from a last-ditch defence, Captain," he said, "is there a plan?"

I pulled the satellite radio from my pack and switched it on. I keyed Easter, to no reply. "Here they come," said Oz, taking aim with his AK. "It's the Chinese."

"I'll see you in Valhalla," the American croaked, eyes flashing. He was as mad as the rest of us. He depressed the trigger, the big fifty calibre chugging and spitting flame.

I dropped, bullets churning the air around me. Pulling out my satellite phone with trembling fingers, I tapped out a message for Marcus: UNDER FIRE QUAANI / GRID REF 38MKE26782602209 / CONTACT WITH CHINESE FORCES / BAD APPLE COMPROMISED OPERATION / MM EXTRACTED WITH EW EQUIPMENT / ENDS

"Whatever you're doing, hurry the fuck up," Oz growled. He ducked as another volley of bullets raked the tower.

Popping my head above the control console, I looked down towards the gatehouse fifty metres distant. Two armoured cars rumbled towards us, covered by a well-spaced screen of Chinese marines and Zambutan commandoes. The headed towards the hangars we'd just left. Those rat-runs would give the enemy plenty of routes to infiltrate behind us. Bytchakov shrugged and swung the MG towards the gatehouse. "The Chinese ain't got proper support weapons, only mortars and UGLs as far as I can see." It made sense. As an anti-piracy task force, the Chinese marines would only have small arms and light support weapons. Their specialist role was meant to be boarding suspect dhows at sea, not war-fighting.

"Put fire down on the armoured cars with the fifty," Oz barked, firing a long burst at two PLA marines. They were making ground under covering fire from the armoured cars.

The American opened fire, marines disappearing in a series of wet explosions as .50 rounds hammered into them. "These Chinese guys have got balls, I'll give 'em that." He redirected his fire at the armoured cars, the jack-hammer noise of the .50 echoing in my ears. Shells smashed into their armoured hulls, the bullets making the dull clang-and-screech of metal-on-metal. "Hey, watch this," shouted Bytchakov, swinging the big machinegun a fraction to his left. Raising my binos, I watched him shoot out the heavy front tyres of both armoured cars.

"Good drills!" I hollered. The American clearly knew the key design flaw of the aging BDRM-2 – the crew can only exit via hatches at the front of the vehicle. Now they were trapped inside. Both APCs were scarred with machinegun strikes, but still their stubby cannons fired. Shells peppered our position, making us hug the deck once more.

"Jesus," said Bytchakov, "See that?"

"BMP," shouted Oz, "incoming!" Tearing past the gate house, the armoured vehicle lumbered toward us, throwing up billowing dust trails as its tracks churned the chalky earth. Next to its turreted 30mm cannon, on a launch rail, was a rocket. Through the smoke and tracer fire I could make out a helmeted Zambutan soldier in the turret. The fighting vehicle was closing on us, advancing jerkily through swirling clouds of dust and grit.

The Chinese marines rallied and fell in behind the BMP, covering its advance with small arms fire. Shouldering my pack, I grabbed Bytchakov and dragged him towards the stairs. We reached the steps as his sand-bagged position and machinegun evaporated in a cloud of metal, 30mm high-explosive shells punching holes through the wall. Crazy rays of sunlight lit up the gloomy tower as it was riddled with fire like a Swiss cheese. "We're screwed," Bytchakov coughed as we half-ran half-fell down the stairs.

"No shit," Oz added. Outside, the BMP's three-hundred horsepower engine whined, metal tracks crunching and clanking as it approached. The AFV was obscured by black smoke from the smouldering aircraft that littered the airfield. It pricked my nose and made my eyes water as we stumbled to escape.

"Follow me," I said, dashing outside and towards the warren of maintenance buildings. Then the top of the control tower exploded as the BMP's turret-launched missile struck, the blast hurling us to the ground. The building began collapsing in on itself, radar and communications arrays positioned on the roof toppling into smoking chunks of masonry and rubble. It was a world of shrapnel and fire, of chest-heaving fatigue and throat-burning smoke. My heart pounded and my bowels heaved. It was war. I'd survived Maysan and Basra, Bosnia and Kosovo, Sierra Leone and South Armagh… by fuck I was going to survive this.

Oz dropped into cover by a hangar door, a pilfered light machinegun slung across his chest. "How's that quick in-and-out job going?" he panted, a smile on his grime-streaked face. I peered through the smoke. The Chinese troops had gone firm by the control tower behind us, the BMP reversing into cover. Two marines were carefully examining the ruined doorway, looking for booby traps like the ones we'd left at the prison. Five more stacked up behind them, waiting to assault into the ruins. We ran through the maze of alleyways between cavernous hangars, mouths covered against stinking smoke. From the number of bodies scattered on the ground, I guessed the rebels had taken heavy casualties. As we withdrew I scrounged a dozen more AK magazines and grenades from the dead, stuffing them into pouches on my belt-kit.

There was no plan now other than to flee. At the last hangar Bytchakov pointed at a row of ageing Ural trucks. He pulled himself up into the cab of the first six-wheeler, V8 engine grunting into life. We climbed in, and the American drove along the apron and onto the runway. In the wing-mirror I saw camouflaged figures combing the rubble as the BMP was nudging its way back over the wall of debris, black smoke coughing from the engine. The 30mm cannon pointed into the sky, too high to depress onto us. "Slow down," said Oz.

"What the fuck? Maybe you ain't noticed, but there's a freaking *tank* chasing us."

Oz pointed a grimy finger out of the window, "Chinese helis, the Z9s!" The American came off the gas. We slowly passed the neat line of naval helicopters, Oz pointing his LMG out of the window. He opened fire, hosing bullets into the airframes. Hot brass fell in my lap as the canopies and engine compartments of the Z9s were spattered with bullet holes. Oz nodded, satisfied with his vandalism. "OK, let's go."

Bytchakov threw the truck across the runway and smashed through the perimeter fence. Then we were bumping cross-country, a range of low hills to the west. I had no idea where we were going and didn't care, as long as it was away from the Chinese marines and the Zambutan armour. I found a plastic bottle of warm water in the cab. I passed it around, sighing happily when it was my turn to drink.

In front of us and to our right cannon rounds churned up plumes of gritty earth as the BMP gunner tracked us. The truck shook as a shell slammed home, Alex hauling the steering wheel down and careering towards a row of scraggly trees. Then there was a noise like two metal animals colliding as the cab of the truck lurched crazily, the front wheel collapsing under the chassis as another cannon shell eviscerated the axle. The vehicle slid, crashing onto its side in the soft grey-orange soil. The cab was suddenly full of smoke, dirt, kit and limbs as we tumbled into each other. "OUT," Oz hollered.

Bytchakov kicked the windscreen clear and rolled from the cab, AK already shouldered. I had blood in my eyes as I followed Oz, scrabbling in the dirt. The sandy soil felt warm against my face, smelt good after the smell of burning aviation fuel. I looked at my right sleeve, slick with blood from shrapnel wounds. "Get up or die," the American growled.

I found my rifle and grunted an affirmative, checking the magazine. Scanning the horizon back towards the airbase I saw the BMP tearing towards us. An extended line of marines advanced behind it. Behind them limped one of the badly-damaged BDRM armoured cars, still coughing black smoke.

They were less than five hundred metres away. "Don't figure we'll get away with surrenderin' this time," Bytchakov said quietly.

Oz shrugged and went over to the truck's fuel tank. Puncturing it with his combat knife, he put an empty soda bottle from the cab under the stream of petrol, then another. Finally he ripped two strips of fabric from his shredded fatigue trousers and stuffed them into the bottles. "Poor man's antitank," he said, passing me one of the Molotov cocktails.

"I bet you pull grenade pins out with your teeth too," laughed Bytchakov.

"How do you walk with balls that big?" I added. We were drunk on fear now, giddy with the hopelessness of our situation. If Oz had done this in the SBS, he'd be up for a Victoria Cross. As a mercenary, he'd get a death sentence and an unmarked grave.

"I need all the covering fire you can give me," said Oz, "I'm gonna hide in those trees and flank them. When I get the chance I'll dump the petrol bombs on the rear deck of the BMP." He had more chance of winning the lottery than getting near the BMP, and we both knew it. Oz winked, nudging the LMG towards me with his boot. Then he darted into the acacia trees and was gone.

Bytchakov was burrowing into the soft earth, trying to fashion a crude shell-scrape in the pancake-flat earth. I grabbed another belt of ammo and joined him, resting the MG on its bipod.

The carcass of the truck shuddered, raked by cannon fire, the fuel tank smouldering and popping. A hundred metres away marines dashed across the open ground, through wafting mauve smoke. I swung the MG around and opened fire, forcing them into cover. The American emptied his AK, desperate to win the fire-fight and buy Oz time. Again I saw the familiar mauve, roiling cloud as they hurled smoke grenades. Through the swirling mist I saw the BMP's distinctive low profile and slanted hull, the pan-shaped turret turning towards us. In the trees Oz loped forwards, trailing smoke from the petrol bombs.

"Cover him," I barked, switching targets.

CHAPTER EIGHTEEN

Bullets churned the earth to my front, bullets hurting by my ears. Then a noise like high-pitched thunder cracked over my head, and the front of BMP disappeared in an orange flash. Another object hit the turret in a geyser of white sparks, the armoured vehicle juddering to a halt. The front of BMP had been torn asunder, a body flopping from the shattered turret. "What the fuck?" I coughed.

"I'd say it was an AT missile," said Bytchakov, "look to my nine O' clock…"

I glanced over. To our flank, three vehicles tore across the scorched ochre plain, straight towards the Chinese. They were pick-ups, two with Dushkas and recoilless rifles mounted on the back, the third equipped with an antitank rocket post. The men crammed into the backs of the vehicles looked like something out of a Mad Max movie – dressed in crash helmets, berets, sunglasses, scraps of ragged uniform and leather jackets. They whooped as they fired rifles and machineguns. I didn't know who they were, but I loved them anyway.

The remaining platoon of Chinese marines, outnumbered, began falling back towards the crippled BMP. The BDRM armoured car lurched to a halt on shredded tyres, turret swivelling and cannon chattering. Tracer fire streaked towards the technicals, heavy shells punching into the bonnet and cab of the first vehicle. It lost control and span like a top, soldiers and weapons tumbling from the groaning wreck. The other two vehicles swerved crazily as they sped by, men plugging rockets into their RPGs as they went.

The American's voice, usually a high-pitched croak, went down an octave, "I guess they're on our side." He jumped to his feet and loped forward, snapping off rounds as he went. Wildly aimed RPG rockets tumbled past the BDRM like demonic fireworks, exploding harmlessly behind it. The rebels started arguing over the RPGs as the antitank crew tried to mount a rocket onto the weapon's launcher at fifty mph. The Chinese troops took advantage of the confusion, falling back and opening fire on the technicals. More mud-caked pick-ups motored past, packed with jeering troops. Black and gold battle flags, gaudily decorated with a stylised leopard, billowed from the vehicles.

A weapon-studded Toyota, painted in crude camouflage, slowed down. The driver, a slim Zambutan wearing desert fatigues and a bandana, peered at us over his sunglasses. "Are you Captain Winter?" he said in a broad London accent, revealing a mouthful of gold teeth. The rebels sat in the back looked at us curiously as Chinese tracer fire popped around the burning truck.

"He's Winter," said Bytchakov, jerking a thumb at me.

The Zambutan-Londoner looked me up-and-down with a shrug. "Stay here. General Abasi sends his regards." He grunted something in Swahili and the technical sped off. Another of the militia vehicles was swallowed by smoke and flame, rebels fleeing as they traded fire with the more disciplined Chinese marines. Zhang Ki's men calmly withdrew, back towards the airfield while the battered BDRM slowly reversed. A rebel buckled as a cannon shell from the armoured car hit him in the belly, disembowelling him with a wet ripping noise.

"If they had as much skill as bravery..." said Bytchakov, peering over the top of his iron sights. A camouflaged technical ground to a halt as another vehicle was shredded by cannon fire. The Zambutan with the London accent started waving furiously, shouting orders. As the Chinese continued to retreat, the rebels fired rifles in the air and sang. Others started dragging the wounded to a harassed-looking rebel medic, wearing a boiler suit and a red-cross armband. A lone rebel fired an RPG at the retreating enemy, the rocket fizzing across the orange desert and exploding harmlessly.

Oz trudged out of the trees, an unlit Molotov cocktail in each hand. "That's the nearest I've been to certain death for *weeks*," he said, a wry grin spreading across his face.

I looked at my hand. It was shaking. I held it and pressed it to my chest, heart pounding.

"You OK?" said Bytchakov, gripping my shoulder.

"I'm fine," I lied. "Listen to those crazy bastards."

It was singing, the rebels of the Free Zambutan Army triumphant. Their dusty vehicles now flew yet more leopard standards, flapping like the sails of galleons in the hot desert wind. We watched their flying column approach, a circus of machine-gun carrying technicals, Russian armoured cars, motorbikes, jeeps, mortar-carrying pick-ups and trucks equipped with an exotic assortment of AA guns and rockets. There was even an ambulance in Red Cross livery, although the men with RPGs sitting on top suggested only a passing knowledge of the Geneva Conventions.

A Land Rover, painted in green-and-umber camouflage, pulled up and General Kanoro Abasi, 'The Leopard of

Zambute,' stepped out. The rebels all stiffened visibly as he appeared, flanked by scary-looking bodyguards. "Captain Winter," he beamed. "Welcome to Zambute." Kanoro Abasi was a neat, wiry man in his late forties, eyes hidden behind over-sized sunglasses. His hair was cropped close, as was his salt-and-pepper goatee. He wore neatly-pressed desert fatigues with the NATO rank patches of a three-star general, a holstered pistol at his belt and a silk scarf at his throat. I knew he'd been a senior officer in Zambute's paramilitary police before deciding to oust President Aziz.

I nodded respectfully as he mentioned my old army rank. I threw up a smartly theatrical salute for good measure. "I'm grateful, General. This is Master Sarn't Bytchakov and Colour Sarn't Osborne."

General Abasi nodded approvingly at the formalities. "Colonel Murray radioed for us to return and look for you."

"Is the colonel back in Kenya?" I said, scraping oily sand from the cut on my cheek.

"No, we only received a brief radio message. He said his helicopter was damaged, I have sent men to search for him." Abasi removed his shades and scanned the skies, shielding his eyes from the sun. "We must go, before the Chinese return with their helicopters." His eyes were heavy-lidded, almost golden-brown in colour.

"We shot the fuck out of their helis," Oz grinned.

"Excellent," the General smiled He said something in Swahili and the men cheered. "You will be feted as the heroes you most surely are. We will see if we can find your comrades. I have more soldiers nearby, in a town called Hagadifi. They will help."

We were ushered into the rear of the General's vehicle, which was air-conditioned. A rebel passed us bottles of chilled mineral water from a cooler. It tasted like Champagne as I swilled the taste of burnt aviation fuel from my mouth. I looked at Alex, who raised an eyebrow and chuckled, his much-scarred face smeared with blood and soot. Ten minutes ago I was preparing for death. Now I was enjoying air con and Evian. I checked my satellite phone. The little green light on top of the handset winked, the screen showing a reply from Marcus. I filtered the message through the decryption software:

MESSAGE RECEIVED / AUTHORIZATION TO EXTRACT EW EQUIPMENT WAS DENIED ONE (01) MONTH AGO / CORACLE WRAPPED / TEAM MISSING / EXFIL MURRAY FROM Z ASAP / MAKE VOICE CALL 12:00 ZULU.

It was now 08:45: twelve hours since we'd arrived in-country. And Marcus had confirmed whatever skulduggery the CORACLE team had planned at the prison was off-policy. The involvement of Chinese forces was a diplomatic disaster, whichever way you looked at it, making Murray an even bigger embarrassment to the UK. I sent a return message:

ESCAPED CHINESE CUSTODY / NOW WITH FZA GEN ABASI / SEARCH FOR MM CONTINUES

The satellite radio Brodie had given me was still in my assault pack. I keyed the handset and tried to raise any of the SIS call-signs, but heard only static. I found myself drifting asleep, despite the injuries I'd sustained. The rear seats of the Land Rover felt like a feather bed, and after swallowing a handful of painkillers I dozed.

I was woken by General Abasi bellowing into his walkie-talkie, followed by the whoosh of rockets. Oz and Alex crouched outside the open passenger doors of the Land Rover. We were parked in a row of trees next to the road, skeins of orange sand swirling about our feet. "It's OK Cal," said Oz, looking at the stains seeping through the dressings on my leg, "try and sleep, mate. It's just a crap air-raid."

Bytchakov's shoulders went up and down as he chuckled. "Jeez, you can buy better air-raids than this at Wal-Mart."

I rubbed my eyes, "is everything OK?"

"Yes," Abasi replied from behind a pair of binoculars. "The air force is desperate. We've already destroyed their ground attack squadron at Quaani, now they send children flying old crates."

Above us, two slow-moving aircraft jinked and dodged glittering streams of tracer. I could see ordnance pods under their wings, but to me they looked like bombed-up training aircraft rather than proper warplanes. The rebels were whooping as their truck-mounted, multi-barrelled cannons spat fire, forcing the little turbo-prop aircraft higher. Other men prepared shoulder-launched AA missiles. "Why are they bothering?" I said, accepting the binoculars the driver offered me.

"Aziz," shrugged Abasi. "He is not a military commander. He always presses an attack, whatever the cost. He is probably on the radio to the pilots himself, threatening them with death if they are not victorious." I watched as two coils of tracer tracked towards the lower of the two aircraft, which trailed dark smoke and fell from the sky like a dead bird. There was more cheering as it exploded. The second plane dropped two bombs, which fell harmlessly out of view, then turned lazily towards Marsajir, to the Northwest.

Air-raid over, our convoy crawled west, along the pot-holed Marsajir highway. The road was pocked with craters and littered with abandoned vehicles and corpses. Going was slow, the scouts at the front of the convoy stopping to check for mines and cluster bomb munitions on the road. The sun shone high, the horizon shimmering like jelly. We passed a clutch of burnt-out APCs smouldering by the side of the road, the corpses of Presidential Commandos splayed obscenely next to them. A troop of vultures tore at the bodies, their faces dyed red with gore. Trees burned and smouldered where they'd been struck with phosphorous grenades. "This was our ambush," said General Abasi proudly.

Alex shook his head, "those must be the healthiest vultures I ever saw."

"Wait until we take Marsajir," Abasi smiled. "The vultures will get even fatter." We arrived in Hagadifi two hours later, a shanty town of rickety shacks bunched around a dusty marketplace. Perched on a low plateau, it overlooked a sludge-coloured river. Townsfolk looked on as we drove through, some waving, others running indoors. The General slapped his hand on the dashboard, the vehicle halting by a grubby general store. The rebels of the FZA dismounted their vehicles and immediately started smoking, drinking from their water bottles and wandering around the fly-blown market. The stalls were selling cigarettes, animal carcasses, weapons and straggly-looking vegetables. General Abasi leaned on the bonnet of his command vehicle and lit a cigarette. He signalled for one of his men to come forward. "This is Captain Ismael," he said, pointing at the rebel we'd met earlier. "His English is excellent, he has lived in Britain. I will make him your liaison while you are our guests."

Ismael nodded. "I'm out of Leyton," he grinned. "So, basically, this is a holiday."

"Thanks," I laughed, offering my hand to Ismael. "I take it you do something different at home?"

Ismael laughed. "I'm a special needs teacher in Hackney. Seriously, this is a vacation. I was born here. My old man was into opposition politics, back in the 1980s. I decided it was time to come home, make him proud of me."

"I'm sure he will, Captain," I replied.

"Call me Tony. Now, wait here and I'll see if there's any news about Murray and the rest of your group." He said something in Swahili to a young rebel and strode away.

I mumbled my thanks and I took a cup of coffee from a young woman who'd appeared with a tray of drinks. The coffee was hot and sweet. I gulped it down and motioned for another, giving her a ten dollar bill from my escape fund. Eyes-wide, she hurried away with the cash. "Cal, shouldn't we just get the fuck out of here?" asked Oz.

"We need to find Murray and the others."

"They might have made it back," said Bytchakov, smacking his lips as he drained a third cup of coffee. Ten dollars bought you a lot of coffee in Zambute.

"I can't get the others on the sat radio," I replied. "We have to assume they're missing and still in Zambute, else the mission fails." We all stood and shared a grim silence. None of us wanted to fail, leave men in-country. Besides, failure on The Firm was never an option. And if I wanted to take advantage of what Isaac Samuels had told me, a few days and a lifetime ago, I had to succeed.

"I agree, Cal, we need to see it through," said Oz finally. He lowered his voice to a whisper, "but what happens when Abasi finds out that MI6 are bugging out of Zambute and his covert support dries up?"

"Well I ain't telling him," Bytchakov replied. "Are you?"

We trudged off wearily through the market, the locals eyeing us suspiciously. After five minutes we reached an abandoned building, a limp red and yellow Zambutan flag on the roof. The building looked Italianate, with crumbling balconies and peeling stucco. A sign in English declared it was The Hagadifi hotel. It had been plastered by artillery fire, windows broken, the ugly concrete façade pitted by shrapnel. We trooped past a burnt-out taxi, into the lobby. We dropped our kit and crashed out on dusty sofas. I pulled up my trouser leg and redressed my bite injuries, Alex producing a first aid kit and a tetanus booster. Tony Ismael appeared with a carrier bag of nuts, hard rolls and palm-fruit. We ate ravenously, washing the food down with mineral water. "We've got reports from the locals," said Ismael. "The locals saw a chopper heading north last night. It was flying very low, on the outskirts of town. They think it was damaged."

"What did it look like?" I asked, following him outside.

"Orange," Ismael smiled, "and painted like a tiger."

"That's the one," said Oz. "But why north? It's the wrong direction."

I asked Ismael if we could see a map. He nodded and spread one out on the sofa. Hagadifi was some sixty miles due west of Quaani, and over a hundred miles north of the Kenyan border. "Their maximum range for a fully-loaded Super-Puma would be nearly five hundred miles," said Bytchakov. He was an ex-heliborne assault specialist, so I trusted his judgement.

"I'd guess your route in would have been two hundred-fifty, to evade radar and come in by sea."

"Yeah," Oz added, "plus Idris was doing some tactical flying. That burns up fuel."

"Sure, the math ain't exact," Bytchakov nodded, "but by the time they flew evasively another sixty miles here... I'd say they would only have a range of another one-fifty, tops."

"Mel said the heli was damaged when he radioed the general," I replied, studying the map. Due north of Hagadifi was nothing but scorched desert, punctuated by low hills and dried-out river beds.

"Let's settle on a hundred," the American shrugged. "Idris' priority would be to land somewhere safe, where he could refuel."

Ismael traced a finger across the map. "In which case, he ain't got much choice. There's Tano Makaa, which is government-controlled. Then there's Buur Xuuq, which I would say was a better prospect if you were on the run."

"What's there?" I asked.

"A manganese mine," Ismael replied. "The Chinese run it. They use choppers up there to move engineers and equipment. There's a heli-pad, I've seen it myself."

There wasn't much else to go on. I'd had no SIGINT from Marcus and no radio contact. "I need to speak to the General," I said.

Ismael nodded, "he wants to help Colonel Murray. He's agreed for me to take twenty men to escort you, anywhere you need to go."

I looked at Oz and Alex. "We need to agree on this," I said. The operation had gone seriously off-track. I wanted the men to buy into my plan.

"We don't have a choice," said Oz.

"We need to move soon," said Ismael. "Aziz's 21st Brigade was to our northeast two days ago. They know we use Hagadifi to resupply, we can't hang around."

Four vehicles pulled up outside the hotel, weather-beaten pick-ups and a Russian jeep. The jeep was a vintage GAZ, festooned with tow ropes, jerry cans and loops of rotting camouflage netting. Mounted on the back was a 120mm WOMBAT recoilless rifle. Rifling through my pockets, I found my prismatic compass. Oz and Alex collected the weapons we'd found at the air base and resupplied with ammunition, grenades and water. I still had emergency rations in my pack, which I broke out between us. We were mounting up when an excitable kid wearing shorts and a camouflaged tee-shirt ran through the market, waving his Kalashnikov in the air. He shouted in Swahili, older men trying to calm him down.

"What's he saying?" I asked Ismael.

"That kid is a scout," he replied. "We send them out on motorbikes. He's saying that they've seen government soldiers to the northeast with tanks."

"Which direction are we going?" I said "to get to the mine?"

Ismael smiled. "Where d'you think? Northeast."

CHAPTER NINETEEN

Our convoy continued north under brilliant blue skies. The men in the front vehicle stopped to change a flat tyre, other rebels stopping to have a smoke and brew coffee. Ismael's truck was fitted with a short-wave radio, used to speak with the kids on motorbikes scouting ahead of us. In my pocket the satellite phone trilled. "Who is it?" said Oz.

"Hold on," I replied. I slid out of the GAZ jeep and walked into the shade of a gnarly palm tree.

"Having a good war?" said Marcus. "To say the brass at SIS are worried would be understatement of the year. The shredders are working overtime."

"This is a clusterfuck," I agreed.

"An overly-generous assessment," Marcus sighed. "I need the CORACLE team out of Zambute now. Where are they?" I explained about our plan to travel to the manganese mine, and our capture by the Chinese. Marcus listened carefully. I could hear the scratching of pen on paper in the background. "I've a couple of observations. First, the plan to capture Chinese electronic warfare equipment was never authorised."

"Who tried to push it through?"

"Duclair and Easter," he replied. "The source of the intelligence was never corroborated. Their department head wasn't prepared to run with the operation."

"So they piggy-backed it onto Murray's rescue attempt anyway?"

"It's a possibility."

"Maybe Easter wanted to try and recover some credibility by stealing the Chinese comms kit and decided to go off-policy?"

"And perhaps she cooked it up with her Chinese handlers?" he replied. "Don't make excuses for the woman, Cal." He was right. That's exactly what I was doing. The more I knew about Easter, the more I liked her. Going off policy like, if that's what she'd done, took balls as far as I was concerned. "Secondly," Marcus continued, "we've been listening in on the Chinese. They haven't a bloody clue why a PLA Special Forces unit is fighting in southern Zambute. They're as worried about it as we are."

"Zhang Ki said he'd been attacked by rebels. He said he was within his ROEs," I replied. "Is there any update on the location of our helicopter?"

"I'm waiting on it," he said. "Their GPS appears to be switched off. I'll keep checking, but I think it's fair to say my access to surveillance assets is diminishing. This job is toxic - arses are being well-and-truly covered."

"Jesus, Marcus, what's going on?"

"I was rather hoping you could help me with that. Crack on, I'll be in touch." He ended the call and I returned to our vehicle.

"Why the sneaking off?" said Oz.

"I've called in a favour," I said.

"What do you mean?" he said.

I sighed, narrowing my eyes against the sun. "I've got a contact in SIS," I said finally. I was too tired to lie, and Oz deserved to know.

"What the fuck? You know the rules."

"Screw the bloody rules," I growled. "And while we're at it, screw The Firm."

"OK, call in Fallen Eagle," Oz scowled, "because if you don't get me killed here, you'll get me killed back home."

I put a hand on Oz's shoulder, felt him flinch. "You're the bravest bastard I've ever met, but you need to stop trusting the bloody Firm. I'll call Fallen Eagle when there's genuinely no hope. At the moment, there still is." I felt a tremble in my body, hand twitching. I pulled it away from Oz in case he felt it.

Bytchakov looked at us both, weighing up the options. "What can this SIS guy do for us?"

"He's trying to track the Puma," I said, itching to tell the truth about my mission to unmask the rogue agent.

"OK," he shrugged. "That's somethin' calling in Fallen Eagle can't do. Anyhow, calling it in might not make any difference."

"What do you mean?" I asked.

"When I was in Trieste, one of the teams went to Kazakhstan on a search-and-destroy operation for the CIA. I was working logistics back then, waiting for an assignment."

"It sounds a different set-up from the UK," said Oz.

"Yeah, I guess it was. In Trieste there's a dude who runs three teams, like a coordinator. It ain't like here – out there you meet the guy occasionally. Anyhow, the guys in Kazakhstan were near the Chinese border. I don't know the operational details, but they called Fallen Eagle. I was with the coordinator when it came in."

I took a gulp of cold water. "What happened?"

"Gerhard, the coordinator, said he'd passed the message up the chain of command. The nearest assistance was from the

CIA in Uzbekistan, and they couldn't get there in time. Three full syndicates were lost, nine guys." Alex shook his head and grimaced. "So all I'm sayin' is that a Fallen Eagle ain't a guarantee. It's a roll of the dice."

Ismael strode over, tapping his watch. "We need to move."

"Fine," I replied, looking at the others.

"Is there a problem?" said the rebel Captain.

"No," said Oz sharply, "let's get on with it."

We continued our journey, crossing drought-parched plains. Now and then a rocky escarpment or scrubby copse of trees broke up the moonscape. Occasionally we passed the bleached bones of an animal, or a burnt-out truck. "Wow," said Bytchakov, "this place is a karmic vortex. It makes Helmand Province feel like Woodstock."

It almost was dusk when the signal to halt came. The highway split in front of us, a new metalled road heading north. A rectangular hoarding, in Swahili, Arabic and English, boasted:

Welcome to the Buur Xuuq Highway
A gift from the People's Republic of China

Ismael hopped out of his vehicle and stretched like a cat. "This road was built with slave labour, paid for with stolen aid dollars," he grumbled. "The mine is part-owned by the Chinese Government. We raid it now and then, so the army have a guard force on site. This bit of Zambute sits on top of the biggest Manganese deposit in East Africa." A kid on a motorcycle appeared. He got off and saluted Ismael, who patted the kid on the head and gave him a cigarette. They chatted for a few moments. "The boy thinks he saw your helicopter, the tiger-painted one. It crash-landed near the mine." The scout begged for another cigarette, received the rest of the packet and returned to his Yamaha.

"Who needs spy satellites when you've got a kid with a nicotine habit?" said Oz.

I turned to Ismael. "OK, how many government troops?"

"Maybe fifteen," he replied confidently. "No more than twenty. When we attack, follow my vehicle. If you get the chance, flank them. My men will go for the guard bunker and take the soldiers hostage. Sometimes they surrender or even join us."

"Sounds like a regular thing," I replied.

"We raid this place for diesel now and then. We either bribe the guards or attack, it depends if the Chinese are there."

"What did you say you did back in England?" I asked.

"I worked with problem kids."

"You should manage our team," Oz shrugged, slapping him on the shoulder.

The field radio squawked, a chattering voice leaking from it. "The scout reports ten or eleven soldiers at the mine," said Ismael. He barked orders in Swahili, the rebels busying themselves with mortars and rockets. The weapon-laden technicals started forming up near the road leading to Buur Xuuq. Behind him a team of rebels were setting up a towed 160mm mortar, neatly stacking bombs and equipment along the side of the road. "M-66, Israeli mortars," said Ismael. "Very good artillery, we can shoot nine thousand metres with this baby."

We re-mounted the jeep, following the technicals up into the hills along the shiny new road. A hundred metres from the top we dismounted. It was getting dark, the sky mauve and blue. Oz handed me his night-vision binoculars. Half a mile away I saw the Buur Xuuq mine, lit by harsh white light. A cluster of low prefabricated buildings nestled in a dip in the ground, overlooked by a whitewashed two-story building, covered with a wall of sandbags. To the east was the depot, a covered area marking the fuel point. A row of trucks were parked by more prefabs, boiler-suited men standing around smoking.

Beyond was the mine proper, a giant semi-circular monster-bite taken out of the hills. A skeletal tower stood over the mineshaft, pricks of flickering amber light marking the pit entrance. Next to it, a giant brick chimney poured smoke into the evening sky. "Check the gatehouse," said Bytchakov.

Focussing my binos on the main gates, I saw two army pick-ups parked by a sand-bagged bunker. A gaggle of soldiers chatted, others in pairs walking the fence-line. They looked as bored as you'd expect from men guarding a mine in a desert. On cue I saw a flash, a giant mortar bomb exploding near the gates. A pick-up was thrown on its side like a toy. "Go," Ismael ordered, weapon raised. The rebel technicals raced down the hill in an extended V-shape, weapons spitting tracer towards the mine buildings. Rebels whooped and yelled as another mortar bomb hit the blockhouse with expert precision, raining sandbags, limbs and chunks of concrete.

"Let's go," I said, starting the engine. Oz positioned himself behind the WOMBAT.

"I guess following up in the rear makes sense," Bytchakov dead-panned, "crazy motherfuckers." We raced towards the perimeter road, another mortar bomb exploding near the gatehouse. Machinegun fire raked the low-rise admin building, windows smashing and guards ducking for cover. Over my shoulder I saw Ismael firing a machinegun at the gatehouse, cutting down a stunned Zambutan commando making for a tripod-mounted Dushka. We cringed as Oz fired the recoilless rifle behind us, the blast bursting in my ears. The 120mm round roared overhead, smashing into the front of a grey-green armoured car manoeuvring outside the admin building.

The familiar glow of incoming tracer danced between the technicals, the high-pitched screech of metal-on-metal as they peppered a rebel vehicle. RPG rounds flashed towards the doomed armoured car. It lurched to a halt, fire-tinged smoke billowing from its hatches. I saw the glare of brake lights at rebels began to dismount. Behind us technicals blazed, bodies scattered around them. To our front, the muzzle flash of small arms fire sparkled from windows and hidden sangars near the main admin building. A rebel croaked and half-fell, shaking as bullets shredded his body.

Bytchakov returned fire with short bursts from his AK. Oz fired another WOMBAT round at it, hitting the rim of the flat roof. The top of the prefabricated building began to sag, then slowly collapse as heavy machineguns, rocket fire and mortar bombs pelted it. A kinetic gang-bang with only one possible ending, the rebels whooped and shouted gleefully at the destruction. The technical next to us was spattered with incoming tracer, the rebel driver's chest and neck torn open by machinegun fire. Oz re-loaded the recoilless rifle, grunting as he slammed a shell into the weapon. "Where's that MG?" he shouted.

I scanned the low-rise prefabs around the collapsed admin building. I saw movement and smoke from a sand-bagged position next to the rubble. I shouted a fire control order to the ex-SBS man. "LOOK LEFT – SANDBAGS BY GREY HUT - FIFTY YARDS - FIRE…"

"SEEN," Oz replied, firing the WOMBAT. The low building shook as the HE shell detonated, and the MG was silent.

"Forward," Ismael ordered calmly into his radio. Dismounted rebels swarmed towards the mine, firing from the hip. The remaining government troops were shown no mercy, gunned down as they staggered from the smoking wreckage of their bunkers. Their bodies were bayonetted and smashed with rifle butts. The rest of the rebels motored through the gate, towards the depot's fuel point. They started stripping bodies, friend and foe alike, of equipment and ammunition. I realised The Leopards were combat locusts, living from scavenging and stealing from the land as and when they could. "Captain Winter," called Ismael, "look over here." He stood by a sullen Zambutan army officer wearing dusty fatigues, face streaked with blood. "This guy has an interesting story."

"Has he seen the Puma?" I asked.

"This is more important," said Ismael darkly. "We'll find your helicopter later, Captain Winter."

"The Chinese were here dealing with a collapse in one of the lift shafts," said the Zambutan officer in good English. "There were miners trapped down there..."

"Miners, you bastard?" snapped Ismael, cuffing the officer around the head. "Don't you mean slave labour? Kids?"

"Kids?" I asked.

"Yeah, twelve and thirteen year olds," Ismael growled, spitting on the officer's boot. "They take them from Marsajir's slums and pay them fifty cents a fortnight."

"Carry on," I said to the wide-eyed officer, his forehead beaded with sweat.

"The Chinese… they worry about production targets," the officer continued in English. "The miners were doing double-shifts when the shaft collapsed…"

Ismael's fists were clenched. "They dynamited the lift shaft to clear it, and to hell with the children trapped down there. He says he released the rest of the kids from their huts rather than let them replace the others down the mine."

"Yes," the officer gushed, voice high with desperation. "I let the miners go! We gave them water and rations, you have my word."

"Motherfuckers," Alex growled.

The captured officer tried to look calm. Two rebels took him away at gunpoint. "Tony, do you believe him?" said Oz.

"I'll find out soon enough," Ismael shrugged. "We'll radio our contacts and see if any kids were rescued. Our men are checking the mine now. Now, as for your helicopter, the prisoner claims earlier today Chinese marines arrived in a helicopter. Their officer ordered a platoon of Zambutans to join them in their search for you. They headed towards Afuuma. That's a port east of here."

"That Chinese colonel really doesn't like you, does he?" said Oz.

"Cultivating enemies is my speciality," I shrugged. "What type of helicopters were the Chinese in?"

Ismael translated. The army officer replied quickly, eager to help.

"He says there was only one helicopter, a big grey one. Thirty men left in APCs towards Afuuma."

We waited by the smouldering admin building as the officer provided more information. Ismael translated that the Puma arrived after the Chinese had left, but no one had seen the crew. A rebel in his teens produced a small coffee machine. He built a fire so he could brew up. "Good drills," said Oz, pointing at the kid and producing a battered enamel cup from his kit.

"He's a natural," Bytchakov agreed. The big American also produced a mug.

"This is Zambutan coffee," said the kid in good English, "the best. Do you have any cigarettes?"

"How old are you?" admonished Bytchakov.

"Old enough for this," laughed the kid, pulling up his shirt to reveal a six-inch scar along his belly, "shrapnel from RPG."

"Here you go," I said, handing the kid a Montecristo. He smelt it and lit it, "for fuck's sake don't inhale." Of course, he did. We all laughed as he coughed his guts up. He got the hang of it eventually, posing like a clown with the *Cubano* to his mates.

Ismael appeared shortly afterwards. At gunpoint were three dishevelled Chinese engineers wearing boiler-suits. "It's true," he spat, pushing them to the ground. The Chinese started babbling, but none of us spoke Mandarin. Ismael levelled his AK at the first engineer and emptied the magazine into him. The body spun like a top, bloody holes blossoming in his chest and guts. "They did it. They dynamited the mine-shaft. It's full of dead *kids* down there." He spat a gobbet of phlegm at the bullet-shredded corpse. The two remaining mine workers started begging for their lives. Ismael calmly slid a fresh magazine into his still-smoking rifle and snapped back the cocking lever. His eyes flashed with hate. I'd seen that look before, the one that says a man hasn't had his fill of killing.

Sometimes I see it in the mirror. "Wait," I said. "I need to ask questions."

"Better make it quick," said Tony Ismael quietly. Right now, I couldn't imagine the man was a teacher, looking after kids with learning difficulties.

"Do you speak English?" I said to the two Chinese.

"Yes, my English is good," chattered one of them. "Don't let them kill me. We didn't give the order to set the explosives, it was the Zambutans."

"Who did?" I grunted. "Tell me quickly and you might live." It was a lie, of course. He'd rolled the dice and got snake eyes.

"The Zambutan trade ministry," he stammered. "We told them over the satellite radio we had problems. We asked for more men and equipment, to excavate the collapse. They said just dynamite it, that's what they would do. We'd never do that. We'd use earth movers and specialist equipment, but the Zambutan foremen used dynamite. It was crazy."

I shook my head and looked at Ismael. Around me prowled more rebels, loathing etched on their faces, "so you let them do it anyway?"

"We had no choice, we have targets to meet," said the engineer simply. He looked at his feet.

"Hold on," I said, "Tony, do you have a video camera?" The Londoner barked an order in Swahili and a few moments later a rebel arrived with a Sony Handycam. I took it and switched it on. "Tell your story, in English," I said to the engineer. It took five minutes for the Chinese mining official to repeat his account, blaming the Zambutan Government for ordering the dynamiting of the collapsed tunnel at the Buur Xuuq manganese mine, killing dozens of young labourers. "Get footage at the mine, show exactly what happened. We'll get that uploaded onto *YouTube* when we get the chance," I said, pocketing the camera.

"Why?" said Bytchakov.

"If I was at Staff College, I'd say we were *dominating the information battle-space*," I shrugged. "Anything that puts the spotlight on Aziz, and not us, helps SIS. Maybe the African Union and UN will intervene."

"They drop poison gas on Syrians and nobody gives a shit," the American shrugged. "The Kremlin's lapdogs shoot down airliners and nobody gives a shit."

"The Syrians don't sit on East Africa's largest Manganese deposit," I replied.

"Figures," he replied.

I ran a hand through my cropped head, felt dried blood and grit. "Besides, it's just the right bloody thing to do," I said, nodding at the faraway mine.

"I make you right," said Oz.

"Fucking A," said Bytchakov.

As we got into our vehicles, the Leopards went about executing the remaining mine engineers. I couldn't put my hand on my heart and say they didn't deserve it. The dead mine staff were hung on the barbed wire fence, like crows nailed to a barn door. I shrugged. I'd seen, and done, worse. I ground out a cigar stub under my boot, "that's just Karma as far as I'm concerned. Speaking of which, let's go and find our old friend Colonel Zhang Ki." The rebels buried their dead. Behind us, the Buur Xuuq mine burnt. Stinking black smoke spiralled skywards as the rebels sang dirges for the dead. "Let's go," I said, hefting my rifle. "We need to find the Puma."

We formed up and patrolled deeper into the mining camp, trying to ignore the cries of prisoners being crucified. Oz nodded towards the torture. "You should put that up on *YouTube* too."

CHAPTER TWENTY

The trembling officer, before he was executed, told us the Chinese landed beyond the giant chimney stack. As we approached I saw it was encircled by rusting warehouses. "There," said Oz.

The tiger-striped heli lay riddled with bullet-holes. The canopy was shattered, engine fluid staining the sand. The churned trail of earth behind the airframe suggested an emergency landing. There was no one inside, although the cockpit was spattered with congealed blood. The radio was smashed, door-mounted machineguns hanging limply. "So the bird gets damaged, makes it this far and crashes. Zhang Ki takes the rest of the team prisoner and here we are," said Alex Bytchakov, shaking his heavily-scarred head.

"Possibly," I replied. "Let's take a look around."

The route to the nearest warehouse was marked by a blood trail. Boot prints led to an abandoned bottle of mineral water and scraps of first aid stuff. Switching on my Maglite, I scanned the gloomy interior. Long-abandoned, it contained little but old mining equipment surrounded by piles of discarded of wood and plastic. Then I saw it, the shape of a booted foot emerging from a pile of junk. We dug the bodies out with our hands. Idris, our pilot, had been executed with a single pistol shot to the back of his neck. So had Steve Bacon, the engineer lying face down in a fly-blown puddle of blood. "The Chinese?" said Alex.

"Maybe," I replied. "What better place to commit murder than the middle of a warzone?"

Oz examined some spent brass. "These are 9mm cases, Winchester Silvertips. They came from one of *our* pistols, Cal."

I checked the bodies. Both had facial injuries consistent with the crash, but hadn't been beaten or tortured. Their deaths had been straightforward executions, clinical and precise. I wondered if the rest of the CORACLE team were buried nearby, brains blown out by the traitor. "We need to bury these guys," said Bytchakov. "I'll go get shovels."

Oz watched the American leave. "What's going on?" he said finally.

"SIS think there's a traitor in the CORACLE team," I replied. I knelt and took a wedding ring from Steve's finger. Maybe he had someone back in the UK to give it to.

Oz grimaced. "How long have you known?" I gave him a look and shrugged. "So we flew into this knowing the shit would hit the fan?" he snapped.

"I didn't have a choice. None of us did. If I told you then I'd be dead." Oz spat on the ground. "I'm sorry," I shrugged. "It's not like The Firm is big on risk assessments, is it?"

"I'm sure you had your reasons," he snapped.

"Yeah, to get us out of this shit alive."

"Or is it your crazy vendetta against The Firm?"

"Leave it," I glowered. That was too near the truth for comfort. Bytchakov returned with shovels. We buried Idris and Steve on the perimeter of the mine, their graves unmarked. We returned to our jeep, the rebels waiting impatiently in their technicals. As ever, they were drinking coffee and smoking like it was going out of fashion.

"So, your friends ain't here," said Ismael. "Where do you want to go next?"

I walked over to his vehicle and took the offered coffee, gulping it gratefully. "The prisoner said the Chinese headed to Afuuma. Where's that?"

Ismael unfolded his map, pointing at a coastal town a hundred miles east. "Afuuma is a port," he replied. "It's in the disputed zone between Somalia and Zambute. It's protected by government troops and the security police. The Chinese warships sometimes use the docks there."

"Is there a garrison?" I asked.

"Yeah, there's an armoured unit based there. It's why we don't raid that far, but we'll need to take Afuuma soon, to cut off supplies headed for Marsajir. That was Colonel Murray's view as well."

"A strategic objective," I said. Marsajir, the capital, was the only big city in Zambute. It relied on Afuuma as a logistic artery. And now the Lion's share of the Zambutan airforce was burning on the runway at Quaani, air supply would be increasingly perilous.

Ismael nodded. "Sure, Marsajir is our next big offensive."

"Do you have sympathisers there?" said Alex.

Ismael smiled. "Of course, but the 21st Brigade has its HQ northwest of town. It's Aziz's best-equipped outfit, apart from the Presidential Commando. My men are brave, Cal, but they ain't crazy."

"General Abasi said he wants to help get Murray back," I replied. "He needs to commit forces to Afuuma now."

"We don't know if Murray's there, or any of the others," said Oz. He pulled me to one side. "If you've got an inside man at Vauxhall Cross, you might as well use him. Don't let these poor bastards start a battle they can't win. Not on our behalf."

I nodded. Oz was right. I pulled out the satellite phone and checked the power indicator, which blinked orange. I guessed I had less than thirty minutes battery life left. Marcus replied immediately. I explained that we'd found the crashed Puma and two bodies. "The rest of your team, along with Murray and Dancer, have vanished. We think they might have been taken by the Chinese to a place called Afuuma."

"Do you still have the device I sent you?" said Marcus, "the decryption for the CORACLE radio nets?"

The device was still with my radio at the bottom of my pack. "Yes, I've still got it."

"Check it," he sighed impatiently. "When you switched it on it would have recorded their comms whether you were listening in or not. It's a failsafe the boffins programmed into the receiver."

"It didn't come with bloody instructions, did it?" I snapped. "What if their radios were damaged or dumped?"

Marcus sighed, "you won't know until you check, What happened in the minutes after that Puma took off from the prison might be crucial."

"I'll listen," I grunted. "It doesn't help me deal with the fucking tank battalion between here and their likeliest location."

"I'm working on it. The Foreign Office is in free-fall. You're The Firm, remember? You don't have rules like we do. Get on with it."

"Get back to me when you've got something," I replied, ending the call. The priority, as usual, was defending reputations and covering arses in Whitehall. I felt a wave of anger wash from the pit of my stomach to my forehead. But anger solves nothing. So, like the Americans like to say, I *embraced the suck* and headed back to the vehicles. I asked Oz to plot a route to Afuuma and rummaged in my pack. I found my radio handset, the decryption device still plugged in. Putting in my earpiece, I found a playback function and rewound the recording of last night's radio traffic after the Chinese arrived. There wasn't much to listen to, the sound quality was poor. All I could hear was the sound of helicopters and mortar fire in the background.

"*Go*," said a female voice, either Duclair or Easter.

"*What the fuck are you doing?*" shouted Dancer.

"*I'm hit*," screamed a high-pitched voice. "*Fuck, I'm hit!*"

Duclair's voice was clearer now, "*shut up, it's a fucking scratch.*"

I heard Idris' voice, scratchy and faint, in the background. He was reporting damage to the airframe in a low, calm voice.

"*New route,*" said Dancer. "*Grid reference… no Mel, we can't go back… put that bloody hand-set down.*"

That must have been Murray's call to Abasi. Then I heard the hammer-blow racket machinegun rounds hitting the heli, the groaning of steel and whine of engines. "*What are…?*" said Easter.

"*Juliet, no,*" Duclair replied, "*Idris, move to the grid we…*"

The recording ended.

All I took from it was that someone had been wounded, Dancer ordering Idris to re-route the heli. I didn't know why – was it part of an impromptu escape and evasion plan? Murray had been on the radio to Abasi, but Dancer stopped him. Again, it was open to interpretation. Was Murray going to squeal on SIS, tell Abasi that CORACLE was finished?

"Have you made a decision?" said Tony Ismael, hands on hips. A cigarette smouldered at the corner of his mouth, flak jacket gaping open to reveal a much-scarred torso.

"Yes," I said, pointing at the map. "This feature, halfway between Afuuma and our current location, is the MSR from Afuuma to the rest of the occupied zone. It looks like a bridge and easy to defend. I want to wait there and go firm, pending further intelligence from London."

"Yes, that's the Afuuma River road bridge. We could be there in four, maybe five hours. And what's an MSR?"

"Brit army terminology for *Main Supply Route*," Bytchakov explained, pronouncing route '*rout*' like Yanks do. "It'll FUBAR the enemy logistic train if we cut it off, which will help the General."

I nodded my agreement. "Have you spoken to the General?"

Ismael offered me a cigarette. "He's sending men with heavy weapons. They should be with us by morning."

"That's good," I replied.

"I suppose this helps," Ismael continued. "The plan is to harass Afuuma and draw in the 21st Brigade. A new offensive is happening, very soon. I think you're right: drawing them into a trap would be a result for us."

I nodded. "Is there anywhere else to cross the river?"

He studied the map. "Yeah, several fords, but heavier vehicles have to use the bridge. If we hold there, the enemy tanks will have to make a long detour."

"The way I see it," said Bytchakov, "this is a win for all of us. An attack on that bridge will stir up a world of shit. It'll make enough of a distraction for us to mosey over to Afuuma for a look-see."

"He's right," Oz nodded. "Cal, we need to move our arses. Murray and the others could be on a slow boat to bloody China by now."

"No problem," the rebel captain replied. "We'll move out and set camp five miles from the bridge for tonight. There's an old herder's track we can use. It's a longer route, but safer." We mounted our vehicles and followed the rebel pick-ups. It was midnight when we pitched camp, sleeping under blankets donated by the rebels. The bedding smelt of oil and goats, but did the job. The rebels ate porridge, fruit, bushmeat and crackers from ageing American MRE ration packs. Entombed in dark brown plastic, it was Cold War vintage scoff. "Shit, when I left the army I swore I'd never eat one of these again," said the American, pulling a face as he chewed on stale crackers. "They taste like dried shit, just not as good for you."

Oz pulled his trusty bottle of Tabasco out of his pocket. It had survived every fire-fight and explosion intact. "Have some of this," he laughed.

"Hey, shit-and-Tabasco," Bytchakov grinned. "Why didn't I think of that?" I ate some porridge and swilled it down with coffee. The rebels sat with us, chain-smoking and drinking horrible local hooch. They wanted to talk about Premiership football in broken English. Oz tried to persuade them to support Ipswich. An urgent order was suddenly barked in Swahili and the men scrambled for their weapons. I picked up my AK and crawled forwards, peering into the darkness.

"It's OK," said one of the rebels in English. They relaxed as a ramshackle convoy appeared, headlights masked with tape so only small rectangles of light were visible. There were a dozen pick-ups, an old ambulance and a rusty armoured car with a boat-shaped hull. The vehicles were covered in camouflage netting and foliage, bristling with Dushkas and recoilless rifles.

"Hello wankers!" cackled a familiar voice. Duncan Bannerman leapt from a pick-up, MG4 still slung across chest. His baggy smock and fighting gear were filthy and torn, face sunburnt. A sullen Ruben Grey waved from the back of the vehicle, arm bandaged from shoulder to wrist.

"You're fucking indestructible," Oz laughed.

"This is true," the ex-Para beamed, "the Gods of Airborne Warfare yet again smile on the Bannerman."

"Airborne, fuck yeah." Bytchakov agreed.

"See? We're brothers really, you ugly Yank cock-sucker."

A grin spread across the American's scarred, meaty face. "I'll take that as a compliment, comin' from a skirt-wearing Scotch goat-fucker."

"Get a room. This is getting like *Brokeback Mountain* with assault weapons." I laughed, shaking Bannerman's hand. "Good to see you both. What happened?"

"A fucking war, that's what happened."

The five of us gathered around the back of the pick-up, smoking and sharing a tin mug of coffee. Bannerman told us that after the Puma took off, Ruben had been hit by shrapnel, gashing his arm. "We just looked at the GPS and started hoofing it south," he shrugged. "We saw half the Chinese army coming over the hill and thought *fuck that*."

"By daybreak I was proper shagged," said Ruben, his usually coffee-coloured complexion ashen. "I reckon I'd lost a pint of blood. We were picked up by a rebel patrol this morning."

"These rebels are top boys," said Bannerman approvingly. "They got a radio message to come up here and reinforce

'The Europeans.' I reckoned it would be you lot and asked if we could come along."

"When are we getting the fuck out of here?" said Ruben. "We've lost Murray, right?"

Oz gave me a look. "Are you going to tell them?" The tone of his voice suggested that if I didn't, he would. I explained that we'd been compromised, but kept it simple.

"Fucking spies," said Bannerman darkly, as if they were a species of poisonous snake. I suppose it wasn't far off the mark.

"They got Raph killed," glowered Ruben. "The Firm can go and fuck itself. I'm not going anywhere until the bastard who gave us up is dead."

"And I'm not going anywhere until I've got my hundred grand," added Bannerman. It's always good work with a man who knows his priorities.

"We're gonna make all those things right," I promised. "And, yeah, The Firm can go fuck itself." Those words tasted sweet in my mouth.

Ruben Grey looked at me with dark, wet eyes. "Do you promise, Cal, we'll get the bastards who did for Raph?"

I gripped his forearm and squeezed. "It's a promise, Ruben."

"I appreciate it, mate." His eyes welled with tears.

I pulled him to me, hugged him tight. The way I would like to have hugged a son. "Ruben, *there's only us*, right? And we look after our own," I whispered in his ear. "Keep it tight and remember: Raph would want you to see this through."

"Yeah, I make you right," he sniffed, wiping his face with the sleeve of his tattered combat fatigues.

"There's no shame in tears for a brother," said Bytchakov.

Then we parked our vehicles together, ate and set up a harbour area. Finally, we got some sleep. I dozed fitfully for a few hours. "STAND-TO," Bannerman hollered, "STAND FOOKIN' TO!" I crawled from underneath my blanket, shivering, and flipped the safety on my AK. It was just before oh-five-hundred. Oz had crept behind the engine block of the jeep and was scanning arcs, AK in his shoulder. Rebel guns spewed fire into the darkness, rockets and grenades lighting up the night like a freakish fireworks display. A parachute flare flooded the desert floor in strange lemony-coloured light. A body lay sprawled fifty yards away. "CEASE-FIRE," Bannerman ordered. Surprisingly, the rebel guns fell silent.

We all knew that the Chinese marines and their Presidential Commando allies were out there somewhere, and the sentries were jumpy. The team patrolled towards the body, weapons ready. A gaggle of rebels followed on. The corpse was that of a skinny guy wearing a grey-brown woollen cloak and armed with a vintage bolt-action rifle. You didn't have to be that ginger bloke from CSI to work out the cause of death was fifteen-odd high-velocity bullet wounds to the torso and head. It wasn't pretty. "Vultures," nodded Ismael, patting down the body.

"We've been up against these bastards before, on the border," I said.

"From the camps?" said Ismael, shaking his head. "They take the name, but they aren't the real thing. These are Xaboyo tribesmen, mercenaries. They hire themselves out to the government as trackers and scouts. Or sometimes they join the *Jihadis*."

"Well this one ain't much of an expert scout," Bannerman grunted. "He's deader than disco."

Ismael sighed and slung his Kalashnikov. "You don't get it. Some of our men are shit-scared of them. They believe the Xaboyo practice witchcraft – it's said that to kill one means you might get cursed."

"You really are a long way from London, Captain," I said.

"Fuckin' tell me about it," he laughed, "and I told you to call me Tony."

"Then I figure I killed the Vulture," said Bytchakov, "Tony, tell your men it was me. I ain't afraid of no curse."

Tony Ismael translated. His men cheered and slapped Alex on the back. "They're very pleased you took the curse for the team," said Tony, grinning. "You mug."

"So the Xaboyo are linked to the Jihadis," I said. "Is that true?"

Ismael sighed. "Sometimes, but we can't fight everybody. The Xaboyo keep to the border and the disputed zone. At the moment, if we see them we ignore them, and vice versa. *Shadow of Swords* is different, if we see those fuckers we attack." I knew General Abasi, like President Aziz, were Christians. Despite being a hard-line socialist, Aziz had been savvy enough to allow religious freedoms. And Zambute's minority Muslim population were Sufis, not usually given to radicalism. "Aziz is a bastard," Ismael continued, "but he's a bastard who slaps down Jihadis. That means the Americans tolerate him for now."

We returned to camp and slept, a golden slice of sunlight splitting the horizon as we stirred from our pits. We brewed rich Zambutan coffee and cracked open more US MREs. I ate peanut butter smeared on crackers, the nutty sludge washed down with sugary coffee. Oz shovelled cold macaroni with lemon powder and Tabasco into his mouth, "this," he said, "is the breakfast of champions."

"It tastes like shit," moaned Bytchakov. "I'd pay ten thousand bucks for a Big Mac right now."

"What about all this 'I'm Airborne' bollocks? I thought you lot were tough."

"Man, we all got our Achilles Heel," the American shrugged. "Mine is food."

Ismael appeared, satellite phone clamped to the side of his head. "Let's go," he shouted at us, "no time for breakfast."

"What is it?" said Oz.

"We have people in Afuuma, spies," he said. "The 21st Brigade is on the move. We've got to cut off the bridge."

"How long do you need to hold it?" I asked.

"No more than a day," Ismael grinned. "But I've heard that one before."

I looked at the motley collection of vehicles behind us and the crew of lightly-armed teenaged rebels. There were no more than sixty men. "Can you do it?"

Tony Ismael shrugged. "I'm only a special needs teacher from East London, but you guys are Special Forces. I need your help, if you'll give it."

"He ain't Special Forces," Oz grinned, pointing at me. The others laughed. That I'd never served with the balaclava-and-beards brigade was a joke that never got old.

"Compared to us he is," Ismael replied, locking eyes with me. The rebel captain suddenly looked like a lost kid. We needed to get to Afuuma. Yet again, a rebel attack would be the perfect distraction. I wanted to help. I knew we could make a difference. Ismael saw the look on my face. "When Abasi sends reinforcements he'll bring antitank weapons. We only need to delay them – we've got mines, MGs, mortars and RPGs."

"They're good lads," nodded Bannerman. "We should try to make something good out of this cake-and-arse-party."

"I'm with the Scotchman," Bytchakov declared.

"It's *Scots*, you ignorant prick," Bannerman sighed.

"Yeah, whatever dude."

Oz nodded his agreement and looked at Ruben. Ruben nodded grimly, "if fighting gets us out of here quicker, then I'm in."

"We vote," I said. Democracy is unusual on operations, not to mention dangerous. But I'd decided to change the rules, and in more ways than one.

"No call to our handler?" asked Oz.

"No way," I replied.

We voted. It was five-nil in favour of going to war. It wasn't a decision The Firm would have approved, which is why making it felt so good.

CHAPTER TWENTY ONE

The Afuuma road bridge spanned a treacly brown river. On the far side lay a rusting tank carcass, just shy of wooded high ground. The trees were skinny desert acacias, grey and with papery leaves, but would provide ample cover for a defending force. Our side of the river was scrubland – an apron of baked mud interrupted by deep ruts and copses of spiky foliage. It was nine in the morning, and already hot as Hades. "That's an American pontoon bridge, a Mark II," said Bytchakov over my shoulder. "I guess it was built, say, twenty years ago?" American peace-keepers had once attempted humanitarian intervention in Zambute, sparking the war that lead to the ascension of Aziz.

An order to halt came over the radio from Ismael. "Wait for the scouts to check out the bridge," he said. A kid on a trials bike zipped across the metal-framed pontoon. He reached the rusting tank when the motorcycle erupted in a ball of orange fire. Tracer spat from the tree line on the opposite riverbank. I heard the hollow cough of mortar tubes firing in the distance, men scrambling for cover.

"That wasn't a very elegant ambush," I said, rolling into a ditch.

"Good camouflage and concealment though," said Oz grudgingly. "I can't see them." Rebels scrambled from their vehicles and took cover, well within killing distance of the mortars. Snatching a shovel from the side of the jeep, I started digging a shell-scrape, feeling the bowel-loosening fear of bombardment.

"That's nae a bad idea," Bannerman laughed, nearby mortar rounds sending up spumes of gravel and sand. The rebels returned fire, Dushkas raking the riverbank. A volley of RPG rounds followed, their impact marked by puffs of grey and black smoke. They unhitched the heavy mortar and began setting up, urged on by an elderly rebel wearing a Manchester United shirt and a Russian-issue steel helmet.

Tony Ismael scurried towards us, falling to his belly as bullets cracked overhead. "Shit, I thought we'd get here before the army," he grunted.

If we retreated we'd concede the bridge to enemy armour. If we tried to defend they'd bombard us with mortars. "We attack," I shouted over the sound of artillery fire.

"Huh?" said Ismael.

"I'll take my team across, further downriver," I said, pointing to a mud-choked ford a few hundred metres to our left, "we'll flank them and draw their fire. Get those mortars to put down smoke, then assault across once we're engaged."

Ismael nodded. "Okay, we can do that."

"We'll pop red smoke when we want you to cross the bridge," I said, "in the meantime plaster that side with mortars and Dushkas. Just keep their bloody heads down." The rebel's giant 160mm mortar coughed, the enemy side of the riverbank shuddering as high-explosive rounds detonated. Men in camouflaged uniforms panicked and broke cover, only to be mown down by rebel machineguns.

Readying weapons and equipment, Oz nosed our jeep along a muddy ridgeline for cover. We'd scrounged locally-made chest rigs for spare ammo, as well as AK74 rifles and Chinese-manufactured grenades. Following the curving riverbank, we had a better view of the wooded plateau where the enemy were dug in. I could make out hastily prepared fortifications covered with camouflage nets, heavy machineguns marked by tell-tale puffs of smoke as they returned fire at the rebels. If they had flank protection, I'd yet to spot it.

Oz stopped maybe three hundred metres from the bridge. The riverbed was little more than a muddy, boulder-strewn ford, Alex and Oz covering as the rest of us waded across. Sludge sucked at our boots as we slapped at clouds of biting insects, trying not to trip on debris from years of fighting: scraps of metal, rotting coils of barbed wire and submerged vehicle tyres. Ruben tripped and fell in the mire, gashing his face on a rock. "Shit, is this entire fucking country trying to kill me?" He fished his G36 from the murky water and checked the semi-transparent magazine, shaking his head. Blood streamed from his nose, attracting a squadron of mosquito-like flying monsters.

"Aye," said Bannerman, stopping behind him. "This place makes Basra look like San Tropez."

"You've never been to San Tropez," Ruben spat.

"I've seen it on the telly," he replied, looking for tripwires and mines, now and then stopping and probing debris with his bayonet. "It's OK," he said. On the other bank we took cover behind a clump of twisted reeds. Oz and Alex joined us, the mud-spattered American carrying an RPK machinegun and an RPG. In the distance the sound of gunfire was more ragged, the mortar fire infrequent. I didn't know the reason for the lull in battle, and hoped it wasn't due to our side running low on ordnance.

Oz scouted ahead into the trees, reappearing a few minutes later. "OK, three enemy up ahead, a hundred metres, setting up an MG to cover the ford. There's an APC under a camouflage net beyond those spiky bastards." He pointed to a dense copse of Baar trees.

"They're setting up a flank?" I said.

"That's what I reckon," nodded the ex-SBS man, "but we beat them to it."

"We advance to contact into the trees and along the riverbank," I said, "and assault the enemy - Ruben, on my signal pop smoke." We began crawling through the reeds towards the HMG position. I heard hushed voices ahead. To our front I spotted an APC, hidden under gauzy green netting. It was an eight-wheeler, a Russian-built BTR80. At the front of the boat-shaped hull was a small turret packing a 30mm cannon. There was another parked next to it, this one without a turret. Boiler-suited Zambutan crewmen stood warily nearby, one talking into a radio, the other smoking. A third guy, who looked like an NCO or an officer, sat on the edge of the tailgate looking at a map.

We lay in the reeds, sweating. Ruben rubbed his bloody nose, smearing blood and camouflage paint over his face "I've got six frag grenades."

"Just take the crew out," said Oz quietly, "Alex, can you drive one of those things?"

"Sure," Bytchakov replied. "It's got wheels, ain't it?"

I pointed at the APCs with the chop of my hand and nodded. We sprinted forward, fire-and-manoeuvring towards the APCs. My AK bit into my shoulder as I hosed down a Zambutan soldier. He fell backwards, bouncing bloodily against the side of his vehicle. "GRENADE," Oz hollered. It exploded between the two remaining Zambutan crewmen, shredding them with shrapnel and killing them instantly. Bytchakov fired bursts from his MG, bounding forward and hosing down the enemy with fire. He took cover by one of the APCs and gave a thumbs-up.

To our right flank I saw smoke and heard yelling as Bannerman and Ruben attacked the men setting up the machinegun. The two mercenaries broke cover, the momentum of their assault sweeping them into the clearing. "Let's go!" I shouted "take the APC – roll up the riverbank and assault from their flank!"

"Roger," said Ruben. "Do I pop smoke now?"

"When we get to that bend in the river," I replied, not wanting Ismael's men to cross too soon. The sound of heavy machineguns and 160mm mortars cranked up again. The inside of the APC was painted a pale grey-green colour and smelt of unwashed men, cigarettes and engine oil. The troop compartment was accessed via the roof, and I clambered past piles of equipment, rations and an ancient-looking radio. I finally squeezed into a tiny seat. I saw Oz's legs in front of me as he settled into the turret to operate the 30mm cannon. Ruben and Bannerman took position by the back of the vehicle, Alex Bytchakov in the driver's seat. Peering through a tiny weapon slit in the side of the hull I saw trees collapse as Bytchakov nudged the forty-five tonne monster through the trees, accelerating onto a track running along the river.

Ruben wriggled through the open roof panel and opened up with his G36 at a startled Zambutan soldier. I heard screaming as the grim-faced ex-marine emptied his magazine and fluidly loaded another. "Incoming!" shouted Bytchakov from the driver's seat, bullets screeching off armoured plate.

Oz fired the cannon, dust and smoke filling the back of the APC. From my vantage point I could see 30mm rounds shred timber and pieces of earth from a sangar, like a buzz saw through plywood. He switched his fire to the Presidential Commandos bugging out of their position, cannon shells raking the ground. "Ruben, gimme smoke," I shouted.

The little Londoner tugged two grenades from his chest rig and hurled them out of the APC. Red smoke gushed into the sky as the APC hit a dip in the earth, barrelling to the right and almost throwing me out of my seat. Machinegun fire splashed against the hull, forcing us back into the crew compartment. By now we were two hundred yards from the wrecked tank, at the foot of a gentle slope opposite the rebels. Cannon-fire hammered the APC, forcing us to stop. RPG rockets snaked towards us, the flash of the launchers popping in the trees. "Blockage!" shouted Oz as our cannon fell quiet.

"RPG," bawled Ruben. The explosion rang through the vehicle chassis, but didn't penetrate the armour. The next one might. We bailed out as rebel vehicles raced across the bridge, a fresh barrage of heavy mortar rounds churning up the enemy positions. Rockets flew in both directions, two of the rebel technicals crashing into the side of the two-lane pontoon bridge, engines ablaze.

"Go!" I shouted, the men splitting into two fire teams. I rolled into cover and opened fire with my AK. Oz and Bannerman sprinted ten yards and threw themselves into cover near the wrecked tank. They immediately poured fire onto the enemy positions in front of them. "Go" I repeated, pulling myself to my feet. Bullets whipped past us, Ruben thrown off his feet as he was hit. I grabbed him by the yoke of his webbing and dragged him with us, increasingly accurate fire sweeping down from the hillside. We went firm near the shattered T-55 tank, Bytchakov spraying the roadside in front of us with his RPK. I could see the body of the rebel motorcycle scout ten metres away, his torso ripped open by shrapnel. I patted down Ruben and found his field dressing. "Where are you hit?"

"It got my plate carrier," he groaned. "It's okay."

The bullet had hit the leading edge of the Kevlar, spinning off and grazing his already injured upper arm. "You're good," I said, pressing the field dressing on top of the bloody bandages.

"Easy for you to say," he grinned. Rebel vehicles sped past us, the 4x4s throwing up clouds of orange dust. The wounded groaned and Dushkas thudded, punctuated by the sharp crack of small arms fire.

Bannerman lay on his belly, scanning arcs. "The wee fuckers are pulling back." The incoming fire was dying out. Battles can be like a flu victim's temperature. One minute it's cold, the next it runs hot. I wasn't ready to relax just yet.

Ismael jogged up to us, sweating, and collapsed in the dirt next to us. "We've lost five men dead, maybe six or seven wounded," he gasped.

"We've won the fire-fight," I replied. "Now exploit it and keep the momentum going. Keep pushing and attacking. Take your guys forward to the edge of the tree-line, 'cos the enemy might well counter-attack. Keep the mortar and a couple of Dushkas on the far riverbank."

He nodded and darted forwards, weapon ready. He was a good man, now I'd seen him under fire. Calm and assured. I reckoned Ismael would make a good infantry officer…

...and none of us heard or saw the enemy jet. A blast-wave, a white-hot monster, tossed me backwards. The sensation of heat and raw energy rippled through my body like lava. I landed in the soft sandy earth and rolled into cover. My hearing came back with a liquid popping noise inside my head. The sound of screaming and gunfire filled my ears. "GET THOSE FUCKING DUSHKAS SITED," Bannerman, the eternal NCO, bawled at a nearby gunner, voice louder than gunfire. The ex-Para strode calmly across the battlefield, his confidence infectious. "GET ME SOME ANTI-FUCKING-AIRCRAFT OVER HERE!"

Oz lay in a heap, rubbing his bloodied nose. I peered over the side of the rusting tank, where another shattered Toyota pickup burnt by the roadside. Further up the road another rebel technical was burning where a trail of rockets had hit. I heard the supersonic rip of jet engines. A dark shape with a blunt nose and swept-back wings zipped past in the distance. It was a ground attack jet, belly bulging with ordnance. "I thought we'd fucked their air force," I shouted at Oz, ears ringing.

"Don't look like it," he shouted back. "But they might fuck us!"

The rebels readied shoulder-launched rockets and AA guns. Ismael swung up onto his vehicle's AA cannon and began shouting orders. Afterburners screaming, a dun-camouflaged MIG-21 broke cover over the horizon and lined up for another strafing run. AA guns opened up, hurling ropes of sparkling tracer across the morning sky. As the MIG thundered overhead, a black oblong-shaped bomb fell into the treeline and exploded, sending up a giant plume of smoke and fire. The sky was a crazy kaleidoscope of light, blobs of multi-coloured tracer firing in every direction.

I lay helpless on my back, coughing and wondering if the gunk flowing out of my ears was my brains. Bannerman appeared and sprinted along the road, a grey-painted anti-aircraft rocket resting on his shoulder. He sniffed the air, nodded and fired the weapon. With a crack-and-whoosh, the AA rocket span off, trailing white smoke as it began sniffing out the enemy jet at MACH-2. The ex-para shielded his eyes as he watched the rocket trail, like a golfer assessing a tricky drive out of the rough. I couldn't see the jet being struck, but I heard the cheering of the rebels.

Pulling myself up, I staggered over to the others. They were surrounded by bloodied first aid kits, bandages and field dressings as they helped wounded rebels. Others were plundering the bodies of the dead government troops, seizing weapons and ammunition. The Presidential Commando had left RPGs, machineguns and a recoilless rifle. Like a train of soldier ants, the rebels returned to their vehicles with the kit. Oz and I jogged to the front of our column. Ismael climbed down from his AA gun and snatched the map from the cargo pocket of his fatigues. "Tony, we need to dig in, fast," I said. We'd won the reverse slope of the wooded plateau, the ground best suited to defence.

The young rebel captain nodded, eyes narrowed. He'd been hit by shrapnel, blood seeping into the collar of his jacket. Two rebels in combat gear sprinted down the road towards us. "*Faru!*" they shouted.

"What the fuck does that mean?" I asked.

Tony Ismael wiped from his face. "Faru is Swahili for *tank*."

CHAPTER TWENTY TWO

"Achtung Panzer!" Oz barked, "three hundred metres."

"Fucking tanks?" Bytchakov was grim-faced, "this RPG ain't even gonna scratch that."

"A lone tank supported by shite infantry? We can take the crew with grenades," Bannerman shrugged.

"Fucking right," Ruben nodded, eyes shining with excitement. "We can do it if we can get close enough." The dirty yellow T-72 main battle tank squatted on open ground beyond our hard-won tree line, next to the Afuuma Highway. The old war machine farted clouds of oily black smoke, gun swivelling slowly in its turret. The tank commander's head was visible through an open hatch. It looked to me like he was arguing with a soldier in a rusting Toyota pick-up.

I'd helped brew-up old Iraqi tanks during the second Gulf War, dug in as strong-points. But back then we had decent antitank systems and air superiority. We'd have to wing this. "Right, listen in," I said, hopping into the driver's seat of our jeep. "Oz, get on the recoilless, when we get up there start putting down rounds on the tank. Alex, engage with RPG to distract them..."

Bannerman looked at me and grinned wolfishly. "I'll work my way through the trees on their flank, with these bastards." He pulled two respirator bags from his assault pack. They were improvised bombs, each fashioned from a block of C4.

"Cover that fucking lunatic," I ordered.

Bannerman exuded coolness and bravery. You wouldn't invite him to the ambassador's reception, but on the battlefield he was unequalled. Shaking his head at the Scotsman, Bytchakov plugged a rocket into his RPG. "Bannerman, you really are one crazy motherfucker," he said approvingly. The Scotsman laughed and bullied a gaggle of rebels forward. He motioned for them to cover him, the men nodding at the grinning, dreadlocked apparition with a sword strapped to his back.

Gunning the engine of the jeep, I burst through the trees. The rear wheels cleared the edge of the roadside, the vehicle shuddering as Oz fired the Wombat. A puff of smoke marked the impact of the shell on the frying-pan shaped turret. The commander dropped down into the bowels of the tank, slamming the hatch shut after him. The T-72s main gun swung towards us, Oz grunting as he heaved another round into the Wombat. As soon as he'd re-loaded, I ground my boot into the accelerator. I fed the steering wheel down, swerving the vehicle to frustrate the tank gunner. In the distance, through the grenade smoke, I saw one bullet-riddled technical chewed up by Ruben's MG fire, infantry on their bellies in the dirt. The second technical was reversing behind the T-72 for cover, glowing red tracer bouncing off metalwork. "Cal, turn right!" Oz hollered as the tank's main gun tracked towards us.

I complied, slamming the gearstick down to third as we bumped off the road, racing through a screen of bushes and thorns. The boom of the tank gun sent up a curtain of dust. The screeching 125mm round missed, sailing off into the trees. Bytchakov's RPG streaked across the field, exploding on the side-armour of the tank hull. The T-72 stopped for a moment, the turret panning away from us, like a monster sniffing out a new threat. "Oz," I shouted over my shoulder, "does the T-72 have that rapid auto-loader system?" I remembered from my army recce days, when we studied Soviet tanks like train-spotters, that a well-trained T-72 crew could fire four rounds a minute from the main gun.

"Yes, it does have a rapid auto-fucking-loading system!" He squeezed off another shot with the RR, the rocket slamming into the heavy machinegun mounted on the turret. Even at this range I could see two black scars our shells had made on the armour.

"Aim lower - go for the driver's viewing hatch."

"It's a *recoilless* rifle, not a fucking sniper rifle," Oz spat. "Now move!"

I drove off, parallel with the T-72 before careering right again, driving straight towards it. "Ruben," I hollered into my PRR, "can you button down that tank?" I heard a squelch of acknowledgement, tracer dancing from the ruined technical and across the tank turret and viewing block. The T-72 gunner engaged us with his co-axial machinegun, rounds sparkling towards us the size of burning coke cans. They made a high-pitched buzzing noise as they whipped past.

Bannerman had covered his first hundred metres, firing from the hip. A covering screen of rebels emerged from the treeline, firing small arms and rockets to cover us. From my position in the driving seat I saw a barrage of tracer and RPG rockets stream across the open ground. Government troops scattered, baffled by the crazy and sudden attack.

The second enemy technical broke cover from behind the T-72, a skinny guy wearing body armour hanging off the rear-mounted machinegun. He swung the weapon towards us and opened fire, bullets tearing into the front of our jeep. I fought with the steering wheel, aiming the dying vehicle towards the nearest cover, a shallow embankment twenty metres away. The engine moaned, steam and water pissing from the shattered bonnet.

Oz's RR barked again as we slewed to a halt, the vehicle exploding in a ball of orange flame and greasy smoke. The vehicle must have been full of spare gasoline and ammo, the wreck spitting and fizzing with bullets and RPG rounds cooking off. "De-bus," I hollered, rolling out of the crippled jeep.

Oz hit the dirt, rolled and scrambled for his RPG. Blood oozed from a six-inch long gash on his upper arm, his shredded sleeve slick with claret. Tracking the scene through my rifle sights, I saw the remaining infantry cowering behind the T-72 as Bannerman advanced through the smoke. Sweat streaming down his face, Oz took a knee, RPG in his shoulder. The rocket sparkled across the battlefield, exploding on the turret and setting light to some rolled-up camouflage netting. The T-72 jerkily reversed behind the trees, the gun trying to depress low enough to hit us. "He can't get us!" shouted Oz. He slid another RPG rocket from the canvas bandolier across his back and reloaded.

Bannerman rushed from the treeline, weapon raised. I saw him bellowing as he hauled himself onto the hull of the moving tank. The remaining Zambutan infantry were pinned down by the scything rebel covering fire. Oz put the RPG down and reached for a field dressing. I put my hand over his wound and pressed. Bannerman slapped two hubcap-sized lumps of C4 onto the tank turret. He leapt from the T-72 and sprinted for the trees, the explosion blasting a jagged breach in the armoured beast, exposing the dirty grey innards of the vehicle. The tank bellowed smoke, moving slowly as it tried to manoeuvre away.

Bytchakov shouldered his RPG and shouted at the other rebels to do the same. A shrieking volley of rockets slammed into the damaged T-72, more smoke pouring from the doomed machine. Like a dying dinosaur the tank juddered, grey smoke billowing from the hatches. The few remaining enemy troops fled, abandoning their wounded.

Tony Ismael shouted for his men to advance. The rebels established fresh fire positions, siting their Dushkas, RRs and RPGs. Three men scurried forward, hurriedly laying mines on the road. The assault had gained three hundred metres of killing ground out from the bridgehead. I watched the mortar team cross the bridge and men treated for gunshot wounds near the old ambulance. "You OK?" I said.

Tony nodded. "I've been on the radio. Our scouts say 21st Brigade stopped five miles further up the road due to the fighting here." The rebels had lost a dozen men, with more wounded, but had taken a good defensive position with ample support weapons. "Reinforcements are on the way," he added. "Two hundred more fighters."

The enemy needed air support and artillery. Without those I guessed the rebels could hold the bridge for some time, with tanks being especially vulnerable in the wooded terrain. "You can hold here," I replied, "but you need cover. Get the men to dig in."

Tony grabbed my shoulder. "Cal, go to Afuuma, find Colonel Murray. The army will need to regroup, but there's an old herding trail you can use to skirt 'round them." We studied the map. The trail meandered parallel with the highway, threading through wadis, culverts and rough ground. It met the outskirts of Afuuma sixty miles from our current position. "Take whatever vehicle you need," Tony said.

"That's very generous."

The rebel captain lit a cigarette and smiled, "I want it back."

After I'd found the others, we went to the ambulance. One of the medics, a stick-thin Kenyan, cleaned and bandaged our injuries. We gave him our spare ketamine, keeping enough for a dose each. "*Shukrani*," he said. "I'm running low on supplies, especially morphine and blood plasma." The best we could do was to give the medic spare field dressings and a sleeve of cigarettes. We headed for the pick-up we'd chosen, a dirty white Toyota Hilux. We chose it not only because it was ultra-reliable, but because it looked distinctly un-military. "You're heading to Afuuma, yes?" the medic smiled. "Afuuma can be dangerous for westerners."

"I'm sure it is mate," I laughed. "But then again, so is this place."

The medic chuckled. "My name is Jimiyu. My cousin's husband owns the Turtle Beach hotel, he supports General Abasi. If you mention my name he might be able to help you."

"Does he have beer?" said Bannerman.

"Of course," Jimiyu replied.

"He can help us then, mate."

"We need civilian clothes," I said.

Jimiyu looked around at the rebels. "You have good uniforms. These men are wearing rags. Of course they will swap if you ask." He said something in Swahili, and soon the rebels were bartering for our German army-surplus fatigues. I kept my trousers and boots, but swapped my combat jacket for a black heavy metal tee-shirt and a faded blue windcheater. Oz, being smaller than me, did better and bagged a South African rugby shirt and knee-length orange board-shorts. Bannerman, Alex and Ruben managed to scrounge civilian shirts and jackets. We looked like tramps, but at least we looked less like soldiers.

Bannerman and Ruben still had most of their original kit. They dug out wet-wipes and toothpaste as we tidied up, Ruben even shaving his beard into a goatee. Finally, I pulled a roll of black duct-tape from Bannerman's assault pack and spelt the word 'TV' and 'PRESS' on the bonnet and doors of the Toyota. We stored our rifles, a machinegun, RPG and other kit under a tarpaulin and studied the map again. "Brew up for five minutes," I said. "I'm going to make a call."

Oz pulled a face but said nothing.

I sat by the rusting tank near the bridgehead and called Marcus. He answered immediately. "I've got you on GPS, located seventy miles southwest of a place called Afuuma," he said. "Apparently, there's a war on."

I explained about the bodies we'd found at the Buur Xuuq mine, that Afuuma was our likeliest bet to find the CORACLE team.

"Less than an hour ago we intercepted a signal from the Chinese anti-piracy taskforce," Marcus replied. "They've docked in Afuuma, reporting the loss of four helicopters and fifteen men to unprovoked rebel action."

"What's the Chinese reaction?" I asked.

"They don't want to get drawn into fighting. The tone of the SIGINT suggests that the commanding officer was too gung-ho. I'd say he's in the shit with his chain of command."

"An officer called Colonel Zhang Ki was in charge," I said. "Marcus, he had pre-prepared statements for us to sign, implicating SIS. He even brought two Chinese intelligence guys to meet us."

"This whole thing reeks. Find the team and don't spare the rod. Find out what the hell they're up to."

"A location would help," I replied. Marcus had the habit of making his office-based battles as difficult as the real one, and it was starting to piss me off.

"I'm sure it would." Marcus' voice softened, "I'm working every angle, Cal. You have my word I'll get you out of there. But the fan is my office is so covered in shit I'm wearing a rubber raincoat."

I found Tony Ismael standing next to his truck, listening intently to instructions on the radio. "Things are happening quickly," he said, keying off the mic. "Our spies report Aziz reckons we're the advance element of a major offensive."

"What does General Abasi think?" I replied, leaning against the bonnet and lighting a cigar stub with my Zippo.

"He says if they want a major offensive then he's happy to give 'em one," Tony grinned. "With two hundred more men I reckon we can harass the south of Afuuma while the General loops up the coast and attacks from the east."

"Just be careful," I said, "and watch your flanks."

"I will, and I love that look," he laughed, motioning at my ragged clothes.

I shrugged and laughed with him. "Take care, Tony."

"Don't worry, Cal, I'll see you in Afuuma, we can drink beer and tell war stories, right?" The young Londoner offered me his hand, which I gripped.

We mounted up, waved goodbye to the rebels and crossed the bridge onto the herder's path. My compass said we were headed due northeast. Oz drove, and after an hour on the road we saw a convoy of military vehicles in the distance on a parallel route. Trucks, armoured personnel carriers and towed artillery rumbled by, stirring up a miasma of orange dust. After another two hours, I estimated we were fifteen miles from Afuuma. To the east we could see a hazy strip of blue, marking the coast. The herder's path ended abruptly, feeding us back onto the metalled road. The terrain became greener, dotted with groves of palm and fruit trees. "Checkpoint," said Bytchakov. He reached for the AK hidden in the foot well.

"Let's see if we can talk our way through," I said.

"Good luck with that," said Bannerman, who'd been dozing in the back of the Toyota.

The checkpoint consisted of two battered Land Rovers and six khaki-uniformed security police. They'd put two oil drums on either side of the road, joined with a heavy duty chain covered in spikes. One of the Land Rovers had a whip aerial, and I could hear the crackle of voices on a radio. I waved as we approached. The cops were scruffy, with dirty uniforms and old FN rifles. Their sergeant stepped towards us. "Where are you going?" he said suspiciously, in sing-song English.

"Afuuma," I replied.

The cop looked us over and crossed his arms. "What is your business?"

"My name is Adrian Clay," I lied. "I'm a freelance journalist. These guys are my security team. I went to cover a story near Hagadifi, but our guide disappeared and we got lost."

"That is rebel country," he sniffed. "Show me your papers."

"That's where the story is," I shrugged, "but all our stuff was stolen by rebels, two of us are injured. Our cameras, laptops, passports are gone…"

Ruben motioned to his bandaged arm and groaned theatrically. The sergeant smiled at our stupidity. He turned to his men and said something in Swahili. They all laughed. I watched Ruben's hand disappear underneath the tarpaulin. I shot him a look. It said no.

"This serves you right, you are lucky to be alive," the sergeant chided. "But if they took everything, how will you pay the tax for travelling on this road?"

I'd been asked for bribes more blatantly, but not by much. I reached into the waistband of my fatigues and pulled out a wad of dollar bills. "Listen to me," I said wearily. "Here's eight hundred US dollars."

"I thought you only found trolls under bridges," Oz sniffed.

The sergeant raised an eyebrow as he counted the banknotes. "I've had a terrible day," I continued. "Can you just radio ahead and say that we've paid our taxes and that we're heading back to our hotel?"

"Of course," the sergeant beamed. "In any case, the road will be closed by order of the army. You are very lucky to be alive." Oz drove us through the checkpoint, the police eyeing us warily as we passed.

"Ruben," I said. "Cool it." The ex-marine glowered at me, but said nothing.

Bannerman put his hand on Ruben's arm. "You'll put this right for Raph, son. Don't worry."

"I know I will," he hissed. "If it's the last thing I do."

CHAPTER TWENTY THREE

Afuuma was a ramshackle port, positioned in a scoop of land overlooking the Indian Ocean. Zambute's only deep harbour, it was strategically crucial to the regime. During the annexation of the disputed zone, Aziz's army had ousted the *Shadow of Swords* and *Al-Shabaab* militants who'd held it for several years. Now it teemed with the usual suspects – aid workers, journalists, UN hangers-on, merchants, spooks, mercenaries, whores and thieves. The local people made their living servicing the foreigner's whims, desires, and agendas. The economy would collapse if they left, which they would as soon as a new disaster or war zone became *du jour*. Then Afuuma would return to its old industries: clan-feuds, smuggling, kidnapping, piracy and terrorism.

"Looks like the fleet's in," said Oz. Three warships sat in the 'L'-shaped harbour. Two were sleek, dangerous-looking destroyers, the third a boxy helicopter carrier. All flew the red and gold banner of The People's Republic of China. I saw a few Chinese sailors as we drove into town, outnumbered by seedy-looking local cops. The Zambutan police wore grubby army-surplus, stood on street corners in armed packs.

We soon found the Turtle Beach hotel, a bullet-riddled dive. Still, inside it smelt of home-cooking, mothballs and bleach, a peeling relic of happier times. The reception boasted cracked tile floors, yellowed fire regulations printed in Italian and faded seventies décor. We found the owner, a wizened old guy called Ibrahim. He spoke broken English, but better Italian. I switched to that language to tell him about the medic we'd met with the rebels. Ibrahim was delighted to meet friends of his cousin, and even more delighted when we gave him a thousand dollars and suggested he keep his mouth shut. He sent up a tin bucket full of ice and a crate of Tusker beer.

It was a thousand dollars well spent. Eyeing the booze, my alcoholic's logic figured it was *only beer*. I groaned with pleasure as I chugged a bottle before showering, shaving and re-treating the scratches, gashes and bruises that covered my sorry carcass. I suggested the guys waited in their rooms and did the same until I'd had a look around.

"That's the best fucking order you've given since we bloody well hit the LZ," said Bannerman. He climbed into bed, sighed happily and popped open a beer. "Call me when it's time for tea and medals." He'd taken a bayonet to his dreadlocks and got Ruben to shave his head in an attempt to look less conspicuous. He'd held onto his Claymore, still sheathed in its camouflaged scabbard. A sword-wielding Scottish skinhead was going to be conspicuous anywhere in Africa, but I wasn't going to argue.

Alex Bytchakov was bandaging a shrapnel injury to his shin while Ruben quietly cleaned his weapons. Oz had gone to buy food and clean clothes with a bundle of crisp dollars from our escape funds. Our weapons, cleaner than any of us, lay on a towel on the floor. We had the MG4 and a G36 plus a RPG, three Kalashnikovs, pistols, grenades and enough ammunition to start a small war. I hoped we wouldn't need to, but the prognosis suggested we would.

Oz returned from the local market, a bustling souk we'd passed on our way to the hotel. "You can buy more or less anything there," he reported. "It's like the world's biggest knock-off car boot sale."

"Car-boot?" said Bytchakov quizzically.

"Swap-Meet," I translated.

Oz dished out clean Chinese copies of popular Western clothes.

"Fucking hell, this ain't bad for snide gear," said Ruben, holding up a pair of not-quite-*Diesel* jeans.

"Snide?" asked Bytchakov.

"Jekyll and Hyde, y'know, *snide,* as in counterfeit, I thought Yanks spoke English."

"They do, they just don't speak your fucking gutter language, you Cockney wanker," Bannerman drawled.

The American scratched his head. "How many languages do you speak in your freaking country?"

"One," Ruben chuckled, "except for the Sweaties. Fuck knows what they speak."

"Fuck off," said Bannerman, popping open another beer. "I speak a wee bit of Gaelic, language of bards and fucking kings. I'll give you fucking Sweaties…"

"Sweaties?" asked the exasperated American.

"Sweaty-socks: Jocks. Scotsmen," Ruben grinned. "You really don't speak any English, do you?"

"I give up," said Bytchakov. "Captain, can you order these monkeys to gimme a break?"

"Fat chance," I replied, rifling through the clothing. I chose khaki cargo pants with plenty of pockets, a counterfeit Ralph Lauren polo shirt and a pair of sunglasses. I was keeping my own boots. I unzipped one of the side compartments of my pack and stowed my satellite phone, video camera, remaining cash and bottled water inside. Shouldering it, I left the room.

My Walther was in a pancake holster, covered by my shirt tails.

It was time to start making shit happen.

Ibrahim told me Graziani Beach was where the Westerners hung out. The wreckage-strewn beach hugged a shabby strip of Italianate shops, a café and two seedy-looking bars, patrolled by feral-looking soldiers. Locals hawked trinkets to Scandinavian aid workers while Chinese businessmen drank coffee and chain-smoked, barking instructions into their cell phones. Rusting taxis, held together with duct-tape and optimism, lined the streets. There would be a brisk trade in evacuations to the airport when the rebels advanced.

The *Afuuma Lounge* appeared to be the most popular joint in town. Faded pink stucco peeled from the shrapnel-scarred walls like a snake shedding its skin. A gaggle of journalists sat in the shade outside, drinking cold Tusker and gossiping.

As a rule, I don't like The Media. Most journalists are lazy and dishonest, a bit like me. I've found their relentless quest for truth utterly conditional, and secrets are something they tell ten people at a time. But when you were in the shit in a hostile environment, I'd found two groups of people who could usually help you out. Prostitutes were one, journalists the other. And there didn't appear to be any whores with high-speed internet access nearby.

Perched at the bar, I sized up the room as I knocked back chilled lager. A surly waiter suggested grilled mutton. The Anglosphere media, made up of British, Antipodean and American journalists, sat in a noisy gaggle in the middle of the terrace. There were seven guys and five women drinking beer and babbling into satellite phones. Their local stringers sat at the next table, chain-smoking and playing backgammon. The journalists wore expensive outdoor clothing, a pile of blue-covered body armour and helmets at their feet.

Their cameramen, bodyguards and producers stood nearby, slagging off the talent. More than a few production teams I'd met took a jaded view of the Muppets in front of the camera. A few of the TV guys I knew from the Balkan wars and Middle East had been injured because of an ambitious correspondent's vanity. On the other side of the bar sat a gaggle of ripe European blondes in their twenties. I made them as workers for an NGO or charity. They were surrounded by a pack of predatory diplomats, aid workers and gnarly PSC operators. I was pleased to see the PSC guys doing the best job of chatting them up.

The last group were freelancers. I'd met plenty of them in war zones, young journalists who got a buzz out of the drama, War as extreme sport. They were having a noisy drinking competition, ignoring the rest of the room. As far as journos went, the war-junkies were OK, a fair few of them ex-military.

But I'd already spotted my man. He lurked solo, in a shady corner. An ageing lounge-lizard dressed in a crumpled beige safari suit, cowboy boots and a black AC/DC tee-shirt, he exuded *been-there, done-that*. Lank yellow-grey hair trailed over his shoulders, eyes obscured by a pair of tortoiseshell Ray-Bans. He looked like he hadn't shaved for a month, a *Romeo Y Julietta* smouldering at the corner of his mouth. A half-empty bottle of local Scotch, probably ethanol with caramel food colouring, sat in front of him. He was scribbling notes in a yellow legal notepad with a pencil, oblivious to the end-of-war party going on around him. I ordered another beer and took a bar stool next to him. "Hi," I said, offering my hand. "I'm Adrian Clay."

"Nice to meet you Adrian," he replied in a raspy Australian accent, "Mike Turpin." He took of his sunglasses, revealing deep-set brown eyes. Offering me his hand, he looked relaxed but amused, like life was a complex practical joke only he understood.

"I'm looking for a journalist," I said easily. "I've got a story."

"Everyone's got a story in Zambute," Turpin guffawed. "There's a fuck-load of journalists over there, mate. They'll chew your arm off for a story, as long as they don't have to leave the bar." He gestured to the foreign correspondents holding court on the terrace.

"They look like wankers," I shrugged. "You don't."

"Flattery will get you everywhere," he smiled, revealing the sort of teeth a druid might dance around. "OK, I might be interested. Unlike those wankers, this is my beat, from Sudan to Swaziland."

"How did you end up here?"

"Ah, the Turpin life-story," he grinned. "I was with Australian state broadcaster, ABC. I got a gig as an embedded journalist with the Yanks during Gulf War One. After that I freelanced, ended up covering the American fuck-up in Somalia. I've been in Africa ever since."

"I missed the first Gulf War," I said, warming to the boozy Australian. "I had a walk-on part in the sequel."

Turpin chuckled and raised his glass. "So what's your story, Adrian, mercenary or spook?" He took in my battered face, scuffed boots and assault pack, the butt of my Walther poking beneath my shirt.

"I'm a mercenary," I shrugged. I could have insisted I was a contractor, protection officer, security consultant or one of the other polite euphemisms for hired gun. But I was tired and in a hurry. "I work for a PSC. We look after energy industry assets."

"Which energy company would that be?" said Turpin.

I nodded as the waiter passed beer and food. I pushed fifty dollars across the bar and motioned for another bottle of Scotch, a decent one. "That doesn't matter," I smiled. "Let's just say they're scary and Russian."

"That means BASNEFT," Turpin scoffed. "OK, what have you got?"

I reached into my pack and put the video camera on the bar, flipping open the screen. "Watch that," I said. The mutton was hot and charred on the outside, doused in chilli. I enjoyed the fiery flavour and gulped more beer.

Turpin looked at the camera quizzically. "What is it?"

"Forty-eight hours ago, the Zambutan energy ministry ordered a Manganese mine to be dynamited at the Buur Xuuq facility."

"And what happened next?"

"There were at least fifty kids down that mine," I replied. "Average age twelve to fourteen. The rebels raided the mine, found out what happened and videoed the incident."

"That video could get you killed around here," he said matter-of-factly. "I suppose the rebels executed the guilty parties."

"Yes, with extreme prejudice, including the Chinese engineers."

"It's a good story, if it's true," he replied carefully. He ran his tongue across his lips. "What do you want for it?"

"A cigar would be good," I said.

Turpin chuckled and pulled a leather case from his pocket. He snipped the end from a *Cubano* with a pocketknife and passed it to me. I lit it and happily rolled smoke around my mouth. Since I more or less gave up Class 'A' drugs, booze and cigars are my only remaining vices. I try to enjoy both as much as I can. "Thanks, Mister Turpin. The camera is yours."

"Call me Mike. What do you really want?" He swiped the camera, which disappeared inside his threadbare jacket.

"What, apart from a cigar? Maybe you can help me with the whereabouts of some Brits who may have arrived here in the last twenty-four hours."

Mike looked at the Scotch I'd ordered, Johnnie Walker, and poured a hefty glass. He threw it down his neck like a man who hadn't had a drink for a month. "I know people in Afuuma who could ask," he shrugged. "Who are they and what do they look like?"

I described them all, except for from Mel Murray. I didn't want to scare Turpin off by revealing that I was linked to Regime Enemy Number One.

"And why do you need to find these people?"

I smiled. "They owe me money. Shall we leave it at that, Mike?"

"Here's my card," he nodded, passing me a grubby piece of paste-board with a mobile telephone number printed on it.

"I take it you won't simply disappear with the story?" I asked.

Turpin looked me in the eye, a smile on his leathery face. "I've been around long enough to know when not to fuck someone over, *Adrian*," he replied.

"Fair enough," I said. We shook hands again and Turpin gave me another cigar.

I drained my beer, finished my food and took a stroll over to the port. Apart from the Chinese navy, it hosted a collection of dhows, fishing boats and cargo vessels. A checkpoint guarded the entrance to the facility, guarded by a nervous-looking group of government soldiers. Sitting down on a rocky premonitory overlooking the bay, I pulled the satellite phone from my pack and called Marcus. "Anything for me?" I asked. "We're in Afuuma. I've put out feelers to find your officers."

"The data you found at the camp, the table Brodie prepared?" he replied, "It looks like Duclair was onto something. Juliet Easter's comms data shows contact to a source in Eastern Zambute and the Somali border at key events during the two compromised operations."

"So you think it's her?" I said, heart sinking.

"At the moment, I'm inclined to. The entire CORACLE team has disappeared – no GPS activation, no compromise protocol initiated. Four officers, vanished into thin air."

I pulled a face. I didn't want the traitor to be Easter, but the evidence was compelling. "What about a motive?" I asked.

"I don't know," he replied. I could hear him eating, mashing and chomping noises on the end of the line. "It's unprecedented, treachery on this scale. Losing *agents* is one thing, we've had that before. But losing *officers* like this? Even Philby didn't do that."

"If they're here we'll find them," I said, sounding more confident than I felt.

"Are you sure their bodies might not be at the mine?" he asked hopefully.

"I don't think so," I said. "If they'd executed them I reckon there would've been more blood and signs of a struggle."

I could hear Marcus' breathing, heavy and strained. "I agree. I find it difficult to believe the Chinese would execute them out of hand."

I explained Zhang Ki had been happy for us to be beaten, but was more eager for us to sign confessions. "Is there more SIGINT from the Chinese?"

"Only that Beijing is furious with the PLA Navy," said Marcus. "Tell me about this Colonel Zhang character."

I thought about it for a moment. "He's in his late thirties, tall, speaks fluent English. The statements prove he knew SIS was involved."

"I'm wondering if he's actually a marine Colonel," Marcus pondered. "Is he an MSS officer with military cover?"

It struck me as possible. "Perhaps, but he's a trained soldier. He's not just playing the part. I suppose you're guys are digging into his background?"

"As best we can," Marcus sighed heavily. "There are only two-and-a-quarter million people serving in the People's Liberation Army, after all."

"We're searching Afuuma," I said. "But the place will be locked down now the rebels are advancing." I didn't tell Marcus we'd spear-headed the offensive. He sounded pissed off enough as it was.

"I'll be in touch," he replied. "In the meantime, get on the internet. I'm going to message you two temporary email accounts. One will have a file, the other the encryption key."

"What's on the file?" I asked.

"The details of the last two compromised CORACLE operations," he replied. "We've looked at the data you found in Brodie's room, and the material Duclair provided. Maybe you can see something in it, now you've been on the ground."

"Okay, I'll take a look."

"Apart from that, you're on your own."

"No change there, then," I said.

"One last thing, Calum" said Marcus.

"Yes?"

"The Firm have been on to the DIADEM. They've asked for a view on the need to implement what they call *Fallen Eagle.*"

"That doesn't make sense, Marcus. I'm the one who implements Fallen Eagle, not SIS." Monty had made that much clear. The emergency protocol was my call as the team leader, The Firm's secret prerogative.

"*What?*" he replied, astonished. "Say that again."

"Fallen Eagle is our last-ditch exfil protocol. I call it as a last resort in the event of irreversible compromise."

Marcus's laugh was bitter. "Is that what the bastards told you? Cal, Fallen Eagle is the protocol whereby you all get neutralised. It's a failsafe to cover The Firm's backside, not yours."

"What?"

Marcus chuckled, "and they've tricked you into calling it in yourself? It's sheer genius."

"What the fuck are you talking about?"

"If your mission fails and The Firm decides it's holed beneath the waterline, they get *you* to call it in under the pretext of a rescue. That's when a CIA team holed up in Djibouti flies in a Reaper and gives you a Hellfire missile or two."

"What the hell have the CIA got to do with it?"

"The Firm has a lot of fingers in a lot of pies. The CIA will write you off as a target on their Signature Strike list. They keep fictional terrorist profiles on the list as spares, for when they need to go off-policy."

"What did the DIADEM say?" I asked. "Did he agree?" Without thinking about it, I scanned the skies. Although I doubt you'd spot a drone, let alone a Hellfire missile, until it was too late.

"DIADEM was disturbed The Firm has such… high level *liaison* within the CIA but he's considering it, to keep things tidy," Marcus whispered. "There's enough *Shadow of Swords* HVTs in the region for them to justify a strike. So, for God's sake, give me some progress to take upstairs so I can dissuade him from doing something stupid."

"Do I dump my phone?"

"No," Marcus sighed. "If you do that you've told The Firm you've resigned. Good luck with the rest of your life. You *should* be fine as long as you don't call it in, Cal."

"So now I'm a High Value Target? I've never been a high-value anything. As for progress, I'll get back to you."

"Remember, Cal, I can help you with The Firm."

"Talk is cheap," I hissed. I jabbed the 'off' button and ended the call. I was getting to the end of my cigar. I enjoyed the last of the smoke and flicked the butt into the murky water. I looked at my satellite phone and thought of doing the same. Then I thought better of it and headed back to the hotel.

CHAPTER TWENTY FOUR

The internet café was three doors down from The Afuuma Lounge. I saw Mike Turpin was gone, but the foreign correspondents were still there, listening to news bulletins about the rebel offensive. Al-Jazeera was reporting that reinforcements camped on the Ethiopian border had linked up with General Abasi's ramshackle army. Although poorly-equipped, it was growing every day as disillusioned Zambutans defected to the rebel cause. And the Ethiopians, no great lovers of Aziz, were turning a blind eye to the military build-up on their territory.

Next up was a gloomy-sounding President Aziz, claiming the rebels were secretly backed by Islamists. The allegations smacked of desperation and no one was buying it. Already Abasi's forces had clashed with the *Shadow of Swords*, uploading videos of executed Mujahedeen to prove they weren't in league with Al-Qaeda's East African franchisees. As a result, the Jihadis were retreating north, towards the Somali border in order to escape the opposing armies. That would drag them towards Afuuma.

I stopped to listen to the journalists loudly discuss the war. "This is a mess," slurred an Australian, draining another beer. "It's a three-way death-fuck. You've got the Yanks, Aziz's forces *and* Abasi attacking the Muj to prove they're on the side of the angels."

"Well," opined a long-nosed Brit with a plummy accent, "as long as the Muj get a kicking I couldn't care less." He drained his beer. "Discretion being the better part of valour, I think it's time I buggered off back to Nairobi." The media pack started bullying their stringers to get them back to Marsajir, camera crews sighing as they asked for the bill and receipts.

The internet café was quiet, a few locals sending email or watching lagging football footage on YouTube. I sipped coffee and logged onto a 90's-vintage terminal, slowly downloading the reports Marcus promised on a dial-up modem. The email accounts were in the name of a company I'd never heard of, using long alphanumeric usernames and passwords. I wore the novelty beer-bottle opener on a chain around my neck. Sliding it into the computer, I saved the file and encryption key onto it. Leaving a handful of dollar bills on the counter, I headed to the market and bought a cheap Chinese laptop computer. Back in my room I found Oz snoring gently under his mosquito net. I booted up the laptop and opened the file using the decryption key. From a field of random gibberish two reports emerged, a warning flashing that they would be wiped when I closed them:

Op. STOWAGE (CORACLE sub-operation)
Objective: Recruitment of key agent in Zambutan finance ministry
Intelligence Requirement: (a) Strategic intelligence, Chinese economic policy in East Africa and (b) fraudulent use of UK aid by Zambutan regime and money-laundering aid payments via third parties
Outcome: COMPROMISED.
OPSEC REVIEW: Zambutan agent cultivated by DUCLAIR and EASTER in Marsajir and Zurich over eight-

month period. A final meeting was arranged in Marsajir to confirm status as SIS asset. Agent arrested by Zambutan security police the day prior to meeting, tried and executed within two weeks. DUCLAIR was on leave in UK at time of incident and was not aware of the meeting location. EASTER was in the field, assisted by JACKSON. Comms data for all suspects examined. EASTER'S satellite phone linked to an untraced number traced to Zambutan location in border region (a commercial satellite telephone number from a Chinese service provider). EASTER'S use of the phone is partially corroborated by images and meta-data acquired by WOODSMAN. The provenance of these images is via suspicious colleagues. SIGINT on day of arrest suggests congratulatory messages were sent from Beijing to MSS listening post traced to Eastern Zambute / Somali annexed territory.

I assumed I was WOODSMAN. There was little I didn't already know in the report, except nobody had mentioned Hugo Jackson's involvement on the mission in Duclair's absence. I scrolled down to the second operation:

Op. TRICORN (CORACLE sub-operation)
Objective: Online penetration of, and disruption to, Zambutan regime financial assets.
Operational Requirement: Covert retrieval of corruptly obtained HMG International Development payments
Outcome: COMPROMISED
OPSEC REVIEW: Cyber-exploitation by JACKSON and BRODIE, leading to penetration of systems at National Bank of Zambute. This enabled CORACLE to trace and identify

laundered assets estimated at UK£175 million across numerous private European financial institutions. DUCLAIR and EASTER managed HUMINT to add value to online operations. Authority granted to penetrate and sequestrate funds to HMG covert accounts. Forty-eight hours prior to JACKSON'S penetration attempt, funds and physical high-value assets were transferred back to Zambute. Data provided via WOODSMAN shows EASTER making calls to the same unknown satellite telephone on six occasions in the forty-eight hour period prior to the compromise. In light of WOODSMAN'S reporting, it is now assessed that Duclair and Jackson's email traffic during this period cast doubts over EASTER'S integrity.

I copied the satellite phone number from the first report onto a piece of paper and closed the document. A pop-up told me that they'd been deleted permanently from my system.

Easter's fingerprints were all over the compromised operations, damned by the calls to the Chinese-registered satellite phone. Although Easter struck me as hyper-professional, she was having an affair with Dancer. That was a big professional no-no, and from Dancer's level of knowledge it was obvious that there had been indiscreet pillow-talk between them. I wished I could ask Dancer's opinion. He would be devastated if he knew Easter had betrayed Mel and the rest of the CORACLE team.

There was a knock on the door. Oz rolled out of bed, Kalashnikov ready. "Who is it?" I called, snatching my pistol from the bedside table.

"Mister Cal, it is Ibrahim," said the old hotel owner.

"One minute," I replied, motioning at Oz to stay out of sight. I held my pistol behind my back and opened the door a few inches.

Ibrahim was alone, a knowing smile on his deeply-lined face. He was wearing a neat brown suit and an open-collared shirt, a cigarette smouldering in the corner of his mouth. "It is only me," he said. "There is a message for you."

"Thanks, Ibrahim," I replied.

He handed me an envelope. "My daughter is cooking for your men. It will be ready in an hour, but I would ask that you eat in your rooms OK?"

"That's very kind of her."

I opened the envelope and pulled out a piece of yellow notepaper from a legal pad.

"What's that?" said Oz curiously.

"I went and did some nosing around," I replied.

The note was short but sweet: *I spoke with a friend. A Brit showed up yesterday at Adoyo Shipping and Transit on the Via Roma (near the police barracks). He's a young guy with spiky hair, looks Chinese but speaks English like he went to Eton. Adoyo is a local fixer and criminal, be careful. Best regards, Mike Turpin.*

"Hugo's turned up," I said. We studied our map and found the Via Roma. The road ran through the centre of Afuuma, north towards Somalia, then dog-legged west towards Marsajir. The police barracks was just over a mile out of town, the road hugging the hilly coastline.

"Doing surveillance on that is going to be fun," said Oz, in a tone of voice that suggested it wouldn't.

We went downstairs and collared Ibrahim. He ushered us into an office at the back of reception, a gloomy cell with a slow-moving ceiling fan. It was furnished with an ancient TV, a fridge and the world's oldest desktop computer. A joss-stick smouldered in the corner, the smell of lavender tickling my nose. "Please, sit down," said Ibrahim through a fug of cigarette smoke. He fussed around with a coffee machine, grinding beans and finding some small china cups. "And how can I help?"

"The message we just received, did you read it?" I said.

"Of course," replied the old Zambutan, eyes twinkling from his weathered, cadaverous face. "You need to know about the shipping office on the Via Roma?"

"Yes," I laughed.

"It is owned by Julius Adoyo. He is from the same clan as President Aziz, so he is a crook." Ibrahim shook his head, "Adoyo is as you say in English, a *front*, for the *maharamia*, the bandits and pirates."

"How?" said Oz.

"If you need a vessel to get in or out of Afuuma you have three choices," Ibrahim explained, counting them off on his bony fingers. "First, you can hope the anti-pirate ships are in the area, as they are now. Secondly, you can trust you have enough security on your ship. Third, you can pay Julius Adoyo to speak with the pirates to leave you alone."

"What sort of cargo are we talking about?" I replied.

"Anything," he shrugged. "The big shipping companies have gunmen on board nowadays, so the smaller operators need Adoyo, or criminals. If you need to smuggle people or drugs or weapons without the pirates seizing your ship, you pay Adoyo. So do the smaller traders who bring in goods from India."

"He sounds well-connected," I said, sipping my coffee.

"Oh, he is," Ibrahim smiled. "The police are his dogs, the pirates respect him and the Jihadists fear him. He does not care if you are Christian or Muslim or Zambutan or Somali. He is a snake."

"I think we'll pay him a visit," I said. "Can we just walk in there?"

"If you have balls the size of mangoes," the old man chuckled, looking doubtfully at my groin. "If you do, make sure you have a proper business proposition for him, because he is a difficult man to fool. His business is next door to the police barracks, for extra protection."

Oz drained his cup, smacking his lips. "If he's from the same clan as the President, why isn't he getting out of town? The rebels will be here soon. Surely he'll be hanging from a rope."

Ibrahim smiled, revealing a mouthful of gleaming teeth. "When General Abasi's men arrive, Adoyo will meet them with tributes, girls and bribes. He will do business with them, and the General's men will spare him. Adoyo can keep the peace in Afuuma for the rebels. They say his skin will shrug off a thousand bullets, that he enjoys the luck of a devil."

We went back upstairs, the others still dozing. After I briefed them food arrived, plate after plate of rice, beans, fish, mutton and freshly-baked bread. We devoured it all, like we hadn't eaten for a month. Of all Afuuma's problems, a shortage of food wasn't one of them.

Ibrahim's daughter was called Fathiya, a slim, proud-looking woman in her thirties. She had high cheekbones and narrow, suspicious eyes. She watched us eat. "Have you killed many government troops?" she said finally.

"Yes," Ruben said solemnly, "but not enough. I'm going to kill more."

"Good," Fathiya nodded, eyes flashing. "Both my sons are dead, murdered by those bastards."

"My brother died forty-eight hours ago," Ruben replied. "The Chinese killed him."

Fathiya walked over to where Ruben was sitting and held his head, fingers ringed with henna tattoos. She kissed his cheeks and smiled. "Repay them in blood, promise me." He nodded, and she hurried from the room, eyes welling with tears.

It was getting dark outside as I gathered the men together. "We need to Close Target Recce and then establish an OP on the Adoyo's office," I said. "It's our only lead to Murray and the others. The problem being it's right on top of the police barracks and Adoyo has them on the pay-roll."

"Why is Hugo cutting about in Afuuma?" growled Ruben. "I thought they'd been taken prisoner."

"That's the million dollar question," I replied.

"Damn right," said Ruben angrily. "And when we find him he's got some explaining to do."

I agreed. And I was tempted to let Ruben ask the questions. It would be a short but bloody interrogation.

"The police station bothers me. Why don't we just slip the local Peelers a grand, ask them to fuck off?" said Bannerman, to guffaws from the others. "It seems to work everywhere else around here."

"If only," I laughed. "Seriously, though, how much dough do we have left?"

We emptied our escape funds onto the bed – there was just over thirty thousand US dollars left. Ruben swore he'd 'lost' his, and I let the blatant theft go. It was an impressive amount considering the average yearly wage for a Zambutan was less than a hundred and fifty. "So, what's the plan?" said Oz.

"If you can recce with Duncan and come up with some ideas for an OP, me and Alex will go into the target and see what the score is. Ruben, you'll run protection for us." I saw the murder in Ruben's eyes, wanted to keep him on a close leash.

"This might help," smiled Bannerman suddenly, pulling a black plastic box from his Bergen. Inside was the spare PD-100 drone. He carefully took the palm-sized aircraft and checked it. "I'd forgotten about this wee fucker."

Oz nodded. "We just need to sit out of sight and fly it in."

"Cal, can we go back to the part where you and me go into Adoyo's office?" said Alex, suddenly alarmed.

"Sure," I replied. "You're perfect."

"Nobody's ever said that to me before," he grinned.

"I get it," said Oz, raising an eyebrow. "Are we resurrecting Mikhail Susenov?"

The rest of the team looked puzzled.

"Yeah, sort of," I grinned. "He was last seen being hunted in Kurdistan, right?" I still had the Russian ink.

"You've lost me Cal," Bannerman deadpanned. "It sounds cool, though."

"We'd better get going, Duncan," said Oz. "This recce ain't going to do itself."

"Yeah, but what the hell are you talking about?" said Bytchakov.

"Welcome to the mafia, *Sasha,*" I said to him in Russian, slapping him on the back. "Tomorrow we're going into the organised-crime business."

CHAPTER TWENTY FIVE

"I'd like to see Mister Adoyo," I growled in heavily-accented English. I felt more confident being someone else, especially a gnarly Russian Mafioso like Mikhail Susenov. Behind me Bytchakov, dressed in a cheap black suit and shades bought from the souk, glowered. And behind him was Ruben Grey, who needed no instruction on gangster-like behaviour. He loitered like a poisonous smell, a sneer on his lips and his hand on a gun.

We stood at the lock-studded door of *Adoyo Shipping and Transit*, a fortified blockhouse overlooking the beach. Last night's recce with the miniature drone had revealed a path to the rear of the building, leading to the police station next door. A small fleet of luxury cars were stored in the compound, BMWs and Mercedes. Three guards came and went, all armed with submachineguns.

The first guard was a big Zambutan wearing green Vietnam-era body armour. He leant by the door smoking, an Uzi slung across his chest. A thick rope of gold hung at his throat, a pistol strapped to his belt. "Is Mister Adoyo expecting you?" he grunted.

I smiled. "I doubt it. A friend suggested he might help."

"Who is your friend?"

Bytchakov was warming to his role. "Tell this dipshit we don't talk to the fucking asshole on the gate," he growled in Russian.

"What did he say?" said the guard.

"He's getting impatient," I shrugged. "Your attitude annoys him."

The guard spat noisily at my feet. I was wearing the most garish and expensive shoes I could find in the souk that morning, pointed patent leather efforts with brass studs. They looked bloody horrible, but would suit your average knuckle-dragger from Solntsevo.

Ruben Grey pushed his jacket to one side, revealing the pistol stuffed in his waistband. "You are behaving like an idiot," I smiled. "We are *Russian*. You understand? We will end up killing you. We'll piss on your corpse. Then we'll speak to your boss anyway."

"Fuck Russians. Who shall I say is asking after him?" the guard shrugged. He'd seen Bytchakov's pistol, held loosely by his side and had wisely come to the conclusion that he was prepared to use it.

"My name is Mikhail Ivanovich Susenov," I announced proudly, as if surprised he didn't already know. The name was common as muck in Russia, roughly translating into Michael Ian Smith.

"Wait here," the guard grunted. He pressed the button on an intercom and muttered something in Swahili. A few moments later, the door swung open. "This one waits outside," he said, pointing at Ruben.

I nodded at the ex-marine. "Please, Pyotr, grab a coffee, have a smoke."

Ruben grunted his acknowledgement and stalked across the road, towards a kid selling sodas on the beach. It gave a good view of the blockhouse. Oz and Bannerman were parked up in the Toyota nearby, heavily armed and ready to go on Ruben's signal.

The door swung open, revealing a bare concrete corridor. A lonely fly did loop-the-loops around a naked bulb. Two wary guards stood at the end, Uzis readied. Both had spliffs, thick as my thumb, dangling from the corner of their mouths. "Your weapons," the first guard ordered, pointing to a rusty metal box.

"Sure," I smiled. I surrendered the Chinese automatic I'd taken from the dead MSS guy. My knife was secured to my shin with medical tape, the suppressed Walther taped to the small of my back.

Swearing in Russian, Bytchakov also surrendered one of his many concealed weapons. We were escorted up a flight of stairs, to a plainly furnished office. It was cool inside, the only light coming from a window overlooking the sea. Sitting behind a desk was a gaunt African man in his early sixties. He wore the local business uniform of slacks and an untucked white shirt with short sleeves. His hair and carefully trimmed beard were grey, eyes hidden behind shades. Apart from the gold-and-diamond Rolex strapped to his wrist, he looked like an accountant. "I am Julius Adoyo," he said in perfect English. He smiled and stood up, shuffling to a drinks cabinet. He had a pronounced limp. "It isn't often we have the pleasure of Russian visitors in Zambute."

"I am Mikhail," I replied in the same language. "This is my associate, Sasha."

Adoyo produced a bottle of vodka and three glasses. "I believe this is customary in your country," he said pleasantly.

"Yes," I grunted, taking the drink and tossing it down my neck. "Thanks, this is good vodka." It really was. Smirnoff Black, no doubt from some unfortunate cargo ship.

"I speak Russian," said Adoyo in that language. "I learnt it at university in Volgograd, in the late seventies."

"Russian or English is fine by me," I replied.

"So, how can I help you gentlemen?" he smiled. He put his vodka down untouched and returned to his desk. He motioned at two faux-leather chairs and invited us to sit.

"We've been in Nairobi, looking for some people who owe my organisation money," I lied. "We know they crossed into Zambute."

"Then they are desperate," said Adoyo. "Why else would you seek refuge here?"

"They think we won't look for them here," I replied. "We asked around for a man who might help us find them. Your name was mentioned."

"Who gave you *my* name?" he said coolly.

I smiled, ignoring the question. "If you can help me, I can pay you a percentage of my finder's fee. I can also put some profitable business your way."

"What sort of business?" he replied.

"A business partner of mine wants to move thirty girls a month from Marsajir to Yemen. His clients enjoy beautiful young Zambutan women. Kenya is too well-policed and Somalia is impossible to work from. He is prepared to pay a fixed rate for safe passage from Afuuma to Aden."

"And where do these girls end up?" asked Adoyo politely.

"Massage parlours and brothels," I replied. "Very few in Russia, most go to Germany and Austria, where old pale men are prepared to pay extra for young, dark meat." I gave the creepiest smile I could muster.

Julius Adoyo nodded and looked out of the window. He sat and played with a string of prayer beads. "I might be able to help you," he said finally. "But first I would speak with your man who traffics girls."

"Of course," I replied. I put the satellite phone on the table in front of me. "I would expect the same."

"But first I would like an arrangement fee for my time," he smiled. "This is customary in Zambute."

I shrugged and pulled a wad of dollar bills from my pocket. "There's a thousand."

"Three thousand," he said flatly. "This isn't the Crimea. You don't hold any sway here."

"Two."

Adoyo smiled, "a deal, Mikhail." I pulled another wad of cash and placed both on the desk in front of him. He took the money, counted it and locked it in a drawer.

I punched a number into the phone, an old contact I hadn't seen since my last operation. It had taken an hour of frantic phone calls to find him, but when I did he was prepared to help. There was a condition, which I'd anticipated, that the favour would need to be returned. "This guy is a German," I said. "His name is Bernard." Bernard Schmidt, the people-trafficker who'd helped me take down The Hunt, knew it was better to have me as a friend than an enemy. We'd spoken the night before, to go through our story.

"Trust Bernie," he'd laughed. "I know the top three traffickers in Kenya and Tanzania." I didn't trust Bernie Schmidt, and never would. But he was all I had.

Adoyo took the offered satellite phone from me. I only caught one side of the conversation, which was in English. Adoyo asked about Bernie's contacts in Zambute and quizzed him about money and logistics. As good as his word, the German had the right answers. Finally Adoyo ended the call. "Your friend knows the right people, but his business is new to Zambute," he said. "Working here is more difficult than Nairobi or Dar-es-Salaam. I might be able to help. We will see."

"Excellent," I said. I helped myself to more vodka. "Mister Adoyo, now we need to speak of my other problem."

"Who are you looking for?"

"A young guy, Chinese-looking but really he's English," I said. "He is a con-man, a computer hacker. He has upset my organisation."

"I presume that was a stupid thing to do," said Adoyo.

"Very fucking stupid," Bytchakov replied.

"The British are the stupidest bastards," I shrugged. "They think the rest of the world plays by their idiotic fucking rules. This kid has ripped us off for twenty million dollars."

I saw Adoyo's snowy eyebrows appear above the rim of his shades. Everybody has got something that gives them a hard-on. I could tell that with Julius Adoyo it was the oldest aphrodisiac of them all. Money. "Mikhail, what is your fee for recovering this stolen money?"

"A million-and-a-half US Dollars," I shrugged. "I cut you into ten per cent of that when I have the kid. Not bad for a ten-minute meeting, eh?"

"You might need to do better than that," Adoyo purred. "I might have done business with this young man and made assurances concerning his safety."

I leant forward. "And you might need to be less fucking greedy, Mister Adoyo. I'm cutting you into a serious deal, just for giving up a name."

He thought about it for a moment then took off his sunglasses. One of his eyes was milky-white, the other golden brown. The effect was unsettling. "We have a deal," he said, offering his hand. I shook it. It was soft and warm, a hand that had never dug a ditch or laid a brick. He tightened his grip suddenly, fixing me with that dead white eye. "I learnt Russian at your KGB School for 'Progressive Elements.' This eye was lost under torture, when I was in the Zambutan Communist Party." I saw Bytchakov tense. Instruction for 'Progressive Elements' was old-school Soviet speak for terrorist training camps. President Aziz himself was a graduate of the KGB academy in Minsk. "So don't insult me, in my own office," he continued calmly. "If you try to fool me, or are even thinking of not paying me, you will never get out of Afuuma alive. Do you understand?"

"I understand," I said coolly in Russian. "But I would remind you, old man, to be a bit more respectful. I imagine we are all men with dirt under our fingernails."

"Personally," said Alex Bytchakov in his strangulated voice, going for an Oscar, "I'd welcome the chance to fight my way out of here and kill your pig-shit stupid guards." He produced his hidden pistol and slapped it on the desk. "If I was going to kill you, I'd have done it by now."

I took the satellite phone from the desk and pushed a button. "Mister Adoyo, our deal stands. Please tell me about the British guy and I won't call my associates on the other side of the road. They have an RPG aimed at this window. I'll walk out of here and you will die."

Adoyo shuffled to the slit in the concrete wall.

"They're in the Toyota pickup, do you see them?" I smiled.

The crook nodded and returned to his desk. "The British man calls himself John Moon, but he looks Chinese and speaks their language. He came to see me yesterday, asking for me to broker a meeting with a contact of mine. I also arranged safe passage out of Afuuma."

"Where does he want to go?" I asked.

"Sri Lanka, after that I do not know. He's paid me for his party to travel on a freighter carrying sugar to India. It is called *The Cleopatra*."

"Who was the contact he wanted to meet?" Alex asked.

Adoyo looked uneasy. "A man called Muxsin Ahmed, a Somali."

Alex Bytchakov slid his pistol back into his pocket, "and why is Muxsin Ahmed so important?"

"Ahmed is the most trusted *hawaladar* in Afuuma, possibly in Zambute," Adoyo replied. "The British man told me he needed a hawaladar. I simply pointed him in the right direction."

Bytchakov pulled a face, "what's a hawaladar?"

"A trust-banker," I said. "Hawala is Islamic trust-banking. You move money via intermediaries. There's no paperwork and no electronic transfer."

"Exactly," said Adoyo. "It is the most popular form of banking here, among the common people."

"And terrorists," I added. "Do you know how much money he wanted to move?"

"No, but it must be a large amount," said Adoyo. "Muxsin Ahmed said I would need never to pay for his services again. Muxsin is not a man known for his generosity."

"Does the trust-banking guy actually take possession the money?" said Alex.

"Of course," Adoyo replied. "He takes the total amount and deducts his commission. Then he instructs another hawaladar to pass that sum, or part of that sum, to the customer in another place. The hawaladars then recompense each other in kind. It might be in London or Paris or Moscow. Anywhere you find Muslims, you will find Hawala."

"Like a series of human ATMs, right?" Bytchakov shook his head, "it sounds crazy. All this just works on trust?"

"It's functioned perfectly well for a thousand years," Adoyo said. "If a hawaladar cheats a customer, he is finished. It is an incredibly safe way of moving assets, I use it myself."

"How do you contact Moon?" I said finally.

Adoyo reached inside his desk and produced a well-thumbed notebook. He tore out a page and pushed it towards me. "I understand he's staying in a villa on the coast road. It's called The Red House. I wouldn't waste your time, the ship is due soon."

I raised an eyebrow, "how soon?"

"This is Africa," he shrugged. "It could be could be tonight, it might be tomorrow."

I took the piece of paper. "I'll be back to pay you shortly."

"I look forward to it."

"In the meantime, call your guards and ask them to put their weapons on the floor," I smiled. "In case you decide to do something you might regret."

Adoyo picked up an old Bakelite telephone and muttered a few words of Swahili. "I take it our business is done?"

"For now," I nodded. I tucked the Walther in my waistband as I stood up. "We'll be in touch as soon as we've located John Moon."

Adoyo sneered dismissively, signalling for us to leave as he cursed under his breath.

I stood my ground. A real Russian Mafiosi wouldn't stand for the insult. "If I discover you've alerted the Englishman, I will return here and kill you. I will kill your family. I don't give a fuck about your local police, your Jihadis, your rebels or your piece-of-shit army. There's no roof here big enough to protect you. Do you understand?" I didn't know if my threats were part of the act or not.

"Go, Russian, and take your stink with you."

We left the office. The two guards stood outside on the landing. I motioned for them to put their weapons down again. I unloaded the Uzis and smiled as we trotted down the stairs. Alex covered them with his pistol as we left. I stepped out of the shadowy blockhouse. Ruben joined us and hailed a taxi. Now I had a location for Hugo and the name of an Islamic trust banker. The SIS report told me Hugo had tried to hack the Zambutan regime's personal bank accounts. Although I didn't have a deerstalker hat and a magnifying glass, I thought I'd figured it out.

Hugo Jackson was the Bad Apple. He'd figured out a way of stealing money from the regime. Now he was trying to move it out of Zambute via the hawaladar, an untraceable method favoured by terrorists. He was the guy who had created the computer modelling for our mission, and whose technical expertise equalled Brodie's. It was Hugo who'd sold us out to the Chinese, probably using Zhang Ki as an intermediary.

What I needed to know was what he'd done with the rest of his team, and how. Was he ruthless enough to kill his colleagues, incur the wrath of MI6? And where did Murray fit in? Maybe there was an explanation for the communications data implicating Easter…

But, sadly, it looked like Duclair and Brodie were right. I wondered if their bodies lay somewhere in the desert, like Steve Bacon and Idris. I pulled the sat phone from my pocket and keyed a message to Marcus: HUGO IS MY BAD APPLE / MOTIVE – THEFT OF ZAMBUTAN ASSETS / STAND BY.

I hoped it was enough to keep the Fallen Eagle from taking flight. The satellite phone burned in my hand. It was my life line and death warrant, the electronic scent that the Predator would sniff. In the end I decided to keep it, another chip in the poker game I was playing with The Firm.

The taxi dropped us near the market. We ran a counter-surveillance route back to the hotel and met in my room. I briefed the others on what Adoyo had told me. "Hugo?" said Oz, shaking his head. "It's always the quiet ones."

"Let me do it," Ruben snarled. "I'll get the fucker to talk."

I looked at the wiry Londoner, into his hate-filled eyes. If I let him loose on Hugo, there was only one way the story would end. Raphael Grey died in a hail of cannon fire, in an ambush set up by the bad apple. I'd watched him ripped to pieces like a sack of meat. This wasn't a game, something I suspected Hugo had yet to find out. "Yes, Ruben," I said grimly. "He's all yours."

CHAPTER TWENTY SIX

"Cops," Ruben hissed, standing watch at the bedroom window. Two canvas-sided trucks chugged to a halt in the town square, disgorging armed men. They formed a line in front of the hotel. A Land Rover pulled up next to the trucks, and two men in smart blue-grey uniforms and sunglasses stepped out. They wore the red shoulder-boards of the despised Zambutan security police. The locals began to melt away. A tinny radio playing local music stopped. In the distance a dog whined.

"All we need now is Clint Eastwood on a horse," said Oz.

"That sonofabitch Adoyo," growled Bytchakov, "he must've given us up."

"Could have been anybody, I reckon," Oz shrugged. "This town must be full of grasses."

"*Grasses*?" said the American. "For the love of sweet Jesus, Oz, speak English. I'm never working with Brits again. You need a fucking translator."

"Snitches," I translated. "Duncan, get the Toyota and wait around the back."

"Roger," he replied, shrugging on his Bergen, sword strapped to the side.

"I've got the first floor landing," said Ruben, snatching his G36. We had a bug-out plan, Ruben holding our floor while Bannerman cleared reception and got the wagon fired up. I watched as the security police barked orders, cops splitting into two groups. One headed towards us, the other fanning out towards the back of the building. They were armed with a variety of rifles and shotguns. "Aw, fuck it," spat Bytchakov, shouldering his AK.

"No," I snapped. "We've got civilians down there." Although the locals had kept their heads down, a full-scale gunfight in the square might still cause casualties. In my world there are two groups of people – those who've chosen to step into the arena and those who haven't. You pick up a gun? You've stepped in. You've done something so bad I'm knocking on your door? You've stepped in. But civilians are off limits, at least in my book. And people who harm them, they step into the arena too. That was another rule I'd set myself, one I'd not heeded as resolutely in the past. That changed, right now.

Bytchakov's nostrils flared as he lowered his AK. "I'll see you out back."

Oz gathered up our remaining weapons and slung his pack over his shoulder, "let's get out of here."

I was still wearing my Russian gangster outfit: shiny grey suit from the market, a black polo shirt and pointy shoes. Tucking the Walther in my waistband, I pocketed a smoke grenade and the satellite phone. I trotted down the staircase, the others already in reception and heading for the back exit. Ibrahim and his daughter were standing behind the scuffed front counter. The old man's face was defiant, an ancient bolt-action rifle held in front of him. "Get out of here," I ordered.

"No!" He replied. "This is my hotel."

Tears rolled down Fathiya's cheek. "Father, please…"

The first security policeman strode towards the front door. He looked confident, head held high. This was his turf.

Raising my Walther, I fired twice, into his face. "Get out of here," I barked. Fathiya shoved her father into the corridor. The second security policeman hit the deck, pistol in hand. My Walther coughed again, a khaki-uniformed paramilitary spinning as the bullet ripped through his throat. Tossing the smoke grenade, I leapt behind the counter as incoming rounds rang out. I crawled on my belly, following Ibrahim, who now understood the sense of urgency. Chemical-stinking smoke swirled around us as I pulled myself to my feet and helped the two Zambutans to the rear exit.

Ruben Grey was crouched in the doorway as we approached, the black snout of his assault rifle pointing over my shoulder. Looking back towards the hotel reception, I saw nothing but smoke. The cops were shouting at each other, coughing as they advanced. They were taking their time, expecting an ambush.

I wasn't going to disappoint.

The back of the hotel was a dusty yard, surrounded on two sides by a crumbling brick wall. A couple of battered cars and our truck were parked near the exit. Bannerman gunned the engine, Bytchakov sitting next to him. "Go," said Ruben to Ibrahim and his daughter. We bundled them into the pick-up, covered them with blankets and equipment. Ruben was climbing in when the first Zambutan cop stepped around the corner, pump-gun ready. The gunfire from my team was instant and overwhelming, a torrent of bullets from the belt-fed MG4 and Kalashnikovs tearing across the wall. The cop disappeared in a cloud of gore and brick dust. Hearing footsteps and barked orders, I stalked towards the exit to provide cover. "Move!" Ruben shouted, smacking the roof of the cab with his free hand.

"I'll cover you, RV at a safe position near the Red House," I shouted to Bytchakov in Russian. Many Zambutans spoke English, and I didn't want to advertise.

"Copy that," yelled Bytchakov, "you take care, OK?" This wasn't the movies, where your mates beg you to get out while you can. I was big enough and ugly enough to make the call, and the men respected it.

The Toyota motored out of the yard, into the fetid backstreets of Afuuma. Slamming the fire door closed, I hurled myself at the wall nearest me and scrambled over, Walther ready. Two security policemen peered around the corner, earning each of them a bullet in the head. Bullets chasing me, I vaulted the car park wall and dropped into an alleyway. My choice was to head south back into the square, or north into the back-streets.

I heard a shotgun blast, then the crash of the door coming off its hinges. I ran north. After twenty metres the path petered out into a baked-mud track. Locals watched sullenly from doorways, tinny music drifting from shacks and lean-tos. I ducked as I heard another shotgun blast, buckshot peppering a nearby wall. I returned fire. Two cops disappeared into cover, back towards the hotel.

I fired two more shots and ran, the labyrinthine backstreets swallowing me. I turned left then right, racing through shady alleyways and dusty, narrow streets. People eyed me warily, a hefty white guy in a crumpled suit. I patted my pocket, checking the precious satellite phone was still there. Finally, I emerged into a larger thoroughfare, maybe a couple of hundred yards north of the souk. I heard gunfire and shouting in the distance, a battered police car trying to force its way past livestock and taxis. Vehicle horns blared, goats bleated, the stink of animals and raw sewage in my nose.

"Over here," called a familiar voice. "Nice shoes, by the way." The Aussie journalist, Mike Turpin, sat in the front of an old Mercedes with bright orange paintwork. The universal word TAXI was painted across the bonnet. A powerfully-built Zambutan glowered from behind the wheel.

"Cheers, Mike," I replied, hopping into the back of the car.

"You seem to have upset the security police," the journalist chuckled. "Luckily, that'll make you more friends than enemies around here."

"Doesn't feel like it at the moment."

"Meet Xaashi," Turpin replied, the Merc accelerating deeper into the back streets. "He's my stringer in Afuuma." Turpin tossed a baseball hat at me. I nodded my thanks and pulled the peak low over my eyes.

"*Jambo*," said the big Zambutan gruffly. He was eighteen stone of glistening ebony muscle, topped by a strangely small head with bulging, manic-looking eyes. He wore a string vest and tracksuit pants, a crucifix dangling at his throat. "Is this story, the one you tell Mike about the mine, true?"

"Yes," I replied. "I saw it with my own eyes."

Xaashi studied me in the rear view mirror. "There is someone you must meet." It sounded too much like a demand for my liking.

"I'm sorry," I said. "Mike…"

The journalist shrugged. "Xaashi has family working at the mine. The BBC took the story, its big news. People are getting worried about their missing relatives."

"I've got to get to the Red House, on the Via Roma."

Xaashi slammed on the brakes, eyes flashing with anger. "This is not a game, Englishman. My brother's nephew ran away last year. The last thing we hear, he is working in Buur Xuuq. Speak with him and answer his questions. *Then* we take you to the Red House." A police car chugged by, the cop's eyes scanning the sidewalks. I hunkered down in the back of the Mercedes. "It is dangerous north of here," the Zambutan continued. He nodded at the cop and shouted something in Swahili. The cop laughed and drove on. "The Jihadist's use the roads as a short cut to Kismayo."

"I can only tell your brother what you can already see on the video," I replied.

Xaashi drove deeper into the old town. "Do you have children, Englishman?"

"No," I said.

"That explains it," he grunted.

"He wants five minutes of your time," said Turpin. "I'll promise you'll make it to where you need to go. Like Xaashi says, the further north you travel the more chance you've got of bumping into those Shadow of Swords bastards."

"The Jihadis are worse than Aziz," nodded Xaashi, shadowy streets flashing by.

We drove for another five minutes. Now the shooting had stopped, people were emerging from their homes. "Seriously," the Australian replied, "Xaashi's older brother is the head of his family, one of the big clans. They've stayed neutral up until now. But this incident at Buur Xuuq…"

"My family will make Afuuma ungovernable," spat the big Zambutan, hammering a fist on the steering wheel. "Fuck Aziz."

"What about Julius Adoyo?" I said.

Xaashi laughed. "Julius Adoyo? That piece of shit is only safe because he is Aziz's kin. He does not worry me, the one-eyed goat-fucker."

We drove on, bumping across winding dirt roads. I was now completely lost, any attempt to orientate myself to the old town's geography doomed. "Here we are," said Turpin. The house was studded with laundry-fluttering balconies, another peeling Italianate pile marooned between two brutalist apartment blocks. A fleet of battered cars and trucks were parked outside, a young kid with a rifle keeping an eye on them. I smelt cooking on the wind, something spicy-sweet and meaty. My stomach rumbled.

"Follow me," said Xaashi, folding his bulk out of the Mercedes. He went to the boot and took out a canvas bag containing fruit, meat and a stubby AKS carbine.

"Everybody carries guns here," shrugged Turpin.

"Yes, we need to protect ourselves from the police," Xaashi smiled. He pointed at the Walther tucked in my belt. "It would be better if you gave that to me. I will return it, of course." I nodded, cleared the weapon and handed it over.

The house was dark and cool, plainly furnished and spotlessly clean. I was led to a yard where a group of men were holding a meeting. They were drinking coffee, chewing *Khat* and clearly unhappy. The mood seemed tense, conversation a low growl. If there were any women in the house, I couldn't see them. All of the men carried weapons, bandoliers of ammunition around their chests.

Xaashi said something in Swahili and a tall, pot-bellied man wearing dark clothing stood up. He embraced Turpin, whispering something in the Australian's ear. The Zambutan had narrow, almost oriental, eyes and skin the colour of teak.

His hair was a glossy mop of oiled ringlets. He nodded at me and smiled, showing crooked but gleaming white teeth. "I am Cawaale Warfa," he said, offering his hand. "Welcome to our home, please, have coffee with us." Cawaale snapped his fingers and a young boy brought drinks. I gulped the coffee, the boy pouring more. It was delicious, thick and sweet. "I apologise if Xaashi was rude to you, or if bringing you here was inconvenient," said the Zambutan, his English excellent and precise. "He is known as *The Bull* in my family."

The other men laughed, Xaashi proving the point by snorting and stomping off. He arrived at a large steel urn and poured himself a brew. "The Warfa's are the oldest clan in Afuuma," Turpin explained. "They own the market and the fishery here."

"We are Somali-Zambutans," said Cawaale, nodding. "We are not Zambutan-Kenyan, so we are hated by the government."

"We are survivors," shrugged Xaashi.

Cawaale nodded. "I will get to the point. My nephew, Idris, is a difficult boy. He is from my wife's side of the family, and they are crazy." A number of the men who understood English nodded and mumbled in agreement. "He was going to work in the market, learn how to be a trader like his father," Cawaale continued, "but he ran away. He got mixed up with a bad crowd, drinking whisky and smoking too much *bangi*. The last news my wife had of him, he had taken work at Buur Xuuq, to pay back his debts."

"We want to know if he is dead," said Xaashi bluntly.

"My sister has to know," agreed Cawaale matter-of-factly. "He is her favourite."

One of the men began to wail when the boy's possible death was mentioned. The others patted his back until he was quiet. "I can only tell you many kids died in the mine," I said. "Maybe fifty or so, but the army officer we captured said his men set the others free. Even they seemed unhappy at what happened."

"And the army officers and the Chinese engineers?" he asked.

"All dead," I replied. "The rebels made sure of that."

"That is only proper," Cawaale nodded. "I have seen this video, but I did not see my nephew. Maybe he is in the countryside."

"He might have joined the rebels," said Xaashi hopefully.

"I was with one of Abasi's men at the mine, a rebel officer called Tony Ismael. He's Anglo-Zambutan, a good man. If you can get word to him, he'll ask around."

Cawaale said something in Swahili. Two of the men nodded respectfully before leaving the room. "I tell them to speak with someone close to General Abasi," he explained. "I have decided to support the rebels. We will help drive Aziz's men out of Afuuma." There was nothing triumphant in his words, just sad resignation.

"Good," said Xaashi. "I've seen bad things over the years, but letting those bastards dynamite children like that?"

Cawaale nodded at his brother's words and gripped my hand. "I thank you for coming to speak with me," he said gravely. "There is nothing more you can do. Please understand that before I make a decision like this, I needed to speak with a witness."

"I understand," I said. And I did. As far as I was concerned, my country had gone to war on flimsier evidence than Cawaale Warfa had asked for.

"Good," he replied. "Now, you wish to travel north on the Via Roma?"

I explained that I wanted to meet my friends near the villa known as The Red House.

"This can be dangerous, I'm sure you've heard about the Jihadis," Cawaale said. "Xaashi will take you with one of my cousins here." He said a few words in Swahili and one of the men stood up, slinging a heavy black rifle.

"Yes," Xaashi replied, looking at his watch. "Let's go."

"Thanks Mike," I said to the journalist.

"Hey, thank you," he replied, a knowing smile on his lips. "I might see you around."

"Not if I see you first." The kid who was watching the cars burst into the room, rifle slung across his chest. He was shouting excitedly in Swahili, the other men swarming around him. "What is it?" I asked Mike.

"The Presidential Commando 2nd Regiment is here, to reinforce the army," he translated. "The kid says there are hundreds of them, and they've brought tanks. The 2nd Regiment is Aziz's own bodyguard, an elite unit."

"What about the rebels?"

The journalist smiled, "Abasi's forces have been reinforced in the south, are advancing on Afuuma. I'd better get down there."

I looked Mike up-and-down, taking in his scruffy suit and cowboy boots. "You're going to war like that?" I said.

"Sure I am. Look at yourself, mate," he laughed. "You're the one dressed up like you wandered off the set of *Miami Vice*."

"This is no time for jokes," grunted Xaashi, grabbing my upper arm and steering me towards the door. "We will take you to the Red House."

"Sounds safer than here," I replied.

The Zambutan's laugh was bitter. "If you think heading north is any safer than going south, then you are an even bigger fool than you look."

I heard the crump of shells as I was bundled into the Mercedes.

The war had reached Afuuma.

CHAPTER TWENTY SEVEN

Xaashi drove fast, car suspension groaning in protest on the pot-holed highway. Black smoke billowed from the docks, tinged with flame. "That's the rebels?" I asked.

"Yes, they have sympathisers in Afuuma, people willing to, how do you say in English? *Make sabotage.*" Then we were speeding along the Via Roma, the road crossing orange-tinted desert. To the east, the Indian Ocean glittered under a late afternoon sun. Army trucks and APCs trundled south, carrying soldiers of the Presidential Commando. They wore red berets and pristine combat uniforms, weapons modern and well-maintained. They looked battle-seasoned and dangerous, not like the men we'd fought at the bridge. They ignored the battered taxi. "Bastards," Xaashi hissed. We left the highway, onto a pitted track. "The Red House is another two miles," he said. "It used to be the compound of a pirate, a Somali. He was killed by the Americans. They said he was with the Shadow of Swords or Al-Shabaab."

"Who lives there now?"

"Nobody, the place is abandoned. To live there is to invite bandits, bastards like the Xaboyo."

I remembered the Xaboyo tribesman we'd shot out near Buur Xuuq, the mercenaries Tony Ismael described. The Xaboyo scout didn't strike me as especially fearsome, but I wouldn't want to fight a battalion of them on their home ground. I saw a long line of spiky trees, fringing dead ground between a series of baked earth hillocks. It's where I'd have hidden if I were establishing a secure RV. "Is the terrain like this all the way to the Red House?" I asked.

"No, it is barren beyond this point. There used to be fields and an orchard, now it is just dead land."

"Pull over," I said. Opening the car door, I walked to the side of the road and waved.

Alex Bytchakov emerged from the bushes nearby, expertly camouflaged with foliage. A smile split his dusty, craggy face. "These are my people," I explained to Xaashi.

"The others are nearby," Bytchakov reported. "We've run recon."

"I'll be OK now," I said to Xaashi. "Thanks for your help. I hope your brother finds the kid."

The Zambutan grunted in acknowledgement. I peeled off a wad of banknotes and passed it to him. "No, I do not take your money," he replied gruffly. "My brother told me to do you a favour. Any debt was paid when you agreed to meet him."

I nodded respectfully. He turned the car and headed back towards Afuuma. "Who the hell was he?" asked Bytchakov.

I explained about my visit to the Warfa clan and the army advancing on Afuuma. "We're well out of it," I said.

The American led me through the trees, to a shady gully. Oz, Bannerman and Ruben were sitting in the shade, brewing tea. They wore a mixture of fatigues and civilian clothes under their body armour. I felt glad to be back with them and began to relax. "I thought it was a cliché, you Brits and the tea thing," Bytchakov chuckled.

"Have they got you drinking tea yet?" I asked.

"Hey, I'm half-Russian, I love green tea. Just not that milky shit you guys drink."

"Ah, Steve-fucking-McQueen returns," said Bannerman. "You made it over the Swiss border, then?" Oz laughed and emptied sugar into his steel mug of tea. Banter was a sign of good morale, although I was sure Bannerman would crack jokes stood in front of a firing squad. Ruben was still quiet, sharpening a combat knife with a whetstone.

"You found your way here OK then?" I said.

"None of us are officers," Bannerman shrugged. "So we can read a map."

Oz explained they'd dropped Ibrahim and his daughter in the old town before escaping. Ruben had mysteriously found ten thousand dollars in his kit, which he gave them for their trouble. They encountered no police and were given directions to the Via Roma by friendly locals, who'd no love for the paramilitary police. "We used the micro-drone to recce the Red House when we arrived," Oz continued. "Then I went for a look myself."

"First things first," I said. "Please tell me you brought my stuff." I looked down at my tragic shoes, which pinched my feet. To corrupt Woody Allen's old dictum, *Hell's fine as long as you've got the right footwear.* The guys laughed and pointed at my assault pack. Inside were my precious Lowa boots and fatigue pants. I changed, strapping on my belt kit and zipping a dusty windcheater over my polo shirt and body armour. Sipping tea, Bytchakov passed me an energy bar, which I wolfed down in two bites. I had a brew, some calories and comfortable boots. Happy with these luxuries, I sat on my pack, using it as a cushion.

Oz drew a map in the earth with a stick. "It's an old villa, three floors with some crappy old sheds and out-buildings to the rear. There's a compound to the front, with a three metre wall. That's old mud-brick, covered in plaster. The villa itself is sort of *Arabian Nights*, you know, domes and stuff with satellite dishes on the roof."

"What about the enemy?" I asked.

"We've seen at least six gunmen cutting about on the plot. They spend most of their time smoking spliff and lazing about in front of the villa."

"No sign of Hugo?" I asked. "Are there any vehicles?"

Bannerman pointed at the sketch, towards the furthermost point of the building. "We've seen at least one person in civvy clothing, they look European but the imagery on the drone is'nae good enough to confirm ID. There are some pick-ups parked in the compound and a jetty to the side of the building. I saw a couple of wee boats at the end of it."

Ruben looked up from his shadowy perch, combat blade gleaming. "We ain't got time to wait for dark," he growled. "Let's slot the locals and get in there, do the business and go home."

He may have been motivated by revenge, but he had a point. I'd learnt the hard way that an average plan executed with aggression and speed is better than a complex plan carried out slowly. The philosophy served me well on The Firm, where we were used to being dropped in the shit and expected to make the most of it. "Oz, what do you think?"

"The walls at the western apex of the building line are weak as fuck, held together with chicken wire and baked mud," he nodded. "I say Alex pulls sniper duty again to keep the guards busy. Meanwhile we ram the wall with the Toyota, win the fire fight then time for tea and medals."

"Shock an' fuckin' awe," Bannerman grinned. He unsheathed the Claymore, the double-edged fighting blade gleaming. "It's about time this beauty saw some action."

Bytchakov shook his head and cackled, "Jesus, Bannerman, you crack me up."

"I'm serious, 'tis the weapon of my forefathers."

"I thought that was the head-butt," Ruben sniped. Banter is like a morale gauge. As long as the men were trash-talking, we were fine. I'd start worrying when they stopped. We readied our weapons and kit until we were happy to go. The only issue was ammunition: I only had four full magazines for the AK, and three for my Walther. We had one grenade each.

"Five bombed-up magazines," said Bannerman, making his G36 ready.

"Four," shrugged Ruben.

"Ditto," said Oz.

"Twelve," said Bytchakov, sharing out his spares, "American ingenuity in action."

"More than I had on the start line in Iraq," I shrugged. I climbed into the driver's seat, gunning the Toyota up onto the track leading to the villa. We drove slowly for a mile, peering into the distance until the domed roof of the villa appeared on the horizon. The Red House was painted in a dark ochre colour, like dried blood. Looking for cover, we drove along a series of sun-baked irrigation channels, stopping a hundred metres from the gate. I parked in the shade of a gnarled tree, providing some cover from the spiteful sun. Bannerman wiped sweat from his face with a forearm. Even though we were only an hour from dusk, we steamed inside our body armour. The gentle ocean breeze was gone. Smoke curled from a fire from somewhere inside the compound.

In the back of the Toyota Ruben crouched, like a pit-bull straining at its leash. "Come on," he hissed.

"Cool it," I said, keying the mic on my PRR. "Alex we're ready when you are."

"Listen to Cal," Oz agreed. "We'll make it right for Raph, OK?"

"OK," said an American accent over our PRR net, "let's get this party started." Our heads whipped around as we heard the familiar *whoosh* as Bytchakov opened fire with the RPG. A shimmering flash erupted along the first floor balcony of the Red House, a vortex of crumbling masonry and smoke. A ribbon of smoke curled along the domed roof.

"Go!" Oz barked. I gunned the Toyota's engine. Bannerman saw movement to our right and opened fire, single shots whipping across the top of the walls. Ruben joined in, both G36s spitting fire. A ragged figure standing on a balcony spun out of sight. "There," said Oz, pointing to the apex of the walls. As he'd described, they were badly in need of repair. Wire and wattle-and-daub had been slapped on to keep them intact, ossified mortar crumbling from jagged gaps in the masonry.

Aiming the Toyota like a battering ram, I braced myself for impact. In the back, Bannerman and Ruben curled up on the deck of the old truck. The truck smashed into the wall, the dull smack of metal-on-stone ringing in my ears. The force of the collision snaked from the steering wheel and along my arms, like an electric shock. Then we were inside the compound, debris from the wall in our hair and at our feet.

"Move," said Oz calmly, hopping out of the shattered truck as bullets zinged off the bodywork. The wall had crumbled low enough to scramble over but provide cover. The front wheels of the truck were perched on a pile of rubble, engine fluid pissing from the engine. More incoming rounds splashed against the chassis. Oz stalked across the compound, Bannerman close behind. Both opened fire, calmly putting down aimed shots at unseen enemy shooters.

"I'm with you," said Ruben, weapon shouldered. I accelerated forward, the truck's belly-plate groaning as it scraped over the rubble. Ten metres from the front door, the engine finally died. Looking into the compound, Oz gave a signal for us to move. Darting towards the Red House, I saw three bodies splayed on the packed-dirt floor. Another ran towards a pair of ornate double doors at the front of the villa. Ruben fired a burst, the shooter falling to his knees. I aimed and fired a single shot from my AK, the bullet blasting through his ribcage. His twitching body rolled into a blood-soaked ball.

"No shoot!" said a heavily-accented voice from the doorway. A wiry Somali appeared, wearing a long grey cloak and sandals. He looked shit-scared.

"Down, on the floor," I barked in Arabic, "*Lasfl 'ela alard!*" The Somali hit the deck. Ruben covered me as I search him, Oz and Bannerman taking position at the doors to the villa. The guy was unarmed, an abandoned AK lying in the doorway. Patting him down, I took two spare magazines and stuffed them in my pockets.

"Sorry mate," Ruben shrugged. He smacked the Somali on the side of the head with his rifle butt, knocking him unconscious.

"Come out," shouted Oz into the villa. "Before the grenades go in."

"It's OK," called a shaky voice. It was Hugo Jackson. "I'm OK, come in. Thank god you've arrived."

"Let me do the talking," I said. "And Ruben, cool it and wait for my signal."

"Yes *Captain*," he glowered. We ducked into the hall and advanced upstairs, onto a landing with marble floors. Another of the guards was curled up in a corner, lying in a glistening pool of blood where the RPG had struck. I gestured for Oz and Bannerman to cover the stairs while Ruben and I walked towards a cavernous room overlooking the sea. It was empty apart from some camping equipment, a breeze gusting through broken windows.

Then movement in a deep swathe of shadow. Hugo Jackson, sitting on a rickety wooden chair, head in hands. He looked in good shape to me, wearing clean outdoor clothes and new-looking boots. At his feet lay a laptop computer and a satellite phone. "We were taken hostage," he said, looking up.

"You look in pretty good shape for a hostage," I replied. "Are you armed?" He shook his head. His usual friendly demeanour had gone, replaced with naked suspicion. I nodded at Ruben, who covered Hugo while I patted the SIS man down. A P-226 was tucked in his waistband. I pocketed the pistol, "funny bit of kit for a hostage."

"My brother was killed, Hugo, because you're a fucking wrong 'un," said Ruben. His voice was raspy, laden with menace. Hugo's face was a mask, eyes focussed on an imaginary point on the far wall. He said nothing. Ruben's voice was larded with scorn. "Oh, you've had counter-interrogation training? What a load of bollocks. Do you think I'm going to shout at you or just give you a slap? Or put you into a stress position, play you white noise?" A strained noise came from Hugo's mouth, the SIS officer drinking up the malice in the ex-marine's eyes. "No," Ruben continued, "I'm going to *peel* you. I'm going to cut your lips off, and your ears and your nose and your fucking *eyelids*." He pulled his double-edged fighting knife from its scabbard, the matte blade gleaming dully.

Hugo started rocking on the crappy wooden chair. It looked like it might collapse. He gazed at me, eyes wide and wet. "Are you looking at *me* for help?" I said quietly. "Tough shit, son, you rolled the dice."

"And you lost, Hugo," Ruben smiled. "Do you know what a sky burial is?"

"Yes," Hugo replied, lip quivering.

"Tell me, college boy," Ruben smiled. "Impress us with your knowledge."

"It's the practice of leaving dead bodies in high places instead of burying them. They used to do it in parts of Mongolia and Tibet. They let the birds and elements pick the body clean."

"Very good, Hugo," Ruben replied, clapping softly. "Bedouins used to do it to Legionnaires, too. Well, that's what I'm going to do with you, except I ain't gonna wait for you to die. I'm going to *peel* you like an orange. Then I'll peg you out on that cliff. The fucking vultures and jackals and insects can eat you alive. It might take them a couple of days."

"Given what you've done, Hugo, I reckon that's generous," I said. "Betraying your team, and my men, for what?"

"Guys, you don't understand," he whispered, tears tracking down his cheeks. "You just don't see the whole-bloody-picture."

"Where's Murray?" I said.

"Murray is alive," he replied. "We were betrayed by Easter, I swear…"

I squatted on my knees, inches from Hugo's face. "Educate me," I said. "You need to understand, Ruben wants to kill the person who betrayed his brother. If someone else did it, then you need to tell us. It's the only way you can save your life…" I knew he'd want a crumb of comfort now, a tiny sliver of hope. He glared at me, trying to take it all in.

"I'm going to need some persuading," Ruben nodded. He ran the tip of the blade across Hugo's cheek, drawing blood. "I think it was you, I can *feel* it."

Hugo's teeth chattered, a hiss of fear escaping his lips. "Oh my fucking god," he said finally. And he told us his story, teeth chattering and crotch wet where he'd pissed himself. "I worked out that Easter was talking to the MSS before the first operation failed, the one we codenamed STOWAGE. She was taking money from the Chinese, her contact was a Chinese marine Colonel called Zhang. He was an MSS asset, working undercover in the military."

"And how did you know all this?"

"I hacked Brodie's network security. That enabled me to trace Easter's satellite comms. She'd been calling into Zambute, the pattern of comms just looked wrong. Then it was just a matter of intercepting the telephone calls, which took a while…"

"Spare me the technical details," I said, looking pointedly at Ruben's knife. "Tell me what happened back at the prison."

"Zhang Ki turned out to be a freelancer, he wanted out of China. He's just a thief," he said. "I had no idea he'd order his men to attack us."

"Why didn't you tell anyone?" I said. "Why didn't you report Easter?"

"I was going to," he replied. "I knew Amelia was suspicious of her, as was Brodie." He sniffed bloody snot, shivering despite the heat. "But after the second job, I realised we had an ideal opportunity to steal the Zambutan government's slush fund. Easter had compromised the operation, and the cash disappeared. I put it to Easter, told her I knew about her treachery but we could share the money if she was up for it."

"So it *is* your fault," snapped Ruben.

"No, you don't understand," he cried. "Zhang Ki was involved in the theft too. Easter roped him into it. I told Easter that after the money was transferred out of Switzerland, it was stored at the same prison Murray was held in. It was an amazing opportunity: we could kill two birds with one stone. But the plan was Easter's and the Chinese ambush must have been her idea."

"That's convenient," I snapped. "So you were just following orders?"

"Yes, for Christ's sake!" Hugo gasped. "*She* cooked up the idea about the Chinese electronic warfare kit as a pretext to getting me into the prison, so I could hack the security system and take the money. That's why you didn't get to see all the plans and learn there was a vault down there…"

"So you were blackmailing her?"

"Exactly," he said hopefully. "I know my hands aren't clean, but I swear I had no idea she planned to double-cross me too.

I got too big for my boots, I realise that now. I'm just the technical guy."

"That doesn't explain why you're still here, trying to employ a hawaladar," I smiled. "We know you were negotiating with one."

Hugo's eyes widened, caught in a lie. "I've got my share," he said desperately, his voice slipping into a near-babble. "We split up. I wanted nothing else to do with her, and it was the perfect way to move my cash. It's totally untraceable."

"And where are the rest of the team?"

"Easter and Zhang took them hostage."

Hugo might have been able to hack a Swiss bank, but he was a poor liar. "What about the cargo ship you've chartered via Julius Adoyo, *The Cleopatra*? You've asked for, what, six berths?"

"Jesus, you're full of shit," Ruben spat. The knife flashed. A quivering chunk of flesh flopped wetly to the floor.

"My ear…" Hugo cried, clamping a hand to the side of his head.

"Cal," said Oz, striding into the room. "You've gotta come and see this…"

CHAPTER TWENTY EIGHT

I left Hugo with Bytchakov. The SIS man sobbed and clutched the side of his head, realising he was now doing a passable impression of Vincent Van Gogh. Oz led me and Ruben into a master bedroom. The domed ceiling had been painted with now-faded frescoes of palm trees. Snakes and lions crept through them, looking for prey.

"Here," said Bannerman, letting out a whistle. "Look at this, it's Christmas, Hogmanay and ma fucking birthday all in one." It was the canvass sacks we'd seen the spooks take from the bowels of the prison.

"Jesus Christ," I said.

"Fuck me," Ruben Grey gasped.

"That's a lot of sweets and Airfix kits," Oz laughed. The first bag was stuffed with glossy green blocks of vacuum-packed bank notes, US dollars, UK Sterling and Euros. The second contained more cash, plus velvet-covered stacks of jewellery boxes. Oz opened several, treasure spilling out onto the floor like a dragon's horde. "I bet these aren't chocolate," he smiled, picking up a gold coin the size of a saucer.

The last bag contained pressurised specialist art containers. I spotted a Renoir, Orthodox icons and a couple of Old Masters, as well as sickly yellow blocks of a resinous substance. A rogue Faberge egg rolled on the floor, golden filigree glinting invitingly. "What are those?" I said, nudging the jelly-like blocks with my toecap.

"That's what I was thinking," said Bannerman, crouching down and picking one up. It wobbled slightly, like rubber. "See inside there?" he continued, pointing at some glittering objects entombed in resin.

"Fuck me, these are diamonds," said Ruben Grey, running an expert eye over the loot. "You don't get shit like this knocking off your local H. Samuel with a sawn-off. These are all at least fifty-point stones, uncut."

The gold glittered in the shadowy light. We'd all heard about conflict diamonds, the forbidden fruit of Africa's vast natural resources. "How much do you reckon?" I asked.

"I dunno," Ruben replied, "but there's a fair few million here, less laundering fees. Those sit at thirty to forty per cent, last time I checked. Jesus, I never thought that plum Hugo had it in him."

"Well, the only question is how we get this loot out of here so we can retire," Bannerman grinned. "I fancy somewhere extradition-lite, with hot and cold running lap-dancers."

He had a point. "Sure, Duncan, after we find Murray and Easter."

"What?" He snapped.

"Listen to Cal," said Oz. "Now ain't the time to get gold-fever. The last thing we need is The Firm after us – you wouldn't live long enough to enjoy the dough."

I wasn't so sure about that, but now wasn't the time. The money would make a mighty war chest for the day I planned on taking the bastards on.

Duncan Bannerman pulled a face, teeth bared like a cornered wolf. He knew we were right, but was too proud to admit it. "I suppose I'll follow orders for a change," he sulked, jabbing a finger at the sacks. "But I want my share."

"You will," I said. "When we get Easter's location from Hugo we'll…"

A burst of gunfire riddled the room, masonry and plaster chopped to pieces by high calibre rounds. Bannerman groaned as he was thrown on his back. I rolled to the floor, bullets blasted more holes in the wall, like a devilish power-tool. Downstairs, I heard return fire, Bytchakov's weapon chattering in reply. "I've got him," shouted Ruben, crawling towards Bannerman.

"On me," I yelled. We scurried from the room, onto the balcony overlooking the hall. A group of grey-hooded men were hurrying up the stairs, weapons ready. They, like the other guards, looked Somali. Oz and I opened fire, hosing the hall with bullets. Two men crumpled and fell, the others ducking back into cover. The muzzle of a rifle popped into view and spat fire. The stairway was a maelstrom of gun-smoke, muzzle flash and hot brass. An injured gunman scrabbled on the ground, our bullets punching bloody gobbets of meat from his body. He twitched like an electrocuted man as he died. More men flooded into view, firing wildly.

I hit the deck. Squinting through the iron sights of my AK, I exhaled and squeezed the trigger, a stream of bullets stitching across the hallway below. I flinched at the volley of return fire, splinters of glass and plaster peppering my face. On the balcony to my right, Oz continued to fire, face calm. It was like watching a robot with a Kalashnikov attached, the ex-SBS man coolly hosing fire into the hall.

I climbed out of cover, the stairwell littered with bodies. Taking the stairs two at a time, I ducked into a small room on the ground floor. I snatched up an RPG from a dead fighter, the bulbous green rocket ready to fire. Glancing out of the window, I saw two rusty pick-ups screech to a halt outside. One of the pick-ups had a recoilless rifle mounted on the flat-bed, a machinegun fitted in front of the passenger seat. The pick-ups were crudely camouflaged in muddy hues, black flags decorated with Arabic lettering fluttering from the aerials.

It was The Shadow of Swords.

I grimaced, imagining a suicide truck or solo bomber wearing a Semtex waistcoat rushing us. I had no doubt they'd think nothing of levelling the villa. Bytchakov opened fire, scattering our attackers. Two men on the pick-up worked a round into the recoilless rifle, flinching as bullets hissed by them. I aimed the RPG-7 at the trucks then looked over my shoulder. There was a wall directly behind me. Aiming my AK, I emptied a magazine into the plasterboard, making a tall U-shape. Kicking and stamping, I made a hole into the corridor beyond. Now I had an exhaust port for the RPG back-blast. As it was I was already likely to turn myself into a boil-in-the-bag meal, but there were too many attackers for our depleted force to fight off with small-arms.

Sighting the RPG on the engine block of the technical, I squeezed the trigger. The back-blast roared behind me, the rocket-propelled grenade zipping across the compound. It detonated a metre high and right of my aiming point, into the open cab of the vehicle. Several bodies were tossed into the air like dummies by the explosion, lacerated by white-hot shrapnel. The first truck was also on fire, gunmen taking cover wherever they could. The recoilless rifle was gone, its crew lying motionless on the floor.

Oz appeared at my shoulder, looking at the smoking hole in the wall behind me. "What did I tell you about firing rockets indoors?" The gunmen retreated to the walls beyond the compound. Oz crouched by the window, his AK aimed at the gate. Incoming RPGs exploded on the ground floor.

"I'm going to see Alex," I said. The American was sprawled on the floor of the main living room, peering over the iron sights of his Kalashnikov. Behind him, Hugo sprawled on his back in a puddle of grey-and-red gloop. The top of his head was missing, like a neatly cracked egg.

"Marksman took him out," Bytchakov sniffed. "He's on a ship out there. Whoever the shooter is, he's good."

Getting on my belly, I slithered across the room. Bytchakov tossed me the flat green video panel for the PD-100. The toy-sized surveillance drone sat in front of him, rotor blades spinning. I manipulated the controls and it took off, tiny cameras panning and tilting as it drifted through the window. In the dying light, I saw the outline of a cargo ship. I guessed it was *The Cleopatra*, the charter Hugo had negotiated with Julius Adoyo. "What's it like out front?" the American asked.

I landed the tiny helicopter on the bare stone floor. It buzzed like a wasp and the rotor-blades powered down. "It could be worse," I replied. "We've screwed their trucks."

"OK, Captain. Let me know when there's a plan."

Crawling back into the lobby, I headed for the stairs. A half-hearted volley of gunfire rang out, bullets smashing into the blood-slicked marble floor. Oz returned fire, muzzle flash lighting up the room. Upstairs, Ruben was kneeling over Bannerman. The Scotsman's face was a rictus of pain, one side of his uniform soaked in blood. "How is he?" I said.

"Not as bad as it looks," Ruben replied, pushing a field dressing onto his shoulder. "The first bullet hit his body armour dead centre, the second looks like it's a ricochet. The bullet's embedded itself in his upper arm.

"It hurts like fuck nurse," Bannerman groaned, eyes watering. "Gimme some disco biscuits."

"Typical Jock, all he's interested in is getting off his tits," said Ruben. I left them bickering and crawled on my belly over to the window. I had a panoramic view, tracking from the sea to the front of the compound. Carefully, I raised my head high enough to take a look. Dead ahead, the ship steamed towards us. It was a rust-streaked tub, fifties vintage, about sixty metres long. It was still too far away for me to see anyone on the bridge much less the sniper lurking on board. To my right, gunmen had taken cover in the trees and behind smouldering pick-ups.

"Ruben, once you've patched Duncan up, can you go and get Bytchakov? I want him up here with the RPG, in case we have to warn that ship off." However grave the tactical situation, we had the loot. If they wanted it, they'd have to either come and get it by force or negotiate. Using heavy weapons would risk destroying their booty, something I was confident they'd want to avoid.

Ruben nodded as he finished tying off a field dressing. Bannerman was sitting with his back to the wall, left arm lying uselessly in his lap. With his free hand he lit a full strength Marlboro Red. "These things will kill me one day," he grinned.

I heard Oz's voice from downstairs. "Cal, come down." I darted across the lobby, the blown-off doors giving a view onto the compound where enemy gunmen lurked. Oz was standing in a tiled room to the rear of the house, in what had once been a kitchen. Stood with him, breathless and standing in a pool of seawater, was Tom Dancer. "Glad you made it," he gasped. Dancer was still wearing the fatigues he'd worn on the raid, soaked through and ripped, his ruddy face bruised and swollen. He had no weapons or equipment.

I levelled my AK at him. "Tom, until you can persuade me otherwise, you're a hostile."

"Agreed," said Oz.

"Cal, calm the fuck down," he said.

"Hugo told me your girlfriend is responsible for this fuck-up," I said. "Am I right?"

"She is," he nodded sadly. "I've been taken for a ride. Put the bloody gat down, Cal. I've just swum half a mile. I had to kill a sentry to get away. Is Hugo here?"

I kept the barrel of my rifle aimed at his chest. "Hugo's dead."

"Good riddance," the ex-SAS man spat. "He was a fucking weasel. Did he tell you about the plan he and Easter cooked up? Amelia and Brodie have the evidence."

"Hugo told us a bullshit version of it, yeah," I replied. "Now tell me yours, because I'm sure you swimming all the way here had nothing to do with the loot upstairs."

"For God's sake," Dancer snapped. "I knew nothing about the money until Easter and Hugo hi-jacked the chopper. They took me out first, stabbed me with some sort of muscle relaxant. When the Puma took ground fire we had to do an emergency landing at a mine complex. The Chinese arrived and murdered Steve and Idris. Amelia and Brodie are still on the ship out there, Easter's holding them hostage."

"If Easter was in bed with the Chinese, why did they shoot down the chopper?" asked Oz.

"Fog of war," he shrugged. "No plan survives first contact with the enemy and all that. Easter's business partner, a

Chinese colonel called Zhang, wasn't in a position to let his superiors know what he was up to. He had to set up a battle instead. Only a handful of his senior NCOs were in on it, they're on that ship with him."

"You haven't mentioned Mel," I said, "remember, your best friend?"

"He's alive, trussed up with the others," he said, looking hurt. "God knows what the plan is for us all? Maybe they want to use the dirt from CORACLE as leverage?"

"So what's their plan?" I asked. "Who are the guys outside?"

"According to Easter, Zhang Ki did a deal with the Xaboyo to provide local muscle. The guys outside are Xaboyo, ex-Shadow of Swords militia."

I lowered my rifle and laughed. "You're telling me MI6 officers did a deal with a Chinese marine colonel and Al-Qaeda affiliates to pull off a glorified bank robbery?"

"It's a lot of money," said Oz.

"Yes, you've got to hand it to Juliet," Dancer winced. "And there was me saying she lacked ambition. I've overheard her speaking to Zhang Ki. I got the gist of their plan."

I pointed to the bodies littering the hall. "Grab a weapon, Tom. Our only option is to break out, get Murray and head for Afuuma. We can link-up with the rebels and head back to Kenya."

"The Zambutan cache is still here?" Dancer asked.

"Yes," I replied.

"Good," he said. "The guys outside are meant to protect the handover. There's a financier coming to pick the loot up, a…"

"…*Hawaladar* called Muxsin Ahmed," I finished. "I know the plan, Tom, we tracked Hugo from Afuuma."

Dancer's eyes were wide, "you've being doing your homework. The money and the diamonds belong to the people of Zambute," he continued. "Mel will be adamant about that. We need to return it…"

"You might need to discuss that with my men," I replied coldly. "They've got other ideas, and Mel's hardly in a position to give orders." Dancer frowned, but buttoned his lip. "We need to get out of here," I said, shooting him a look. "And we need a vehicle. Then we can worry about loot."

Dancer looked around, running a hand through his hair. Oily seawater trickled through his fingers. "We were held here before they put us aboard the ship," he said. "The outbuildings to the north by the cliff-edge can't be flanked. If we could work our way out there, maybe we could hit the Xaboyo with enfilade fire. If Alex is prepared to play sniper, we should be able to do it."

Like I said, an average plan committed with speed and aggression… "Let's go," I said.

Dancer nodded sadly, face battered and grim. He snatched up a Kalashnikov and peeled a chest rig from a dead Xaboyo gunman. "Don't forget the money."

"Do you mean *the property of the Zambutan people*?" I replied.

Dancer, scowling, disappeared into the gloom.

CHAPTER TWENTY NINE

Alex kept overwatch as we crept across the compound. It was dark, the only light coming from the bridge of the approaching cargo vessel. Low cloud scudded across the moon, covering the enemy's position in shadow. The men waited while I jogged to the edge of the wall nearest the shoreline. There was a hillock of trash there, pieces of broken wood, leaves and mouldering furniture. Our crippled pick-up was still parked nearby. Taking a jerry-can of petrol from the flatbed, I emptied it on the trash and lit it with my Zippo. With a whoosh, a pillar of smoky flame shot into the air. I wanted a distraction for the gunmen waiting outside, maybe even enough to draw them in to investigate.

I crept back to the rest of the team, waiting at the wall until our natural night vision kicked in. Our NVGs and other kit was either lost or out of battery life. Oz, Ruben and Dancer each lugged one of the sacks while I supported Bannerman. The Scotsman had taken a Ketamine spray and was in fair shape, except for a few broken ribs and soft tissue damage from the ricochet. As long as we prevented the wounds from becoming infected, he'd be OK.

"There," Dancer whispered. At the side of the villa was a rusting metal side-gate. Beyond lay a dark clutch of buildings, built from mud-dried brick. As Dancer said, the terrain was bare-arsed except for a patch of dead ground ten metres from our position. Back towards the compound I saw the amber tips of cigarettes as the Jihadis kept watch. Dropping his canvas sack, Dancer duck-walked forward, rifle shouldered. For a big guy, he was surprisingly stealthy. He finally raised his hand, thumb-up.

"Go," I whispered to Oz, my AK pointing at the forlorn-looking sheds.

We advanced toward the buildings, finally going firm in an old workshop. All that remained was a broken bench and a scattering of rusty tools. "We need to go through this wall then follow the compound around to the front," said Dancer. "It looks like a couple of decent kicks will do it."

"Just like Afghanistan," whispered Bannerman, voice shaky with medication. "Y'know, blowing the shit out of compound walls tae get to your target."

Ruben lit the wall with the torch fitted to his pistol. I tapped the mud-brick. With no roof, years of rain and sea-air had shot-through the crude mortar. Putting my shoulder to it, I felt some give. Seeing what I was doing, Oz joined me. Dancer nodded and fell back to the doorway to keep watch. Rocking backwards and forwards, we forced our fighting knives into a weak section of brick. The wall buckled and groaned. Then, finally, a section gave, half a dozen mud-bricks tumbling away.

We all froze at the sound, weapons pointing at the gap we'd created.

Silence.

Nodding at Oz, I began prising more bricks away as quietly as I could. A few long minutes passed, and we'd made a gap big enough to wriggle through. Oz slid through, weapon first, and disappeared into the night. Ruben helped Bannerman next, then Dancer. "I'm going to get Bytchakov," I said.

Dancer nodded, "we'll be in cover on the other side." He hauled the sacks of loot through, piling them next to the wall.

I doubled back into the compound. I'd found a pebble earlier, a big flat stone of the sort you'd enjoy skimming across a lake. I hurled it at the gaping upstairs window, the sign I'd agreed for the American to join us. Thirty seconds later he prowled across the compound, painting arcs with his AK, "are we good?"

"As good as it's gonna get," I replied. "You OK for ammo?"

"Sure, I checked the bodies. I've got six magazines."

I led him through the out-buildings, to the rest of the group. Dancer touched me on the shoulder, pointing into the murky night. His voice was barely a whisper, "look right, acacia trees twenty metres."

"Seen," I acknowledged.

"That's our flanking position for the trucks out front. I expect there to be a sentry or two, but if we take the position we've got the enemy bare-arsed."

I heard the metallic whisper of Ruben drawing his combat knife. "I've got the sentries," he whispered. We lay in the shadow of the compound wall as Ruben crept forward.

"I'll head towards the trees," Dancer hissed.

I watched Ruben crawl ten metres when a shot rang out. There was a fizzing noise and a flare spiralled into the sky. The ex-marine was illuminated with a splash of silver light. Immediately, he dashed, dropped and rolled. But the deadly arc of light from the parachute flare lit him up like a target on a fifty-metre range. He sprang to his feet, ready to sprint, as the first bullet struck. He spun on his heels as a second round slammed home, more bullets chewing the ground into a tempest of dust and grit. Ruben's knife tumbled to the ground. He tried to get back up, but a final shot struck his head. A gout of dark liquid splashed onto the dirt, and he was gone.

We were already returning fire, scrambling to escape the searchlight-arc of the flare. Another popped, the sickly wash of vanilla light revealing our positions. "Drop your weapons," said a voice over a bullhorn. "Drop your weapons immediately." I recognised the clipped English. It was Zhang Ki. Shapes moved in the shadows around us. I heard the sound of weapons being readied, the crunch of boots on gravel.

"Bollocks," Bannerman spat, drawing his Walther with his good hand.

"I'm sorry," said Dancer, levelling his rifle at my head. "But I suggest you listen to the Colonel's orders." A warning shot hit the ground next to Bannerman's feet. He glowered at Dancer, face twisted with hate. The red sighting dots of a half-dozen weapons settled on us, floating slowly from our chests to faces. "Grow up," Dancer sniffed. He stepped back, weapon covering us. "I'd prefer not to kill any more of you. It doesn't mean I won't." He patted me down and tugged my sat phone from a pocket.

One by one, flaming torches lit up the night, fuel-soaked rags wrapped around long metal poles. The Xaboyo gunmen loitered warily around us as the Chinese approached. They wore hi-spec outdoor kit, assault rifles ready. I recognised some of the NCOs who'd tortured us at the airbase among them. The ugly sergeant I remembered said something in Mandarin, and three of his men hefted the sacks of loot away. Colonel Zhang Ki strode towards us, an amused smile on his handsome face. "What now, Dancer?" he asked curtly, jutting his chin at us. He glanced at his watch then lit a cigarette.

Dancer looked nervously skywards. "We need to get them inside, and be very bloody careful," he replied. "You've seen how dangerous they are."

"We should kill them now," Zhang shrugged. "The woman's plan is too complex."

"Not now," Dancer snapped. "Just get them inside."

The Colonel hissed something in Mandarin and stalked off towards The Red House. One of the Chinese seized our weapons and took them over to the Xaboyo. The militiamen nodded and shared the guns and ammunition between them. Gunmen barked orders, herding us towards the house. As we walked towards the compound, past the smouldering pick-up trucks, I saw the cargo ship anchored offshore. Torchlight raked the beach, a small launch bobbing in the sea. It was too dark for me to see who the figures sitting upright in the boat were, but I knew one of them would be Juliet Easter.

Inside the house, the Chinese had cleared the main hall. An arc light rigged to a generator bathed the room with a harsh white glow. Hugo's body had been brought from upstairs, the contents of his skull spattered down the hard stone steps. The rogue Chinese marines bound us at the wrists and ankles with duct-tape, ignoring Bannerman's howls of pain when they yanked at his wounded arm.

Zhang Ki stood examining his cigarette in the wash of the arc light. I saw he was wearing a well-cut civilian suit. Apart from the supressed machine pistol slung over his shoulder, he looked like he was dressed for a business meeting. Jarringly, two of the Xaboyo gunmen stood behind him, dressed in their distinctive grey cloaks and festooned with weapons and bandoliers of ammunition. "A shame about Mister Jackson," Zhang Ki smiled, cigarette smoke drifting from his nose, "although one less Hong Kong 'Chinese' is no loss."

"Was this his idea?" I asked.

"No, but his expertise made it possible. I guess my share of the money has increased now he's gone. What is it you English say? *Look on the bright side?*"

"You sound very calm for a man about to feature on the Peoples' Republic's most wanted list," I said. "The MSS have long memories. You must be crazy."

Alex Bytchakov nodded. "You think you'll get away with taking independent military action like that? Man, you started a war."

"Ironic coming from mercenary scum like you," Zhang replied. "You know nothing about China, and nothing about MSS."

"How many of your helicopters did we shoot down?" Oz said. "Or destroy at Quaani?"

"That is no longer my concern, but I concede you put up a good fight," he said quietly. "Bravo, it was a solid effort."

"Fuck off," Bannerman hissed, voice dripping with contempt. "You were shit. I've fought harder on a Friday night in The Gorbals."

A cruel smile flashed across the Chinese colonel's face. "Dancer will be gone for five minutes. Personally, I think it would be easier to kill you all before he returns." He raised his machine pistol, its black suppressor scanning slowly across us.

"Do it then, you fucker," Bannerman continued. His face was phantom-white, rivulets of sweat dripping from his brow. "Don't just give it the big one. If you're gonna do it, *do it.*"

"Leave it Duncan," I ordered.

We sat in an uneasy silence while Zhang Ki lowered the weapon and finished his cigarette. One of his men stomped in as the minutes ticked by. He sat behind his boss, rifle across his legs.

Dancer finally returned. He'd changed into dry outdoor clothes, body armour over a sweat shirt. He wore a web-belt with a holstered pistol, my sat phone in his hand. "Does this still work?" he said, "I thought you didn't take any non-issue comms kit in the field?"

"I picked that up in Afuuma."

"Who did you speak to?" he said, voice going up an octave.

"My handler," I lied. "They've lost interest now the wheels have come off."

"Really?" he said suspiciously, examining the GCHQ-engineered satellite phone. "How do I find the call register on this thing?" he huffed.

I talked him through it. "Press that button, the code there is my security PIN."

Dancer followed my instructions, entering the code I'd memorized and tapping the ENTER key. Turning the device off, he clipped it onto his web-belt. "Keep an eye on them," he said to Zhang, stepping into the hallway.

"What now?" Zhang sighed.

"The hawaladar is almost here," he replied. "We need to decide what we take and what we leave."

Zhang Ki shrugged. "Let's take it all and to hell with this hawaladar shit. Leaving a king's ransom with some fucking *tribal?*" He said something in Mandarin, and the marine sitting behind him laughed.

Dancer's eyes flashed angrily, "*Hawala* has been the most efficient method of covert money-transfer since the eighth century. Your contempt for these people is starting to piss me off."

The Chinese marine lit another cigarette. "You English, always wanting to play T.E. Lawrence with your noble savages. Like the idiot Murray. Don't forget these morons attacked your base long before they were meant to." It was beginning to make sense. Zhang Ki wanted the Focus Projects base razed, loose ends stamped on, after their escape. But the Xaboyo had screwed up.

The two men stepped into the doorway to continue their argument. I tried to listen. Zhang Ki remained calm, his voice barely a whisper, but I was used to Tom's booming voice. He liked the sound of it too much. I got the gist of their conversation, which was that the Xaboyo gunmen might side with the hawaladar if there was a disagreement or double-cross. Their alliance was on shifting sands. With that much wealth at stake, it was always going to be. I wriggled slightly, testing my bonds.

The Chinese marine NCO raised an eyebrow and hefted his rifle. "No," he barked. I reckoned it was the only English he knew.

"How are you?" I whispered to Bannerman.

"My arm hurts like fuck. I need Ketamine."

"No," said the Chinese guy.

"Fuck you," I said. "Do you understand? *Fuck you.*"

The Chinese guy had obviously seen enough Hollywood movies to understand the 'F' word. He grunted and punched me in the face. A sharp pain hammered through my jaw, a tooth dislodging itself. My mouth filled with salty blood.

"What the hell's going on?" said Dancer, striding back into the hall.

"Bannerman needs pain relief," Oz snapped. "Your guard, on the other hand, wants to dish out beatings." I heard more voices out in the hall. One of them was female.

Dancer took the Chinese guy's assault pack, waving him away when he protested. He rummaged around and pulled out a first aid kit. "Morphine," he said.

"No," said the Chinese marine, raising his rifle.

"Fuck off," Dancer spat, swiping the barrel away from him, "fucking half-wit." Dancer snatched his rifle, checked the safety and set it on the window ledge. The marine glowered, spitting something in Mandarin.

"Please," Bannerman groaned.

Dancer sighed as he pulled the old-fashioned morphine needle from its brown card packaging. I looked at Oz, blood trickling down my chin. Oz pulled a face and nodded at Alex, who looked back at me. "Tom, for God's sake release Bannerman's arm," I said. "It's screwed, he took a bullet."

The ex-SAS officer pulled a small knife from his pocket and slashed the duct-tape away. "Bannerman, I'm going to give you the morphine, but if you make any moves I'll have you shot. You need to understand none of this is personal, OK?"

The Scotsman nodded, his blood-stained fingers trembling as he took the needle. "Cheers," he smiled. "This stuff is fucking marvellous." Grunting with exertion, Bannerman jabbed the needle-tipped morphine Syrette in Dancer's neck, straight into his brachial artery.

"Fuck," Dancer gasped, eyes screwed up in pain. His hands flapped at the needle sticking out of his neck, a bead of blood like a full stop against his skin.

"Have that!" Bannerman grabbed the handgun from Dancer's drop-thigh holster and shot the Chinese guy in the chest, hitting his body armour. Howling, the marine snatched his rifle and managed to fire a shot over our heads. Bannerman fired again, the bullet piercing his throat. Gurgling and flapping like a fish, the Chinese marine rolled into a bloody ball. Bannerman shot the prone figure again, before flopping forwards, grasping at the dead man's belt kit.

Oz snatched my boot knife from my outstretched leg. I looked over at Bannerman, now shivering and groaning. The Scotsman kept the pistol levelled at the door as he took something from the dead marine. "You fucking idiots," said Dancer woozily. He'd taken a 3cc dose of morphine intravenously. Usually you'd pop the drug into the armpit, and it wouldn't work for twenty-odd minutes. Dancer, on the other hand, had taken it the *Trainspotting* route. "The Chinese will kill us all."

Zhang appeared for a moment in the doorway. He raised his submachinegun and fired, bullets stitching along the floor. Bannerman returned fire, forcing the colonel to back off. There was shouting in the corridor, in Swahili and Chinese and English. Spent brass rolled on the concrete floor, trailing smoke. Alex reached the dead marine's assault rifle when a black object bounced off the concrete floor and exploded. My ears felt like someone had smacked the side of my head with a cricket bat, my eyes blinded with a searing light.

I'd been flash-banged before, and knew I was fucked.

Men groaned and swore. I heard boots ringing on concrete, weapons being readied. Orders were barked at us in languages I didn't understand and boots were planted in my guts with great force.

"For God's sake, Tom," said an exasperated female voice. "Are you OK?"

Dancer coughed. "They stabbed me with morphine," he said woozily.

My vision slowly returned. Stood in front of me, looking lithe and alert in fresh clothes and body armour, was Amelia Duclair. "Get the others in here, Zhang," she said coolly, aiming a rifle at us. "I've had enough of this fucking about."

CHAPTER THIRTY

"I don't get it," I said.

"Well clever old me, because you weren't meant to," Duclair replied.

Zhang Ki's finger curled around the trigger of his machine pistol. "Duclair, with the greatest respect, we need to kill them now."

"Colonel, *with the greatest respect*, I left fighting to you and extraction planning to me. This needs to look half-convincing if we're all to enjoy a productive retirement."

Alan Brodie appeared, holding a rifle like it might bite him. The GCHQ technician pushed a badly beaten woman in front of him. Covered in filth and bruises, it was Juliet Easter. She smiled at me through swollen lips. "Credit where credit's due, Cal – this bitch totally fooled me."

Despite everything, I felt a surge of relief she wasn't the Bad Apple. "You've set her up," I said to Duclair. "Easter's the fall girl, right?"

"No, *he* set her up," smiled Duclair, nodding at a spaced-out Tom Dancer. "You couldn't help yourself, could you, Juliet… an affair with an upper-crust ex-SAS hero? Too much pillow talk, I'd say. You really are a sanctimonious cretin, lecturing *me* about operational security?"

"Fuck you," Easter grunted. She was wearing the clothes she'd worn on the prison assault, ripped and blood-stained. Her hair was matted, eyes blood-shot and swollen.

"Duclair tried to get me to report you to SIS," I said to Easter. "Amelia said the whole team had their doubts about you."

"My whole team were bent," Easter spat, "and I never saw it coming."

"Gag them," Duclair hissed. "Tom, for God's sake get up and head for the ship. We're going to leave two bags with the hawaladar and take one with us."

Dancer swayed slightly, hand clasped to his neck. "But we agreed…"

"Just do it," she barked, eyes narrowing. "You're not in any state to make decisions. I've compromised with Zhang on this one, and that's it."

Zhang Ki nodded respectfully. "Yes, Miss Duclair. Thank you." Dancer staggered out of the room, hand clamped to his neck.

"Where's Murray?" said Duclair, motioning at Brodie.

"I'll get him," said the GCHQ man, "he's in the dinghy with Zhang's men."

It made sense now, the photographs and comms data I'd found in Brodie's room. They were stitching Easter up, fabricating evidence that tied their dirty satellite phone to the team leader. "They put together a fake comms package," I said. "A lot of work went into making it look like you were making the calls to Zhang Ki."

Easter pulled a face, "how could I have been so blind?"

"They could put the blame for mission failure on you," I continued. "They had data, photographs, everything…"

"I'm sure they did," she replied. "And now, I suspect, comes the carefully orchestrated executions, to tie up any loose ends for their exfil plan."

"Shut up," said Duclair, eyes darting around the room.

"Can I ask one more question?" I said. I shook my head as a Chinese marine went to gag me. Duclair shrugged. "Why did you do it? And where were you when Operation STOWAGE was compromised? That was your alibi, wasn't it?"

"That's two questions," she smiled. I guessed she was enjoying this, a fully-fledged risk junkie. There was adrenaline and dopamine pumping around her system, playing high-risk poker in one of the most dangerous places on earth.

"I suppose it is," I shrugged.

"Perhaps the answer is the same," she shrugged. "I was on leave in the UK eighteen months ago, visiting my sister-in-law. My little brother died in Afghanistan, an IED attack. His first child was born a month later. I loved my brother. Matthew meant more to me than anything else in the world."

"That doesn't explain anything."

"Oh, it does. Rachel, my sister-in-law, was left with nothing. She was given a medal and a shitty widow's pension, less than the profit on a flipped MPs mortgage. So, Cal, let me throw the question right back at you… *Why?* Why were we in some godforsaken medieval country, trying to tame *savages*? *Why?* Every time you see some lying bastard politician on the TV, talking about how essential it is, don't you want to wring the bastard's neck?"

Next to her, Zhang Ki nodded. "I understand these sentiments."

Duclair tightened her grip on her rifle. "Why does every bastard politician who starts one of these stupid fucking wars end up a millionaire? Why don't they ever send *their* kids down a two-way range?" Her eyes flashed as she drew breath, "and why do *we* always end up with the shitty end of the stick?"

"If you want to ask questions like that, lady," said Bytchakov, "you shouldn't have joined. You weren't forced, and neither was your brother. He sounds like he was a better person than you…"

"Didn't I tell you to gag these men," Duclair yelled, face flushed. "Zhang, have them gagged, except for Easter and Winter. When Murray arrives we finish this." Zhang Ki translated and his men roughly wound tape around the men's faces. Duclair took a knee, close enough for me to smell her perfume. She was clean and wearing fresh makeup, her voice low. She smiled her vixen's smile. "There's your answer, Winter. People like us take all the risk for shit pay and no thanks, while the creatures above us thrive. So I decided, sitting there with my sister-in-law, trying not to notice that she's on a bottle of vodka a day to numb the pain… that if I ever saw the chance I'd take it. My nephew will never want for anything again. Neither will his mother and neither will I…"

"And you took the rest of your team with you?"

"They didn't take much persuading. It was a theoretical challenge for Hugo, and Brodie hated Juliet so much he'd do anything to see her screwed over. Never underestimate a geek genius with a sexist grudge."

"And what about Dancer," I said.

"Dancer, well he's a piece of work." Duclair chuckled throatily, tossing her head at Easter, "after he'd fucked you, Juliet, he'd come and tell me everything you discussed for me to pass on to Zhang. Then I'd fuck him, while he still smelt of you." Easter ignored the barb, just stared blankly at the wall. Duclair laughed. "I served in the army with officers like you, Juliet. Oxygen-stealing creeps who thought the whole thing was worth a toss. All for some shiny medals and your head patted by the brass. Jesus, I despise you."

Brodie came back into the room, pushing a quivering Mel Murray in front of him. Murray, like Easter, had been badly beaten. He was a broken man, eyes black pits of despair. Brodie pushed him to the ground, the ex-SAS colonel collapsing into a gibbering ball.

"Well, here we are," said Duclair brightly, like we were at an English country picnic. She pulled on a pair of surgical gloves and tossed copies of the statements Zhang Ki had tried to force us to sign. Of course, they corroborated the narrative she'd fabricated. "I have a deal. Sign the statements and you'll die quickly and cleanly. Refuse and I'll leave you to the Xaboyo. They make ISIS look like social workers when it comes to their treatment of prisoners."

"Your generosity is staggering," I replied. "Fuck you, I'll take my chances."

"As you wish," she shrugged, uttering a few words in Arabic. A tall Xaboyo warrior entered the room, Kalashnikov levelled at me. His face was a study in cruelty, narrowed eyes flashing with hate.

Duclair couldn't have known I spoke Arabic. She told the Xaboyo to kill us slowly, that we were the worst type of Zionist-loving western *Kaffur*. Then she explained that two of the Chinese marines would wait for the hawaladar, to hand over the last sack of cash. She warned that if the sack wasn't delivered, then the Xaboyo would be hunted and killed by the Chinese. The Xaboyo leader growled at being threatened by a woman, but agreed to her instructions anyway. No doubt they were being paid handsomely for their trouble. "Good luck," she hissed at us. "I'm sure you'll go down in SIS lore as brave chaps, dying at the hands of Johnny Foreigner on a mission for Queen and Country."

"If you change your minds about the statements, we'll be in screaming distance for another few minutes," said Zhang Ki. He chuckled and shouldered his assault pack. His men dragged the dead marine's body away, washing away the blood and policing the scene for any clues they'd been there. "It was nice to meet you, Colonel Murray." Murray was still curled in a ball, eyes wild.

The tall Xaboyo started issuing orders. More militiamen rushed into the room, jabbing us with rifles and the tips of machetes. Outside, I could hear the flames from the fire I'd started, smelt the stinking smoke drifting through the open window. "What now?" Easter whispered. A Xaboyo tribesman answered her question, kicking her in the belly then grasping at the waistband of her fatigues. The rest laughed as their leader unbuckled his belt.

"I would 'nae do that if I were you," said Duncan Bannerman, ripping off his gag with his injured hand. He staggered forward, into the middle of the hall.

The Xaboyo looked up. Bannerman held a fragmentation grenade in front of him, the pin dangling from his finger. I realised it was the item he'd taken from the Chinese marine's belt kit during the earlier melee. "Get away from the woman," he hissed. "Or I swear to God we'll all die."

I translated Bannerman's threat into Arabic. "He has nothing to lose, he will kill us all. If you think Duclair will keep her word, you're a fool."

"What do you mean?" the Xaboyo leader grunted, buckling his belt.

"This is a trap, for my country's traitors," I explained, sounding more confident than I felt. "I was sent to catch them by my Government. Take me to the hawaladar and I'll explain."

"No, I gave my word to the Chinese," he said proudly.

"Alex," I said, "you can take the gag off."

Alex ripped the tape away and got to his feet, pushing away the rifle muzzles. Some of the younger fighters saw the look in his eyes and retreated.

"Is the nearest CIA SAD station in Djibouti?" I whispered. Rumour had it the US Special Activities Division operated a covert Aerial Interdiction Program in East Africa, codename URGENT STEPPE. That was spook jargon for a deniable Reaper Drone team. They had three birds constantly in the air, sniffing out High-Value Targets.

"They moved it last time I heard," he replied.

"How long does it take them to respond to an urgent HVT?"

The American shrugged. "It depends on how much due diligence they have to run, and whether they've got a bird on-station. Assuming it's in Kenya…"

"Let's say zero due diligence," I replied. "A juicy HVT, top five say?"

"Speak in my language," ordered the Xaboyo leader. He recognised the English acronym for *High Value Target* and was all ears.

"Wait," I replied in Arabic, "this is important, I swear. Our lives depend on it."

The Xaboyo told his men to shut up, be calm but keep their weapons readied. Bannerman grinned, waving the grenade slowly in front of him. The look in his eyes suggested he'd be happy to use it. Bytchakov did some math in his head. "A Reaper MQ9 flies at three-hundred miles per hour; if it's on station then I guess they could be sighted on target in a half hour?"

The English word *Reaper* got the Xaboyo's attention too.

I glanced at my watch. I estimated it was at least thirty minutes since Dancer had taken my phone, maybe longer. "That could work," I said.

"Cal, what the hell are you talking about?" Bytchakov replied.

"I activated *Fallen Eagle* on my satellite phone, when Dancer asked how to figure out the call register. It's geo-located to the handset."

"Where's the phone?" Easter asked.

"Clipped on Dancer's belt," I replied. "And he's drugged up to the eyeballs."

"Englishman, start talking," the Xaboyo hissed. "Or we will kill you. I say to hell with your crazy friend and his grenade."

I pushed past the crowd of gunmen and jogged to the open window. The cargo ship was edging along the coast, lights twinkling on deck. "Give me until the hawaladar arrives," I shrugged. "Until then, watch the sea."

The tall Xaboyo roughly grabbed my shoulder, breath sour in my face. I smelt the sharp tang of his sweat as he went to say something…

…And *The Cleopatra* exploded with a sound like a thunderclap, a ball of white flame rippling from the centre of the hull. A secondary explosion rocked the cargo ship, tossing it like a child's bath-time toy. We watched it disappear into fizzing black water, leaving nothing but burning wreckage bobbing on the surface. All of us, Xaboyo and Westerner alike, watched the fireworks together in awe. Easter laughed giddily, like a mad woman. "Burn, you bitch!"

"That was Fallen Eagle? It was meant to rescue us," said Oz, eyes wide.

"There's a lesson well-learnt." I looked at the tall Xaboyo. "You know what that was, don't you?"

"*Hellfire*," whispered the Jihadi in English, invoking the word like a curse.

"Yes, it was Hellfire. There are thirteen more on that bird. If you don't let us go, you're next. The drone is circling now, but if it sees you leaving this place you'll be unharmed. You have my word."

"You try to trick us," he hissed.

"No, I'm giving you a chance to live. To the south are the rebels. They want to destroy you. To the west are tanks from the Zambutan 21st Brigade, and the 2nd Regiment of the Presidential Commando. Guess what? They want to kill you too. To the east is the sea…" The tall Xaboyo bawled at his men, telling them to return to their vehicles and head north. "Yes, my friend," I said in Arabic, "and above us is a Predator MQ9 drone, controlled by The Great-fucking-Satan. If I were you, I'd leave that sack of money and head back to Somalia."

The tall Xaboyo looked at me for a moment, rage burning in his eyes. Then he sucked in his pride. He glanced at Bannerman and saw the grenade, realised the crazy Scotsman was as good as his word. He swore and hissed, but kept his weapon lowered.

"The bags," I said. Stepping forward, I scooped up the Claymore from Bannerman's assault pack and unsheathed it. Bannerman laughed. "Give me the bags," I repeated, the sword blade flashing in the torchlight. "Or as God is my witness, you'll fall under the shadow of *this* sword." It was a tad theatrical, but I was in the mood. I stepped forward, the edge of the blade ready to strike.

The Xaboyo hissed an order and backed away. Bannerman limped towards them, brandishing the grenade. "Fuck off, the lot of you!" he bawled like the madman he was.

Oz and Alex picked up Murray, Easter snatching up a rifle. She passed the weapon to me and picked up another. Outside, The Red House was streaked with dirty smoke, the compound swathed in fire and still-smouldering vehicles. Flaming sparks carried on the smoke, into the scrub where fresh fires flared.

The tall Xaboyo stepped closer. Behind him, two of his men carried the bulky grey sack. I pointed at the stars. "Do you see the drone, that bright light?" I was bluffing. The Reaper would be too high to see.

The Xaboyo looked skywards anyway. "Take the money, *kaffur*," he spat. "I hope it brings you nothing but misery and death."

"You have a nice day too," I replied. The Jihadis melted into the desert night, the engines of their pick-ups revving as they fled. They'd decided today wasn't theirs for martyrdom.

Oz was still shaking his head. "The bastards were going to blow us up?"

I nodded. Our little group staggered towards the road. In the distance I saw headlights on the Via Roma, heard the metallic trundle of military vehicles. "I hope that's the rebels," said Oz.

I clutched Easter's trembling hand, "So do I."

CHAPTER THIRTY ONE

Antwerp

"The cheque will clear in seventy-two hours," I said, my breath making clouds in the chill December air. "The account is with a bank in Zurich, called *Tete Noir*."

Juliet's hand rested on my arm. "Thanks, Cal."

Killing two birds with one stone, I'd accessed the safety deposit box the week before. The code Isaac Samuels had given me was good, unlocking a long-forgotten steel tray in the bowels of a Swiss bank vault. The contents, reams of typewritten reports, were more valuable to me than any diamonds.

Juliet and I strolled along Wisselstraat, towards the Christmas market on the Grote Markt. People walked happily through the bustling, brightly lit streets. Snow had fallen earlier, the city resembling a Victorian Christmas card. It was scenic, but I'd chosen the route because it would be a nightmare for a surveillance team.

Everybody knows Amsterdam is the centre of the world diamond trade, which was why I'd chosen Antwerp. Belgium's diamond industry is almost as big as the Netherlands', but twice as discreet. The old Jewish guy, a central casting *Hasidim* with glasses like the bottom of coke bottles, was happy to move our share of the diamonds. Of course, that was less a fifteen per cent handling fee. We were paying another fifteen to launder it, but I'm one of those old-fashioned guys who reckon seventy per cent of a tax-free haul of cash is better than none.

Juliet squeezed my hand, her face gaunt. "This feels wrong," she said.

"Cheer up," I smiled. "You're not in debt and you can look after your brother properly now." Juliet had used her share of the loot to buy her disabled sibling a specially-adapted house near the family home in Winchester. That and the best medical treatment money could buy, for the rest of his life.

"I know," Juliet replied, a wan smile on her face. "I should shake myself out of it." She wore a waxed jacket, jeans and knee-boots, a thick woollen scarf around her neck. She looked good and smelt good, the scars and bruises from Zambute faded. Well, the physical ones, anyway.

"It takes time, dealing with stuff like this," I said gently. Since Zambute my nightmares had stopped. Learning more about The Firm helped too, the gaps between the bars on my cage were getting wider. Soon I'd blow the cage apart.

"Mel was right," she continued, "about the diamonds. It's not our money."

"You know the rest of the money went straight into General Abasi's bank account," I shrugged. The rights and wrongs of what we'd done were academic – given the circumstances I reckoned it was a fair compromise. "It's a no-brainer - you look after your brother or watch Abasi buy more guns and gold-plated limousines?"

When the rebels arrived, shortly after the Xaboyo fled, I asked for them to radio Tony Ishmael. The rebels relaxed when we mentioned his name, had heard of our tank-busting exploits at the Afuuma road bridge. While we waited, Oz and I buried Ruben Grey overlooking the spot where his betrayers had perished. He was a spiteful little bastard. I liked to think he'd have appreciated the gesture.

Tony Ismael showed up a few hours later, delighted to see us alive. His men had smashed straight through Afuuma, the Presidential Commando diverted to defend the westward thrust of Aziz's forces. The rebel general, backed by a surprise Ethiopian false flag operation, had tanks and warplanes at his disposal. The Ethiopians had been an uneasy ally, reluctant to commit troops until they knew Afuuma would fall. Marsajir fell quickly afterwards, Aziz was bundled in front of his palace and shot by a firing squad.

Sometimes history turns on a pivot. General Abasi reckoned the Afuuma road bridge was his. Had the government forces taken the bridge, Afuuma would have never fallen. Tony Ismael was promoted to Colonel on the spot. "Here," I said, handing Colonel Ismael the sack of loot. "This belongs to Zambute, I suppose."

Behind me, Duncan Bannerman looked like he was sucking lemons. In his imagination, he should have had more treasure. Still, we'd kept one block of the diamonds, which we split between us. After I'd sliced the block of diamond-studded resin five ways, we had fourteen carats worth of stones each. For the clarity and size of my rocks I ended up making a shade under three-quarters of a million Euros, even after thirty per cent laundering costs. The money went straight into my war chest. War is many things, but most of all its expensive. And it was war I was planning, on The Firm.

We were escorted to Afuuma, the rebels bemused by our honesty in handing back the stolen money. The Chinese warships were gone, the news full of stories about Beijing furiously denying culpability for the outrage at Buur Xuuq. In

Afuuma, Juliet contacted SIS and filed an initial report. Within twenty four hours a team of UK Special Forces were bundling us into a heli. The next stop was a dusty Kenyan army base.

We were left in situ, while Juliet and Mel Murray were spirited away the same evening. Juliet was taken for debriefing in Nairobi. She played it straight, leaving out nothing except for the diamonds sewn into the lining of her kit bag. She confessed to her relationship with Dancer, that she'd shared secrets with him she shouldn't have.

As for us, The Firm sent us to Serbia for decompression while the dust settled. Juliet told me what happened next, over dinner in Belgrade, six weeks later. We sat on a terrace overlooking the Danube, enjoying the late autumn sun. It was warm enough for Juliet to wear a strappy summer dress, her feet in simple leather sandals. "SIS thanked me for my honesty and hard work," she explained. "Then they invited me to resign. *With all the good will in the world, Jools, this has been a major fuck-up*," she laughed, mimicking her upper-crust bosses. "*You were having an off-policy relationship with a man who turned out to be a major security threat to HMG.*"

"What then?" I asked, topping up her glass with *slivovica*.

Her eyes, grey as flint, narrowed. "It was the most reasonable sacking ever," she explained, emptying another glass. "They offered me a job working with Mel Murray at Focus Projects. Mel's going to be away for a while, recovering from what happened…"

"You got Dancer's old job?"

She nodded. I looked at her. Her face was still tanned and weather-beaten, a spray of freckles across her perfectly-imperfect nose. Her russet hair, fine and gold-flecked, fell across her face. Juliet, I decided, was one of those most appealing of women: a beauty that didn't fully realise it.

I'd offered to manage the sale of her diamonds, over that drunken dinner in Belgrade. She reluctantly agreed. Early the following morning, when she shared my bed, Juliet's crying woke me. We made love, urgently, both of us knowing it was unlikely to happen again. And when we were spent, we fell asleep to the noise of the wind in the trees. "What are you going to do next?" she said when we woke. Her arm trailed across my chest, her belly hot against my flank.

"I'm going to be a better man," I said.

Juliet laughed. "Good luck with that, Cal Winter."

We kissed then she wriggled on top of me with a wicked smile. When I stirred at sun-up, Juliet Easter was gone. We'd only spoken once since then, to arrange the meeting in Antwerp. I left her alone, figuring that if she wanted to see me she had my number. Juliet had the chance to live a good life, and the last thing she needed was me in it. I wanted to ring, of course. Why wouldn't I? She was beautiful and smart and brave…

…but I didn't make the call. I'm the fly in the ointment, the oil slick on a pristine beach. I know that.

We left the Christmas market and stepped into an old Flemish-style tavern. Bannerman, Oz and Alex were sitting in a corner booth. The men were drinking foaming glasses of beer, laughing and goofing around. They quietened when they saw us. "It's done," I said. "Your cheques will be in your Tete Noir accounts by Christmas Eve."

"That calls for another drink," Bannerman declared, wiping froth from his lip. He'd exaggerated the story about me threatening the Xaboyo at the Red House with his Claymore. Now it sounded like something out of *Braveheart*.

"Nothing for me," said Juliet. "I'm sorry. I'm flying back to London tonight." I tried to catch her eye, but she looked away. I wondered what she was doing for Christmas and the New Year.

"How's Mel?" asked Oz.

"He's slowly getting better," she replied. "Although he doesn't want to talk about Tom or what happened in Zambute. He's shaken by the disloyalty, I think. Mel's very old-fashioned."

"I'm sorry, Miss Easter, but that sonofabitch Dancer is better off dead," Bytchakov shrugged. He drained his beer and motioned to the waitress for another, "and so is Duclair."

"Yes, I suppose you're right," she said quietly. "Thanks for everything you did. You saved my life. If I can ever begin to return the favour, you know where I am. Consider Focus Projects at your disposal." And, with a shy nod of her head, she was gone.

That left The Firm, and the truth about Fallen Eagle.

When the rebels took us to Afuuma I picked up two fresh sat phones. I sent a message to Marcus on the first, telling him to expect Easter to show up in Nairobi with the full story, and that his Bad Apples were all dead. I hurled the phone in the sea and powered up the second device. "You're alive?" said Monty. There was no disguising the disappointment in his voice.

"Tell me, Monty, how did you plan to rescue us with a Hellfire missile?" I replied.

"There were crossed wires with the Yanks on Fallen Eagle," he wheedled. "You know how it is. I'm grateful that you accomplished your mission, Cal."

"I lost two men."

"Yes, but we won't hold it against you. The job was challenging, to say the least."

I liked this new, emollient Monty. I could get used to it. "I don't believe you. I think it was a tidy-up mechanism, designed to kill us."

The handler was silent for a moment. "Is there any point making an issue out of it?" he replied. "You're alive. The mission was a success, of sorts."

"Where does my knowledge of Fallen Eagle leave me?"

"Do the rest of the team know the truth?"

"Negative," I lied. "I thought it was best to keep them in the dark. I'm sure you'd agree."

"Yes, I a-agree," he stuttered.

I rolled cigar smoke around my mouth. The view across Afuuma's harbour would have been peaceful, if it weren't for the executed security police hanging from cranes. "I hope it guarantees their safety."

"I'm not saying…"

"You don't need to, Mister Montague," I smiled. Sometimes you need to roll those dice more than is strictly healthy. The story from the old forger in Old Street was my loaded pair, which hopefully would come up Lucky Sevens. "Or is it OK for me to call you Owen?"

I listened to the intake of breath at the other end of the line. "How the hell…"

"It doesn't matter, *Owen*, I thought a bit of mutually-assured destruction might keep us both in line. Are you in your office down in Kent?"

"What do you mean?" he hissed. "You can't *threaten* me."

"I just did," I growled. "I'll find Declan Cross's family, you know, the lunatics from the Real IRA? Together we'll look you up, for old time's sake. I'll forget how much I hate Republicans if it means screwing you over. Remember that." I switched off the phone and tossed it as far as I could, into the sea.

I left the guys in the bar and walked into the glow of Christmas lights. The tickets for Lapland were in my wallet. I was taking Sam Clark and the kids to meet Santa Claus. Yeah, I know what you're thinking. I was one of those phony, flash bastards, throwing money around to fix broken promises. Snowy slush seeped into my shoes. I hailed a taxi. Being a phony, flash bastard would have to do for now. I guessed it was better than being a dead one.

EPILOGUE

I sprinted the last hundred metres along the beach, waves lapping at my ankles. My time was good; I'd knocked three seconds off yesterday's effort. The six-mile circuit was part of my daily routine. I towelled down and returned to the hire car, ducking inside as it started to rain. Fishing an isotonic drink from the glove-box, I switched on the radio and listened to the BBC World Service. There were wars everywhere, more than a mutt has fleas. Bombs, rockets, incursions, slaughters and massacres, too many to report or comprehend. It would be a busy time for The Firm, doing stuff Governments didn't have the guts to do for themselves.

Yet the phone hadn't rung. No Monty, no Marcus and no Firm. Since I'd threatened Monty I'd only had coded email, on the first of each month, telling me to maintain my cover. I'd taken precautions anyway, dropped off the map, lest men with guns were out looking for me. I doubted they'd find me in northern Iceland. You might as well go to Mars. The farmhouse was in the middle of a bleak volcanic nowhere, in a place with a name I couldn't pronounce. Stepping out of the car, my fingers brushed the grips of the pistol tucked in the waistband of my sweatpants. There were no fresh footprints in the muddy ground leading to the porch, no vehicle tracks. "Hi honey, I'm home," I said.

"Yo," Oz replied, sitting at the kitchen table. He'd run twelve miles already, was eating a bowl of porridge. "When's the last time you had a drink?"

"Three months."

"Good effort. Do you want one?"

"I could murder a Scotch," I grinned.

Oz tapped the pile of papers on the table, arranged chronologically. Next to them lay reference books, notepads and a laptop. We'd spent our time productively, corroborating the information from Marcus and the material in Harry's safety deposit box.

"Harry must have wanted to fuck The Firm over as badly as we do," I said.

"I make you right," Oz agreed. "The question is what now?"

"Are the others ready?"

"Bannerman's in Scotland, waiting for the call. Bytchakov is deployed in Thailand, he's back next week. He says he'll be ready when we are."

I studied the maps, plans and photographs plastered across the walls. They listed the management structure, order of battle, logistics and intelligence capability of The Firm from 1953 until Harry's retirement. It was my old handler's paper hand grenade, which he'd gifted me to throw. I didn't know why, but had no doubt I'd find out. Once upon a time, it transpired, The Firm had been a force for good. We decided the point of compromise, the moment the tree was poisoned, was September 12th 2001.

I wanted to turn back the clock.

"We've got two options," I said finally. "We either kill every bastard with his or her fingerprints on The Firm…"

"Or...?"

"Well, you know my preferred option."

Oz raised an eyebrow, "you still think that's possible?"

"Yeah, I do." I stood and walked to the window. A watery beam of light lasered through the clouds, alien mountains sparkling in the distance. I took a lungful of clean, cold, air and shivered. "I'm going to be the better man."

THE END

Printed in Great Britain
by Amazon